Mario 8

Captivated

Mario 8
Captivated
by
George
Hatcher

Casa Hatcher Press is an imprint of Pretty Face, Inc. Pasadena, CA 91103

For details, contact:
    Casa Hatcher Press.
    http://casahatcherpress.com
    (818) 519-2976
    Mario 8: Captivated

Book and cover designed by Casa Hatcher Press
Cover photos
©pv/adobestock.com; Leolintang/shuttterstock.com
©George Hatcher interior art by Tarik Chraiti

Mario 8: Captivated by George J. Hatcher
First Edition May 2020
LCCN 2020936882
ISBN:978-1-7332351-1-2 (Hardback)
ISBN:978-1-7332351-2-9 (Paperback)
ISBN:978-1-7332351-3-6 (E-book)
R: 20200505

Dedication

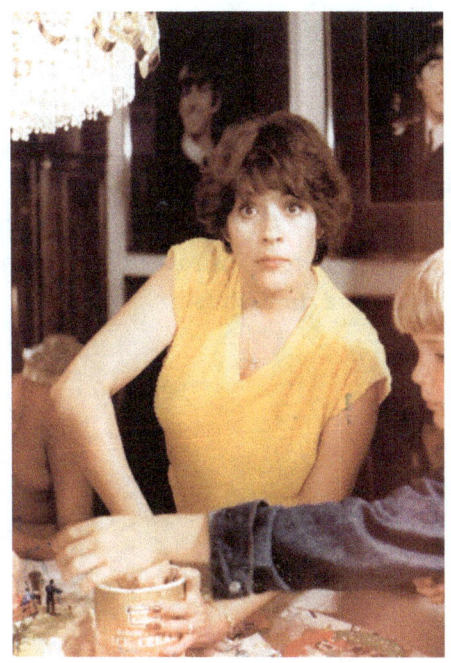

Molly

You are my sun during the day and
my moon at night.

Love,

George

Acknowledgements

Tarik thank you for your quick hand and artistic eye. Your artwork enhances these pages.

If it were up to my editor, Allie Bates, this book would still be in edits. I had to pry it out of her grip while she was still marking up. Every pass makes it a little better, she says. Just let me proof-read it one more time, she says.

WARNING!

Adult matter

This book is intended for adults. Violence and sexual antics are not intended for minors, sensitive readers, or people living in the real world where there are sexually transmitted diseases which are incurable. Mario is a work of fiction. The people in the book lived and died only in my imagination. Any resemblance to actual people will be only in your imagination. The story is purely a product of long plane flights, random flights of fantasy, the wild goose-chasing of ideas like what if this (or that) happened on top of my experience in wrongful death cases. Like Mario, I am no lawyer. I do not employ nubile sex groupies or toss people out of high-rise buildings when they get on my nerves.

Works by George Hatcher

Ambulance Chaser Series

Mario 1: Woman in Jeopardy

Mario 2: Coming of Age

Mario 3: Risky Business

Mario 4: Free Fall

Mario 5: Afire

Mario 6: Marked

Mario 7: Aftershock

Mario 8: Captivated

Single titles

Gabi

Coming Soon

Billionaire Dollar Rainmaker

Mario 9

Arabe

Prologue
November 2, 1991 (Saturday)
Off the Coast of Puerto Vallarta, Mexico
Mario

Letty is holding my hand. The plane is hurtling down with terrifying force. The cabin is dark, and the dark magnifies the screams. The noise is terrible, but across from us, I hear Pixie and Lainie making up at the top of their lungs. They've been estranged for so long.

"Mom, I've been such a creep to you. I'm sorry, Mama. I'm sorry. I don't want us to die, Mama."

"We're not going to die. I promise."

"Baby, I love you!"

The plane is cracking around us, agonizing, as if the metal is alive and screaming just like everyone else. I look back where the dim shadows where Pixie and Lainie had been. The whole tail of the plane is gone, and with it, Pixie and Lainie. So, it ends.

No one should die, not Captain Largo who is doing his best at the helm, not his copilot, not the other first officer and his copilot, not the four stewardesses whose presence is just the luck of the draw, not Jo and Niley whose management of my apartments has taken flight, not Andrea, my assistant at GAL (GAL, which has given me another new lease in life when I've already had so many), not Pixie and Lainie with their burgeoning rags-to-riches singing career, not Betty and Storm with their magic massage hands that have soothed my aches away, not Tangles whose joy keeps a smile on my face, and most of all, not Letty, who is as vital to me as the air in my lungs. There are eighteen souls on this plane. Are we going to die?

No one should die, but we're in a plane over the Pacific ocean and dying is what we are about to do, dying while flying to Camila's funeral in Bogota. I am surrounded by almost everyone I love, and the engines have failed. I thank the Virgin that at least Aunt Carmen is safe in Pasadena. Flying is now falling, and everyone else I love is on this plane with me, falling, falling faster, speeding toward death in the dark, unforgiving ocean, words of the stewardesses in my ears. Brace position. This is how I die, in brace position, crouched in the seat of a plane, head down, clutching the hand of my best friend, everyone I love dying with me. My ears are full of their screams, screams of the whole world dying with me, slamming into the ocean, lights off, wind, metal and all the hearts beating around me, all my loved ones screaming. The plane bounces when it hits the water the first time, and here I am again bargaining with the Virgin of Guadalupe. Spare them all. Please take me.

And everything goes black.

Splashdown
November 2, 1991
Pacific Ocean
Mario

Above me, the whole world was navy blue with white sprinkles. And wet. I blinked a couple of times. The sky was incredible, huge and blue and twinkling with stars. I'd never seen anything like it. I don't think that before this, I've ever been floating on my back offshore after midnight, staring up at the night sky. I touched the life jacket, found the cord, and pulled it. It inflated with a hiss.

The ocean around me was quiet and dark. The waves moved gently, rocking my view of the clear night sky. It was dark, but the millions of stars in the impossibly bright night sky were reflected in the water. I could hear no one, only the sea in my ears, and the lapping of water on some distant surface. The horizon was a flat line in a circle around me. I had no idea which direction land was but supposed it might be in the direction where the sky was slightly brighter. I was alone. Back in Pasadena, it dropped to fifty degrees on November nights. Here, wherever here was, it felt like spring. I had no idea how long I'd been floating on my back, or what time it might be. All

I knew is that we took off just after eleven, ate dinner in the cabin, were roused from bed, hustled to our seats when we lost the first engine, and minutes later, lost the second engine. It had to be in the sixties or seventies and the water was even warmer. Thank God for the Mexican climate. Thank God for Captain Largo.

"Where is everyone?" I yelled. "Is anyone here?"

"I'm here!" I heard a distant voice.

"Letty, thank God it's you. Who else is out there?"

"I'm over here."

"Tangles, Tangles!"

I started swimming. "Letty, say something. I'm swimming that way."

"I'm swimming too," she replied.

"How did we get so separated?" Tangles yelled. "I'm swimming to your voices."

Over to my right, maybe two hundred feet away, I could make out the vaguest image of the plane jutting out of the water, rocking side to side slowly with the tide. Everything behind the wings was gone. The moon was invisible, but thousands of stars lit my way. I looked up and saw Letty swimming toward me. Over to my left, I caught a glimpse of Tangles.

We came together almost at the same time. I embraced both of them.

"Are you hurt, injured, anything?"

"I'm good," Letty said. Her lips pressed against mine.

"Me too, Boss," Tangles said. "I'm good, but I want some of that, too."

The three of us embraced, treading water, checking each others' life jackets.

"Look over there," Letty said, pointing. In the distance was a big ship.

It was lit up like Christmas, and two large bright lights were scanning the water in front of the ship. Its brightness blinded me. Everything else was suddenly darker. The beam floated over us, highlighting Letty and Tangles, bedraggled but always beautiful.

"Thank God," I said, raising my arms and waving at the approaching ship. "Over here! Help!"

"Lifeboats," Tangles said, pointing.

The three of us were yelling and waving wildly at the big ship. As Tangles pointed out, the ship was lowering two large lifeboats.

"We see you. Stay where you are. We'll come to you," a male voice said in perfect English over a public address system. "Keep away from what's left of the plane. Stay where you are. Lifeboats will be there in a minute."

"Is that a commercial or private yacht?" I wondered aloud as it drew closer.

"Who cares? It's beautiful," Tangles said. "Beautiful that they are rescuing us. But where are the others?" She started crying.

"Suck it up, buttercup," Letty said. "Swim now, cry later."

"Don't cry. Tread water. We will find the others," I said. "We'll search for them as soon as those boats get here."

I don't think of myself as a worrier, but I would be relieved when Letty and Tangles were safely aboard. The sea was calm, but I had a sense of a world of marine life swarming around us, and now that the yacht had brought lights into the picture, the sky and water looked black. One of the boats pulled alongside. The men aboard were stocky and wore wetsuits. It was hard to tell anything else about them.

"My name is Lucas, and this is Simon. Is anyone injured?"

They hesitated before pulling us aboard, probably concerned about making any trauma worse.

"I don't think so," Letty said.

They introduced themselves as they pulled us aboard. I made sure the girls were aboard first.

Another boat with two men manning it was twenty feet behind them. They were waving. We waved back once we were in the lifeboat.

We shook hands with Lucas and Simon. I could smell the fumes of the lifeboat's loud diesel engine.

"Simon has medications he can give you right now if you are dizzy, nauseous or in pain," Lucas said.

"I'm a medic. No one is hurt?" Simon asked.

"I don't think we're injured. It's a miracle," I said.

"Nothing broken, no bad pain?" Simon asked.

"We're good," Letty said.

"My name is Mario Luna," I said. "We can't thank you enough. This is Letty and Tangles."

"Thank you for rescuing us," Letty said, taking a seat.

"Si, muchas gracias," Tangles said, sitting beside Letty. I took a seat between the girls.

Simon handed us giant towels.

"We'll feel better if we can look for the rest of our people," I said, vigorously making use of the towel.

"How many are missing?" Lucas asked. "Our patron has been on the radio with fisherman in the area. Fifteen people have been pulled from the water, not counting you."

"That's fucking wonderful!" Letty blurted out. "Oh, sorry," she said in Spanish.

"Are they all okay?" Tangles asked.

"If they have fifteen other survivors, no one is missing," I said.

Simon dug a walkie talkie out of its holster and spoke into it. "Patron, we have one male and two females. They say that there were eighteen on the plane."

"In that case, everyone is accounted for," the other speaker replied. "Are you returning your passengers here or to the shore?"

"Do you want to go to the patron's boat," Lucas asked, "or should we take you ashore where your friends are headed?"

"Ashore," I said without hesitation. "We will pay a visit to your patron to thank him at a later date."

"Si, Senor," Lucas said. He relayed our response into the walkie-talkie.

Lucas sped toward the shore, a beam of light at the front of the boat illuminating the way. The ocean rose sharply before us, and we rose and fell with it. It felt like a very long wave, a swell.

"What's happening?" Letty asked, clutching my hand.

Simon said, "It's the plane sinking. I'm surprised it was afloat that long. We saw the plane land on the water and break apart."

"I don't understand how we got separated," I said.

"That we didn't see," Lucas said. "Ahead is the Krystal Hotel Beach where the fishermen took your friends. Radio chatter says the Red Cross is there attending to everyone from the plane."

"Great," I said. I was hoping for a miracle that no one was hurt. Look at us. We got out without a scratch.

"I see the lights," I said.

"So do I," Letty said, pointing. "Over there."

"Oh, God! I want everyone to be okay," Tangles said.

Everyone turns to God when there is trouble. I should know. I do it through the Virgin of Guadalupe. If it is true that everyone had been rescued, it is a miracle. After the plane crash landed on the water and split in two, it is unbelievable that any of us are alive. I needed to see the others to believe it.

The boat sped over the shifting water, sea air washing over us. I hung on to Letty and Tangles as if I could never let them go, their heads resting on my shoulders as we bounded our way to shore, riding high on the water. I felt their love flowing to me like my own heart's blood. The boat could have held twenty or more, and only the five of us were aboard. It felt like the perfect moment to be alive, and I was inexpressibly thankful for it. My senses were attuned to everything: the water, the wind, the sound of the engines, the voices of our escorts, the staccato background chatter from their radio dulled by engine noise, some raucous, unexpectedly nocturnal sea bird. I would never forget the intensity of this moment. It had been a very long time since I realized how great it is to be alive.

November 1, 1991 (Friday night)
Bogota
Olga

At eleven his time, Mario called me from the airport to let me know they were aboard and were ten minutes from being wheels up. They were going to have a midnight supper on the plane, and be in Bogota by seven a.m.

"It would be nice if we were all together here at the big house," I said.

"Big house it is."

"Safe trip, Amor."

"I miss you calling me Amor."

"We never talk much anymore," I reminded him.

"We should talk more," he said.

I didn't agree or disagree.

I did not tell Mario how much I miss him. Even before I ended our engagement, we had not been constantly together, but we were always in touch. We'd had an open engagement, an understanding. At least, we'd had an understanding until Mario brought home a hooker named Lola, who had turned out to be a federal agent. Camila ordered her executioner to kill her.

He shot her, but she hung on to life. Camila ordered another shooter to finish her while she was in the hospital in a coma. That shooter ended up dead before he could finish the job. Lola recovered and surfaced again to tell Mario that she wanted a million dollars in compensation for the pain and suffering she had endured from the attempts on her life. If she didn't get the money, she threatened to kill Camila and me.

Mario delivered her message to us in person, treating her whole scenario like one of those plane crashes he used to handle for lawyers where the family is entitled to compensation.

"Pay the million," he said. "Who knows what an angered cop can do."

"I'm not paying," Camila insisted, but eventually she gave in.

After endorsing her blackmail (he called it compensation), Mario had continued to see the bitch cop. That's what pissed me off the most. After she blackmailed us and threatened to kill us, he still sneaked off for sex with her. Not to mention, she was a cop whose job it was to take Camila and me down, along with our business. Someone took her down, though. Lola died when her car blew up. I don't know who did it, but I'm grateful to them. Her death did not forgive Mario's involvement with her. At the time, it was unforgiveable, and it still is. I was devastated. I didn't care who he fucked but how could he continue with a woman who threatened to kill me, his fiancée?

I had nothing to do with the orders to go after Lola. Camila never told me or consulted with me. I didn't even know about it, not until after the second failed attempt. That's when she told me about it. There was no way Lola or anyone else knew Camila (or I for that matter) had anything to do with it. Still the bitch blackmailed us, and got away with her money, using my fiancée as her messenger.

Mario ran GAL aviation leasing for LAI. Camila *was* LAI since she owned all the stock in LAI. Now that she'd died and I'd inherited, he would be running it for me. I'm glad he was infatuated with the business, because I needed him to stay. Then again, why would he want to leave? He was making more money than ever before. When I broke our engagement, Camila had been worried that he might walk. But he didn't leave.

That was a relief not only for Camila, but for also for me since if he left, she would have blamed me.

I have never been officially adopted into Camila's family, but we were sisters. My father had worked for her father. I grew up in the Camacho house alongside Camila and her brother Pepe. They were all the family I had.

Before this, I have never leaned on anyone for personal support. But now that they are both dead, without them, I feel like something is missing. Camila's death has left me feeling insecure. I can't remember a time when I felt like that, not even when my father's death left me orphaned.

Now Lola is dead, Camila is dead, Pepe is dead. Mario and I have been apart since I broke it off. I have never been so alone. I have no one at all except my companion Riana.

It hurts that Mario and I are not whatever we were before.

Camila, may you rest in peace my dear sister. I shared him with you, and you shared him with me, and there was never an awkward moment between us about it. Lola was a different story. Her intrusion between Mario and me felt like being knifed by my best friend.

In a few hours, he'll be here. We will sleep under one roof again, maybe in one bed. I can't help thinking that tonight we might be in bed together. Does he miss me as I miss him? How can I be wanting him, Camila, with you trapped forever in your permanent sleep? I am so anxious.

Riana has been a godsend. Handling the preparations for the funeral has been grueling. I have been sitting back and letting Riana do the lion's share of the work. She's been delicate about it too, coming to me the way I used to come to Camila, and making subtle suggestions about telling the servants this or that. This afternoon, she came up to me with changes in the menu for the dinner after the funeral. I grabbed her hand as she held the typewritten menu out to me. I took it, but for all I noticed, it could have been written in Chinese.

"Riana, Amor, feed them whatever you want. Whatever you say, it's fine with me. The chef will do it. I can't deal with this right now. I'm torn."

"Don't worry. I got it totally under control. It's not like I don't have a lot of help."

We have over sixty on staff at this Camacho house.

"Thank you, Amor. I love you," I said.

Riana leaned over to embrace me, her lips on the top of my head, then my forehead. She walked in a cloud of light fragrance that was comforting to me because it was hers.

"I promise I'll be back to normal," I said. "I can't stand being like this."

"You're fine," she said. "All you need is the time to heal."

I was lying in bed, sleepless beside Riana when the house phone rang on her side of the bed. She answered it. Her face got very still, and her voice quiet.

"I see," she said on the line, then turned to me with the phone out.

Riana said, "You need to take this call. It's important."

I wanted to pull the pillow over my head and ignore the problem, whatever the problem was, but Riana would not be giving the phone to me if it were not urgent. I sat up in the dark and took the receiver. The lacy strap of my gown dropped off my shoulder, and I pulled it back up.

"This is Olga. Who is this?"

"Miss Olga, this is Ava."

She was Andrea's assistant at the Los Angeles GAL office. She had been Mario's assistant, but positions there were fluid, and change as needed.

On top of the sadness I was feeling over losing Camila, I felt a sense of dread. Ava would not be calling at five a.m for good news.

"What is it Ava?"

"I just took a call from the NTSB about one of our planes down near Puerto Vallarta."

"What did you say?"

"I have no details yet. I know a plane is down in the ocean, and it can only be Mr. Mario's plane."

I felt my heart stop. The wrench in my chest blocked my breath, but I managed to respond as if I were sane.

"You have the manifest of everyone on that plane," I said. "Call them and get right back to me. We have protocols for a downed plane. Follow them. And call me the instant there is news. I want constant updates."

I got up and walked to the foot of the bed where there was a sofa. I sat down. Behind me, I heard a soft tap, and a bedside lamp switched on. I closed my eyes against the light, dim as it was.

"Yes, Miss Olga, right away."

Ava hung up. I sat there with the phone in my hand. Riana took it and hung it up and returned to sit beside me. She took both of my hands in hers, and chafed them, gently.

"Mario's plane?"

I nodded. The tears rolled down my face.

"Turn the TV on," I managed to say. "The news."

There was nothing of it on television, at least not here in Bogota.

Ava called back. "I called every cell number I have for everyone. I get a ring but nothing else."

"Are we in touch with anyone in Puerto Vallarta?"

"Mason's in Los Angeles but he said he'd get right back to you."

Mason was a licensed psychiatrist and lawyer who didn't have patients. He used his know-how to solve cases. He was my private investigator. For the right money, he would do just about anything.

I curled up on the sofa in my bedroom, my face pushed against a cushion, my back to Riana who was hugging me. I cried, at times, loud and hysterical, then quiet and inconsolable. I rambled. I cursed. I prayed.

"Riana, pray for him. I forgot how to pray. Please Riana, pray."

She mumbled something in return. I have no idea what. All I knew is that she was there.

Riana and I leapt at the sound of the phone ringing. It was only minutes since the last call but felt like hours. Riana's lavender negligee floated around her, and when she moved, it felt like slow motion to me. The seconds ticked away. Riana went to the nightstand and answered it.

"This is Riana. Who is this? Mason, hold on."

Maybe Mason had news. I was anxious to hear, but terrified that the news would be bad.

I took the phone.

"Did you find out anything?" I asked. It was hard to breathe, and the bout of crying had left me hoarse. Riana was holding me, her face beside mine, listening to the call.

"ATC says that the plane touched down on the ocean only a few miles from Puerto Vallarta. He can't confirm officially, but eighteen living survivors have been rescued. I have Rodney on the other line with the Krystal Hotel where the Mexican Red Cross is set up."

"Mason," I said his name, and there was a long pause as I struggled to sound normal. "Stay on this. Call me right away with any news."

"He's okay," Riana said. "You can't kill that man."

I fell again into sobs. I had not cried this much when I learned of Camila's death. At least the feeling I had now was relief. I opened my dresser and stood staring at the piles of black clothes inside. Riana handed me an oversized t-shirt. I recognized it as one of Mario's and put it on. Irrationally, I felt better immediately, like I was somehow closer to him.

I went down the hall and into the small bathroom off the den. Stucco walls. I could remember when Camila chose the cool mint colors it was painted in. Even that memory hurt, but not so much now that Mario, at least, was still alive. I washed my face with cold water and couldn't believe the mess I saw in the mirror. I was bare-faced but swollen from all the tears.

When I came out, I brought a damp washcloth with me to help repair the damage. Riana was still in her peignoir waiting for me. She'd put on matching scuffs, little wisps of lavender fabric.

"If he survives this, I will forgive him, and I will never, ever, mention Lola again."

Riana hugged me.

"I adore him," I said.

"I know," Riana said. "I know."

She brought me my cell phone. I looked at it, turned it over and over in my hand and willed it to ring, but time passed, and it was silent.

We had gone back to my bedroom, Riana and me. I refused a sleeping pill. If anyone called with news, if *he* called, I wanted to be awake.

Riana inhaled and exhaled softly beside me, but I rolled around restlessly for two hours in the dark, turning fitfully, and trying to find a comfortable position in a world that had no comfort for me. My cell rang. My heart raced. I knew who it must be.

"Baby, I don't know if you've heard, but we had a little mishap on the way to Bogota," Mario said.

"Mario," I said. My voice sounded normal. I was feeling anything but.

Riana had sat up with the first ring. I handed the phone to her. She knew what to do.

"Mario, Olga needs to get hold of herself. Don't hang up. We're so happy you are alive." Riana put her hand over the phone and said, "Mario says everyone is alive."

I put my hand up, one finger up. One moment. That's all I needed. I took a deep breath.

Once I was hijacked by my own security crew. I was raped, then I shot and killed the turncoats, went into the cockpit, killed the pilot and co-pilot, and managed to fly the DC-9 to Bogota and land safely. My heart beat wildly during that crisis, but it did not compare to how it raced when I heard

Mario's voice on that call.

　　I took the phone back from Riana.

　　"Amor, Amor, Amor, I adore you, I adore you."

　　After I talked to Mario, I had the Learjet that we kept for domestic flying, and my DC9 manned with crews to head to Puerto Vallarta. I sent the Lear to fly the crew to Los Angeles where they were from. My plane would bring Mario and his group of nine to Bogota.

　　I left Riana, and walked alone into the living room, a huge, bright, beautiful room with seating for fifty or more. The thermostat said seventy-two, the perfect temperature, but I was freezing. I sat beside one of the wing chairs Camila had favored, a blanket around me.

　　"Mario almost didn't make it to your funeral," I told Camila's chair as if Camila were in it, "but you know him. He just won't die."

　　I closed my eyes. A picture of him played in my brain. I knew Mario was traveling with the girls, and Camila was lying in a refrigerator waiting to be buried. Earlier this morning, I had been broken by Mario's death. Well, at least he was alive. I willed myself not to think about the dead lady cop. The harder I tried to banish Lola from my thoughts, the more persistently she lodged in my brain.

　　My personal house assistant, Gloria, prepared a bath for me. Bogota in November did not get very cold, but it was winter. I didn't ask her where she managed to find the bucket's worth of rose petals that floated around me as I submerged up to my chin. I lay back on the bath pillow and drifted away.

　　I complained to Gloria when I woke up.

　　"Next time, wake me right away," I said. "I wanted to savor the moment, not sleep through it."

"Count on it, Miss Olga," she said in Spanish.

She always smiled. I loved her. She worked at my house in Bogota, but all my personnel had come to the big house to provide extra help in preparation for tomorrow's funeral. Gloria was here to look after me. I put my hand on the crystal pillar behind the marble tub and gave the other to Gloria as I climbed out.

She joined me in the shower. I sat on the marble bench, water cascading from three different sources in the ceiling. Gloria washed my hair and sponged me with a soapy puff. I was like a yeti with soap instead of fur, then the water washed it away. Her own hair was up in a ponytail, long and black and sticking to her bare skin.

I heard Riana outside the shower door.

"I can see you are in good hands. I'm going back to work on the funeral buffet."

"Si, Amor, thank you."

Gloria rarely voiced an opinion, but she spoke up now.

"Miss Olga, I was pleased for you that Mr. Mario was saved."

"When I heard his voice, the entire weight of trouble I had on my shoulders vanished," I said. "Still there is Camila's funeral. It is so sad, so hard to bear. I cannot say goodbye. This house is so empty without her."

I looked up from the bench where I was sitting as Gloria made the sign of the cross. Hot water poured down on both of us.

"May Miss Camila rest in peace," she said.

I opened my arms and hugged her, still sitting.

"You are so special," I said.

"Thank you, Miss Olga."

I kissed her stomach, and she giggled. Her merry little laugh lifted my spirits. It felt good to be spoiled. It was a distraction from everything else.

My plane arrived in Puerto Vallarta at noon. I was not on it.

I heard from Andrea who should have been taking it easy after the near-death experience.

"The media has been swarming since we arrived in the rescue boats. I guess that would be expected considering it was a plane crash, but now that they know Pixie and Lainie were on board, there is a mob. The hotel security people are trying to figure out how to get us out."

"Helicopter, of course," I said.

"Yes, but we don't fit in one helicopter. Don't worry, we'll be in Bogota. We'll get out of the hotel one way or another."

The news hit television in Bogota. The big story was how everyone survived and then all about Pixie and Lainie being on board.

I called Jaime, owner of De La Rosa's department store in Bogota. His store was twelve floors of everything, and it was one of my favorite places to shop.

"My deepest condolences for your loss, Olga."

"Thank you," I said, feeling the familiar knot in my throat. Camila had loved De La Rosa's also.

"Jamie, I need a favor."

"Anything for you, Olga."

"You heard of the plane crash in Puerto Vallarta?"

"Yes. Of course."

"The passengers will be flying here in a couple of hours. Nine women, one man. They need to shop. That includes Pixie and Bebé."

"Whatever you want, you got, Olga."

"What is your closing time?"

"Nine."

"They may arrive here after hours. They will all need clothes, every-thing from the skin out, sleepwear, changes of clothes, and especially some-thing for the funeral tomorrow. The man is large, athletic, six five. That's 195.58 centimeters. You may need a few tailors to work all night. It has to happen tonight because the funeral starts at noon tomorrow."

"I will open the store for them," Jamie said. "Just give me a call before you leave so we can be perfectly ready."

"You are a sweetheart, Amor."

"I love you dear friend."

"Bill me for everything. I'll see you at the funeral tomorrow."

"It's getting late, so hurry on this," I told my assistant Elisa. "Buy ten cell phones with domestic US and international coverage, and bring them to the house, activated and ready to use."

"I will get it done, Miss Olga," Elisa said.

"Thank you," I said.

Elisa Sarmiento wasn't a domestic, but she was a member of my house staff, at least technically. She manages international office duties in my place when I am not here, and is a personal assistant when I am. She looks like the twenty-two-year-old college student she is, though she never has given up her impressive waterfall of braids. (Bo Derrick has nothing on her.) She was born to a family who has been in service to the Camachos for gen-erations. We had paid for her education when she proved to be gifted in languages. For three years, when she was still in high school, she spent six months abroad in language immersion programs in Italy, France, Portugal, Spain, Germany, and Holland. Once she enrolled in the university, she continued mastering those languages. Her own family spoke Creole English, Spanish and a local African dialect. She'd grown up in the Santa Catalina Islands, where my family once had an estate that Pepe sold when he got out of the drug business. She called herself a Raizal. What I liked most is that in spite of her education, she kept her lovely Afro-Caribbean lilt when she spoke English.

She purchased them, set them up, and presented them to me returned to their boxes, with their Colombian phone numbers written in ink on the outside of the packages.

"Miss Olga, I heard the good news on television. Everyone is safe."

During the short crisis of not knowing anything, I only thought and worried about losing Mario. I had not once thought of the others.

"Yes, Elisa, all safe, thanks to God."

"We're going to be wheels up in twenty minutes," Andrea said on the plane's phone, a little after five p.m., calling from Puerto Vallarta. "We got out of the hotel, finally."

"I am glad you made it. What would I do without you? How is everyone?"

Andrea was a serious person and a realist right out of the box, but she was sounding downright spiritual. "We've all been marked by it, but there are no broken bones, no blood. We're good. No, we're amazing. We're walking miracles. Boss is waiting to talk to you."

"Amazing," I said. "Let me talk to Mario."

There was some static.

"Did you have to force anyone to board the identical plane?" I asked.

"Storm was a little balky. It's only her second time on a plane. I doubt she recognized that it is the same model. Your plane is not identical inside."

"Storm?"

"Betty's assistant. Purple hair? At least, it is purple now."

Betty was Mario's masseuse. I vaguely recalled a pink-haired girl with Betty the last time she worked on me.

"I've arranged for all of you to go shopping."

"I'll let everyone know. We're kind of a mess." Mario's laughter was music to my ears. "The hotel stores were closed. Only the gift shop was open. We look like a hotel gift shop exploded."

That put some pictures in my head that made me laugh aloud. I would have asked for details, but his statement reminded me of killing time one afternoon Mario was in the gym, and his team and I were all in a hotel gift shop trying on hats. I had bought all the hats they had, and Pixie and Letty had spent the rest of the vacation giving hats to everyone we met. It was—as Letty put it—a blast. It was twice as much fun because Mario had no clue why Letty was giving hats away and scratched his head over it for the whole trip. Had we been staying in the hotel, or were we just there at a restaurant? I couldn't recall exactly where it was—Hawaii, Jamaica, the Bahamas—but I realized that moment how glad I was that none of the girls had died. I felt a serious wave of emotion.

"Amor, I thought I had lost you."

"That makes two of us," he said in a low voice. "The plane fell, then hit the water, and broke apart. I thought we had all breathed our last."

"I am glad you were wrong. Amor."

"Me too."

"I'll let you go now. Safe travels."

"We'll be there before you know it."

"Si, Amor, Si."

November 2, 1991
Puerto Vallarta
Letty

If any of us had a camera, I would have used it. The pictures of us would be hilarious. The Red Cross gave us scrubs. Even Mario got some that fit. The medical exams were brief, but it was slow, and there were eighteen of us. Mario arranged a room for each of us, all on the same floor except for the crew who were down on the second floor. We had six hours to shower and sleep before Olga's plane was scheduled to arrive. Boss gave us an option to go back home or continue on to Bogota. All of us except Storm had known Camila. She had touched our lives. We all felt obligated to pay our respects and be there for her funeral.

"I came with you. I'll go home with you," Storm said.

Mario had kissed her.

"Brave girl," he said.

After the sun came up, we met in a waiting room on the top floor where the helipad was a few steps outside the door. Andrea had us sign a simple one paragraph affidavit of citizenship that attested under penalty of perjury we were citizens of the United States. Andrea was still an Italian citizen, so I guess her paragraph was different.

"Olga arranged with customs in Bogota to issue a visa without a passport to each of us. On our return, our attorney in Los Angeles will arrange to let us enter without a passport providing we have this affidavit. It's a good thing that all of you are US citizens. I'm not, but I'll manage," Andrea said.

I seriously doubt she got any sleep at all.

Tangles whispered in my ear. "I'd fuck Andrea if she was a boy."

I whispered back. "Have some respect. We're going to a funeral tomorrow. And since when did somebody being a girl keep you from fucking them?"

"What are you to up to with the whispers?" Mario asked

We just giggled.

I should not have mentioned a camera because, of course, Mario heard, and bought one and handed it to me on the plane. It was just one of those plastic instamatics where you point and shoot, but I took loads of pictures of us with no makeup, in matching scrubs like some kind of hospital music squad or majorettes or drill team flying to some competition, with no underwear, sitting in the plush seats of Olga's tricked-out plane, and poor Mario, the only guy. We were scrubbed clean like the Mormon Tabernacle choir only I'm pretty sure they wear underclothes. Not a drop of makeup among us, and don't let me start on the hair. The scrubs were clean, and so were we, but it was pretty obscene with none of us in underwear. There was no place open at the hotel to buy anything like that. Of course, Pixie and Lainie look like pin-ups. I know the paparazzi snuck a couple shots of them. There were some bulb flashes at the airport. I'll have to get my pictures developed somewhere special because the paparazzi would go crazy over these pictures. But they're just for us.

The pilot just announced we're cruising at 30,000 plus feet. Mario's regular pilots don't usually make that kind of announcement, but this is Olga's regular flight crew. I can't remember the last time I flew in Olga's plane. I guess she expects her cockpit crew to be like an airline, or maybe they are just doing it because it's a full house. I mean, this big plane is nowhere near full, but we're used to flying three at a time, and ten almost feels like a crowd. Earlier we had the full drill about emergency exits and fasten your seat belts, etc. Except for Storm, we all know the drill. My heart raced a little, especially when she did the oxygen mask demonstration. I remembered when the oxygen masks made their appearance before we lost the second engine. I paid attention like we were going to be quizzed on it, and believe you me, I wasn't the only one.

November 2, 1991 (evening)
Bogota
Mario

Olga and Riana greeted us at the door. There were lots of long hugs and kisses in the foyer under a crystal chandelier about twenty feet overhead. Pepe Camacho had been buried on the big Camacho estate in the private cemetery, so we had been to the big house before. Twenty-one bedrooms with ensuite bathrooms. Over thirty-five thousand square feet of house.

"Thank you so much for coming to celebrate Camila's life," Olga said. "I am horrified by the crash but thankful that all of you are alive. After dinner, you can all go shopping. My treat."

"You'll be sorry," Tangles said.

"That's for sure." Pixie giggled with her special giggle.

"The store is expecting you in an hour and a half, so we have an hour for dinner."

"I'm starving. Let's eat," Lainie said.

The table was huge by any standards, and probably hand-made for that particular enormous dining room. At least a dozen empty chairs not in use were parked against the wall. Staff brought in trays of hamburgers, pastramis, tortas, burritos, spareribs, chile rellenos and sides like baked potatoes, refried pinto beans topped in melted cheese, and elotes, and put them on the buffet, flavoring the air with chili and cumin. As we carried our plates and filled them up, Olga walked the table and hugged each of us.

"Let me see what happened to you," she said to Letty.

Letty pushed her plate away and stood. "I have to pull my pants off, and I have no panties," Letty said, laughing, and reaching for her waistband. Olga laughed with her, and put her hand on her shoulder, encouraging her back into her chair.

"Eat," Olga said. "It's almost time to shop."

"You are my family," Olga said, "Even you, Storm. It means so much to me that you wouldn't let a plane crash stand between you and remembering Camila."

On arrival at the store, a shy little man waved a large red handkerchief at me to get my attention. He came over to me with a clipboard in one hand, chalk in the other, a pencil behind one ear, and a measuring tape looped over his neck. His shock at seeing me in scrubs was comical, and it was about the only thing he did not talk about. I followed him into a lavish dressing room where he apologized profusely for bothering me, then made busy use of a dressmaker's tape, chattering in a low voice the whole time. A very tanned young man with a long mullet walked in carrying an ironing board and an iron, which he set up in an adjoining room. Meanwhile the head tailor took each measurement twice and marked the numbers on a drawing of a dressmaker's dummy on his clipboard. He did not give me his name but introduced me to the young man he called Mr. Dias whose job it would be to follow me and collect the items I would need to have altered. The tailor talked about the clothes available in the store, how hard it must be for me to find clothes that fit, offered condolences for Camila whom he said he'd never met personally though he had altered many clothes for her, and apologized at least seven times for intruding in my private spaces.

"How else would you get the measurements?" I asked. He didn't respond, having launched again into lavish descriptions about the selection of funeral-suitable big and tall menswear available upstairs, and then gave me some very involved directions on how to get to the exact place where my sizes might be found.

It was past midnight when we got in the caravan for the ride back from the department store. The store reminded me of Harrods in London only smaller. Olga had not gone shopping with us. Ahead of us was a police car with flashing red lights, then a Suburban full of security. We were in the second Suburban. Countless bags followed us in the third Suburban. Trailing us were four motorcycle cops, their red lights flashing. It felt more like a midnight parade than an emergency expedition to secure mourning clothes for the funeral.

"I can't believe this," Storm said, impressed by the experience.

"This is Olga to a 't,'" Letty said. "Extravagance and security. Camila was the same way."

"I wanted to pay for my purchases," Jo said. "My wallet is somewhere in the Pacific."

"Mine too," Niley said.

"Don't worry about it," I said. "Olga would never had permitted you to spend your own money."

"I had no problem packing it up," Andrea said with a laugh.

"I bought eight pairs of panties," Letty said.

"You're wearing more than panties to the funeral tomorrow, right?" Tangles asked.

She took the words right out of my mouth.

"You saw the dress I picked out," Letty said, poking Tangles in the arm. It only made her laugh.

"We bought a ton of stuff. We were shopping in the same area as we're about the same size."

"The tailors are working all night to get your clothes done in time for the funeral tomorrow," Letty said.

"I know. I met the tailors." I pictured my luggage that had gone down in the plane. "Yeah, it's crazy when you think of the full closets I have at home."

"But you aren't home," Betty reminded me.

"I bought myself everything nice," Storm said softly, her face turning pink.

"I feel like a leech compared to you," Betty said, "My name is on four full bags."

The store had sweatpants, sweaters and jeans that fit; and I had gotten two of each. I found only one t-shirt that fit, plain white cotton, but it felt like silk. I found three pairs of leather shoes and two pairs of tennis shoes and one pair of sandals. My clothes for the funeral had been snatched up by Mr. Dias as soon as I had found them.

When we pulled in front of the house, Olga and Riana had an army of staff on hand to carry everything inside. Our clothes went straight to our rooms, but we went straight to the buffet table. The desserts we didn't have time to eat at dinner were served. The coffee, cocoa, and specialty candy were delicious. Tangles and Letty split dishes of every dessert there, just to try them. They had candied figs, a baked coconut cookie called *cocadas* similar to macaroons, cassava cake with guava jam, flan, *milhojas*—thousand sheet pastries with a variety of different fillings—and *merenguitos* which were hard little meringues. Fredo the bartender had no takers for the score of dessert liquors from Olga's bar, nor did Margarita for the assortment of cigars and joints she offered from an engraved silver box.

"Tomorrow, perhaps," I told Margarita.

"Yes, Mr. Mario."

Everyone kissed and hugged before leaving the dining room. I kissed Olga and Riana, then I hugged Olga a second time. "I am tremendously sorry for your loss," I said to her.

"Si, Amor, thank you. Her passing is a loss for everyone. She will be missed. She will never be forgotten."

Camila had been one of the hottest ladies I had ever met, that is until I met Olga.

Eventually we were escorted to our bedrooms where our purchases were waiting. The bed was not as large as mine at home and there was no mirror over the bed, but it was bigger than a standard king, and long enough for me to easily stretch out. The walls were wood halfway up, and where the wood ended, they were papered up to the crown molding with scarlet fabric. A glass wall opened to a balcony with a view of the old estate. It was a manly room, so huge that even with several large freestanding wooden wardrobes, dressers, desks and chairs, it felt open. It's possible it may have been Pepe's room. I wasn't going to ask.

I went through my shopping bags and put everything in one massive empty wardrobe. Mr. Dias had taken a suit and four shirts that had needed alteration, and he assured me that the clothing would be here before the funeral.

Just before three in the morning, I turned off the lights and hit the bed. Less than five minutes later, I heard the door open for a second. I expected it to be Letty, but I knew by the fragrance that it was Olga. I came to life all over. I sat up in the bed.

"Amor, it's me. Is it okay?"

I had left the curtains open for the night view of the estate, and so the sun would wake me in the morning, but there was not much light coming in. I could barely see her. I opened my arms.

"It's been too long," I said.

She tossed her robe over the back of a chair.

She moved on top of me, her lips on mine.

She mounted me in an easy, swift move, taking my breath, not in a bad way.

"I couldn't wait, Amor. I'm sorry."

She spoke into my mouth. It had been such a long time since we had been together. It was both familiar and excitingly new.

"Am I dreaming?" I whispered.

"Amor, Amor, I promise you are not."

Before and during our engagement, Olga and I had sex for one, sometimes two hours, slow, fast, hard, every which way. We sometimes lingered all day in bed, or had others join us, like Letty or Riana for marathons that took all night. We had been in unusual places, like in the ocean, pool, on a beach, in a high rise building in construction, and of course, aboard a plane. That night in a secluded bedroom, we were both spent in five minutes.

The Camacho house is designed for entertaining. A funeral was not entertaining, but it was certainly a massive event. A large crowd circulated through several rooms on the ground level of the house. I had no idea of the number of guests. All the rooms connecting to the entry were engaged, including a large area outside of the house, plus the front parlor, a den, the dining room, a living room and a few bedrooms for use as coat closets. Those who were here for the funeral circulated freely. I hadn't asked Olga how many were working to keep everything moving smoothly, but I had counted fifty Camacho staff just inside. There were dozens more outside managing the cars and seeing to the guest's needs. In addition, plainclothes guards armed with automatic weapons were scattered from the basement to the roof tops, from the street to the wooded folly, and, of course, the private cemetery on the grounds.

About five blocks from the back of the main residence was the family cemetery. About a block from the residence was a helipad with Olga's helicopter. In front of the house, half of a mile from the front gates were two more helipads where guests were being delivered. I could hear the helicopters landing and taking off as I was walking around the back of the house.

My grounds at Casa Luna are large but a matchbox in comparison to this property. I saw guests walking in small groups following a cobblestone pathway. Wrought iron park lights had been erected just for this occasion to guide everyone from start to finish. The lights themselves were things of beauty, the metal hand-crafted, coiling into the shapes of vines and leaves crawling up the posts. The path led from the house across the lawns, around fountains and gardens to the cemetery. Golf carts weaved along the pathway. Walkers moved out of the way for the small vehicles carrying people who couldn't or didn't wish to walk.

Jack Fino arrived.

Olga walked him over to where I was standing. She stayed only as long as was polite, and then excused herself to continue with her rounds of the guests.

"I was shocked when I heard about the plane going down," Fino said. "I'm glad this isn't your funeral, that you made it out alive, and equally glad I wasn't aboard."

I had asked him to join us on my plane. I patted him on his shoulder like a pal does.

"It was a bad experience, but it could have been much worse," I said. "I'm glad you didn't come along with us. Life is strange."

Jack shrugged. "I'm returning to LA right after the service," he told me. "I can't believe Camila is gone. After the shooter took a shot at her the first time, she should have done something."

It was my turn to shrug. "Jack, how the hell do you manage that kind of surveillance if you're not a king, or the president of the United States?"

Jack went silent, then nodded. "Yeah, you're right."

"Olga will go to every extreme to learn who did it. I'm sure that Mason and his team will find the responsible party," I said.

"Of that, I'm certain. Hand's down," Jack agreed. "I miss our lunches. We never see each other like before."

I put my arm around him.

"Jack, I'm working office hours now at GAL. I miss you too, my friend."

"Let's do something about making time for us again."

"Yes," I said.

He turned to shake someone's hand, and I saw Letty and Tangles walking toward me. They were gorgeous. A day ago, they had been bedraggled and barefoot on the beach, with salt in their hair. Now they were dolled up like the GAL executives they are. They can hold their own in any situation.

Riana's father, Felipe Carrera, arrived late. The funeral hadn't started but was about to.[1]

Shaking Carrera's hand reminded me of when Olga confessed that she'd bedded him. The confession had been years ago, a sexual encounter that she said was 'only business'—to launch his bank accepting large sums of green cash for deposit. Knowing Carrera had led Olga to an introduction to Riana, who was now practically Olga's shadow. I was glad Olga didn't have to fly everywhere alone. I searched the crowd, and found Riana circulating among the guests, as I expected, a shoulder's length from Olga.

There were several distinct groups of people who came to pay their respects. I paid attention, and counted first three, then four, maybe even six distinct groups. What I mean is that they sat separately, moved together, and did not mix. Some within each group stared at the others malevolently.

Maybe it was my imagination.

They seemed to get lost in the crowd when we all went outside for the walk to the cemetery; but when they stood in the cemetery, they sep-

---

[1] I had spoken to Carrera on the phone in his capacity as banker, and head of a lending consortium of bankers that financed whatever part of a lease GAL cut them in on. If GAL put up half the money and the consortium the other half, the monthly lease payment would be split in half. It was a good deal for both parties. Andrea was the instrument between GAL and the consortium. I didn't always give the consortium a steady flow of business because I wanted GAL to keep more of that monthly income. When they noticed, Riana's dad or someone from the consortium would complain to Olga. Someone would bring it to my attention, and I would turn the faucet back on.

arated again. Olga introduced me to a handful of people. They were from the government, and included the vice president of Bogota, the chief of police, and a few military generals. I shook their hands, mumbled a greeting, a comment about Camila, and something about Pepe's funeral where I had met them before.

Now they were here for Camila.

I cannot say how much it all reminded me of my all-time favorite movie, *The Godfather.* I prefer my excitement and brush with the underworld to be in movies. I couldn't tell who was who.

I didn't need to know. I didn't want to know.

Okay, maybe I am a curious man. I did want to know, but it was safer not to.

I counted fifteen golf carts moving along on the grass, loaded with people. Jo, Niley, Letty, Tangles, and I were walking in our own group. A short distance behind us were Pixie, Lainie, Betty, Storm, and Andrea.

"Melina called," Letty said. "She sends kisses. She called Olga to let her know she didn't fly in because of the difficulty with her pregnancy."

"I talked to her before we left. I know."

She had always been afraid of pregnancy after forty, and then she went and did it anyway.

"I met the Mayor of Bogota," Tangles said. "Said he'd like to take me to lunch."

"Maybe you'll get another six-carat from him like you did from Pepe," Letty teased.

"I wouldn't fuck this guy. Give me a break."

"Shh," I said. These two could get loud.

"Actually, I would fuck him for a six carat."

At least she spoke in a lower voice, and the last line had been in English which I doubted many of our fellow guests understood.

Tangles stopped and dug a stone from under her high heel.

"I don't know how you walk in those," Letty said. "You knew we would be walking on grass and dirt and cobblestones. Why did you wear heels? In heels, this is a walk and a half," Letty said. The boots she was wearing were not exactly flats, but compared to the stilettos Tangles was wearing, they might as well be.

"This is nothing," Tangles argued.

"Shh," I said.

At noon the next day, Pixie, Lainie, Letty, Tangles, Jo, Niley, Betty, Storm, and Andrea left Bogota for Los Angeles. Betty and Storm had their massage business to get back to. Pixie and Lainie had tours lined up. Jo and Niley had their business managing all my properties waiting; and everyone else worked at GAL.

Andrea was my second in command at the GAL office in Los Angeles. There was another office in Italy. I had lived there for a couple of years while Andrea and Jules taught me the business.

"You don't have to rush back to work," I had told Andrea. "I won't be here long."

Andrea always said she was married to GAL first and her husband second.

"I'm fine. I'll be at work tomorrow. You take your time."

I hugged Letty and Tangles. "I need to stay to sort out some things with Olga. I'm sorry to be letting you go back alone."

"Oh, Boss, we're not alone. We have a plane full," Tangles said, being her typical literal self.

"I love you, Boss. Take a step back and think about what you want," Letty said.

"I know what you mean."

They were family to me, but our kisses were filled with passion, not the way you kiss family.

"I'll be home before you know it."

I did not go with them to the airport.

November in Bogota was in the eighties, too warm for the sweaters I had picked out. My shirt sleeves were rolled up to my elbows. About the time Olga's plane was wheels up, Olga, Riana and I were having lunch in an old gazebo covered in vines and flowers, with water falling all around it into a koi pond. Olga was between Riana and me. The main swimming pool on the grounds was about fifty feet away. Olga's helicopter, probably the one I cruised in with her on a prior visit, was sitting ready on a helipad two hundred feet away. For all I knew she owned more than one helicopter.

"There is nothing in this world I would not do for either one of you," Olga said. "We are going to talk about delicate matters that I am now faced with. I need your input and support."

"What is it, baby?" I asked.

"The five families Pepe had arrangements with were here to pay their respects yesterday. They are not friendly with each other. They are rivals. What they have in common is that they get their cash deposited into banks by Camacho. In a few days I will be meeting them one by one to go over their current deposits and to discuss the future of doing business together."

"I think I may have noticed them," I said. "Strange that they were here in such close proximity to the vice president of Colombia, and all those military officers."

"Amor, it's not like the movies where the heads of cartels are hiding in caves. Look at this house. Every person in Colombia knew who Pepe's father was, and look how he lived."

"I never gave it much thought, but you are right, Olga, they don't hide," Riana interrupted.

"Baby, go on," I said.

"When Pepe died, Camila thought we might be done, but after she met with the families, they agreed for Camila to stay aboard for three more years. Although she told me it would be nice if we folded the money laundering business, Camila didn't really want the business to end. The money was too good. The thing is that Camila told the families that she was the one with the global bank connections. They had no idea that I'm the one who made the bank connections so we could deposit millions in green cash in the families' accounts. The families agreed to continue sending their cash and agreed to the time limit. But because she claimed the bank connections were hers, there is a possibility I can quit. I can claim the connections died with her."

"Sounds like you got a way out," I said.

"I need out. I will have my hands full with LAI, especially when we go public. There is much to do. I don't have time to be escorting millions of dollars all over the world. And who knows? I'm not so sure I have a way out. They may know it is me that has the connections. I barely know these people. Pepe always kept me away, and after she took over, so did Camila. I don't know what they will think."

"You really want out?" Riana asked.

"I'm tired of looking over my shoulder at airports, waiting to catch a bullet like Camila did. I'm burned out. I made enough money for myself and for Camacho."

"Good," I said.

"You never made a deal with the families," Riana said. "Why should you have to live up to a promise someone else made?"

"That's right. I didn't make any deal."

"You shouldn't be on the hook," I said.

"If I manage to get out without anyone getting killed, I'll be very happy."

"It used to be our dream," I said. "It was my dream."

Olga didn't confirm that it had also been her dream. When she had been my fiancée, we talked about her getting out of the business. I had not known quite what business it was. I had believed she was hauling drugs from Colombia to other countries in her big plane. On her end, she always said, soon. Soon never came.

"Did you talk business at the funeral with them?" I asked.

"Not a word. Condolences only. Each of them was warm and polite to me."

"Maybe your meets will go the same way. You can tell them that the people you messenger are not rooted to you as they were to Camila, and that without that connection, there's no possibility of multi-millions of dollars going into secret bank accounts on a regular basis."

"You talk about it like you know the business, Amor," Olga said. "You are so smart."

"I just figure they will understand that the chemistry and the trust has to be there."

"Rooted is an apt description," Riana said. "My father is rooted with Olga. If he were not, he'd shut the door on accepting cash deposits."

"Don't say that too loud," Olga said, though there was no one else in sight. "Remember, I'm not the one with the connections." She looked around as if she was expecting spies or something. Riana and I laughed.

"I hope they back away amicably," Olga said. "I'm not doing this anymore, even if it means a war."

"Why war?" I asked. "This isn't a territory thing. What am I missing?"

"What you're missing is how much these enterprises need this service. Pepe's father, he had money warehoused in houses, buildings all over the world, wherever he sold his product. The money just sat there uselessly in storage. Pepe started investing it in properties, then found a way to bank some of it. I came along and found a place for all of it. Just as Pepe's father did, the families here in Colombia lost millions. Buried cash—and by buried, I mean hidden, stored—buried cash succumbs to mold and deterioration. So now the cartels have had years to get accustomed to having a way to move their profits into usable legitimate bank accounts. They may go crazy when I pull the plug and reality sinks in."

I nodded. "Got it, baby. You got to convince them you are nothing without Camila, no matter how big of a lie that is."

"Amor, I'll get it done."

November 4, 1991
Pasadena
Storm

I was pretty rattled. I almost died in a plane crash. How many people live through something like that? I was desperate to get home. I figured I'd get some comfort there. I walked up the flight of stairs to the apartment in scrubs, the clothes Olga bought in the Louis Vuitton bag she gave us to carry them in. Lugging the bag up the flight of steps was a return to reality. I could not picture Olga hauling her own suitcase, much less walking up an outdoor metal staircase to a squalid little second story apartment whose only view was an inner city parking lot that needed paving. Still, it was good to be home. It was still daylight, so I banged on the door, but nobody answered it. I used my key. The door squeaked real loud and when I opened it, the smell of the apartment hit my nose: mold, old pizza, beer with a hint of garbage. One step in, I could see the kitchen trash can overflowing.

My guy Rick, he's not much of a talker, but I figured I'd be able to talk with him about my feelings. I needed to vent over being on a plane and surviving the crash. It was only now that I walked in that I remembered how pissed off he was that I'd gone in the first place. When I left for the airport, he threw a bowl of chili at me. It was dried on the wall and looking like some topographical map of Death Valley. With beans. I left in the middle of the argument.

I dropped my Louis Vuitton bag on the patchy shag carpet so I could drag the trash out on the front step and shut the smell outside—some of the smell anyway. Rick was smelling pickled. He was zoned out on the couch beside an ashtray of roaches and a pile of twinkie wrappers. Judging by the heap of crushed cans on his lap, I guessed he'd polished off a six pack, eaten a whole box of cakes, then zoned out in front of MTV. I dragged my clothes into the bedroom, then came back to him. He didn't wake up when I gave his shoulder a shove. I returned to the bedroom, shut the door, and though it wasn't even dark yet, went to sleep.

November 5, 1991 (Thursday)
Bogota
Mario

Riana had gone off somewhere, leaving Olga and me alone in a second-floor den that Camila had been using as her office in this house. We were surrounded by antiques, walking on Persian rugs on highly polished Brazilian wood floors. There were anachronisms though—an office phone with multiple lines, a steel file cabinet secreted in a closet, a couple of state of the art computers side by side on a wooden table that must have been two hundred years old. All the deep reds and blues of the room were taken from a disturbing Salvador Dali original that hung over the computer table.

Olga pulled open a heavy red velvet curtain so that light streamed into the room, brightening a section of a thick, intricately-figured Persian rug in shades of burgundy. A small, old-fashioned door opened to a balcony with a table, chairs, and glider of wrought iron. The heavily padded cushions looked inviting, but, between Colombia and Puerto Vallarta, I'd had enough time to melt the winter from my bones. and I declined Olga's suggestion that we go out there.

"I'm perfectly happy staying in your central air conditioning," I said.

I was still in my shirtsleeves from lunch.

"Amor, I need you to reassure me that you will stay with GAL."

"Not if you fire me," I replied with a grin.

"I am serious, Amor. If I even think you will leave, I'm going to include the company in the public offering. As Camila did, I want to keep it a separate company. Please stay, Amor."

I nodded.

"I'm staying," I said.

The door to the hall was open. I only noticed because of a soft tap on wood that made me look in that direction. I recognized Olga's assistant Elisa standing in the opening.

"Pardon me," she said in her lilting accent. She is not a domestic, but she came in with a bottle of red and two glasses, poured, and set the bottle on the marble table in front of the sofa where we were sitting.

"Thank you, Elisa," Olga said.

"Shall I close the door?" Elisa asked.

"Please do."

When she was gone, we clicked our glasses of wine.

"Salud, Amor."

"Salud."

Olga took a sip, placed her glass on a tumbled marble coaster, and leaned forward. "What do you need to keep GAL growing?"

"As much money as you can give me to cover the cost of each lease."

"Fifty-percent, Amor. Give the other half to the consortium, straight across the board. If you do that, no sweat."

I preferred keeping more than fifty percent, but I wasn't going to argue now.

"I can do that," I said. "As long as the consortium can keep up with me."

"Amor, of course they can keep up. If they can't, find other banks. The company is solid. The idea of splitting the lease cost and income is solid. But you won't have to find alternative financing. Riana's father and his partners have tons of money."

"I'm sure," I agreed. "Remember the option we discussed when I came in? I want to buy in."

"Amor, let me get my feet wet with this huge undertaking I now have. After going public is off my plate, I promise to have that discussion with you."

I felt impatient but nodded. "Sure."

"Thanks, Amor. By the way, you need to be able to get around. Let GAL lease or buy you a plane."

I laughed. "I'll lease. It's a tax write-off how ever it's handled."

"Good, Amor. Any plane you wish."

I felt a rush of affection for her, and the wild extravagance that is so much a part of her.

"I love you, Olga."

"I still adore you, Amor."

I noticed her glass was empty and refilled it. Her eyes were downcast. I waited a moment and she said nothing.

"*Peso* for your thoughts?"

Her head jerked in my direction.

"This used to be Pepe's office," Olga said, the faraway look still in her eye. "Camila redecorated. All of the furniture is different."

"We don't want to talk about him," I said.

Camila had always decorated with a heavy hand. The fabrics she had chosen were always heavy, and the furniture was always antique. She had favored red, and the color combination of red and gold. I could not picture what this room had been before she changed it.

"For sure, Amor, we don't."

I changed the subject.

"I hope your Rio house came out the way you wanted."

Olga nodded. She inched closer to me on the sofa, one of many in this room. This one was red velvet like the curtains.

She trailed a long, perfectly manicured nail down the inside of my elbow to my wrist, giving me chills and goosebumps. She kicked off one shoe and ran her stockinged foot up the side of my leg.

"It's almost perfect," she said. The way she looked at me telegraphed the message that the only thing missing in Rio was me.

"This room is almost perfect too. I know exactly what we could do to exorcise all the ghosts."

I heard a knock at the door. It went unanswered, and whoever it had been went away. We snuggled together. Soon we were engaged in sexual aerobics, feeding the fierce appetite for each other that never is fully sated.

Riana was back for dinner. We ate on an outdoor patio attended by a lot of servants who were practically invisible. A huge steak was put before me by one of these invisible servers. Riana and Olga had some kind of broiled fish accompanied by a fruit salad. I was happy with my steak, though it really wasn't as good as Miguel's. A sommelier uncorked my favorite Argentinian red wine. I laughed when Riana drank hers over ice, reminding me of Pixie. She tipped her wine glass, so a little red wine spilled on to her fish before she ate it.

"What do you think happened that both the engines failed?" Riana asked.

"Who knows? The second engine should have been able to get us safely to the airport. A whole bunch of investigative experts have that same question, including the engine manufacturer, Pratt Whitney. All the agencies will be in on working to figure it out. It is a miracle we are alive. I still can't believe we all walked away."

"Ava called me that the NTSB had contacted the office. That's how I found out it was down," Olga said. "I was devastated."

"That's history."

"We should consider compensating the girls," Olga said.

"I am sure that Storm thinks the shopping trip was more than enough compensation."

I laughed. Storm was the only one aboard who didn't know the business inside and out. "Seriously though, I don't know that they want compensation. Let me think about it," I said. Storm could probably use the money. Betty could probably use some money, too.

When I was handling plane crashes, the cases that I signed tended to be families of victims who died in the crash, not those who were injured or who survived close calls like our crash.

"When I get back, I'll start the claim to collect the property damage on the loss of the plane," I said.

"Ava has already filed a claim. You do whatever else you need to do to get the money."

"Property damage won't take long to collect."

"Amor, it's not like we need the money, but yes, get it."

We had already had sex once that night and were lying in Olga's bed with the lights out. If this were a cartoon, we would both be smoking our after-sex cigarettes. No candles were lit as there would be in my bedroom at home. I was in boxers, and Olga in a short silky gown. The central air conditioning was set somewhere in the sixties, and the whirr of the incoming air was pretty loud. It was strange to think how the furnace would be on at home, and a wood fire burning in my bedroom fireplace. November in Colombia is not the same as it is in Pasadena.

"What about us, Amor? Are we going to be engaged again?" Olga lifted her left hand. There was little ambient light, but I could see it was covered in rings, none of them mine. "I want my engagement ring back."

She had millions of dollars invested in jewels, fine jewelry, unparalleled gems, cut and uncut, closets full, maybe even warehouses full. She was certainly not lacking rings. With Camila gone, she would have tons of jewelry to inherit.

I turned on my side to face her. "Neither one of us wants to get married. Tell me the truth. Do you want to get married?"

Silence. She didn't answer. I heard the rustle of sheets and felt her hands on my shoulders pushing me on my back as she moved on top of me. The position wasn't about sex at that moment. She sat upright on me, and we were just talking.

"Amor, I don't know if I want to get married. What I do know is that I don't want anyone else to have you but me. I don't mean you can't do what you do with your team and other lady-friends here and there, but I don't want it to get serious. I'm so selfish. I'm sorry."

I shook my head, but I wasn't surprised. "You haven't changed in all these years."

I made a joke out of it, and she laughed. We'd been down this path before.

"Don't tease, Amor. I adore you. Fuck who you want, just don't get serious. Letty and Tangles live with you, and I never said anything about them. Letty, she's like a wife. It's okay because I know Letty is not looking to get married to you or anyone else, and Tangles is the same."

It was my turn to laugh, and I did. I did not contradict her, but I was pretty certain that if I asked Letty to marry me, she'd say yes.

"Baby, we had this arrangement when you broke up with me." I snapped my fingers. "Just like that."

I wasn't upset. I was just reminding her, that's all.

"Amor, I promised never to mention this again, but I have to say it. I was hurt when you kept seeing the cop Lola. It wasn't just a fuck. It was fucking a woman who threatened to kill me and Camila. It was fucking her after you paid her the blood money she asked for. I never laid eyes on the bitch in person, so I didn't know if she was serious or what. It felt like the worst kind of betrayal."

It wasn't so dark that I couldn't see the devastated expression on her face. I raised my hands like she had a gun pointed at me to show truce.

"We put that behind us. Lola is dead."

"She's dead but she's still in this bed between us," Olga said, but she nodded. She gave me the peace sign.

For once, Olga's position did not turn sexual. She collapsed against her pillow. Both of us were on our backs, staring at the ceiling. If she had turned on her side, I would have held her, but she didn't. I waited for her to turn, but she never did. It was a long time before I fell asleep.

Olga had always been a mix of contradictions. Maybe that's one reason why she fascinated me.

She claimed she wanted complete sexual freedom for both of us, but she wanted me all to herself.

She'd displaced Melina from my life.

Melina was a woman I had wanted to marry. We never would have married because Melina had had a problem with our age difference. We were never officially engaged, but we were on the brink several times, even got as far as Vegas once, then didn't do it. Melina was convinced that her being ten years older than me would eventually be a problem. Soon after we met, I had moved into the same high rise Melina rented; and when she bought a house in Pasadena, I bought the property across the street, which is now Casa Luna, or I should say, the rebuilt Casa Luna because I've remodeled and rebuilt at least twice. Melina was a smart cookie who saw the writing on the wall long before Olga became a threat to our relationship. When my relationship with Olga got serious, Olga offered Melina six million for her house. Melina moved ten minutes away, far enough that Olga didn't feel as threatened. Olga never moved in the house, but leased it (house, Melina's former staff, furniture and all) to Pixie, after Pixie started making it big as a singer and performer. Melina had eventually married, and I wished her well; I didn't believe she loved her husband as wildly and passionately as we had loved each other. But like so much that has happened, that is ancient history now.

"Take my plane to fly home, stubborn man," Olga said.

"Thank you, baby, but no. Waste of money. It's just me. While we are on the subject of your plane, let's think about getting you another plane and moving this one on to someone else. I'm uncomfortable with you flying a plane identical to the one I crashed in."

"Si, Amor. Look for something and let me know what you find. I'm totally comfortable in the meantime. Besides, they aren't identical. My engines are Rolls Royce. Yours were Pratt Whitney."

There was no winning with Olga.

My life was filled with mysteries, I didn't expect to ever be satisfied with the investigation's findings. The reason why two engines stalled on my plane would be just another in the long list of unknowns in my life. Even if they found answers, the investigation would be years in the making.

"Baby, to use your words of how you say you feel about me, I adore you. I truly do. You are special to me. I was devastated when we broke up. You probably think I could have done a better job of showing it, but it's just the way I am. I don't want to go through that again. I'm not thinking of getting married any time soon, and you just told me the same. Who knows? Some young dude may come along that you will fall in love with. Let's be the best of friends. Let's be pals. Let's be close like you are with Riana. We don't need to be engaged to be that way."

"You just got even for me breaking up with you by turning me down. Embarrassing, Amor," Olga said. She pouted at me, and I don't know how much of the expression was real, and how much was playacting to make light of the situation.

"I think the world of you, Olga. Let's keep it simple, argument free," I said, hugging her.

We made love, followed by an hour of nasty sex. We slept together every night I was there. The last night Riana joined us, not for the first time. In spite of Riana passed out on the bed with Olga and me, our mutual appetite persisted.

Our last night before I left for home started with me kissing Olga with such force it may have hurt her, but she said nothing except begging me to crush her. I made love to her roughly, the way she liked, and when we were spent, we hugged in silence. Some time while we were wrapped up in each other, Riana went to her room.

In the morning we had strong black coffee and homemade dough-nuts on the balcony off of Olga's room. It wasn't hot yet. I could smell flowers from the gardens, and it melded with the scent of the coffee, fruit, and pastry. I wasn't really hungry. The backdrop behind Olga was an impressive view of the estate. In my head, I was thinking about everything I needed to do when I got back to Pasadena. The weather was warm and lovely here, and Pasadena was in the grip of November, but I was ready for home.

Olga sent the servants away.

"Amor, it doesn't matter any more, but I want to tell you this."

"Shoot."

We were alone on the balcony. Olga held a steaming cup to her lips and watched me over the rim.

"Camila sent enforcers twice to make the hit on Lola. She arranged the hit when Lola was shot getting into her car; and when Lola survived, she sent another shooter to finish the job at the hospital where Lola was in a coma. He was killed by the detective that was there. I hated Lola and still hate her now that she's dead, but I had nothing to do with the attempts on her life. Camila paid the million Lola wanted because you recommended it. I don't think she was ever convinced that Lola deserved compensation, but she was hopeful that it would make Lola go away."

Olga had denied being involved in Lola's shooting several times already. I did not remind her of it but stood up to kiss the top of her head.

"Thank you," I said. "Thank you for telling me."

"I'm no saint, Amor. Camila did not ask me. She acted alone when she gave the orders."

I nodded my understanding.

November 6, 1991
Pasadena
Storm

When I woke up, Rick was gone, and a cat or something had gotten into the trash outside the door. I got a broom and dustpan, scooped the mess back into the trash, and took it down to the dumpster downstairs though it was Rick's responsibility. Betty picked me up for twenty-four hours' worth of massage jobs, and when I got back mid-day, Rick was on the couch passed out again. The smell of the rancid trash had almost dissipated. I felt better with more than two hundred in my pocket from five separate massages. I lifted up his legs, flopped down, and let his limp legs drop over my lap.

"I'm back," I said.

He let out a big boozy snore.

"I said, I'm back." Louder.

The third time I yelled it.

He woke up.

He looked at me for two minutes straight before he got it together enough to talk.

"You're back," he said. "So, how is Queen Betty of the ten fingers?"

I stiffened. That was what he had called Betty when I'd told him I had to fly with her to the funeral. He had wanted me to stick around the apartment.

"You were right about not flying to Bogota," I told him. "The plane was big like a commercial jet, but it crashed halfway there. We ended up in the ocean. No one died though. They fished us out, and we got taken to a hotel in Puerta Vallarta, then the same day, they flew us to Bogota, and we stayed at this big ...I guess it was a plantation in Bogota. The funeral was right on the plantation in an old graveyard. I felt like I was in a movie, and Vito Corleone was going to come out smoking a cigar, and Clemenza was going to hand me my panties with a fish inside and say 'It's a Colombian message that I sleep with the fishes.'"

The dope just looked at me sleepy-eyed. "So, you're back."

"Do you get it?" I said. "I was in a plane crash. I was on my first plane trip and the plane crashed in the ocean."

He lifted his feet off my lap and sat up to pick through the ashtray looking for the biggest roach. He lit it up, sucked air, then looked at me again like he was surprised I was there.

I stood up from the couch. "They checked me over after the crash. Nobody got killed. As for me, no injuries. Can you believe it? Just a bruise on my ass." I pulled down my sweatpants and showed him the dark purple bruise that covered the back of my left leg from the knee up. I pulled my pants back up.

"Where'd that come from?" he asked.

He sucked another hit and offered me the roach. I slapped his hand away.

"You're such a dope," I said.

He laughed. "You been paid this week? I spent my disability check on this." He pointed to the remains of the pot in his ash tray. "Rent's due."

"You gotta find it somewhere else, dude. I'm out of here."

I dumped everything I had, clean and dirty alike, into a couple of boxes, and carried them out to my stupid car that wouldn't start. I tried a couple of times, but the battery was dead, and my jumper cable had walked off somewhere. I was lucky Rick wasn't paying attention. He didn't ask why I was carrying boxes of my stuff out. He'd figure it out sooner or later that I was gone, but it might take a year or two. I needed to use the phone but didn't want to go upstairs.

I remembered the phone that Olga gave me. I've never had a cell phone before.

I pulled it out and called Betty. No answer. I tried Letty.

"I need a ride."

Letty was there in twenty minutes. She jumped my car.

"Follow me home," Letty said. "We can talk over dinner."

So that's what I did. I followed her to Mario's. Betty came over for dinner. Letty, Tangles, Betty and I all had tomato soup and BLTs. Miguel had made the soup from scratch. I didn't even know people made tomato soup that didn't come from a can. It was so delicious that I didn't need those little fish crackers to make it taste good. The BLTs had watercress in them and were cooked in a panini press. I never had watercress before.

They were all discussing what I should do. We weren't in that huge dining room of his, just in the breakfast room off the kitchen, but still I felt like Queen for a day.

Betty thought I should move in with her. She and her boyfriend had an extra room. I was afraid I'd be a third wheel at their house.

Tangles and Letty said I could stay at their apartments, then they got into one of their quarrels about which of their apartments I would be staying at. They both turned to me, said I had to go with them, and choose which one I wanted.

"Choose now," Tangles said.

"No need to choose," Letty said, changing course. "Boss will be back tomorrow. We'll deal with it when he's back. We are picking him up at the airport."

Betty had an appointment for us, so after dinner, I went with her for a four-hand massage at Melina's, then Betty handed me my cut—a hundred dollars—and dropped me off at Casa Luna. Caro took my boxes and told me not to worry about it. She'd have everything back to me tomorrow, fresh from the dryer. I put on a huge old shirt—Letty had a drawer full of Mario's old t-shirts.

I spent the night in Letty's bedroom with Letty and Tangles, the three of us lying in bed talking. At midnight, Letty decided to go down to the kitchen and bake chocolate chip cookies. Tangles and I sat at the counter watching the magician toss it all together, helped her break up two handfuls of Hershey bars, and helped her eat the results. The cookies and milk were delicious.

I saw more of the house that night than I had seen before, including the kitchen and the gym. I got to wander around the basement, or first floor, whatever you want to call it. There was a fancy bar that Letty called the wine room. It had a disco ball that came out of the ceiling when Letty pushed a button on a remote control. The light dimmed and the ball spun and glittered, and we sat down on the crazy round couch to watch it. There was an actual bar, and a door to a wine cellar. Next door, there was this fancy arcade room that was full of pinball machines and games and a popcorn cart, and it had fake windows with window scenes that you could push a button, and change from Italy to Mexico to Paris, and a whole bunch of other places. Once I was down there, I made one big mistake though, asking how they kept so slim and fit. Next thing I knew I was in the gym—also on the same floor—working my ass off, clumsily following what Letty and Tangles were doing. My workout was a joke, but this morning when I could barely move, we all went to the hot tub downstairs and soaked, and they made me do a bunch of stretches that made me feel better. I can't believe they do that all the time.

Afterwards, we went to the kitchen, and Miguel fixed eggs for us two ways. I had easy over, Letty had scrambled with veggies and peppers in it and salsa on the side, and Tangles drank some nasty-looking green concoction she had Miguel mix up in the vita-mix. Tangles has weird taste in food.

After breakfast, it was late in the afternoon. While we had been doing stuff, Caro had brought all my clothes back in baskets, perfectly folded.

I stood in the hall staring at the baskets.

"I need my boxes back," I said. "I don't know where I'm going. I guess I can just bring the baskets back when I know where I'll be living."

"No worries," Letty said with a wave of her hand. "I have a feeling something will turn up."

Letty and Tangles spent an hour deciding what they were wearing to the airport. I was picking through the stuff in Letty's closet for some blue suit she was looking for. She and Letty were arguing as usual about who would wear what, and whether or not they should match.

"Can I come with you?" I asked, interrupting the flow of their repartee.

"Only if you drive," Letty snapped back. She started laughing, reached past the suit I was holding out to her, and handed me a professional-looking uniform with a cap. Then Letty and Tangles were both laughing. I wasn't in on the joke.

I put on the long-sleeved white shirt like a man's only cut to fit, the man-style tie, and the black military-looking coat that had gold bands on the wrists, and a double row of gold buttons down the front.

"You look sharp," Tangles said when I put it on.

"This will do the trick," Letty said.

Tangles nodded.

I looked at myself in the mirror. I looked like I had just graduated from Annapolis or West Point. Tangles slicked my hair back with gel and gave me a hat. It didn't matter that I wasn't in on the joke. They make me feel like family.

November 7, 1991 (Thursday)
Pasadena
Mario

Days after my team left Bogota, I took the LAI Learjet to Los Angeles with a stop in Mexico City. When they were refueling, I told the crew that I'd be back in a couple hours, and a taxi took me to the Villa of the Virgin of Guadalupe. I had thanked her before when Melina had survived a shooting. I had to thank her again for granting that my loved ones on the plane be spared from death. I had tried to make a bargain. I asked the Virgin to take me and spare my friends. I have faith that she spared me, though heaven only knows why. I have tremendous faith in the Virgin of Guadalupe.

The sun was on the verge of setting when the plane landed at Van Nuys Airport. I said goodbye to the crew and went down the plane stairs. Letty and Tangles were on the tarmac waiting, great big smiles on their pretty faces.

I enjoy sport cars and I've had them, but I'm six five or so. I fit better in a Rolls Royce. My car pulled up beside the plane. First, I was busy hugging and kissing my two ladies, then I looked over at the car to greet Raul, Pixie's chauffeur. He usually drives me when Pixie is on tour.

I did a double take.

Storm was in the driver's seat.

I walked over to the driver's window which was open and gave her a peck on the lips.

"Good to see you," I said. "I thought you'd be hanging out at your place getting over the crash."

"I'm over the crash, Boss. Just a few bruises left. One big one, actually. I can show it to you anytime you want to see for yourself."

"Fresh, bitch," Letty said.

"Fresh is right," Tangles echoed.

A plane roared by so loud all I could do is see their lips moving. Then it faded off in the distance, and once again I could hear them sniping at Storm loud enough that some of the plane crews hanging out in earshot were looking our way. I couldn't help it. I started laughing.

Letty elbowed Tangles, who stopped in mid-gripe. They both looked at me.

"What are you laughing at?" Letty asked, giving me what Tangles likes to call the stink-eye.

I didn't explain.

Finally, I was in the back seat with Letty and Tangles, headed home.

"Boss, Storm needs a job. She can't cut it with part-time massage work," Letty said.

"Boss, can Storm be your driver, please?"

A few minutes before both of them had been poking at Storm. Now they were lobbying for her to become my driver. I looked in the driver's mirror and saw a shocked look on Storm's face. Whoever had been in on this plan, it hadn't included Storm.

"Done," I said.

"Oh, Boss, thank you," Storm said. "You'll learn to love me," she said.

"I already love you."

"You can get a limo like Pixie's," Letty said.

"No way," I said. "I love this car. Besides, we don't need a privacy window if Storm is driving."

"Oh, Boss, I want to park right here so I can go back there and kiss you!"

We were in a fast moving lane with busy lanes on either side of us. The freeway was ahead.

I did not need to point it out. Letty said, "Drive, Bitch. Eyes on the road."

Storm shifted into the lane that fed the freeway.

"You'll get used to us," Tangles said.

Storm laughed, easing on to the freeway.

"I'm so happy, guys!"

She stuck her finger in her mouth and whistled, reminded me of Jo. Jo used to whistle like that. Not when she was happy though—just when she broke up family quarrels or hailed cabs when we were in foreign countries.

In the lane heading the opposite direction, I heard a metal on metal impact. It was loud, disrupting my thoughts. My heart went mad for a second, and I again heard the plane hitting the ocean.

I think I managed to keep my composure, or maybe the girls were dealing with their own responses to the noise. We had moved on, and the accident on the other side of the freeway was behind us.

"It's okay," I said. "We're all okay."

Letty and Tangles gripped either of my hands. I guess I was right that the sound had bothered them too. I nodded at Storm, our eyes meeting in the mirror.

The sound of the plane hitting the ocean and coming apart is engraved in my memory. How can anyone forget a thing like that? It's like being in a tin can while it is being ripped apart. When I was in the ocean looking at the stars, I had no certainty any of us were going to make it. At least I am home now. My treasures are here with me.

We should talk about the accident. I'm not sure where I first heard it was good to talk about a tragedy that happens to you or a loved one, but it is something always told to the families who lost people in tragedies.

I didn't want to talk. I'd rather smother my loved ones with hugs and kisses.

I showered and met the girls in the wine room. Miguel was five minutes from serving dinner at the round table in a niche in a bay window facing a garden. Letty sat across from me to my left, Tangles across to my right. Three canvas placemats were in front us, an empty wine glass, a full water glass, silverware, and for each of us, a napkin folded to look like a swan. Of course, Letty and Tangles swans started pecking at each other. Sometimes they act like they are nine.

"Boss, are you and Olga engaged again?" Letty asked, putting the swan into her lap without unfolding it.

Tangles looked up expectantly, silently, but she was watching.

"No, we're not engaged again."

We were not. Sex with other partners didn't matter to Olga. I don't think anything had changed much. Olga still wanted me not to care about anyone else but her. How, I ask you, can anyone control who they care about?

I had not been able to control my infatuation with Lola.

Miguel rolled in a cart carrying platters of food. A couple of steaks (my weakness), platters of vegetables, condiments, bread, baked potatoes. Storm walked in with Miguel, and she was wearing a red plaid apron made out of the kind of red and white cotton one sees on picnic tables.

"Hey, you're my driver. You don't need to work the kitchen," I said.

"Boss, Miguel is a chef of chefs. It's okay."

"Storm, get some flatware and join us. Draw up a chair next to one of my wives."

That made everyone laugh. It wasn't the first time I had referred to them as wives.

"Can I sit between you?" she asked Letty and Tangles. She took off the apron and tossed it over the back of her chair. Miguel snagged it on his way back into the kitchen. He brought out a place setting, glasses and a linen swan, and arranged it all in front of Storm.

And that was the beginning of Storm's new position on my team. She could have died in the plane owned by a company where I was the CEO, and the girl was not complaining. She was too busy thanking me for the job.

Letty and Tangles filled Storm's plate far too full, each trying as usual, to outdo the other.

"Boss, Storm's between apartments right now. Is it okay if she bunks up with me for a while?" Letty asked.

Storm looked from Letty to me, her jaw hanging open in surprise.

"With all the empty bedrooms in this house? If she wants, she can pick out a room of her own, and stay as long as she likes," I told Letty, then looked at Storm. "If that is okay with you."

Storm teared up. She took her folded swan and blotted her eyes.

It's times like this that I'm grateful to be financially solid. I hope I made Storm's day, first by giving her a job, and then by giving her a place to stay. She was a dynamite massage therapist. When she came over with Betty to help out, I paid her well, but she only worked with Betty part-time, as far as I knew. I don't know the story behind her financial woes.

"Make yourself at home," I said as Miguel wrested the platters from Tangles and doled out steak and potatoes to the rest of us. I had a porterhouse, and the girls the choice of bacon-wrapped filets, rib-eyes or strip steaks.

"I don't need driving often. I usually drive myself to work, but we'll keep you busy."

"We can teach you stuff at the office," Letty said.

"Good idea," I said. "It's up to Storm. No pressure."

"Boss, I'm in all the way."

"Now that sounds nasty," Tangles said, not taking her eyes from the huge steaming baked potato she was putting the works on. The works included a variety of minced herbs, crisp crumbled bacon, a couple of cheese sauces, cold shaped butter, and sour cream with chives. Miguel knew me well enough to stop offering caviar and truffles as toppings unless Olga was here.

"Was that supposed to be funny?" Letty asked.

Tangles raised her free hand and gave Letty the finger.

"It was funny," Storm said, cooling the jets between Tangles and Letty.

I smiled at the banter between them. Jo used to do the same thing, soothing the conflicts between Pixie and Letty whenever things got rocky. Storm fits in as if she's always been here.

November 7, 1991(Thursday)
Pasadena
Tangles

I have it made. I live in this big mansion with Boss and Letty. Being together like we are right now is like a gift. Just having dinner is beyond anything I can describe. I was so sure we were all dead. The plane finally quit moving, and I found myself in the dark with a life jacket on, and realized I was in the ocean. I took three deep breaths and forced calm throughout my body. I was preparing to die. A black belt wasn't going to help me out there in the dark ocean.

But we made it home. Life is wonderful.

Storm is on board. She thinks she's being cool making eyes at him. Letty will kick her ass. Funny. Everyone wants him, especially Olga. I know Olga wants him back. Don't go back Boss. I put my cool glass of water against my forehead and thought about it very hard. *Don't go back to her, don't go back to her.* I sent him a mental note, but he probably didn't hear me. His ears were blocked by the huge steak he's eating. He looked up, met my gaze. His brain got what I sent him. Yeah. I can tell. I'm going to smother you with kisses and anything else you want from me. Just wait and see, Mario Luna.

November 7, 1991
Pasadena
Letty

Storm is Betty's find. Boss opened the door fast for her. I just hope she doesn't turn out to be a Lola. I would have let her stay in my room, but maybe that would have been insulting to Storm, with all the free rooms in this place. Boss mentioned Olga is sending Elisa from Bogota to Puerto Vallarta to reward our rescuers lots of cash. The fishermen, the Red Cross workers, the hotel workers, all would receive a bonus.

"I talked by phone to the owner of the yacht. His name is Manuel Real, and he's from Acapulco. I told him I want to meet him one day soon to thank him personally for rescuing us."

"How did you find the yacht owner?"

"I didn't. Olga had Mason do it."

"You need to do something nice for this Manuel guy," I said.

"When you think of something, tell me."

"Whoever Manuel is, he must be loaded to own a fucking boat that big. Rich people and their toys," Tangles said.

It struck me that Boss's toy, that airliner, is broken and at the bottom of the ocean. I'm just glad we're all still breathing.

November 11, 1991
Pasadena
Andrea Jones

It's a good thing my husband Dan is in love with his job. He gets why I came back from Bogota and the next morning, I was at the office. My assistant Ava is good, but she can't delegate, and she can't manage. Without Mario or me around directing traffic, the entire team is out to lunch. I had credit checks piled up from my days off and ran them right away. Credit worthiness of a customer who wants to lease a multi-million-dollar plane is not even a decision. On my end, it is based entirely on that credit-worthiness, cash flow and years in business. Boss can go by his gut, but not me.

I am at GAL because Camila's brother Pepe sent a headhunter to steal me away from the big leasing company in London that I was working for. Once I arrived in Milan and started working for GAL, Camila wasted no time teaching me about being with a woman. Camila was seldom in Milan, so we were occasional lovers. When Mario came on board in Milan, he moved into the big Camacho house there, and sometimes he and I fooled around. When Mario opened the office in Los Angeles, he asked me to move there as second chair. I totally lost track of Camila. I was not as hurt when she died because there was distance between us at that point.

Once we were in Los Angeles, there wasn't much room for me in Mario's bed. Letty and Tangles pretty much fill it up, anyway. They are always around at work, plus they are living with him.

It freed me up to marry Dan. Dan and me, we're both workaholics. I'm happy here in LA, and the wedding ring helped with my green card. Soon I'll start working on getting citizenship. I hope Dan's telling the truth when he says he's happy. We still have two apartments in a building owned by LAI, the parent company of the aviation leasing company, GAL. While my apartment is a fringe benefit of my job, Dan pays rent. My first week in America, we met in the laundry room. When we started fooling around, we'd do it at my place, then go mess up his bed at his place. We have agreed to give up his apartment since mine is free. My married life is like a slow-motion movie. We put off almost everything because we're so devoted to our jobs.

November 11, 1991
Bogota
Olga

After Mario left for Pasadena, Riana and I moved back to my Bogota home. The big house had too many bad memories of Pepe Camacho. It's silly to be angry at the dead, but I hate that house. It was where he raped me during one of his drunken binges, had two of his bodyguards follow suit, and then shot them.

Camila remodeled that house and used Pepe's former bedroom as her own when she stayed there. She had her own house in Bogota, but she found comfort in the big house that had belonged to her parents. She often stayed there for an extended period of time. She was a Camacho by blood, and that was the family estate.

For me, the house is the opposite of comfort.

I thought long and hard about my meetings with the families and how I needed to lay out my case. I was going to tell them how, without Camila, I could not do anything. The bankers would be spooked dealing with me on matters she had setup in secrecy. I was just the messenger who followed orders and made deposits to client accounts. I would tell them that the bribes I paid to the bankers were setup by Camila. Lies.

They would only know that someone from their organization gave custody of millions in cash to Jeronimo Valencia and somehow it got to the banks.

Valencia was secretive and well-versed in communication methods that couldn't be tracked. He used his skills to stay in contact with a web of underlings woven through the cities where I had friendly bankers who accepted cash deposits. I knew I had to speak to Valencia for his input on my stepping out. He had to be the closest person under my control that had a relationship with the families who depended on us to get their cash in to banks. I hated the words money laundering.

After Camila died, he'd refused my calls. I had gone down to his place with a show of force. Nine of his security people were killed by my security people and the soldiers who had accompanied me to his house. I had to make the point that I had inherited the business.

One thing was certain. He knew not to ignore me again.

We never talked business on the phone, so I arranged for him to visit me.

"I'm back at my house. Can you come over in the morning?"

"Tell me the time and I will be there, of course."

My Bogota house is straight out of Architectural Digest. It had taken two years to build, and it was less than ten years old. After the funeral, and after Mario's visit, I was relieved that Riana and I were finally alone there, except for my staff of course. Now that the funeral was over, everyone who had traveled here was back at home, and the locals were waiting to see who would die next. Morbid, I know. Isn't that what life is? Aren't we all waiting to die? In the meantime, we bury those who were called before us.

I didn't want to go to war with anyone, but I knew that telling these families that I was done cleaning their money was not going to go over very well. They had armies of people. They were distributors, regulated only by their own conniving and violence. The Camacho family had once been like that, back in my dad's day. I am glad we weren't in the drug business any longer.

If I failed to extricate myself, if they gave me trouble, I knew how to handle it. I wondered how much I'd would need to offer the general to do whatever was necessary to get out from under. Easier said than done. The families knew the same people I knew, including the general. The split had to be amicable. Jeronimo Valencia gave me an alternative.

I met with Jeronimo the next morning alone in my home office.

"How would you like to retire?"

"No need, Miss Olga. I am at your service."

"Jeronimo, since the last time we talked, I have been thinking. There is no way I can continue flying all over the world. LAI and GAL require my attention. I need to get out of what I was doing. We all made a lot of money, and I will miss some of the excitement. The families will no doubt miss a money dump. How do you think the families will take it?"

I was scoping out Jeronimo's perspective. When I'd gone into his compound guns blazing, it had been because he had ignored my calls. But maybe he had plans to continue without me. As long as I wasn't involved, I wouldn't care, but he didn't have the bank connections. He was money delivery, nothing else.

"I don't think they will expect you to do anything," he said. "They know Camila is no longer with us. You were chosen as the contact and delivery person because you were young, smart, and could get away with playing a jetsetter. Why are you worried?"

"I'm not worried," I lied. "I want an amicable separation. That's all."

Jeronimo only knew his part: distribution. I could now tell that he thought all I did is escort the money.

"Miss Olga, I have to believe that the families know it's over. I haven't heard anything from any of them."

I took a deep breath and lied through my teeth. "Truth is, I can't continue. I don't have the influence with the people we delivered cash to. The contacts were Camila's and Pepe's, not mine."

"Exactly, Miss Olga."

"I will be taking over the legal Camacho assets, a full-time job. It would be full-time if I were twins."

"LAI is a giant, and the families know this," Jeronimo said.

"How should I handle the families?" I played up to him. He was an old man, but I could see interest in how he looked at my legs crossing and uncrossing. I got up and sat beside him and could tell he got nervous. I can't blame him. After Camila died, I pointed a gun at his wife, and demanded his submission and loyalty. I patted his thigh.

"Tell me, Jeronimo. How should I handle this? Should I meet with the families, one by one?"

He stared. We both went silent.

He had a plan of his own. Instead of me, he would talk to each family. He said he had been dealing with them for years. He said they trusted him. He said he had their ear.

It had been Pepe and Camila who had their ear, not Jeronimo, but I decided to let him talk to them.

"I don't want a war," I said.

"Miss Olga, there won't be a war. You had no deal with them. You are no Camacho. Camacho employed you. They will want to confirm if you have the connections. I will explain that you do not. They already know this. It's the truth. Camila always said that she was the key to the entire operation since Pepe died. The families never met with you about this business. It was Pepe until he passed away, then Camila. You were a just a messenger, trusted because the Camachos considered you family, going back to when your father was alive and in service to Camacho."

"Jeronimo, I will be very generous if you get each family to confirm that the business is done."

I was glad I hadn't killed him when we had our little disagreement.

Suddenly I was filled with hope.

"Miss Olga, I am a rich man. The Camachos were generous with me for decades. Before the money changing deal, I worked with Camila's father. I kept track of how many tons of product we cultivated and shipped all over the world. You need not give me anything."

I kissed his right cheek, then his left cheek. I patted his crotch. I was not sure he could get it up. The man turned red as a tomato.

"Jeronimo, I will find a way to repay you for settling this matter."

I saw him smile. He stood. I stood. We walked to the office door where I kissed him again.

November 19, 1991 (Tuesday
Bogota
Riana

Camila had been dead for a month.

We were sitting at the roomy glass table having breakfast on the balcony off the second-floor family room. The deck extended out twice, maybe three times farther than the balcony off the master bedroom. The railing was an etched picture of Roman Chariots, a talking piece if Olga ever were to entertain at this house.

"Olga, let's kill a day at Camila's house. You said you need to," I suggested. "Let's do it."

Olga agreed. "We're going to need a locksmith. She has three safes, all of them spin combinations."

"What are you going to do?"

"I'm going to call in Pino, a friend of my father's. He's old as sin, but I bet his safecracking skills are still intact. He worked for the Camachos after my father died, an enforcer."

I love how Olga is filled with surprises.

Camila's house is not as modern as Olga's house, but it is modern, and twice as big. She had twice the number of servants working at the house, another house with no use.

"Are you going to sell this place?" I asked Olga.

"I am, fully furnished with an agreement that they keep all the help for at least five years."

"Seems like you been thinking about it," I said.

"When we walked in today, that's when I made the decision. If I can find a buyer for the big house, that's going too."

The safe in the master bedroom was big, tall and wide. It took Pino less than an hour to crack it. While Olga looked it over, Elisa took him to the home office to open that one next.

I stood beside Olga as she opened drawers.

"So many times before, I've stood at Camila's side, right where you are. I know where most everything is," Olga said.

She pulled out four drawers with jewelry inserts. One had only rings. Olga's safe has jewelry too, but not like this. No one had what I was looking at in Camila's safe.

Olga handed a tray of rings to me. "Pick out anything you want and take it with you. No arguments."

"I got enough jewelry already," I said, "But thank you anyway, Olga."

"I said no arguments."

I put the tray down and sat in a chair. Olga's back was to me as she continued going through the safe. I looked at the waterfall of colors and shapes in my lap. Millions of dollars worth of rings, right here. It's hard to believe. Most of the gemstones were clear, bright colors: blue, clear, red, amber. Some had subtle tints.

"Are you surprised with what you are finding?"

"No. I've been here when Camila showed me a new piece of jewelry or handed me something for the banks."

I put the tray on my lap and started counting and looking them over.

"There are fifty-six rings. Five of them have matching necklaces, and earrings. They're not in this tray but there's a sticker. At least I think that's what this sticker means."

I tried a few of them on. They were a little big, plus I was unaccustomed to wearing stones as large as these. I found one I liked that fit, and I liked the way it looked. It was a red rose carved out of Sardinian coral, which being Spanish, I favor. The ring was probably the least flashy one there, but I'm pretty sure it was vintage. I bet it was a hundred years old. I could just imagine a Sardinian coral necklace that probably matched it.

"This one fits perfectly," I said.

November 19, 1991 (Tuesday)
Bogota
Olga

My back was to Riana, but I turned every so often. She was having a ball trying out those rings. I thought maybe I would give her the whole tray to surprise her.

"I could swear this is the engagement ring that you gave back to Mario."

I didn't turn around; I knew the ring. Riana was right.

"Keep it for yourself, Amor, seriously."

"No, this is way too much. Got to be worth a mil or something."

"Money doesn't matter. Do you see how many more trays there are? And this is just one safe, and no telling what we'll find at the big house," I said. "Doesn't matter. If you like it, I want you to have it."

Riana quietly kept trying on the rings. I would have turned around but on top of a stack of cash, was a note. When I picked it up, I saw it was a letter folded to fit in an envelope, but there was no envelope.

Riana said something but the words went in one ear and out the other. I was high on finding this letter from Camila.

My dearest sister, Olga, my Amor,

If you are reading this, I must be dead. Of course, you called Pino to open my safes. Who else could you trust? I know you so well. We're so much alike, Amor.

I have no idea when you are reading this, but I wrote it after one of my security guards was shot. I wouldn't be surprised if it was a sniper that killed me. I'll never know. I thought the sniper had been caught and I was safe, but just in case I wrote this to you.

My Swiss attorney, Noah Witzer, is the architect taking LAI public. He kept pestering me about a will. It is apparently part of the paperwork for going public. I have no intention of dying but I signed off that you would be my successor. If we both die at the same time, the estate is fucked.

Everything I have is yours, Amor. You already sign on all bank accounts for LAI and my personal accounts. No more flying money around. LAI is already a giant. Your job now is to make it bigger. You are now a billionaire, Amor.

Do not give my clothes away. Burn them if you must. Do not sell my house. I don't want anyone else to have it. Burn it if you don't want it, but don't sell it or give it away. We always worried that the government would confiscate the big house because of the business. Now that there is no business of any kind, there is no reason to sell it. Maybe it should be a museum? Do what you want but do not sell it. The Camacho houses we have in Rio, Rome, Hawaii, Bahamas, New York, do whatever you want with those. You decide what to do with them. I hope you keep them.

Give all our help a fair amount of money as a gift from me. Whoever wants to leave, let them leave.

Don't fight with our Mario. GAL's success depends on him. Andrea is not strong enough to do what he does. I did not plan to take GAL public. Now it is your call to keep it separate or bundle it up.

You can trust Noah Witzer. He has the accountants, and an entire team working to take LAI public. He knows nothing about our business or the history of how LAI became what it is. Perhaps he suspects but he doesn't know. Keep it that way. On anything else, trust him. You need someone like him to deal with the paper and the regulations. You cannot do it alone. You have Mason. You can trust him with anything at all. I love you, Amor. Wait until you see what I have stashed in my safes. It's all yours Amor.

I love you with all my heart.

Camila

After Jeronimo visited with his family, I got a call from Santiago Dominguez. He was in his early sixties, was married to Liliana, and had two daughters and two sons. Dominguez's estate outside of Bogota covered many hectares of land, though it is nothing compared to the Camacho family estate. Only Camacho senior had had the cojones to live the way he lived when everyone knew that he was one of the biggest drug lords in the country.

I told Santiago to visit me at the big house to keep this business away from my place. The servants admitted him and led him to the room I was using as an office—Pepe's former office that Camila had remodeled. I still felt her presence here.

Pepe used to sit at the desk and receive visitors like he was some kind of a king. I followed Camila's model—when Elisa brought him to the door, I got up from behind the desk and met him halfway.

My father always said to trust no one. Maybe now was a good time to start following his advice. Santiago was darkly tanned, wide bridge to his nose, hard brown eyes. His hair grew upward like a shrubbery, and he was cleanshaven except for a little spot the size of a quarter just below his bottom lip. Was it a face I could trust? I don't know. I saw only sincerity there.

"You are a very rich lady now," he said in Spanish.

I replied in kind.

"Santiago, I was already rich. The Camachos paid me very well for the hundreds of trips abroad I made for them." We walked toward a sitting area instead of the desk.

"I spoke to Jeronimo," he said seriously. "He says we are out of business because you are not the person with the bank contacts."

"Camila arranged it all. My orders were to open the accounts for you and four other clients, deposit money, make sure that we had a receipt to carry money on the plane, and make sure the cash was deposited into the right accounts. The bankers know who I am, but I never made the arrangements."

"I am familiar with the banking protocol in every bank that has my money."

I sat on a chair, catty-cornered from a lush sofa. He took the hint and sat at the sofa. There was a carafe of light white wine on the table, and I poured two glasses, handing him one.

"Of course, you are," I said.

He thanked me and took a sip. I saw appreciation in his face for the quality of the grape.

"Olga, I wanted to bring you the condolences of my entire family for the loss of Camila in a more personal way than when I attended the funeral. I remember how you two grew up together. You were sisters. It is very hard to lose a sibling."

My eyes watered instantly. "Thank you, Santiago. It is very kind of you to remember."

"I know there are changes going on. I don't want you to feel alone. At the same time, my motives are not completely humanitarian. I am a businessman, and there is real opportunity here. If you have need of an investor, I will be more generous than you can imagine. With LAI going public, I would love to buy in with the same kind of collateral we have been using."

I knew he meant he would like to buy stock with green cash.

"LAI will be a whole new landscape. I promise to let you know if I see an opportunity for you to give me cash and somehow get you stock for it. It will take me some time to learn the ropes. Pepe and Camila were artists of the deal, the way they bought bankers, the way they moved the money."

"Yes, they certainly were," Santiago agreed. "I understand you are a mathematician. You have the schooling that they don't have."

"I have to be good in math just to keep track of your accounts."

"Pepe and Camila did me good, but don't sell yourself short. Without you, the money would never had gotten to the banks."

"Pepe was the clever one. He came up with the business and did it himself before I finished school. Camila too."

We laughed as if we were best friends.

I really didn't know him at all. Everyone in Colombia knows his face, including me, but this was the first conversation of this type that we've had.

"Don't sell yourself short," he said. "You are one smart lady."

We talked for a few more minutes, then as he was leaving, I stood and shook his hand.

"You are a very rich man, Santiago. Solid clean money in banks around the world. A billionaire."

He smiled. "I have more money than I or my family can spend, yes. Thank you."

"The thanks go to Camila and Pepe," I said.

He reached into his pocket and pulled out a handkerchief. Spotless white linen, no lace, embroidered around the edges, no frills. He touched my face with the tip, refolded it, and wiped away my tears. I could tell by the crisp lines of his pocket square that it had been ironed.

"You are beautiful, mi hija," he said as a father would.

I hugged him. "Don't be a stranger, Santiago. Come back with the family."

"You owe me a visit," he said.

I walked him to the office door where six mean-looking bodyguards were standing outside. We hugged again. He kissed me on both cheeks. I put my hands on his face and kissed his forehead as a daughter would.

Soon I got another call. Another family had met with Jeronimo. I did my best to be gracious and invited them to come to the big house at the first opportunity. Two of the families had many questions about their money deposited all over the place. None of them seemed as savvy as Santiago. I was as patient as I could be. After each meeting, I felt the beginning of a bond. I wanted to tell all of them to dump the drug business and enjoy the hundreds of millions they had banked, but I held my tongue.

I had been in Bogota over a month. I had no scheduled flights, no plane landing for me to take to Amsterdam or Rio or Paris or London. I wasn't sure when I'd leave or where my destination would be. I had all the time in the world. It was strange that I would never again be expecting a call from Jeronimo that my plane was ready for me to be flying out to some bank in a faraway place.

Though I had no flights out, there was still business to be done. I hosted the architects of public companies—the Swiss agency that Camila had hired—at the big house. We discussed many things, like what would be expected of me when we went public.

GAL was an Italian corporation with offices in Milan and Los Angeles. I decided that GAL would not be a part of the public offering, nor on public exchange. Noah Witzer arranged for GAL stock to be mine as Camila had wished.

At noon, I met Noah out on the gazebo where I provided a private lunch. The staff brought out pitchers of sweet iced tea, and an array of all types of arepas—stuffed arepas, fried sweet arepas, and grilled arepas. He was a German who worked for a Swiss firm, and he found these ordinary corncakes very exotic. I wanted to know him better. I massacred a cheese arepa, minced it to bits, stirred it around my plate and hid part of it under a lettuce leaf because I would be meeting Riana for lunch after this meeting. I did drink the tea, and I watched him over the rim of my glass. He certainly had an appetite. We sat in partial shade, but there were dapples of sunlight here and there. His eyes were blue, wide and squinty, the color hidden beneath a prominent browbone that barely left room for his eye. He was already getting a five o'clock shadow. Flecks of silver here and there glinted on his square jaw just as they did in his thick brown eyebrows. The squareness of his face reminded me of that actor, Patrick Swayze. His hair was very well cut, the receding hairline hidden by perfectly cut bangs that swept across his forehead, and the color was the kind of brown that looked like it might have been blond when he was a child. I don't think I've ever seen another person with eyebrows that grew so low on his face. It gave him a perpetually worried look. At first glance, I had thought he was in his thirties, but now that I was seeing him closer, there were subtle lines around his eyes, mouth, chin, and neck. He was probably in his fifties.

"Camila trusted you," I said. "That means I trust you. Don't fuck me over. If that were to happen, I would not be as nice as you may think."

"I will earn your trust," Noah said.

"Do that, Noah."

After we were done, he excused himself and went to join his team working in my office. I joined Riana in a private upstairs den where we compared notes. She had been hanging out with the Swiss accountants like a fly on the wall.

"All I can say is that they seem to be very organized, and never once lapsed into German or Dutch while I was in the room. They all seem very open."

"I'm so happy that Camila left me that letter. If there is something havey-cavey going on, it will be my secret weapon."

And it was a secret. I had told no one but Riana. If I ever needed that letter, then and only then, would I pull it out. It wasn't my only secret. In one of Camila's safe was a bundle of cash—ten million.

I stash money too. I had two million in my safe at home. We were alike. Emergency money.

The Swiss accountants were in a rush to make their departure, wanting to get home well before Christmas.

Riana and I returned to investigating the bedroom safe. In a large drawer at the bottom of the safe were twenty-one VHS tapes numbered in red.

"Not sure what these numbers mean. They range from six to ten," I said.

Riana handed back a tray of bracelets I had pulled out for her to check out while I continued going through the safe.

"Probably an X-rated video," Riana suggested.

No telling how long this project was going to take. Pino had left me combinations for all of the safes he had cracked. There were more safes out there, and as I came across them, we would let him loose on them. Eventually I would get through them all. The letter was worth more to me than anything else.

I handed one of the tapes to Riana.

I opened another drawer inside the safe, then heard Camila's voice coming from the television. I turned around but furniture blocked my view. I walked over to the loveseat where Riana was sitting watching Camila on all fours. The ass of a man was taking up most of the screen as he pounded her.

I watched for a minute then took the remote control from Riana and turned off the television.

"We don't want to see this, Amor."

Riana frowned but only for a moment.

"You're right, Olga."

I wondered if all the tapes were of her and lovers. Camila and I had been lovers for decades, ever since we were teenagers. Men were what we really craved but we were avid lovers for years. I supposed we ought to screen the tapes or burn them.

I talked to Mario daily.

"You been there a long time, baby."

"I have gotten a lot accomplished."

"You sound happy."

"I'd be happier if you were with me, but yes, I'm happy. Amor, you haven't seen the Rio house."

"When you settle all you have going, I'll meet you there," he said.

"Si Amor, Si."

"What are you going to do with the big house?"

"I'm thinking of making it a museum or something. Not sure yet."

"It's a beautiful house," he said. "Way too big though. I remember when Pepe was going to sell it."

"I don't want to sell it," I said. There was no reason to tell him about the letter.

Mario changed the subject.

"How is your project?"

"Amor, I think it's settled. I'll tell you when I see you."

I hung up and looked across the room at Riana. It struck me that it was a new year.

"Rio. Pack now."

I made the call to my flight crew. Taking action energized me. Riana had to run to catch up.

"Talk about last minute decisions."

I stopped packing long enough to hug my friend.

"Amor, I keep thinking I've got to run and catch a plane filled with money. I don't have to do that anymore! It takes me by surprise."

"We're going to have so much fun!"

Riana was all smiles.

I did not call Mario back to say I was headed to Rio and to meet me like he said he would. I'd be in touch from Rio. I wanted to be with Riana. I wanted to have fun, night clubbing like we'd done in the past. I want to let my hair down and have a blast.

Mario can make love for hours, and he has a huge bat between his legs. He's strong as a gorilla, yes, and those wonderful abs of his get me hot. But Mario was right. I wasn't ready to be married.

In Rio, there are plenty of men equipped with the same hardware. There was a whole world out there, with choice of size, width, length, color. Hairy, hairless, I'm horny just thinking about it.

Riana noticed my pause.

"Are you okay?"

"Of course, why?"

"You're blushing."

I grinned.

"I think I just had an orgasm."

The pilot came on the speaker.

"Miss Olga, we're going to pull back now."

We sat in our favorite seats across from each other, a window for each, a table between us. We buckled up. It had been weeks since I'd been on board my plane. It felt like we were falling back into the old routine, though I knew that wasn't what was happening.

"The bankers that I had deals with are going to wonder what's going on," I said.

"You never really got back into it after things got hot. When my dad asks me, I'll tell him it is still too hot, and maybe you're out of it for good. He's got so much money, but I know he'll miss the opportunity."

"Good idea, Amor. You are so smart."

"I'll wait till we fly there."

"Maybe we need to do the rounds to speak to the others."

"No need, explaining. Both LAI and I have countless accounts at all those banks. We'll go about it like we were never doing any business. I assure you no one will call wondering."

"Riana nodded.

"Amor, I love you," I said to my best friend as we were wheels up.

"If you were a boy, I'd marry you," Riana said,

I blew a kiss at her. "We are married, Amor."

It was a routine we went through all the time. Riana has this funny bug-eyed look when she is happy. I knew she was happy. She was radiant.

She was also so sexually charged that it was getting me excited.

I licked my lips. The plane was roaring down the runway.

Our eyes met.

"If I had a dick, I'd fuck you, Amor."

"Promises, promises," she said with an adventurous look. "Don't let that stop you."

Rewind
February 19, 1991
Pasadena
Lola

It is three in the afternoon when I walk out of the hotel room. I have my overnight bag and purse. I am wearing jeans, a sweater, and a short ski jacket I would never wear in Miami. I take the elevator to the lobby and switch to the parking lot elevator. I dial Mario as I wander through the maze of cars on the second level.

"About to leave the hotel," I say, "if I can just find the damn car."

"I hope you got some sleep."

"I slept," I tell him. "How about you?"

"No sleep. Going home soon as I hang up. Thanks for a lovely time."

"Thank you too."

"You're leaving for Miami next week?"

"I am. I'll call before I go."

"Be sure to."

"I found the car. Don't hang up. Let me get in. Keep me company for a minute."

"I'm here for as long as you want me."

I open the door to the Plymouth, toss my overnight bag and purse on the passenger side and get in the car. I close the door. "Okay, I'm in my rented wheels."

"Be sure it's your car. Don't want you arrested for getting in someone else's car." He laughs.

I laugh.

"Mario, thanks to you, I feel like the most beautiful woman in the world. That's how you make me feel. I'm sorry we started off with a web of lies from me. It was a job."

"Say no more. That's all in the past."

Holding the cell phone with one hand, I insert the key into the ignition.

"I had a crush on you going way back to the beginning, back when the team and I first started watching you from afar. I guess that goes back to when you first met Pepe. That was after you got back from Venezuela, when you'd been kidnapped back in 1975, like...fifteen years ago. That's a long time to be dreaming up ways of getting up close to you. Eventually my handler came up with the prostitution idea. Now that I've been with you, it's worth the wait. How lucky am I, getting what I've been wanting for so long?" I laugh, turn the key in the ignition.

I heard a distorted noise, loud enough I pulled the phone away from my ear. Maybe she had dropped her phone.

"Lola, are you there?" I repeated myself a couple of times. I got up from behind my desk, walked over to the television, and turned it on.

I went back to the desk, sat, and dialed Lola's number. No answer.

I had a bad feeling. I could hear my own heartbeat, steady, regular. I quietly put my cell down on my desk. The office was quiet, but active. I could hear the heat being pumped through the vents, the muted voice of someone walking past my door, elevator music being piped in. Everything sounded normal except that unnatural blast I'd heard through the phone. It was like nothing I could compare it to. I grabbed the phone and hit redial.

Nothing.

"Oh my God," I prayed aloud. "Don't let it be what I think." I was repeatedly hitting redial. With my free hand, I called Letty on my desk phone.

She and Tangles walked in chattering with each other about some client thing. I was pretty agitated.

"Something happened. I can't get her on the phone."

"Her who?"

"Her—Lola. It's Lola. Something happened. She was in Beverly Hills. She just got in her car, then the phone blew up in my ear. I was talking to her. There was a loud blast. I mean boom! She was just getting in her car and the line went dead. Now she won't pick up." I was anxious, talking away like I was high on something. I hate feeling helpless.

Letty said, "Let's go there, Boss. Why mess with the phone?"

I nodded and grabbed my coat off the coat tree. Letty stood there watching me redial. She didn't say anything. I didn't say anything. She reached out, and put her hand over mine, trying to stop my dialing. I shook her off. She looked over my shoulder, pointing at the television. The silent screen was showing a Channel Five helicopter circling above Wilshire Boulevard, smoke pouring out of Lola's hotel.

"It's Lola," I said. "They got to her."

We watched the screen in horror.

"Boss, I don't think we should go there," Letty managed to say. "Not if you think Lola is at the center of what we're watching."

If this was a movie, Lola would have called by now to say some explosion knocked off our conversation, and I would be filled with happiness that she was okay. In a movie, I would be driving like a crazy person from downtown Los Angeles to the hotel where I had left Lola.

This is not a movie. Until I knew for certain, I could hope that Lola was not a victim. So far, the police were not saying it was a car bomb. I knew better. There was nothing I could do for Lola. Beyond our adventures in bed,

I knew almost nothing about her, no hint of her family beyond her home being Miami.

I wanted to mourn. It was too soon. I was too angry.

I prayed in silence. It's disgusting that my prayer only happens when I need something. I'm totally overdrawn with God and the Virgin of Guadalupe. I'm a horrible Catholic.

God, Virgin of Guadalupe, please intervene. She was a federal agent wanting to take the Camacho family down and maybe even me. A cop doing a job, she doesn't deserve to die in a car explosion. Please let me be imagining this. Don't let her die.

Present Day
January 3, 1992 (Friday)
San Juan, Puerto Rico
Lola

I told Mario I had resigned from the agency. The million he made the bitches pay me would give a jump start in my new life. The bullets that nearly killed me helped me get a medical discharge. I get a nice chunk of change each month from Uncle Sam for my service and injuries.

Not all agents go out with a bang like I did, but I had no choice. The Camachos would have come after me to finish the job. Maybe I shouldn't have threatened to kill them if they didn't pay me. But a million was chump change for what they put me through.

I still hurt. I should have demanded five million.

When it blew up, my car had a dead body already in it. The explosion practically vaporized the car and the dead occupant. I knew I had to take that way out, but it hurt. It meant I lost the possibility that Mario and I would have something going one day.

Long shot.

Still hurt.

I was deep undercover. Tracing me back to my actual identity would be impossible. My Los Angeles persona died for those who knew me there, but I didn't have to go into witness protection. If Mario ever went looking for me, he'd be poking around Florida where I never lived. My parents in New York State were glad to hear I was out of a job. My two brothers and one sister are spread between Washington, Chicago, and Buffalo. My brothers are cops like me, Nico in the FBI, Ugo in Washington with the ATF. They know I—or at least my cover—got taken out by an explosion. They wish they could talk about how I ended my part in the Camacho investigation. It's a hell of a story.

I don't know if I'll ever get married, but I do fuck and have a life. My two-bedroom condo is a block from the beach. I don't have a job and have no plans to. If I get married someday, I'll let the old man support me. If I don't get married, I get my monthly check.

I'll never spend the entire million on anything crazy. It's my nest egg.

Once a cop, always a cop. I keep fit. One of my bedrooms is a gym. I have a treadmill, elliptical and stair master. I have just enough barbells to keep me toned. When I was in the academy, a long time ago, I kicked ass doing sit-ups and chin-ups. I still do. In my bikini, you got to be really good to figure me for forty-one. I look the same as I did when I was twenty-five except for the scar on my abdomen that the tattoo is supposed to hide.

The fed team I worked with for years resulted in no Camacho family arrests, just a ton of data and surveillance. I'm not in touch with them. They know I'm not dead. I can't be around them for at least five years, but who is counting? We ran into bad guys—federal criminals who got in the way, but we never had to testify. We referred the crooks to other agencies who picked up on the cases as we came across them. The years spent on the Camachos was not a total loss to the government.

My brother with the FBI calls me. Though he has nothing to do with any ongoing investigation of Olga or Mario, he has his ear to the ground. He let me know Camila had been shot and when she died at the hospital in Mexico. Camila being shot didn't come as a surprise, but that she died, that was a surprise.

Maybe it was karma. She had it coming. I came close to breaking out of my protective cocoon when my brother told me about Mario's plane crash in Mexico. Luckily there was an immediate update that everyone on the plane was rescued, including Mario. But in that short window of time, I called his cell number. I got no answer. The phone probably went down with the plane. I took a terrible chance that he would answer. What would I have told him? *I'm glad you didn't die in the crash, and oh, by the way, the explosion didn't kill me. Want to come see me? I live in Puerto Rico.*

What a stupid move. It's just that I miss him. As a cop I watched them all for so long hoping to catch Pepe, Camila and Olga doing something we could make a strong drug case out of. I never meant to fall in love with him. How would I know what love is anyway?

I miss him.

The last two times Mario and I were together at the hotel in Beverly Hills, I had a camera in the bedroom. I didn't tape it for the Feds. It was for me. I'm such a dumbass.

I watch the videos when I get down and out. Such a stupid thing to do. Then I am down and out and horny with no dude to take care of me.

Financially I got it made, but when I think about having to lie low, it's a bummer. Maybe one day I will get into private security at one of the hotel casinos here. At least no one knows me.

January 8, 1992 (Wednesday)
Rio de Janeiro
Olga

We were on our fifth day in my new house in Paradise when I had Mason come see me. He was installed at the Camacho beach house where he could enjoy the castle on the beach surrounded by eager personnel. Riana and I went over to meet him.

"I'm not questioning how good you are, though I should. It's been forever, and you haven't solved the Mario attacks."

Mason started to say something. I raised my hand.

"The Mario investigation is growing whiskers, but you need to put it on hold. Focus your energy on Camila. Her murderer is out there. I need to know who did it. The person who did it may be a threat to me."

"I'm all over it," Mason said. "It was a mistake to hush the shooting the way we did in Mexico City. We could have had help from the authorities. That would have been helpful if the shooter is from Mexico."

"Mason, please. I do a lot of business in Mexico. What makes you think you would get anything done by the cops in that crooked city?"

"It's not like it used to be," Mason said. "By the time my men found the sniper's nest at the terminal hundreds of feet away, we found nothing to help us. If the cops had been told more right after the shooting, we might have gotten some leads."

"We can't change what is done. Camila would have said to keep it hushed. How could we know that it would be front-page news in Colombia for days? Not sure how they got the story, but once they had wind of it, they kept writing. Her funeral only brought it back to page one. Now that it has simmered down, I want you to keep me informed on a weekly basis regarding the investigation."

Riana was as silent as a bird with a cover on her cage.

Mason nodded his understanding.

"I'm sorry you are unhappy about the slow progress on the Mario case."

"Mason, I love you. Camila loved you, she trusted you and so do I, but...."

He raised his hand and nodded again. "I understand."

"All that matters now is finding out who killed Camila."

"May she rest in peace," Riana said.

As Riana and I were about to return to my place, Mason said, "I've had three dreams that Lola is alive. The last one had concluded she shot Camila."

"She's dead."

"Dead or not, it was a dream."

"You're the one who assured us Lola died in the explosion of her car."

"Yes, she's dead," Mason said. "I thought I'd share this stupid dream."

"In your dream, what evidence did you have to conclude she had been the shooter?" I asked.

"I don't remember that part of the dream."

"It was just a dream," Riana said, "Lighten up, Mason. You're a psychiatrist, not a psychic."

We were in the back seat of a Lincoln limousine on the drive back to my house. It was dark out on top of having dark film on the windows.

"Amor, what do you think?"

"Olga, Lola is dead."

"Hug me, Amor."

"Come here, my sweet," Riana said.

I was shaking from anger, uncertainty, hate or all the above.

January 10, 1992(Friday)
Pasadena, California
Tangles

Matthew Martinez was a lawyer who was forty-one, divorced with a six-year-old daughter and five-year-old son, and worked for Jacobs & Jacobs, a law firm on the third floor in the same building where Letty and I worked for GAL. I met him on the elevator. Matt is a flirt, and so am I. It started with lunch in one of the restaurants on the ground floor and escalated to passionate sex at the Hilton Hotel on one afternoon when I cut out from the office early. Second time, same hotel. It was a dinner date, but we never made it to the restaurant. The third time was in my apartment right after the housekeeper made her weekly pass to change my sheets and freshen everything up, just in case I had to move back in.

Letty and I were in the kitchen at Casa Luna. We'd just finished having dinner at the counter. Boss, who hadn't come home after work like he normally does, was out somewhere.

"I hope we don't end up with AIDS because of you," Letty said.

"Ease up, already. We use condoms for everything. Haven't you heard condoms stop the disease from going anywhere? Besides, Matt doesn't have AIDS."

We walked into the den on the same floor. I put my arm around her as we sat on a sofa facing a television that was on mute. Letty resisted but not for long.

"You're adorable," I said. "I love you, Letty."

"Tramp," Letty said, but I could tell she wasn't mad.

"Takes one to know one." I said.

We kissed.

"Are you getting serious with this dude? I don't care if you are. Nothing wrong with you getting a life outside of here, for sure."

"Not serious. Only sex."

"With all the sex you have, why are you still out hunting for strange? You are a freak."

I kissed Letty again.

"You right," she said. "I'm a freak just like you and just like Mario and everyone else that shares the master bedroom up on the fourth floor."

Letty looked at the big clock in the room. It was mostly glass so you could see the clockworks.

"I wonder where he is?" Letty changed the subject.

"Probably fucking Storm." I laughed

"He fucks her here," Letty said, as if I didn't know. "She's driving him around somewhere. Maybe he wants some strange pussy, and he's out looking."

Letty looked serious.

"That's what I'm doing with Matt. Strange dick."

Letty broke out in a laugh. "Bitch," she said, still laughing. "What are you going to do with your doctor friend? I don't hear you talking to him on the phone anymore."

"Since he got his license, he's so busy at that Urgent Care that he has no time for me. At least he's making money now," I said. "Besides, he just wants me to give him head. He can't go more than five minutes when he fucks me. I like him, but he doesn't trip my trigger."

I spent Friday night out with Matt and got to Casa Luna Saturday morning about ten. I did not see Boss as I made my way to my bedroom, but Letty was sitting on my bed as I walked in.

She read me the riot act.

"This is not my house, so I have no right to talk, but you need to treat Boss with respect. This is not a hotel. You can't stay out all night, not call to let me know you haven't been beat up, shot or raped, and then come in like this is your house."

Letty was right. I didn't argue. An hour later I was at my apartment with two suitcases I had packed in a rush. I got out of there without seeing Boss. I would see him at the office on Monday or I'd go over and talk to him. Letty was right.

Sunday morning, I got a call on my cell. The ring woke me from a sound sleep. I lay there for a second in my bed getting my bearings. When I'd gotten home last night, I'd taken a bath to calm down, and like a dope, went to sleep with wet hair. My hair is pretty short, but I could feel it was a mass of curls, and I'd have to take a shower, and do some heavy duty brushing and ironing to get it straightened out. I groped for the phone without opening my eyes, hoping it was Letty or Boss calling to have me come home.

"Good morning. This is Tangles," I said.

"Tangles the whore," a female voice said. "Hello whore. This is Mrs. Martinez, Matthew's wife."

I felt like someone had delivered a roundhouse to my gut. I opened my eyes, kicked off the covers and sat up. As Letty would say, "Them's fighting words!"

"Come over here and call me whore to my face!" I said.

"Leave my husband alone, whore. If you don't leave him alone, you will be one sorry whore. Get it?"

"You're divorced," I yelled back. She was loud. I was loud back at her. Some women won't let go, even when they get their separation papers. Matthew had his walking papers, and she needed to acknowledge it.

"No, whore, wrong. Not even close to divorce!"

"You're still married," I said flatly. It sank in. Matthew was toast. I don't fool with married men. I don't even hang with married men. "If I had known he was married, I wouldn't even have had lunch with him. Your beef is with him babe, not me."

I didn't say anything else. I disconnected the call and didn't answer my cell for the rest of Sunday.

I couldn't recall a time I cried so much. I wasn't even sure why I was crying. I sure didn't love the guy. I barely liked him. He was just a body in my bed. I cried for being so stupid. I'm a whore all right, but I would never break up a marriage.

I hit the bathroom and faced the reflection. Bad hair Tangles on steroids. Good thing nobody else was here to see.

I went in the shower, turned it on, and let the water stream down my body. I ran a mantra through my head, but my emotions were still churning. Tried leaning against the back of the shower in the eagle pose. It's the one where you rest the top of your right foot against the back of your left shin, bend your knee and do this twisty thing with your hands in front of your face. Letty, damn her, can hold this pose for three days. After a few minutes, I have to lean against the back of the shower to keep from falling on my face. Enough of that. I cream rinsed my curly mop and got out of the tub to blow it dry then iron it straight with my little flatiron hair doodad. This takes forever, so I entertained myself with practicing slow motion karate moves in the mirror—slow motion, because I didn't want to fry my ass with the flatiron. Then I put it down, and did a couple of vicious defensive moves, and a couple of offensive moves. I pictured both Matt and Mrs. Matt, but it was Matt who deserved an ass kicking. His wife was just the victim of his lying ass. What else did I expect? He's a lawyer. If his lips are moving, he's lying.

I thought of confronting Matt. I could punch him silly. I've been practicing karate with the best. He had no idea what I can do. I took a sleeping pill that night. I hadn't yet decided if there would be a confrontation. I was all in favor of it, but maybe Letty would tell me to cool my jets. For sure, I'll bounce it off of her, but one thing was a sure bet. That bastard would never touch my body again.

January 12, 1992
Pasadena, California
Mario

I wanted a Falcon jet as my personal plane. Olga had suggested I let GAL pay for my plane—buy and lease back or something like that. My last Falcon was secondhand, revamped to be better than new, and after I had it the way I wanted it, Andrea leased it out for me. GAL is a good Falcon client, and Stan the VP of sales gave me a generous discount as thanks for past business. I wouldn't want to call it favoritism, but I did feel like I got the red carpet treatment when Stan realized the plane was for my personal use. The brand-new Falcon, a gorgeous creature, came to me factory-made as a VIP plane. Mine was ready to go except for one thing: the convertible seating needed to open to a bed two inches more than my height. Stan had this done for me. His parting words were how he was looking forward to our doing future business together.

The plane itself was built in France. Letty and Tangles joined me on the flight to Arkansas where the final touches like painting and special interiors were done—my second trip here, first time for the girls.

We wanted to take our time, so we got rid of the rep showing us around before we walked through the almost-finished aircraft.

"Totally different from the plane Olga bought you," Letty said.

"Boss, you will miss the bedroom," Tangles said.

"I don't think so. The bed was there just taking up room unless we were on it," I said. "This is a second cabin where the seats and lounge chairs will be. The bigger area up front is the main cabin. Three seats will face the cockpit with a pull curtain behind the seats to give relief pilots and flight attendant a place to sit and snooze." I pulled the brass handles of the mahogany double doors that closed off that part of the plane.

"Your other Falcon had a single door," Tangles said. "And this is a queen, not a king."

"It's a little tight, but my legs won't hang over."

"Love it, Boss," Tangles said, eyes wide.

"I love it, too," I agreed. "I wanted to get Olga one, but she likes her big plane. I'm not going to argue."

"Bigger plane, and bigger bills," Letty said.

More costly, but Olga could afford to fly whatever she wanted.

On the lobby level where our office was located, I visited a banker I was acquainted with.

"My accountant says I should put half down and finance the other half. I understand you handle planes."

I borrowed ten million from the bank and paid the other ten out of pocket.

We sat in the wine room at Casa Luna sipping some fabulous special wine, not the red I like from Argentina, but something like.

"My life is a miracle," Tangles said. "Not that long ago, I was working with Betty and struggling to keep a roof over my head. You wouldn't believe the things I did to get spending money. And now, look at me."

Letty glanced at Tangles and waved her wine dramatically. "I'm looking at you, kiddo. My life is a miracle," Letty said. "Before Mario, Uncle Miguel and I lived on the road, moving from gig to gig. Every time his job was up, we'd hit the road for his next chef job. We were in Pasadena for Tio to get hired on at one of Melina's markets. We got here, and the post had already been filled. Melina said we'd be a good fit for the guy across the street, who turned out to be Mario. Mario hired us on Melina's word. Pixie was here, and Jo and Niley. They took me in. Everybody but Pixie thought Uncle Miguel and I were a thing. They didn't know what to have me do around the house, so I did a little of everything. Including Boss." She giggled.

She looked at me.

"Remember? I paid you a thank you visit."

"I remember the shirt you were wearing," I said, not mentioning that I didn't see the shirt until she put it on after our surprise tryst. "My life is a miracle," I said. "When I was growing up, my aunt barely made a dollar an hour as a bookkeeper at a sewing factory and moonlighting as a midwife. Our rent went up, and her hours got cut, and the television got repossessed by the furniture store. To me, at ten years old, that was intolerable. I got a job working for Cosmo so that a few weeks later, I was able to bring back the TV. And now, I'm good for ten million dollars and covering a check for the other ten million and change. That's a miracle."

By the time I was back in Los Angeles, my four adult kids had heard from me a dozen times, assuring them that the crash had not killed me. The bruising was not serious. Two are in college, one is in the Army and the other in the Navy. Two of them were my sister's children. She had been killed by a shooter that was after Mario. Both got shot, but only Mario survived.

I didn't meet Mario until after my sister's death. He, Pixie, and Jo dropped into the apartment that Tanis and I had shared and changed my life. He put me in business making gift baskets for his girlfriend's market. Eventually I joined his team, first working on auto, train and bus accidents in Los Angeles, and later working plane crashes. Jo was Mario's first team member, then he hired his childhood friend Pixie while she and her daughter were living with his aunt, then I came along. He was a lifesaver. Thanks to him, I made good money and was able to support my family and surround them with an extended family made up of Jo and her kids, and Pixie and her daughter Lainie. I know the world calls her Bebé now, but to me, she'll always be Lainie. I loved working beside him and the rest of the team.

Jo and I caught on that the company maintaining his properties was overcharging. We figured that we could cut his costs by half, do a better job maintaining his properties, and double our salary. And it was a substantial salary to begin with. We saw that opportunity, and, more importantly, convinced Mario of it. Jo and I became partners managing his apartments. When we started, he had about one thousand units.

Our management company now employs thirty-five people to overlook every aspect of his three thousand plus units. We have a team just to work the tenants late on their rent. With more than three thousand apartments, we had tenants who have earned the right to be kicked out, but before we initiate proceedings, we fax Mario all the details: how far overdue the tenant is, how many live in the apartment, who is working, what the tenant's history of past payment performance is. He only approves two out of five evictions.

Jo gives Mario grief over it. "If word gets around that we are soft, no one is going to pay rent," she says. If Mario let a tenant off the hook for past due rent, current rent had to be kept current. Jo would make that deal with the tenant. If the tenant failed to keep that agreement, they were out.

"He can't forget his past," I reminded Jo.

"I know."

Jo has everything so organized that we can keep banker's hours. Our answering service handles calls after hours. The sun never sets on problems.

In the course of taking LAI public, Camila divested a lot of LAI businesses headquartered in LA, and when Mario took title of them, he gave us a shot at branching into managing an assorted mix of businesses: donut shops, liquor stores, and a Mexican pastry bakery that employs over a hundred employees. There's even a tortilla company with a hundred and forty-one employees. That's a lot of tortillas. These were all businesses that have been around East Los Angeles for decades at the time. Mario purchased them for LAI. Plenty of work for us and we have plenty of staff to keep everything running smoothly.

Being a business owner is a total turn-on. Jo is married, and even though she's more domestic than me, she's the numbers person. She's sharp as a pin. I tell her she should own a bigger piece of the action because she's the brains of the operation. She laughs that off.

"Fifty-fifty was the deal, and that's the way it is."

After the crash, Jo had fewer bruises than me. She had three different types of scans because she had a lump on her head.

She's fine now. We're at the office every day. We stay busy and seldom discuss the crash, the rescue, the rush to Bogota, or the funeral that had put us on Mario's plane to begin with. We did speculate whether Mario and Olga would marry or if their engagement was truly off.

It's only fifteen minutes from our offices to Casa Luna, but we seldom visit. For a while, we had Friday dinners together in Mario's big dining room. Those turned to monthly dinners. Now we messenger over monthly reports. On Thanksgiving and Christmas, we exchange gifts, but we celebrate the day in our own homes with our own immediate families. When I do get to see Mario up close and personal, like on this horrible trip, I come away day-dreaming that he would share the feelings that I have always had for him. Sex with him is just about perfect. He treats me like I'm the most important person on the bed. He's that way with all of us. When I joined the team, we had countless duo events and it was wonderful.

My raising four kids scared guys away. I doubt I'll ever marry, though Jo tells me I still have my looks, and for sure, she has too. We're both toned.

Jo and I have black belts. Karate for us is just exercise now. We're not diehard competitive like we used to be. I work out on my own and do at least four hundred sit-ups a day, punch a bag, and flip around on the mat I have at home. I have a great five-bedroom house. My live-in nanny just keeps the house and does the laundry now that the kids are gone. Nanny Delores lives in a guest cottage in my backyard. When the kids come home for the holidays, they all still call her Nanny. Hell, so do I.

Friday afternoon, I drove into my garage at fifteen minutes past four. I went into my home gym, worked up a sweat, and went straight to the shower.

Now what? I could drive over to El Patio, have some drinks, maybe dance a little and hook me a winner I can bring home. I poured myself a glass of chilled Santa Margarita, and played a cd of Lainie, then one by Pixie. Hearing her voice made me feel sentimental. I dug out my phone book and made a call.

"Guess who?" The quality of the connection said she was not local.

"Niley. Bitch, what a great surprise! Where are you and what the hell is going on?"

"I'm just home. Where are you?"

"I'm in Buenos Aires. The concert here starts tomorrow."

"Lucky you," I said.

"What's wrong?"

"Life couldn't be better, but I'm fucking bored to death. The routine is killing me."

"That's when people take vacations," Pixie said in her big voice. "I wish I was there. I'd bring you out of that gloom of yours. I can feel it all the way over here."

"I miss you, Pixie. It was good seeing you and Lainie."

"Call Mario or one of the girls and head over there. Kick back for the weekend. Or go to my house, live in luxury for as long as you like. Make my help work for a living, for once." Pixie giggled.

"You're sweet," I said. "That's a good idea. I think I'll call Letty, maybe I can invite myself. I want out of here for a few days."

Letty was happy to oblige.

"Come on over. You can give me head all weekend," Letty said.

I said, "If I give you head, you got to give some back."

"Deal, bitch. You can sleep in my room or have any guest room you want."

"Where is Boss?"

"He's at the office. Tangles moved back to her apartment. Long story. She may be coming back. We all talked about it over dinner Monday night. She got crushed by some asshole who played her."

"Tell me when I get there," I said. The excitement in my veins felt good. "Do you think Boss will mind me coming over just like that?"

"You know damn well he'll love having you as will I. I'll even make you some cookies and anything else you want to eat."

I always liked Letty. She's a firecracker like Pixie. In short order, I was in my car driving along Atlantic Boulevard towards Pasadena.

January 17, 1992
Casa Luna
Letty

"Hey Boss, guess who is coming over for the weekend?"

"It's not Pixie. She's in Argentina."

"Niley."

"Great," Boss said, as I thought he would.

I gave Tangles a call.

"It's Friday. What are you doing for the weekend?"

"I'm home. I was going to call you."

"You don't have to call me, I called you. So, what's up? You moving back or what?"

"I'll come over and do like I used to. I don't want to take advantage. Like you said, Casa Luna is not a hotel."

She used to come over and stay for dinner, stick around for a while and go home. Over that time, she only stayed overnight when Boss requested.

"Niley is coming over for the weekend."

"She's likeable. I mean, I like her," Tangles said.

"I miss you. It's okay to come home, you know. You're family."

I heard a sigh. A little silence. A sniff. I felt a tear run down my face.

"I miss you too, Letty."

Her voice was full of tears.

January 12, 1992
Monterey Park, California
Jo

I stuck the phone between my ear and my shoulder. I was making dinner as my eldest was coming over with the new baby. I stirred the mac and cheese and took it off the heat so it wouldn't burn while I got distracted. I turned the temperature down on the frying chicken so it wouldn't cook too fast.

"In case you need me, I'll be at Mario's until Sunday," Niley said.

"Really, when did that happen? It's good you get out. You will have fun."

"I need fun," Niley said.

"You sure do. You've been so gloomy lately."

"I'm so grateful we didn't die, and that your head injury turned out to be a false alarm. I'm just feeling down."

"We should talk more," I said. At the office, it's always business.

"I can hear you're frying something. I don't want to be the cause of you burning dinner. I was just checking in," Niley said. "I'll be okay. Actually, it was Pixie who suggested I call Boss, but I called Letty instead. She seemed excited for me to come over."

"If I wasn't married, I'd be right there with you." I laughed, knowing damn well I would if I could.

Back in the day when it was just the two of us working, when Mario and I were in the field, the spontaneous sex we had was out of this world. We were so young and full of life. We were living on the edge, but I miss those days.

I set the table for dinner, and as I put the dishes on the table, I thought that I must do something for Niley. Maybe push her to take a vacation or something. She's so beautiful. I wonder why hasn't anyone latched on to her. Maybe she doesn't want to be latched.

The sex Niley and I had with Mario and Pixie was always hot. I have no regrets that the four of us let our hair down like that. Looking back gets me steamy when I have sex with my husband. Before we were married, he was no angel either. If he knew what went on in my mind when we get it on, he'd blush. I wonder one day if we'll bring Niley into the picture, but I'm a little scared to bring it up. What if he likes Niley more than me? She's so beautiful.

Only he knows how faithful he is now. He's always on a construction site, surrounded by temptation. Do I sound jealous? He has female employees, carpenters, plumbers and other trade people. I've seen some of them. He tells me that he tells them to keep their distance, or I'll kick their ass because I'm a ninja. He does exaggerate, but I think he does it to make me laugh. I don't laugh when he says I'm the love of his life. When he looks at me the way he does, I believe him. I hope his feelings for me never cool.

Rewind
February 14, 1989
Los Angeles
Mario

The big news was that on Valentine's Day, Melina eloped with her liquor salesperson, Ronnie. I found out from the horse's mouth, when Melina called me directly from the bathroom of her honeymoon suite.

"Cuz, I love you. Please don't stop being my friend because I got married."

"How could you do this without telling me?"

"It was easy, Cuz. We got in a car and drove to Las Vegas and did it."

I thought of all the times we almost left for Las Vegas to tie the knot, and it never happened. Melina always backed out on the basis she was ten years older than me.

"I love you, Melina."

"I will always love you," she said.

"I'm crushed," I said.

"Cuz, please. You have a dozen chicks in your bed, and at any moment you could be married to Olga, who, by the way, you should inform of my current situation, so that she has nothing to worry about where I am concerned any more."

That night when sleep finally found me, I was still brooding over Melina getting married. Letty joined me some time in the night. I did not wake up alone.

Present Day

I was talking on the phone when Letty stormed into my office. I raised my hand so she would wait until I was off the phone.

"This can't wait. It's an emergency!"

I could see in her face it was not good.

"I'll get back to you," I told Felipe. "Something has come up that I must attend to." I was off the phone in a split second.

"What is it?" I asked, standing up, with my arms crossed, a little skeptical that it was a real emergency. Letty was entirely capable of claiming she was starving, and that was the emergency. Unfortunately, she wasn't kidding.

"Melina tripped on the stairs coming down from her office at the Echo Park store. She's in an ambulance on the way to Queen of Angels."

The news all but knocked me off my feet. I sat down, feeling a little sick. "She's pregnant," I said. It was her miracle baby. "Any word on her condition?"

"No word Boss. I think she's still on the road. Tangles is already down in the car and Storm is driving."

I grabbed my coat, and we headed for the elevator. I had a strange sense of déjà vu. I remembered years ago, in the middle of an informal open air meeting with the lawyer I was working with at the time, I had heard cars colliding on the street. I ran there and was first on the scene to pull a beautiful girl from her car.

That girl was Melina. The ambulance arrived, and it carried her off to the hospital. When the ambulance drove off with her, her purse was hanging over my shoulder. It was my way into the case. They weren't going to let me in to see her till I said we were cousins. She'd been calling me 'Cuz' ever since.

In the elevator, I said, "Queen of Angels. That's the hospital she was in after I met her."

"I remember the story, Boss. You rescued her from her burning car after an accident on Broadway in front of the Grand Central Market."

Close enough. I wasn't going to correct her. I had pulled Melina out of the car, then the car burned. Everybody in LA called me a hero that week because the reporter got it wrong. Her Spider did blow up, but it didn't catch fire till after Melina was out of it. 1972 had been a terrible year. That November 5th, Tanis had been killed, and I was shot. Tanis had been a good friend, and was Niley's sister, and I mourned her loss for a long time. My getting shot and rescuing Melina had gotten me some unwanted notoriety. For a little while, everyone and their brother had recognized me as that guy in the paper. More importantly, Melina and I had become fast friends. I moved into her apartment building, and a couple of years later, followed her to Pasadena, and bought the house across the street from hers, where she had lived until a jealous Olga had bought Melina's house, so she'd move further away.

Now, all that mattered was that Melina was okay.

I sat in the passenger side over the objections of Storm and two passengers.

"Drive," I said. "You know the way?"

"I got it, Boss," Storm said.

She didn't leave rubber, but she got us out of the parking lot fast enough. I managed not to tell her to hurry.

"Boss, I'm sorry," Tangles said. "I know how important she is to you."

"Stay positive," I said. "Let's not bury her just yet."

"I didn't mean that," Tangles said.

I sighed. "Of course, you didn't." I turned around to face her. "I love you, Tangles. Forget I said that."

I remember being out in the ocean with them, worried but positive. I turned to face forward, my hand on the seat belt.

"Melina is strong," I said, speaking loud enough so the girls in the back seat could hear me.

A few years ago, she got shot in the parking lot of one of her markets. She'd survived several surgeries. It took a long time for her to find her new normal, but she pulled through. She underwent therapy, returned to work, and before long was working long hours again to keep her markets running efficiently and smoothly like she ran her life.

Melina was tough. She was going to be okay. She had to be.

My cell phone rang.

"This is me," I said.

"Boss, Jo and I are on way to Queen of Angels," Niley said.

"We're halfway there."

"See you there."

I told the girls. I heard them talking to each other, but in my mind, I went to God again, via the Virgin of Guadalupe. I prayed in silence with my eyes shut as Storm weaved through the traffic mess of downtown Los Angeles.

When Melina had been shot, I'd asked the Virgin of Guadalupe to save her. That time, I had promised I would give her my thanks. I did go to the Basilica Church in Mexico City to give her my personal thanks, crawling on my knees. The crawl had reminded me of many such submissions in my childhood in East Los Angeles, and now I remembered how I had looked up at the painting of her in the blue starred coat of the heavens, surrounded by gold, and the feeling of communicating with her came back to me.

"Virgencita, please let Melina and her baby get through this," I said in Spanish in my head.

Ronnie, her husband, came out and saw us in the lobby, his eyes swollen and bloodshot. We shook hands, then embraced. He's a much smaller man than I am, and he felt frail to me.

"How is she?" I asked.

"Fractured ribs, a broken right ankle, and some serious-looking bumps on her head," he said. He did not mention the baby.

We did not all go in to see her together but were allowed in for a brief moment. Ronnie returned to her side. After a few moments, I joined them.

Her eyes were closed, and she was so still I wondered if she was conscious. Her face was pale, bruised, and washed free of makeup. There was no hint of gray in her dark brown hair, but I knew the gold streaks came from a hairdresser. I'm not saying she looked like she did in 1972. That was twenty years ago. I'm forty-four. She's fifty-four, and time has dealt gently with her. If anything, she is more beautiful than ever, even bare-faced. There is compassion and sweetness in her face, but I saw new lines of sadness etched in.

I walked up to the bed and without saying anything, took her hand in both of mine. Her hand was so cold that I wished we had brought a blanket for her. I brought her hand halfway to my mouth and kissed her on the knuckles. I would have kissed her palm, but that seemed too intimate with her husband in the room.

Without opening her eyes, she said, "Mario. I knew you would come."

I wondered if she had recognized me by touch or scent. I didn't ask. Then her eyes opened.

"I guess I was not made to be a mom," she said to me. She smiled, but it was a wobbly smile, with her lower lip quivering. I knew the tears were barely at bay.

As soon as I touched her, I felt her sadness. I don't know what I said to her. Something appropriate, I hope.

There was a limit of two visitors to the room. Letty came to the door, and I left. As I walked out, I heard Melina apologizing.

"I'm sorry I lost our daughter," she said to Ronnie. "I'm too old and stupid to be carrying a baby. I'm so, so sorry."

My prayers were answered for Melina, but not for her baby girl. It was a disaster that the baby had passed away, but at least Melina was alive. If something fatal had happened to her, I would be a wreck. As it was, I could barely keep my composure.

I sat in the waiting room on her floor as the girls visited, one by one. Niley and Jo paid their visits. Betty arrived and paid her visit and joined us. Storm hugged her with tears in her eyes. She and Betty had been Melina's team of masseuses.

Ronnie came out to see a man and woman and three other younger people. When he noticed us, he introduced us to his parents and siblings, and thanked us for coming. He had a sister and two brothers. The girls hugged and kissed him. I shook his hand again.

"She's going to be out for hours," he told us. "They gave her something for pain and sleep."

We paid our respects for the loss of the baby. It would have been Ronald Junior if it had been a boy. None of us asked the girl's name.

In the old days, all of us would have camped out at the hospital. That's what we'd done when she was shot. Melina would need us, maybe. I hoped that her husband would be there for her.

We went home, straight to the wine room. Niley and Jo joined us.

I seldom thought about being a father, but I thought about it now. It had not been part of my mindset when I was sure Melina would become my wife someday or during the years I was engaged with Olga. I sort of assumed that it would just happen one day.

It came up, sure. Melina sometimes said she was too old to be a mom. Olga would say, "Our children someday," never mentioning that both of us were getting older.

That Melina allowed herself to get pregnant only meant she wanted a baby. It would not be to please her husband Ronnie. I felt bad for her. Drinking, smoking pot and talking with each other didn't block the gloom inside me.

Jo went home. Niley stayed with us.

After the weekend she spent with us, she didn't need to be urged by Letty or Tangles to stay the night.

"You'll need to provide undies in the morning," she told the girls with a little laugh. "I didn't come prepared."

Letty said, "For your information, the trend is still no panties. Where you been?"

I joined their laughter. The pictures of Melina going through my brain were replaced with pictures of Niley's sister Tanis who I'd been crazy about. Weeks before Melina and I met, Tanis was shot and was yanked from me forever.

Death lies in wait. Nothing we can do about it.

Tangles didn't go home that night, nor did Niley. We had hours of each other in bed. I could see that Letty was happy that Tangles was there, and Tangles seemed equally as happy. Their love for each other so evident. It was almost like Niley and me were alone on the bed, but that was okay.

Eventually everyone was asleep. I stared at the ceiling. No one had said anything of the baby girl's name. I didn't need to hear it. I pictured baby Mellie, the image of her mother. The tears flowed, and I was grateful no one was awake to see them.

February 13, 1992
Los Angeles
Letty

Brian was a vice president of purchasing at Western Sky Airlines, a fast-growing operator headquartered in El Paso, Texas. Andrea had assigned him to Tangles and me to work on getting six new Boeing 737s. He flew to meet with us on our revised proposal for the leases he was looking to get. We met in one of the conference rooms at the office, plush with wood paneling, a big conference table, comfortable chairs, carpeting, and a killer view of LA. There were two glass walls-one to the outside, and one facing the hall. Both of them had drapes and vertical blinds. The one facing the hall was closed, giving us our privacy. The other blinds were pulled open as far as they would go, showing us a high-dollar view of the city. We sat at one end of the long table.

"Congrats," Tangles said. "If you get this approved by your board, you'll have the planes."

"As I said on the phone, you are all approved on our end," I said.

"Our board was impressed by Western's steady growth, your credit history and the cash you are building up in your bank accounts," Tangles said.

I didn't mention that we don't have a board. Olga owns the company. Mario and Andrea make the decisions about everything, including high-dollar leases like this one.

Brian paged through the proposal and the lease. There were no surprises for him to find. He rejected our first proposal, and we had made changes, the biggest one being Western's option to buy the planes if they wanted to do that at the end of the lease.

I didn't think Brian was going to go through the entire lease. He would take it back to Texas for his group to make their decision. Tangles and I watched him in silence. To keep our hands busy, we sipped iced tea, crossing and un-crossing our legs under the table.

Andrea didn't even come in to say hello to this customer. Mario must have told her to let us run with it on our own.

It was amazing how Mario trusted us with such a big deal. The money Tangles and I would make if this lease went through would be the biggest score of our lives. The money was important to me, but the accomplishment would be more important than the commission. I am sure Tangles felt the same, though we hadn't talked about it. I wondered if I had to fuck him to get the deal signed, if I would do it.

I knew Tangles would do it in a heartbeat. Nowadays, she'd be doing it with a condom.

As for me, I didn't know. If I did it, it would be the first time I'd had sex with someone other than Mario in years. Before I met him, I'd fuck anyone I liked in a heartbeat. I don't remember Mario asking me if I've stepped out. He would never ask me something like that.

He's absolutely paranoid that me or Tangles believe he wants us just for himself. He's always been that way about anyone on the team that goes to bed with him. We're free agents, at least technically.

I watched Brian read. He wasn't handsome or ugly. He was just your ordinary looking middle-aged guy, in glasses, losing his hair, maybe losing some muscle tone from younger days, not that I'd seen his younger self. He just didn't stir up any juices in me.

"Looks good to me," Brian said. "I'll get it signed, notarized as you've indicated on the instructions, and we're done."

I said, "If you are totally good with it, I'll send you home with originals. If you look close, what you have is a draft."

Tangles got up.

"It will take less than five to print it for you." She stood beside him, looking down at him. He was still seated. She gave an excited little wiggle that almost made me break out into laughter. I wasn't sure if she was just excited or coming on to Brian.

"Do it," Brian said. "The board will approve it. It's exactly what they wanted."

February 13, 1992
Puerto Rico
Lola

Mickey's Bar is a high-end hangout for drinking exotic drinks, checking out available partners, and watching a hot DJ playing hotter music. I didn't know the regulars, so I didn't recognize who was out to be hired, or who was someone just out, like me.

I'd met a couple of bartenders on the beach. They were my buddies and had invited me here. They pointed out a couple of hookers to me. The management let the hookers slide as long as they weren't obvious or pushy. The house made money for allowing them on the turf.

If I only wanted a fuck, I'd take a for-hire stud and show him the door when it was done. I know it's cold, but it is what it is. Fifty bucks gets me fucked once, twice, with an orgasm or two, and that works for me. Once in a while, I go with a charmer who shows interest in me. We roll around on a bed in sex-driven heat in a nice hotel that he pays for. I am gone in the morning unless the dude beats me to it.

When I want to be at home, I play an X-rated movie and give myself an orgasm. My favorite videos are of Mario and me at the Beverly Hills Hotel.

My life is the pits now, and it was the pits when I was with the agency, too. I felt boxed in, trapped. I was enamored with Mario from the beginning. I fell for him. Our team had hundreds of photos of him, Pepe, Olga, and Camila. Mario was never a subject of investigation. I had enough influence to keep the team focused on the real bad people. The petty shit Mario was doing—buying up property for Pepe Camacho using cash—was nothing compared to catching the big-time drug runners.

"We're looking for the biggest bust of the century," I used to tell the team.

A complicated crime like money laundering is difficult to get a conviction on.

Our team was me, Lisa, and three men. Off hours, we were crazy. We smoked pot. We fucked each other too. You get stir crazy on extended missions like the Camacho watch. It's possible we fucked it all up ourselves, and that's why we never got anything solid to run against them. Our supervisor was in his late fifties. He looked good in a suit but not without clothes. He didn't arrange a meet very often. When he complained about shutting the team down, I took him to a hotel and fucked the living daylights out of him. Twice Lisa went with me. One time when Lisa and I double teamed him, and I thought we killed him. He was so out of breath I was ready to give him mouth to mouth.

All of us were obsessed by the gig, the travel, the private federal jet to keep up with the Camachos when they traveled, the kicked-back life of watching and writing reports. We were totally straight officers of the law who got mesmerized by such intimate study of the Camacho lifestyle. We lost our idealism in the long process of trying to make a case against the Camacho family.

"Bring over a stud," I told the bartender. I palmed him a five. I was here to pick up a guy. I'd left the murphy bed down at my place. The bed was made. Hell, I even spritzed the sheets with cologne and fluffed the pillows.

Normally I stay away from beer because it has a way of sticking around my waist, but I had two. Nothing beats a cold one in Puerto Rican weather, even when the temperature was perfectly cold in the bar.

The bartender's Puerto Rican stood beside me because all the stools were occupied. This guy was a tall, big mother. I bought him a beer.

I whispered, "Less than two hours. We can walk to my place."

When we got to my place, we didn't waste any time. I pulled my shirt off. I wasn't wearing a bra. I could tell he appreciated it, but his eyes and cock got big when he saw the tattoo over my scar.

"Your art is hot," he said. I could tell by the bulge at his crotch he meant it. I'm glad when they love the tattoo. It saves explaining the scar from when I got the bullets taken out of me. Tattoo or not, I never tell anyone where the scars came from.

"Use one of mine," I said, handing him a condom. He was out of his clothes in a New York minute. I guess I could call it a Puerto Rican minute. He was clean enough that I didn't ask him to shower first.

He put the condom on and pulled it down tight. I dimmed the lamp and watched him. He was well-built and handsome. His eyes were a toasty brown, and I could see he was appreciating me.

"How you want it?" he asked.

I turned around, went down on fours, and raised my ass up high.

"How is this?" I wasn't asking.

"Just perfect," he said in a hoarse voice.

I felt his big hands open the cheeks of my ass. I felt his tongue on my clitoris, making me even wetter, ready. His tongue got stiff and he found my backside entrance and expertly probed.

"I don't want it there."

"Want me to stop?"

I hesitated; he hadn't stopped.

"No, don't stop yet. It's good."

"Miles knows about good ass," he said between probes.

I couldn't remember the last time I'd had a tongue there.

His hands moved on my hips, then one hand teased my clit. As his big finger touched, his tongue penetrated me from behind. I exploded in grenade-fashion, an orgasm that made my legs weak. I collapsed flat on my stomach, his hand never moving from my pussy. A moment later, his stiff cock was in my pussy. I pushed up against him as he lay on me.

When Miles left, I gave him a hundred instead of the promised fifty.

"Can I come back?" he asked.

I was standing at the door, bare ass naked.

"I'll see you around," I replied. I closed the door and locked it.

I went straight to the shower, and when I returned to the bedroom, I stripped the bedding and put on fresh sheets and pillowcases. I put the linen in the laundry room and went to bed. I tossed and turned.

I should have let him stay.

I'm such a bitch.

I can be stupid. I hadn't had that kind of satisfaction in a long time. It was the kind of satisfaction Mario Luna left me with every time we had sex.

March 13, 1992
Bogota, Colombia
Olga

Riana and I were in my sitting room at home. It's a cozy little niche off of my bedroom with not much furniture: just a couple of recliners, a table I sometimes use as a desk, and a bookcase full of books I am always meaning to read. I had a device you place the mouthpiece of a phone into to make an ordinary house phone work as a speaker. I used it after I called the main number to GAL in Los Angeles. The receptionist recognized my voice. Letty, Tangles, and Mario joined me in a conference call.

I said, "Hello my dears. I'm on the speaker. Riana is here with me."

"Long time no see. Miss you," Riana said from the recliner next to mine.

"Miss you, too," they said.

"I just heard about the lease Letty and Tangles finalized last month. I want to congratulate you. I am so proud of you," I said.

"Thank you for the congratulations, but we should be thanking you. After all, you are the boss and without you, Boss and Andrea, it would have never happened."

"Amor, I know you are as proud as I am."

"Absolutely," Mario said. "I just signed their checks."

"Olga, he got me a red Ferrari! Can you believe that?" Tangles interrupted, excitedly.

"He got me a black one!" Letty said.

"You deserve it," I said, laughing at their enthusiasm.

Riana clapped and whistled. Everyone laughed,

"Letty and me, we owe you big time, Olga," Tangles said.

"No, no, you owe Boss Man, not me."

"Yes, we do, and Andrea too," Letty said.

"Amor, let the girls come visit me. I'm going back to Rio tomorrow. I'd love to have them over for as long as you can spare them."

"It's up to them," Mario said, as if he has nothing to do with decisions like that. Or maybe he was wondering why I was not inviting him.

"We have couple of possible hot deals cooking on the stove," Letty said.

"Of course, we can come if you want us," Tangles said.

"Yes of course. Thank you, Olga," Letty said.

"I can send them in my plane," Mario said.

I said, "Once we're in Rio, I'll send for you. My plane will pick you up. It's settled, Amor. I got it covered. Hopefully I get to see you soon. I miss you."

March 13, 1992
Los Angeles
Mario

At noon the next day, I was on my new plane with Niley headed to Paris. I planned to visit the GAL office in Milan on our way back.

"You can't imagine how badly I wanted to get away from the grind. I'm dreaming," Niley said, sitting across from me.

We were waiting for the plane to pull back.

I reached across the table, wine glass in my right hand. She met me halfway, and we clicked.

"You're not dreaming. I had to get away too," I said. "I'm having a bad time thinking of how Melina is going to feel when it sinks in that her baby is gone."

Niley said, "I love her too, Mario. We go back long time. You know she's strong. She'll be okay. You'll see."

I nodded in agreement. We clicked again, sipped and the pilot came on the speakers.

"We're going to be pulling back. Please fasten your seat belts."

Niley had such a beautiful smile.

"Tell me we're not going to crash."

"I promise, we're not going to crash."

Five minutes later, we were wheels up.

I showed off the fabulous lounge with a television and comfortable seating, then I called for our attendant Krystal to fold out the puzzle of a bed. As we sat in two of three seats that were not part of the bed, I admired the cream and suede interior of my new plane.

The bed came together like magic under her fingers, then Krystal made the bed with black percale and four pillows with matching cases. We destroyed her handywork as we tumbled under the sheets and tugged up the goose-down comforter. We fooled around for a little while and took the edge off, then sat propped up facing the television. I could have lain flat. The mattress was a little over six feet five inches long.

Niley flicked on the movie. "I wonder what tape you put in there," she said.

Credits for The Godfather came on the screen.

"Marlin Brando," she said. "He's not what he used to be. But you've held up pretty well." She ran her hand over my chest and arms, then lower. "You're hot stuff, Boss. I can't believe I've got you all to myself," Niley said. "Brando in his prime has got nothing on you."

"My favorite movie," I said before kissing her.

"Unmute it," she said, her lips moving on mine as she spoke. "You can watch it. I'll just play on you and entertain myself."

"Maybe later," I said. "I have some playing in mind, too."

Our kiss became a long passionate connection.

Her hands roved all over me. I touched her and found her ready.

All the years I'd known Niley, and we still ignite the sheets.

One Christmas Eve, the girls and I had been in the George V Hotel in Paris when we got word Pepe had died when his plane was shot by a shoulder missile during takeoff. Knowing what I now know of Pepe, I wonder how Camila and Olga had appeared to be so sad. Pepe's memory was no longer sacred to me, and that was okay. I liked the George V, and that history did not cast a shadow over the hotel for me. The presidential suite was not available but that's what happens when you're spontaneous. The suite that was available was beautiful enough for a king.

There were two walk-in closets. Niley's suitcase went in one closet, and mine in the other. The bellboy set up our suitcases in the bigger of the two bedrooms. Once I tipped him and told him I didn't need any help with how the television, gadgets, and remote control curtains worked, he left.

"This is plenty grand. We have three bathrooms. Dig it, Boss."

After the bellboy left, Niley ran from room to room like an excited kid. I could remember her doing the same thing many times in many places, back when we'd been flying all over the world to get cases from plane crashes. The Presidential was superior to this, but Niley was right that what we got was grand.

March 14, 1992
Rio de Janeiro
Riana

Olga walked ahead of me carrying a towel. She flung it over the railing at the foot of the stairs and turned on the outdoor shower to wash away the sand before going into the house. I don't know what there was about it that pleased me so much, but I love this outdoor shower. We were dry so most of the sand had brushed off by the time we got here. We had spent an hour today just strolling down the beach. Olga rinsed her feet, then I lingered a few minutes under the fresh water with the scent of the sea, the drumming of the waves, the salty breeze off the beach, the sound of sea birds. Olga lit a joint and we sat on wicker loungers on the patio letting the sun dry us off.

"You look so happy," I said to Olga. "I love seeing you like this. Does it have to do with Letty and Tangles visiting soon?"

"Maybe. I used to be jealous of Letty. I didn't want her around Mario, day and night."

I laughed. "That man lays anything he's attracted to. She might be devoted to Mario, but I highly doubt it is the other way around."

She nodded. "I feel different now. I love those two girls."

"The attention they give you in bed is what you love." I was kidding, but not really.

Olga laughed. "Yes, that, too. Both said they owe me big time. The four of us are going to have fun."

"You're so naughty," I said.

"Me, naughty?" She giggled.

Her expression changed. She paused and gave me a serious look. I wondered what she was thinking. I didn't have to wonder long.

"Remember when Tangles told me off? She was new to all this, our openness—I guess she didn't understand our open relationship. She didn't think I could care for Mario if I was sharing him. I think she was more than a little infatuated with Mario at the time. Camila was on the bed with us. Anyway, Letty jumped out of bed and hauled Tangles out of the bedroom. The next morning, she apologized. She'd been doped up on pills and booze, and it went to her head. I let it go. Camila didn't. Camila sent an enforcer after her."

The sun had moved overhead so that I could not see her face, but I squinted in her direction.

"After Tangles?"

"Yeah. You know how Pepe was fearless. I hated him, but I have to give him credit for knowing how to extinguish his enemies. He was meticulous. If he was after one person and that person was in a group, Pepe didn't care. Collateral damage didn't matter. He'd order a bomb or grenade to be thrown in the crowd to ensure that the target was taken out. Innocent casualties did not matter to him. Camila had the same angry blood. She turned on Tangles. The enforcer she'd hired was supposed to toss her around a little and be gone. But Tangles found the woman breaking in her apartment. They threshed it out, then Tangles shot her, and the police hauled her off. Tangles never saw her again, because Camila had the woman bailed. She never showed up for court. I felt so guilty. Tangles got beaten black and blue before she shot her attacker. After I found out about it, I bought her a gift or two. I understand being jealous, and she was just jealous. I never was mad at her. Camila was another story. Camila could hold a grudge like nobody's business. She just sent the woman back to Colombia where she'd had found her."

"Rest in peace Camila. I'm glad I was always on her good side," I said. "Camila was a bitch."

"Camila loved me. It's a wonder she let it go."

"Letty always says fuck-me," I said. "Well, fuck-me. Why are you telling me this?"

Olga turned in her chair and reached for my hand. "I love you and trust you. I carry so many secrets I have to let go sometimes."

"I love you too," I said, getting up. "Scoot over." I squeezed in beside her and gave her a kiss. "Tell me anything you want whenever you want."

"Thank you, Amor."

We snuggled facing each other on the one chair, our legs stretched out. Olga dozed off and I tried following her lead. Memories kept me awake.

I owe Olga my life. She'd saved us both when her security team mutinied at thirty thousand feet. We'd been at their mercy, but Olga endured a rape, conned them, and bought us some time. She shot and killed all of them, plus the pilot and copilot, took the flight controls and landed us safely in Colombia. I had been terrified, but Olga never lost her cool. I really admire her for that. In retaliation, Camila ordered the executions of the relatives of Olga's treasonous security team, a lesson that treason is not tolerated by Camacho.

Two family members survived and set out to get even with Olga in Milan. They were trying to avenge their families. She and Mario were getting off her helicopter at the Milan house, and they attacked. It's a good thing that Mario was there, because it could have come out very differently. That attempt on her life was how Olga learned Camila had exterminated the minors along with the rest. She was furious with Camila when she learned that Camila had ordered that minors be included in the executions. I hated that Camila killed the minors, but she was right that they come after you, eventually, if you let them live. I've never said it aloud, but I believe that the person who shot and killed Camila was connected to those relatives that were executed

March 16, 1992
Paris
Niley

He is like I always remembered, considerate, tender. He'd check to make sure I had an orgasm. I was soaking wet. We joked around, and I laughed so hard I cried. We reminisced about that time in Texas, Boss and I were on a case, tipsy from drinking wine. We filled the hotel tub with bubbles and got in. Bubbles went everywhere. We made such a mess, but it was fun. Why do I always remember that? Here in Paris, we have a huge handcrafted stone tub. We spent a long time in it, steaming hot, jet streams of water probing from every direction. Tickles, laughter, fun!

We didn't even feel jet-lagged. He's an expert of when to sleep to manage jet lag. His thing doesn't know soft, and that's okay with me. My body needed the sexual workout. I won't call it lovemaking. The sex was fast, hard, intense, far from lovemaking.

We were in the dining room of the suite and ate just a little. Strawberries and champagne followed. He ordered wine. I filled the glasses at our intimate little table. The lights were turned down low in the room, with candles burning like at a romantic bistro. He was so beautiful to me in the flickering light, like a hero from a romance novel.

"You could have brought anyone or everyone. Why did you bring me?"

"I wanted to spend some quality time with you."

He picked me up piggyback style. I rode him, my arms around his neck, my mouth on his right ear. I rode him piggyback to the master bedroom where we started all over again. We weren't strangers by any means, but it was like our bodies had been doing this for years, without the long dry spell between us that there had been. He found my heat and needed no guidance to enter. It was like a honeymoon, but Mario is the wrong person for a honeymoon. I don't care. I only want to be near him. I want more of him.

March 18, 1992
Milan, Italy
Mario

After five nights in Paris, our next stop was Milan where I planned a half day at the GAL office. I almost always stay at the Camacho mansion when I am in Milan. It is my home away from home. I lived in the mansion for two years with Letty and Tangles. I felt uncomfortable taking Niley to the mansion. I had taken many lady friends to the house when I was working and living in Milan, but this felt different. It was still my residence by virtue of my position at GAL, but maybe my unease was because I was no longer living there, or because my relationship with Olga had changed. Andrea arranged for Niley and me to have the presidential suite at the Bulgari Hotel.

Olga reached me on the cell.

"Amor, you're in Milan and checked in to a hotel instead of staying at the house? What's wrong with you?"

"Baby, I'm only here two days. I'm okay where I am."

In Milan, Niley and I made up for the shopping we didn't do in Paris. Milan has every designer store you can think of, and we visited them all. They don't carry much merchandise, but they did have Niley's size. I noticed what she liked and kept buying everything that put a smile on her face.

"Mario, please don't buy me so much. I'm just happy to be here with you."

I grinned.

"Don't burst my bubble, baby. I'm having fun." I said.

Niley must have serious bucks in the bank from her half of the management company.

I know how much work she and Jo were handling because my assets were what their management company managed. It was big money, but they charged me less than any other management company would. Jo and Niley were family to me. It didn't matter how much their fees turned out to be each year. I didn't just want them to be well off. I wanted them to be rich.

Niley modeled the purchases for me. She came out in pastels like the rainbow, and then in black and white. She stepped out like a model, turns and all, even with nothing on but a nightie. A couple of them, she stripped off, tossed them in my direction, then went off to model the next one.

"You are such a turn on," I said. "You're so hot."

"Tell me that again. I need it."

"You are as gorgeous as when I first met you," I said.

Niley stepped out of the nightie. Martial arts had molded a body that showed no signs of wear and tear. She didn't run to make another clothes change but sat on my lap.

"Tell me that again, Boss. I love to hear it."

She stood, placed her hands on her breasts invitingly, and licked her lips. She backed away.

"Are you just going to sit there?"

From about ten feet away, I stood there staring at her looking like a wet dream. She backed up till she was against the bed, then sort of melted till she was on her side and raising her head to face me. She crooked her finger at me.

When the short vacation was over and it was time to return to Pasadena, I felt somber. Normally, I'd be anxious to get back.

March 18, 1992
Somewhere over South America
Letty

Tangles and I were propped up on pillows on the king-sized bed in Olga's plane. *Basic Instinct* was on, and the television was muted. Two glasses of ice were on the end tables beside us, sweating condensation and waiting.

I popped open a can of coke, poured and the soda sizzled in the glass. The first sip was perfect, crisp, harsh, refreshing.

"I didn't think Niley would become competition," I said.

"He's known her like forever," Tangles said.

"Not forever," I said. "But he used to date her sister. They have something special."

"We all have something special," Tangles said, argumentative as usual. "Anyway, she's got it made. Doesn't need Boss."

"I know I sound jealous but I'm not. I suggested he take her to Paris. She needed to get away. She was close to a meltdown."

Tangles swatted my thigh and laughed.

"Listen to the drama, already. So what if you are jealous? You know how he is."

"Yeah, I know how he is."

"Don't bum us out," Tangles said. "Cheer up. We're on vacation."

"Hug me," I said, "I'm not going to bum us out, I promise."

Olga and Riana picked us up at the airport. We got in the four-seater with Riana and Olga, Olga piloting. A second identical helicopter with her security aboard took our luggage. We knew she was a pilot, but we had never been up with her before. This helicopter looked smaller than the one I'd seen parked in Bogota. She handled the chopper like it was an extension of her hand, and only tried to scare the shit out of us one time.

"Your pad is bitchin'," Tangles said as we got the ten cent tour.

"Way bitchin'," I agreed.

She said how she'd ordered a lot of the furnishings and appliances from the US, and how she'd had trouble getting her builder to stay on track.

We had a great late lunch and went to bed early, but there was no sleeping. Rio is only four hours ahead of L.A. so it's not like there is much jetlag. The thing in bed was like it was planned, and we all got off without a hitch. Tangles and me, we romanced every inch of Olga with kisses and nibbles. Riana sat on the bed and watched, smoked up a storm of pot, and egged us on with claps and laughter. She was funny. She was beautiful. She got no action from us, but Olga had so many orgasms I lost count.

In the morning, we ate breakfast, beachside.

"Here's the scoop," Olga said. "I got a call early that I need to be in Geneva to meet with my attorney and the team preparing to take LAI public. Normally I tell them to come here, but I need to be there to sign papers."

"Aw, gee," I said.

"No aw gee. You're here, and you are going to have a ball. That's an order from the CEO."

Olga laughed. Riana laughed.

Tangles and I moved to the Camacho mansion on the beach. We had all the servants, guards, chauffeur, and even a pilot on call to take us by helicopter wherever we wanted to go.

"I feel comfortable in this house," I said to Tangles.

"I can't imagine owning something like this." Tangles said. "If I owned it, I'd use the hell out of it."

"I'd live here," I said, and wondered if that was true.

When we went out, it was in a three Suburban sandwich, with guards in front and back, and us in the center car.

With Olga, Camila and Boss, we had been to Rio nightclubs before. The guards were not obvious, but they were close by. By the time we arrived, the Rio was already swarming with the writhing bodies of locals jamming to the music. After ten minutes of standing, we were wondering if we should stay or split. Lunes the head guard appeared and wound us through the crowd, leading us toward a little table by the main dance floor.

Ringside seats.

"This is Juan Carlos, your waiter," Lunes said. "For anything you need."

The music was blasting, and we were in the thick of the action. Tangles and I were impressed, but given the decibel level, our eyes did the talking.

Juan Carlos bent his head close to us and yelled without seeming to. "What can I get you to drink?"

"Something to make us feel good but not get us drunk," I said.

"Caipirinhas," he said.

Tangles and I nodded. He returned with two great-looking glasses filled with a clear drink, muddled limes in ice.

"Sip slow. You will enjoy."

He watched us take our first sips, and we gave him a thumbs up. It was difficult to drink slow. Too good. The flavor was like a spiked limeade that started off very strong, but as the ice melted and we drank more, the drink got lighter and sweeter. I didn't recognize the liquor, but it was delicious.

When two young guys approached, Juan Carlos blocked them as though he was on our security team. I waved to get his attention and he read my lips.

"It's okay."

The guys were in loud mod silk button-down shirts, the collars unbuttoned just so but not too much. Their denim jeans were new. The guys were all smiles, attractive, personable, and, we soon found, energetic. We accepted their invitation to dance. Once we started, the dancing was non-stop. I danced with the guy who asked me until the end of the song. The main dance floor was large and packed, and as soon as one song ended, another song and another partner appeared just like that. I lost track of Tangles but caught sight of her dancing now and again. Around us were dancers with their skin gleaming with perspiration. It was strenuous, perhaps, but not for Tangles and me, conditioned by karate. It takes more than a little dancing to get us to sweat.

After a couple of hours, Tangles flashed me a sign and I returned it. I mean, I didn't have a code or anything, but I put my knees together and

took a couple of steps like I was desperate to pee. Classic. We declined Lunes'
escort and headed for the rest room. He waited by the table, and I made out
two of our security-detail with eyes on us as we opened the door marked
Damas.

"Are you digging it?" Tangles asked.

"I'm digging it," some woman said from inside a stall.

"I'm digging it, too," I said much too loud. Lots of other voices
chimed in. Everyone was digging it, and we were all laughing.

"Let's take a couple dudes back with us," Tangles said.

"Not a good idea. We don't know anyone here. And I'm not comfortable bringing strange men to the Camacho house."

"Probably right," Tangles said.

We returned to the dance floor.

After the bathroom break, we didn't dance any more but the music,
mostly American Rock, was to die for. We bade farewell to Juan Carlos, and
I told Lunes, "Copacabana Palace."

"Nice choice," Lunes said.

The Copacabana Palace was a fabulous classy hotel across the street
from the beach like all the hotels. The exclusive night club was a little stuffy,
the music was loud and good, and the dance floor busy, but not as packed.
Around us, guys were in sport jackets, khakis or jeans, no ties. We were in
our cayenne clubbing outfits, which meant sexy designer with enough spice,
glam, glitter and skin showing to be drop-dead sexy. When we were shown
to a table, Tangles slinked her way across the floor like a Bob Fosse dancer. I
almost laughed aloud, but every eye was on her. Tangles was on the hunt.

A guy about Boss's age came up to the table. He was a looker, but of average height, physically an ordinary guy, not even close to Mario's ballpark. He introduced himself as Jordão and invited me to dance. I wasn't worn out, but I'd had enough dancing.

"I just danced so much at the Rio I'm not feeling it right now. But you're welcome to have a drink with us," I heard myself say. I didn't look at Tangles, but she didn't voice any objections.

When the music stopped, there was a little gap. We took the opportunity to exchange a few words.

"Can my friend join us?" Jordão asked. "We're in Rio together for a few days."

Tangles shrugged and said, "Sure. Where is he?"

He pointed him out. A guy a little younger, taller and better looking than Jordão approached the table. Jordão introduced his friend as Joao.

Tangles smiled.

We talked in the ladies' room. "I want to fuck Joao," Tangles said. "Let's take him home with us."

"He's not a gift," I laughed.

Tangles pouted.

"Olga's house is not our hotel. I'm not comfortable bringing fuck buddies over without her permission. And I'm not going to call and bug her in Geneva."

"They're staying here," Tangles said. "I can fuck him here."

"You're wasting no time," I said.

The bathroom wasn't as crowded as the Rio's had been, though it smelled as strongly of beer, perfume, and liquor. There was dark paneling on the walls with Hollywood lighting circling the mirror. Tangles leaned close and examined her face and whipped out a lipstick. She waved her hand to emphasize her words.

"Olga split on us. Let's have fun," Tangles said, reining in her lipstick hand to apply it carefully. She blotted her lips and gave her mirror image a little air kiss. The way she did it, and the way she wobbled on her high heels was evidence that she'd had a couple more drinks than I had.

Two hours later, I'd had nothing to eat and a glass of wine. Jordão asked me to his room.

"Hold that thought," I said, and excused myself ostensibly to hit the bathroom, but it was also to have a word with Lunes.

"We're going to stay here," I told him.

"Whatever you say, Miss Letty. Are you sure you don't want to go back to the house?"

I hesitated. "It wouldn't be right."

"As you wish, Miss Letty."

Tangles and I conferred in the restroom.

"I told Joao about the security guys, take it or leave it," Tangles said. "He asked if we're movie stars or rich." She laughed. "Open your purse."

"Checkpoint? What for? Who are you now, the NSA?"

"Just providing you some party favors," she said. She gave me a drunken grin and dumped a handful of condoms in my purse. I must admit the girl travels prepared.

I snapped my purse shut. "Thanks, and be careful."

Tangles made a face like I'd made a joke. As if either one of these guys could take us. "You too."

I knew what she meant. She was a warrior. We both were though we weren't packing our guns. (It gets serious in Rio if you get caught with a gun.)

We didn't need guns.

When I returned to the table, two security guys were obviously following me. Jordão was still there, swirling an untouched glass of wine. He looked at the security guys. They weren't quite dressed to fit in.

"I'll go with you to your room," I said. "But two men will be outside your door for as long as I'm there with you. Can you live with that?"

When Jordão saw me naked, he whistled.

"Where did you get those abs? Damn."

If you said that kind of thing to Mario, he'd do a back flip just to show off. I didn't do anything, just said, "I work out a little bit."

I whipped off the hotel bed's top cover and blanket, and we got on the sheets, and necked a little bit. I looked at his dick. It was big enough I wouldn't have any complaints.

He made a move for me, and I put a condom on him. He didn't complain, but I had no practice with condoms. He went soft. I gave it a couple tugs, and it came to life.

"Hurry, Letty, I can't wait."

He got on top of me. I wrapped my legs around him, and he fucked me for a long time. I didn't have an orgasm, but I felt good. It had been ages since I had been fucked by a stranger. We rolled around on the big bed. He was enamored by how toned I am, especially my abs. He went between my legs, he cupped my ass with his hands and pulled my pussy to his mouth. I came instantly. That didn't stop him. He kept going until I shuddered with orgasms.

March 20, 1992
Gal Offices, Los Angeles
Mario

"Boss, you won't believe this, but we have a walk-in. This lady here wants to lease a plane," Andrea said over the intercom.

"Really," I said. "By all means, bring her in."

I had barely enough time to sign my name on the letter I was finishing up when there was a light knock at the door. Andrea opened it, leading in a tall, statuesque blonde.

I recognized her right away. The first two times we'd met, she'd introduced herself as Margaret Johnson. She had a headful of straight blonde hair cut chin length by some brilliant hair stylist, light gray eyes that looked green in certain light, and looked as Scandinavian as Greta Garbo with fair skin, rosy cheeks, and high cheekbones. I had met Margaret twice before, and both times she'd said right off the bat that Johnson was her married name, she was full-blooded Mexican, and her family went back to the Aztec Indians in Central Mexico. Maybe I am spoiled by my team, because I noticed she was lean the way a model is lean. The deep v of her fine ivory suit

(Chanel or Gucci or some other such name) revealed a collarbone that looked more bony than sexy, and no cleavage though the décolleté plunged halfway to her waist. Only the top three of the jacket's six chunky buttons were closed. I wondered if she had a shirt-or anything—on underneath. She walked in pulling off alligator-skin gloves that matched her alligator heels. A deep slash in the side of her pencil-type skirt allowed her to take reasonable steps. I saw all of this in a matter of seconds thanks to Melina's long-ago lessons in haute couture.

I didn't give her time to re-introduce herself.

"Margaret Johnson," I said, crossing the floor to take her hand. "Marge, whatever your lineage, you are gorgeous," I said.

She seemed surprised that I remembered her.

I was surprised to see her. Margaret was a walk-in to our offices. That's unheard of. Plane leasing is not a walk-in trade. No one just walks in and says I want to lease a plane, but she did. Andrea took my handshake in stride.

"If you know each other, there's no need for an introduction," Andrea said, reading my glance to see if I wanted to handle Margaret. I took it from there. I could have let Andrea attend to her, but Margaret is a looker.

Turned out that the plane lease she was seeking was not for herself but for a rich widow in Mexico City.

"I'm an advisor for your prospective buyer. Buying planes, I know about, but not leasing. My client wants to lease. I know you're the man for that."

In my Rolls, Storm drove us to Van Nuys Airport where I kept my plane. Our eyes met in the mirror, and she grinned and flashed me a subtle thumbs up. No privacy window in the Rolls, not that I needed it. I explained to Margaret many details of plane leases, and how a plane lease is similar to a car lease except for the difference in price. At the airport, I gave her a plane tour.

"It is beautiful," she said. "It's brand new."

"Yes, it's new. What you are looking at runs twenty million plus. On a lease, that translates to two million down. From what you have said of your client, if she leases it for five years, it's quite within her means, providing she needs this much plane."

I talked about the range of possible choices, showed her the extras, the cabin that converted to a good-sized bedroom with a queen-sized bed. Margaret was a fast note-taker, never asked the same question twice, nor to repeat something. She struck me as very savvy, or I would never had left my busy desk to show my plane. She struck me as a serious buyer with the means to afford it. Her gray pinstriped suit was business casual, but sharp. Margaret was dressed like a person that could afford to lease a plane. I trusted her judgment that her client could afford it, but of course we would do our due diligence.

"If we lease to your client, we'll need the usual credit information and financial details," I said on the way back to GAL.

"Money is no object. My client can buy the plane. Her asset is oil wells. She doesn't need to lease, but she heard about leasing, and likes the idea of not having to maintain an asset like an expensive plane in her name."

Immediately I thought of drugs. Next, she would offer me green cash to buy the plane and forget the lease.

"Should I ask why your client doesn't want the plane in her name?"

Margaret took a sip of the 7 Up I had just poured into a crystal glass.

I swigged my chilled coke in the bottle. Okay, maybe not swigged. I made some effort to match my companion's manners.

"It's complicated," Margaret said. "She likes her privacy. Will you sell her a plane, or do you only do leases?"

"Sure, I can sell or lease, anything she her heart desires. If she wants a lease, leasing makes more sense, but it's up to your client."

"Will you sell your plane?"

"I just got it. I waited long time to get it fitted. We're not even sure this is the plane that your client would want or need, but if she wants one with similar design, I am sure it can be done."

"I love your plane," Margaret said.

"I love it, too," I said with a short laugh.

On her second visit a few days later, she targeted my plane. I was reluctant to sell it, but if she was fixated on it, I would be sure to make a substantial profit on it.

"My client wants to buy your plane," she said. "Can I smoke in here? I need to loosen up a little."

Margaret sat down across from me, my desk between us. I slid a marble ashtray over her way. It was on my desk for looks, but what the hell. The customer is always right, right?

"Sure, go for it."

She crossed her legs. Nice legs. I wavered. I was keeping my plane. I waited to tell her my plane was not for sale.

I figured she'd take out a pack of cigarettes, but she pulled out an ivory and gold cigarette case filled with tightly rolled joints. She selected one and held it out to me. I noticed her manicure. Specks of gold in her polish to match her metallic gold business suit, nails so long there was no way she could do anything productive with her hands.

"We can share," she said.

I waited until she lit up and took a drag.

She held it up for me.

Instead of accepting it, I said, "If I have that I won't be able to do the work waiting for me." I waved my arm, indicating a stack of papers in my inbox. "Enjoy, Marge. I love the smell."

"You don't smoke?"

"I do, but not here." That was not entirely true.

She took two more drags then pinched it out and put the roach back in her cigarette case.

"How much for your plane?"

"Marge, your client hasn't seen the plane. We haven't discussed what it's going to cost you to operate the plane per hour. You or your client haven't flown in the plane either. The plane is not for sale."

I thought of a number to discourage her and quoted her a price double what the plane should cost. It didn't even make her blink.

Twenty minutes later, I asked Andrea to come in my office.

"I've agreed to sell my plane to Margaret's client. I'd like you to take it from here. Margaret has seen the plane, but I never got into the pilot requirements, cost of operations, and everything else she needs to know."

Andrea handled it like a pro. She didn't ask any silly questions like why are you selling or why your plane and not something else.

"Did you agree on a price?"

"Twenty-eight million."

Two days later my bank called to tell me I had received a wire from the Dominican Republic for $28 million U.S. dollars. I paid off the loan I had taken from the bank. I cleared about five million.

"I had to sell it. I'm in the business," I told Olga on the phone. "How are you and the girls?"

"They're on their own," she said. "I was called to Geneva. I, of course, was able to go at the drop of a hat because I have a plane. What will you do if you need to fly? Silly man," she said. "Now what? No plane? Do you plan on flying coach?" She laughed hysterically.

"I'll take the advice you gave me originally and get a company plane, what you told me to do."

Olga said, "You deserve it, Amor. Go shopping, and let GAL buy it for you."

"How are the girls managing without you?"

"They're having a blast. They paired off one night at the Copacabana with a couple of dudes. They didn't want to bring them to the house thinking I'd mind. I set them straight. I don't care about little things like that."

Olga caught me off guard. I thought of Letty having sex with a stranger. I wasn't even sure it was true. Tangles fucked around, and it was no secret. I wondered why would Letty do that in Rio and not here. I urged her to get out, to date, and she always shined me on.

I thought about calling Letty. I argued with myself all the way home.

I'm not going to call.

Let them kick back and enjoy themselves.

Letty with another man?

Why would Olga drop that on me, snitching the girls out? Maybe Olga doesn't think of it as snitching. No, it was something else. She deliberately told me this to jab me about my live-ins. I don't own them. She should know I don't care. Maybe that's the wrong phrase. It's not that I don't care. It's just that like Aunt Carmen always said, 'What is sauce for the goose is sauce for the gander.' If I can be a free spirit, then Letty and Tangles can be too. Who am I to set their boundaries? Still, the thought kept coming back to me of Letty with another man.

Miguel served me dinner in the wine room. There was a huge steak in front of me, a salad, a baked potato, and an entire strawberry shortcake.

I wasn't hungry. I pushed some pieces of lettuce on a fork, nibbled and poured some wine in my glass. I used the remote, turned on the television, flicked through the channels and turned it off. Miguel's food was as delicious as ever, but I might as well have been eating sawdust. I heard the clock ticking and turned on some Neil Diamond to drown it out. His music made me feel even more blue. I went into the arcade, turned on some machines for noise, played a game or two, and returned to the wine room to poke at my dinner with the radio on.

I don't like being alone.

I turned off the music so I could hear the phone and called Niley.

"Hey, how are you?"

"Boss, so good to hear from you."

"I'm home tonight. Want to come over?"

I waited. She said nothing at first, then...

"I'd rush over, but I have horrible cramps. No doubt you'd show me to the door after the first five minutes to avoid hearing my moans and groans. I'd hate to inflict that on anybody."

I told her to come over anyway but was unable to talk her into it. Niley was not going to show up with cramps.

I sat there. The arcade noises from the next room didn't blot out the sound of the ticking clock. I called Storm's room.

"Are you in?"

"Sure, Boss. Want me to drive you somewhere?"

"Want to have dinner?"

"Oh, Boss, Miguel fed me like I hadn't eaten in a week. Where are you?"

"I'm in the wine room."

"Want me to come down?"

"That would be great."

I watched her walk in, so young and beautiful and bare-faced. I remembered how dolled up Margaret had been in her heavy make-up, designer duds, gold flecked nail polish, alligator shoes. Here Storm was in her ridiculous cat-foot house slippers (a house tradition), rattiest jeans, and a t-shirt that was probably as old as she was, and she was positively radiant. I wondered if she was working out with Letty and Tangles but felt like it was an imposition to ask.

"You're beautiful. You know that?"

She waved it away like it was nothing.

"So are you, Boss."

"I need to confess," I said as I poured her a glass of wine.

"Confess?" She gave a little laugh.

"I'm taking advantage of you. I was sitting here feeling lonely and sorry for myself, and I reached out to you. I shouldn't have interrupted your evening."

Storm laughed at me.

"My evening? Boss, I was having an intimate moment with Deep Space Nine. I was just realizing who that Ferengi Quark reminds me of—

that lawyer friend of yours, Jack."

"Really? I haven't seen it."

"Oh Boss, I've taped every one. Do you want to see?"

"Sure," I said.

She got up to go.

"Hang on," I caught her by the hand, and got Caro on the intercom. I could tell Storm was embarrassed to have Caro fetching for her, and wanted to get them herself, but she didn't argue.

"Caro, I left a stack of VCR tapes on top of the tv. Could you bring them down to the wine room? I'm talking about the ones marked DS 9 in big red marker."

"I'll be right there," Caro said, and the line clicked off.

"I'd rather spend time with you than watch that dumb TV," Storm said. "Please reach out more often."

We clicked our wine glasses.

"Cheers. You're gorgeous," I said.

"Cheers, Boss. You're the gorgeous one."

She put down her wine glass and ran her hand over my bicep, and took another sip of her wine, sighing.

"Those guns of yours should be outlawed," she said.

"Really?" I laughed and pulled off my button down, so I was down to my t-shirt.

Her eyes got big. "Very Marlin Brando of you," she said. "Stanley Kowalski."

My dinner was starting to look good to me again, and I pulled the plate of steak in front of me.

Caro arrived with the tapes and put them beside the TV console.

"Goody," Storm said, hopping up like she was on springs. She bounced on over to the VCR, selected a tape to insert, and pushed it in.

"This is the first episode," she said, beaming with enthusiasm and pausing the tape which had just begun. "In this one, we get to meet Benjamin, the guy who runs the space station, which is like a way station for space craft just off a planet called Bajor." She looked at my steak, poised to push the button. "This really deserves popcorn," she said.

"I'm good with this T-bone," I said, shoving the cake plate in her direction. I don't know what wine would go with cake, but Storm wouldn't care about that, anyway. "If you still want popcorn later, you can fix some fresh in the arcade."

She sat down cross-legged beside me, cut herself a big slab of strawberry shortcake, and we settled back to watch tv. At least she was watching tv. I paid enough attention to follow the plot, but mostly I was watching her, sitting there lost in the story, holding her plate of untouched cake and whipped cream, and stopping every so often to explain something she felt needed clarification. She was so enthusiastic.

I was still missing Letty, but at least I wasn't doing it sitting in the dark listening to sad songs.

I felt a hundred percent better. Storm has what Pixie would call 'a positive energy.'

March 25, 1992
Gal Offices, Los Angeles
Storm

"Are you happy driving me?" he asked.

"I love it, Boss."

"Is there anything else you'd like to be doing instead of driving me, I mean, for me?"

I smiled, rolled on top of him, kissed him savagely.

"I'll do whatever you want, when you want. I mean, anything."

It was Wednesday. Letty and Tangles had been gone for a whole week without calling. I don't know how they could go that long without checking in. He was so down earlier today. We watched tv till he got bored, then we went upstairs. I had Mario all to myself.

I realize I got it made. I don't live in the personnel house. Even if I lived there, that's like a palace compared to where I was living. My room is a door down the hall from Tangles. I have nothing to spend money on and I've never gotten paychecks this big. Maybe I'll straighten out my life. I love the man for making it possible. There is nothing I wouldn't do for him.

April 1, 1992
Headed Home
Letty

What a wild two weeks. Lunes and the rest of the security team probably figured we were nymphos. Embarrassing. No doubt, Boss knows everything. After the night at the Copacabana, Olga called me.

"My house is your house. Don't worry about proprieties. Let your hair down, enjoy yourself. Don't sleep in hotels."

And that's what we did. We went out every night, fishing, caught what we wanted and brought them back to the Camacho mansion on the beach. In the morning, one of Lune's men drove them back to where we found them.

One afternoon, I had a massage by Juan, one of two massage therapists on call to the Camacho residence. He was younger than me. Before the ninety minutes were used up, I put his hand on my wet pussy. I felt like I'd taken an aphrodisiac that tripled my hormones. After an hour of straight penetration, I was like the nympho battery bunny. I fucked Juan until he went so soft nothing could bring it back.

Tangles said she had done the same with her masseur without sharing any details. Even after that, Tangles and I still went trolling after dark and screwed the night away.

I don't know what drove me. I haven't done anything of the kind since I met Mario Luna. It's not money. I have the money to do anything I want. I always made good money and staying at Mario's for years means I don't have to spend it. The after-taxes check I got on my last deal was $318,000 dollars.[2] I have six hundred thousand[3] in the bank, more in CDs and stock. I am so independent it's spooky.

The only thing different with these guys is that I am in control. If I wanted it doggy, doggy it was. It was not pay for play either, but I controlled the shots.

All good things come to an end, and our two weeks of vacation were finally over. I was ready to come home. The plane was waiting.

A Learjet is not as quiet as a big plane like Olga's. We took off from Rio in a Camacho Learjet, the same plane Boss flew home in from Bogota after Camila's funeral. It didn't have a bed. It did have killer flatbed seats that actually went flat. The interior of the plane was a luxury piece of work, lots of leather, plush carpet. A narrow aisle split the plane, and Tangles and I took seats beside each other with the aisle between us. We both had a window. If I stretched my arm toward Tangles and she to me, we could almost hold hands.

The flight attendant lowered the blinds when we reached 10,000 feet. Our plan was to sleep until we landed in Houston for fuel and U.S.

---

[2] Adjusted for inflation, $318,000.00 in 1992 is equal to $579,348.03 in 2019.

[3] Adjusted for inflation, $600,000.00 in 1992 is equal to $1,093,109.50 in 2019.

Customs.

Tangles said, "By my count, we got laid fourteen times in fourteen days."

I looked toward a seat a few rows ahead, but not having ex ray vision, I had no clue what was happening on the other side. The flight attendant Melia who works for Olga was sitting there, just outside the cockpit.

"Shh. Keep it to yourself."

Foghorn Tangles lowered her voice but just barely. She went on. "That doesn't count how many times with each one. My pussy is deliciously sore."

I laughed but muffled it.

I turned on my stomach and put my hands on my ears. The sleeping bag option that we chose was all cotton, zipper on sides to enter and exit easily. The pillow was so perfect, I thought of taking it home. My mouth pressed against the soft material of the bedding. The cabin was close to pitch black except for the emergency lighting and stuff. I didn't want to hear. I didn't want to be reminded that my pussy wasn't sore but could have been. Didn't want to be reminded that I went to Rio to kick back. Instead, I had sex with a different stranger each night we were there. I couldn't believe it, after all the years of monogamy with Mario. Okay, there had been women, but no other men. There wasn't anything to see in the darkened cabin, but closing my eyes gave me twenty-twenty vision on what's going on inside of me. I like being in control. Who knew? Just as I was about to figure out what control was, I passed out.

April 1, 1992
Headed Home
Tangles

I looked over at Letty. She hasn't moved once in the past hundred miles. She's dead to the world. I wish she was awake because I'm feeling stupid about our little vacation. I don't want to get sick.

I'm not as smart as I think I am. When I get home, I'm going to confirm with Nate that there is an AIDS test that really works, and I'm going to take it. Three times I didn't bother with the condom. Fuck, what is wrong with me? God, I promise never to have sex without a condom again, but please don't let me have caught anything from these guys. Amen.

We don't use condoms with Boss, and he fucks whoever the hell he wants, and always bareback. For all I know I already have AIDS.

What am I saying? If I've got it, we all could have it.

I tried sleeping but keep looking over at Letty. I don't know how she is out like a light. I should wake her up. Or count sheep. I'll try that. But maybe my imagination is broken. I can't see sheep. And the words keep rolling around.

I'm in the bed. I need to sleep. I need my dreams my soul to keep.

The jumping sheep have from me fled.

Where the fuck are you, sheep? Are you under the bed?

Are you chasing me in a phantom plane? Are you tottering after me lame with a cane?

Come on, sheep, help me out here, quick,

Because I was bad and used a raw dick.

No sheep. I should have taken a pill. Now I keep thinking that last stupid line, I was bad and used a raw dick. I was bad and used a raw dick. The sheep are just going to let me suffer.

We were on the ground in Houston for less than an hour. I did eventually fall asleep and didn't want to tell Letty about the idiotic dream I had, something with me dressed as little Bo Peep, chasing around naked men in green pastures, putting condoms on them whether they wanted them or not.

Letty and I left the flat bed seats and sat in club chairs that faced each other with a coffee table between us. Executive Catering delivered hot meals, including Philly sandwiches. The sweet potato fries Melia gave us were hot like they were right out of the fryer. By the time we were wheels up, half of our sandwiches were history and both of us were on our second coke, drinking it straight from the bottle. No straw.

"I didn't want to leave Paradise."

"Got to get back to work," Letty said.

"Fuck, we did good with that lease."

"We did," Letty said. "And we have more on the stove."

"I got four hundred and change in the bank," I said.

"Don't you love it? I was never solvent before Mario."

My mouth was full of Philly. I put my fist out and we bumped fists. I put my hand up for her to hold that thought till I could swallow the big mouthful I'd taken.

"Never dreamed I'd have anything close."

I don't know why I thought of the hand jobs I did when I lived in that closet in Hollywood before Mario. I got whatever the traffic would bear. Sometimes not even five dollars.

I've come long way, baby. I'll look back. Looking back will keep me from ever going back to that life. I'm never going back.

Melia cleared our trash from the table. She went in the cockpit to feed the pilots, and while she was gone, we took the opportunity to talk about Olga. Melia went back and forth bringing food, and napkins, and things.

"I figure she brought us all the way to Rio to do what we did to her that first night, and then she split to Geneva. She knew all along she had to leave," Letty said.

I thought about it. It was probably true about Olga. "I forgot about that first night. I guess that makes thirteen guys, not fourteen. What's the difference?" I said. "We had a blast. We were treated like princesses."

"I'd say, Queens," Letty corrected me, giving me a royal bow within the limitations of our seating arrangements. She straightened an imaginary crown on her head. "We were better off they left. More freedom, yes?" I winked. "And who's counting? I mean, there were the masseurs, right?"

"Damn right, freedom, yes. To hell with counting," I said. I still wasn't going to tell her about the Bo Peep dream.

It was getting dark outside. We were less than two hours from landing in Van Nuys Airport.

"If I could just go straight to my apartment, I would," Letty said.

"What are you talking about?"

Letty shrugged, suddenly looking sad. I looked closely. No tears. Close though.

"It's like when I told you that Casa Luna was not a hotel, and you packed your stuff and went home to your apartment."

"But you were right," I said. "I stayed out all night and it was stupid to sneak in during the wee hours. I could have gone to my apartment."

"I'm doing the same." A big tear rolled down her cheek. "I can't fuck around and then go home to his mansion. It's not right."

"That means I'm doing wrong, too?" Maybe that explained my dream. Or maybe not. Mario had not been one of the naked men in my dream. Maybe it was just guilt over not using condoms three times.

"I don't know what to think."

She sniffed.

I handed her a tissue, and she blew her nose. Quiet, but juicy with tears.

"Mario doesn't care. You feel this way because you been the on call girl."

"I am not a call girl."

"I'm not saying you are. You're on call for when he wants you. I been doing the same, but I get out when I want to. You don't."

"Don't put it that way, Tangles. It's not like that. If I'm on call, it's because I want to be, not because he expects it."

I double-checked Pixie's concert schedule, which I keep a copy of in my wallet, then used the plane's phone to call Pixie's driver. Raul was always available when Pixie was away. Right now, she was somewhere in Mexico

City singing her heart out. I arranged for him to pick us up at the airport.

"We're going to Casa Luna," I said firmly.

Letty looked at me. She nodded her okay.

"I need a couple hits," she said. "Will you light one for me?"

I looked in my purse and came up with a Marlboro cigarette box where I had stowed three joints. I took one out and lit up. I took a long drag and handed it over.

Less than an hour later, we were in Pixie's limo headed to Pasadena. Thanks to killer doobies, we were feeling no pain. I remembered the anxiety I'd had earlier when I was trying to sleep, but the feeling was gone. I pictured the faces of the strangers I'd had sex with, all of them at the instant they got their jollies, and that image set me to giggling. Letty laughed with me, but she had no idea what pictures were running through my brain.

April 1, 1992
Casa Luna
Letty

We were less than ten minutes from Casa Luna when I called Boss on his cell.

"Hi. Guess who?" I couldn't help a little giggle.

"Baby, are you back?"

"And me," Tangles said.

"Five minutes from the house," I said.

"Can you handle us?" Tangles yelled in my ear loud enough for him to hear without the phone.

Boss laughed. "I can do that but not tonight."

I looked at my watch. It was past midnight. "Boss, are you in bed? I'm sorry I didn't check the time."

I figured he had someone in his bed, probably Storm.

"Is it okay if we go to our rooms?" Tangles asked.

"Letty are you on the phone?"

"Yes Boss, it's me."

"Why is she asking me that? Casa Luna is your home."

I shoved Tangles and put my fingers to my lips for her to shut up.

"Thanks, Boss. We smoked a little. We're kind of buzzed."

"Love you," Boss said. "See you in the morning."

We took the elevator to the third floor and parted in the hall with a fast hug and kiss.

I stood in the doorway looking in. The room Melina had once decorated was not what I saw. I'd added my own touch, moved the king-sized bed by the window, put my own pictures on the dresser. That wasn't the biggest change. Covering one wall was a handmade tapestry I'd been given in Belgium from a grateful widow when Boss and I had worked a plane crash there. I think of Boss every time I look at it, because he'd convinced me it was okay to accept such a priceless artifact. I'd found a comforter and curtains to match, even sheets. On one wall was a charcoal sketch of me, done in Florence at a street market while Pixie and Niley were making faces at me trying to get me to laugh. This was Boss's house, but the room was mine. I've done a lot of living here.

I soaked in a hot tub filled with bubbles. It is ironic that I once suggested that Boss let me put a shot of Clorox in Lola's bathwater back when she was masquerading as a hooker. I had heard that Clorox would kill anything, and I was scared she was carrying AIDS. We had no idea she was a Fed. Now I am worried about my own exposure. I thought of bleaching my bath water but didn't do it. I did sit on the bidet and douched thoroughly as I had done every day in Rio and before we got on the plane for home. And I had used a condom every time. I returned to the tub and turned on the hot water to get it steaming again. I lay back on my tub pillow, closed my eyes and dozed off.

April 2, 1992 (Thursday)
GAL Offices, Los Angeles
Storm

I dropped Boss off early at the front entrance and drove a block to seventh street to the carwash for gas and a wash. While I was there, Betty called.

"Hey," I said. "We tried reaching you last night. Boss wanted a massage."

Saturday when Betty didn't answer her phone, I called a service who sent out two therapists, both females. I massaged him until they got there, then we both got a massage, side by side, on Saturday and again on Sunday.

"I was worn out. You were there. Did you give him the massage?"

"I did," I said.

"I'm still pissed off that you left me without notice," Betty said.

We'd been through this before. Betty shared some of her massages with me, but she never got more massages by having me around. I thought she'd be glad to get rid of me. When Letty and Tangles put me in the chauffeur's uniform, I'd thought it was a gag, not an interview. I was totally surprised when Boss agreed to hire me. By the time I called and told her, I'd already accepted, and it was a done deal. I couldn't jerk around a boss like Boss.

"I can tell you're pissed off, and I'm sorry. I only have this job because you introduced me to everyone."

I guess she really holds a grudge. I'd been working for Mario for six months, ever since early in November of last year, right after we got home from Camila's funeral. Seems like she would have forgiven me by now.

I drove back to the office, parked on the first level of parking in the spot reserved for Boss's car. Three spots next to him were reserved for Andrea, Letty and Tangles. Andrea's car was there, but not Letty's or Tangles's. They were probably tired after the trip from Rio.

Andrea kept me busy during the day doing grunt work: filing and other clerical work, but nothing heavy.

"If you get bored, go take a break, a walk, shopping, as long as you stay close. Don't be more than a few minute of walking through the door in case he needs you."

Andrea was good to me. Last weekend I had forty-eight hours of luxuriating in that fab mansion, spa, swimming, dining like royalty, not that I would know about royalty. I'd been to bed with Boss before and not always alone. He makes me feel beautiful. We even did it in the steam room.

I called Letty. "Hope I didn't wake you," I said.

"No way. We did a late workout. We'll be at the office at noon."

"It will be great to see you. I can be home in a jiffy."

Letty gave a wicked sounding laugh.

"Tangles and I are going to break in our Ferraris. See you in a bit."

"Exciting," I said.

She didn't hang up right away. "Boss said he was busy last night. Did you sleep with him?"

"I can't lie to you. I was with him, yes."

Letty said. "It's okay. You don't have to keep anything secret. I have no ties on him."

There was another pause, then she said, "Did he fuck you good?"

I detected a slight attitude, so I hit back. "Way too good. You know he knows what goes where, and never fails to please. I had a blast. Well, two. Well, three."

That surprised a laugh out of her.

"Are you sure you're okay with that?" I asked in all seriousness. I thought I detected hurt feelings or something. I don't know what. Call it woman's intuition.

"Like I said, I have no ties binding him to me. All I have to say to you is you go girl."

I laughed because she expected me too. "See you when you get here. Drive safe, please, even if it is a Ferrari."

Letty said, "Kisses, Storm."

"Kisses back."

After I hung up, I almost wished I'd lied. First Betty, now Letty. No doubt about it, the girl is upset. It made me wonder how Tangles will be when I see her.

While they were gone, Boss complained that they never called him from Rio. He didn't seem angry, but he wasn't happy. At least their absence gave me a chance to smother him with love while he smothered me with explosive orgasms.

April 2, 1992
GAL Offices
Mario

Just before noon, Letty and Tangles charged into my office like a herd of rowdy sorority girls. I mean, they don't knock, they walk in, kind of a take it or leave it.

They were a sight for sore eyes.

I got up from my desk and caught Letty and Tangles as they ran up to me, like little girls. I lifted Letty off her feet. She was blushing with excitement. Her cheeks reddened as we kissed. I did the same with Tangles. I used to do that to Olga and a long time ago to Melina.

"Boss, I love my car! Thank you, thank you, thank you!" Letty said. "I drove it here."

"That's a ditto, Boss," Tangles said. "Got to be so careful not to get a ticket. It's so tempting to roar away in it."

"Careful," I said. "Fuck the ticket. I don't want you getting hurt or hurting someone else. Treat them like trophies. They are trophies you both deserve."

I grabbed a fresh tie from my desk. Letty gave me a look and stepped close to tie it for me. It was an intimate moment, and I almost kissed her again. It was so good to have her back. There was something off, though. She wouldn't meet my eyes.

"Going somewhere?" she asked.

"I've got to run to Burbank. I'm going to take a look at a plane we took in on a lease. Maybe I can use it."

"What about your plane?" Letty asked.

"If you had stayed in touch, you'd know I sold it."

The smile on Letty's face disappeared. She looked like I had slapped her. She took a step back from me and her hands fell to her sides.

Tangles eyes opened wide. "What?"

I didn't say any more, because Andrea joined us. She hugged the girls, then in her brisk manner, commandeered them.

"Just the ladies I want to see. Work is piling up on your desks," she said.

It was all in the timing. Storm drove me to look at the jet. Letty and Tangles stayed at the office.

The 737 Executive Jet had come into GAL less than a month ago. I didn't read the plane condition report, but if I liked what I saw, I would. The plane looked its age. The interior was dated. The queen size bed was in a paneled bedroom with an ensuite bathroom. The interior needed work. The design was tacky.

"Tacky is okay, Boss. It has a bed." She bent down to sniff the sheet. "At least it's clean." A moment later her slacks were in a puddle on the floor, and I was staring at her bare ass while she was face down.

"I dare you," she said.

Down went my pants. I let my slacks fall to my ankles, shoes on, shirt on, tie on. I positioned myself on top of her, my hands on the mattress in pushup position. My body covered hers, but I put no weight on her. She raised her ass and I entered her wetness. I had never heard her moan like that before.

She was at the wheel, and I was in the passenger side next to her. I touched her bare thigh.

"It was really good for me," I said. "Spontaneous sex like that is a thrill."

"I loved it," she said.

We went straight home from the airport. We did the wet steam and the ice-cold spa. Betty arrived to give me a massage. Storm insisted I was getting four hands.

"I'm sorry I didn't answer your call, Boss. I had a bad weekend. I was totally out of it."

Betty was so apologetic, it moved me.

"No sweat," I said. "Are you okay now?"

"I'm fine. Please don't fire me."

"Fire you? Are you crazy?" I laughed.

A little bird named Melina had told me that Betty was pissed that Storm had come to work with me without giving her notice. I assumed it was true, but Betty said nothing to me about that. The massage was wonderful, as usual.

I gave Betty two thousand dollars before she left.

"Boss, why all this money?"

"I owe you," I said simply.

Storm pretended not to notice.

I named the nine-year-old plane GAL, signed a six million dollar contract with my plane renovator, and ordered her name and logo painted on the aft section at the vertical stabilizer. When I get her back, she will have new engines, a major mechanical overhaul, new interior, seating for eighteen, and a new black paint job like the plane Hefner sold in 1975. She is going to look and fly like brand new. Maybe someone will fall in love with this plane too, but since GAL owns the plane and not me, I seriously doubt I'd sell it until I had another plane ready for me to jump into.

If I had purchased a new plane, I'd have spent much more and not ended up with an airliner-sized executive jet. She costs a bundle to operate, but it's worth it. I have been making a lot of money for myself and a bundle of money for GAL, namely, Olga.

The next six months delivered some major events.

LAI went public. Olga held on to enough stock to control the company. She had been a billionaire when she took over the Camacho assets and since then, added a number of billions more when company went public. The company was attractive because of its mass of real estate holdings, almost all of them solid income producers. Still, I could understand why they didn't want the bakery, donut shops, liquor stores, etc. that I ended up buying when Camila was alive.

I flew to Geneva to celebrate with Olga. I went alone in my refurbished plane. Olga only had Riana with her.

I joined her on the bed in her suite where we shared lusty sex. I don't know how else to explain it, but it felt impersonal. The personal flame was not there for me, and probably not for her, either. I would always love her for what we had once been together, though it had not worked out for us as a couple. Afterwards, she fired one up, and we lay in the dark, the only light being the red ember of her joint, which I declined.

"This is new," I said. "You usually aren't the one calling to smoke pot."

I heard the rustle of the sheets as she shrugged. "Like I said, I gotta learn to live a little."

In the dark, the flame glowed bright red, and then burned out.

"I'm going to give up my seat as CEO and COO," she said.

"What are you going to do?" I asked.

"Acquisitions, but I'm not going to kill myself looking. I want to enjoy my life. I'm not quite sure how I can do it, but I'm going to try."

"I'm so proud of you," I said.

"Thanks, Amor. I'm proud of you, too. What you continue to do with GAL is amazing. I'm glad I didn't include it in the public offering."

"Without your funding it would still be a gold mine, but we'd make less money."

"If you stopped funding half of each lease, I would have to give the consortium a bigger piece of the pie."

"I have plenty of money. Don't worry Amor. Keep your magic going. You provide a fabulous return on my investment."

"No pressure," I said. "If you want to put in less, just let me know. We have so much volume, we can afford to make less on a lease."

The light burned out. I heard the rattle of the ash tray on her nightstand as she put out the roach, then rolled on top of me.

"You lie," she said, laughing. "You want to maximize the income on every single plane."

I laughed, "I do, but it's not the end of the world if we end up with less."

"Amor, what if I told you I thought about getting married then changed my mind?"

"Who was the lucky guy?"

"Noah Witzer."

"Who?" I could not place his name.

"My attorney, the man who took me public. He's so smart but I like my freedom and he doesn't have a lot of money so that could be a problem for me when we get divorced."

I laughed. "Maybe you wouldn't get divorced."

"Oh yeah, I'd get bored. I don't love him. I don't like the way he fucks me either."

"Something made you consider marrying him," I said.

"Yeah, he's an important person. Well known, highly respected by his peers. I figured it would rub off on me if he was my husband."

"Did he know you were thinking of marrying him?"

She laughed. "Of course not."

She was still on top of me and laughing like I'd made a joke. She reached to turn on the bedside lamp.

Olga was making fun, but I believed her.

"Would you marry me, Amor?"

Now it was my turn to roll her over and be on top.

"Thanks for turning on the light," I said, my eyes on hers. "I need to see your face."

She looked up at me, almost serious, but there was still mischief in her.

"We have already been down that road. I'd rather have you as my dearest friend, as we are right now. Marriage would ruin what we have. Besides, how many billions do you have now?"

We both laughed.

"You know, Amor, if I were to prepare a will today you would own it all. I have no one else. Riana is so rich she doesn't need it. When I think about it, I get to thinking about a family. I'm too old for children, but maybe not too old for a husband. Then I think I'm just not ready."

I said, "I'm kind of rich myself. I wouldn't know what to do with your billions. Stick around, baby. We all need you to brighten our lives."

"You're so sweet. Amor, I adore you."

Her legs went around me, and I entered her hard, the way she likes.

"You sure you adore me?"

Missionary style. She matched my rhythm, hard, fast, slow, and then fast again.

"I will always adore you."

Our lower bodies were working like pistons.

"What if I get married?" I asked. Why would I want to get married?

"Makes no difference. No matter who you marry, you'll be back to do this with me. We're addicted to each other. We have magic between us. I adore you, Amor."

I was just thinking how the personal magic was gone, but I didn't say that aloud.

Letty and Tangles still lived at Casa Luna, but something had changed. They presented me with boxes of condoms, suggesting I start using them when I had sex with them.

One day I was a bit pissed because the action was hot, but I knew Letty didn't want me to fuck her without the rubber.

"Boss, if I knew you always use a condom when you fuck others, I wouldn't care."

"Now that you're fucking every Tom, Dick and Harry, you shut me down. Do you make them use a condom, too?"

"Believe it, Boss, that's the way it is."

Tangles was on the bed, too.

"Is that true?" I asked like a dummy.

Tangles said. "Boss, it's a deal we made. Boss, use the condoms, you got at least seven different kinds to choose from. Come on, let me put one on you, then you fuck both of us, pussy, ass, anything you want."

"The condom protects you from me, that's the way I see it. What I don't see, is what do you put on to protect me?"

Letty said, "Boss, you need to do some reading, experts..."

"Fuck those experts. They are looking to make condoms the next General Motors by marketing it as safe sex."

I didn't refuse to use rubbers. Just, when the time came, I simply didn't put them on. Intercourse stopped. They still joined me in bed, and we still had sex. When they slept with me, it was all about touching. I still got them off and they still got me off. It did seem backward to go from where we had been to what we became. Still, it was hot, erotic, sexy. I didn't care that we took a break from actual oral and penetration. Life goes on.

But I griped about it. I turned to Storm who seemed to have no limits.

"Storm, I hate condoms. I lose the feeling. I've tried. I go from hard to soft in less than a minute." I wanted her to know we didn't have to have the kind of sex that could transmit a disease. I wasn't convinced that anyone really knew a damn thing about how the disease was transmitted.

"Boss, I've been such a tramp, I'm not worried about catching anything around. I love having sex with you."

Like Niley and Jo before them, with a little guidance from me, Letty and Tangles purchased a twelve-unit apartment building on California, a fabulous Pasadena Street. The building had great curb appeal, a swimming pool with cabana, gym and party room. They had one vacancy, the biggest apartment. I encouraged them to put up half the sales price each and forget a mortgage. If they ever had a partnership argument it would be easier to buy out each other if there was no mortgage company in the picture.

"Boss, we're never going to have a problem," Tangles said over dinner.

Letty raised her glass, "That's for sure. Let's toast to that."

They vacated the two apartments they had been renting for years and moved into the empty apartment in their building, which was the largest one, a three bedroom, three bathroom unit. Their garage had a direct entrance to their unit and plenty of room for their two Ferraris.

"You don't have to move," I said.

But move they did, totally.

This reminded me of when Olga suddenly announced she was no longer my fiancée and gave me back my ring. As I did with Olga, I held my tongue. Nothing last forever. I keep telling people that, and here it is, coming around to me.

I almost reminded Letty of all those times she'd tell me she would never leave until I showed her to the door. I wondered if she was waiting or hoping I would stop her.

I didn't try.

Tangles and Letty were gone from under my roof, but Storm lived on at Casa Luna and was on payroll to drive me. She hung out at the office waiting for me to go somewhere or go back home.

"I can put you to work in the office to learn leasing. You're here anyway," I said.

"I'll do it if you want me to do it but I'm just not good at numbers, and I get confused easy. I'd rather just look after you. I mean, I'd rather be your driver and anything else I can do for you, when you want."

I hadn't seen any evidence of confusion or problems with numbers, so I pushed her to get into the swing at the office. You never know if you don't try, right?

Sometimes I had lunch with Letty and Tangles, but not frequently. I always invited Storm to go with us, but she always declined politely, all smiles. We ate in my private conference room and sometimes at a restaurant in the building or walking distance from the office. Conversation was almost always about business, a lease they were working on, or I would talk about something I was working on. I was in the room with them, but it was like there was a barrier up between us. I missed our being a real team. I didn't really understand how we could have all been so close, sharing everything, our thoughts, our bodies, our lives, and now we were inches from each other but miles apart.

"How's Storm?" Letty asked.

Her phone rang, and she spoke softly into it.

"Fine," I said, waiting until she'd hung up the phone. I wondered who was on the line but didn't ask. "But you know that. You saw her today at the office doing some filing for Andrea."

"You must be fucking the living daylights out of that girl," Tangles kidded.

"Is that true, Boss?" Letty asked.

"Wrong," I said looking at the roast beef sandwich I was about to bite into. "I'm fucking the lights out of her."

"Lucky girl," Letty said.

"Boss, we'll come over anytime you ask us," Tangles said.

"You know you don't need an invitation. Come over anytime."

Letty's phone rang a second time. She answered and got rid of whoever it was, quick.

I hope I didn't blush. It bothered me to think it was some guy she may be seeing, fucking or just dating. For a long time, I felt like Letty was all mine. I mean, I never told her that, but that's just how I felt.

After lunch, I had Storm drive me home early.

"Why so silent, Boss?"

"Storm, sorry, just thinking."

It wasn't good. I was jealous. I missed Letty, terribly. I missed Tangles but I realized that afternoon how much I missed Letty.

Gorgeous Storm was living in my house, just waiting for me to call upon her.

But it was Letty I thought of, Letty I missed, Letty I reached for in the middle of the night.

Team Letty and Tangles closed two leases, not as big as the six new planes, but the deals were solid. Providing the operators didn't go bust, GAL stood to make a lot of money and the girls were happy with their hefty commission checks.

I had breakfast one spring morning out by the pool. Miguel had fixed fajitas and scrambled eggs and brought me a sizzling plateful to roll into burritos.

I invited him to join me.

Miguel is a buff guy. He is the only one of my regular staff who makes use of my gym. He goes in there about three times a week to lift weights and is careful not to go down there while I'm working out, not that I'd mind the company.

He nodded and went back inside to fetch something. The morning was quiet. I could hear lawnmowers in the distance, and smell some of the fuel used to power it. I heard the fountain in the koi pond, and the scrape of the chair as Miguel pulled it back to sit down. He'd brought a coffee cup and plate. He sat down and quickly rolled some meat and egg into a tortilla, dashed some hot sauce on it and ate a bite or two. We ate in companionable silence, then he filled both of our coffee cups. He sat silent until I noticed he wasn't eating.

I looked at his handsome face, dark passionate eyes, dark hair, finely textured skin. I'd never have known he was gay if I hadn't been informed of it. He and Letty were both remarkably good looking, though fortunately

Letty did not have her uncle's moustache.

Miguel looked stiff and tense, which was very unlike him. He's a very easy-going guy.

"Boss, I don't want to spring this on you cold, but I have an opportunity I can't turn down."

"By all means, Miguel," I said, having no idea what was coming. "I would never stand in the way of opportunity."

"I have a chance to work in West Hollywood. I mean, I found a building down there, and I know a guy. It's more than that. I'm opening a restaurant in West Hollywood."

I nodded, gulped down half a cup of scalding coffee. I was surprised. I was speechless.

Miguel noticed I didn't stop him. He got over his nervousness and began making sense. He kept talking.

"My friend and I are going into a business venture together. Boss, please give me your blessing. It has always been my dream to have a high-end restaurant, a small place with room for maybe forty people. My friend is also a chef. Between us we have two hundred thousand dollars to start up. I will stay until you find a replacement. I can't leave you without a chef."

I gave him my blessing of course, but I went to work with a heavy heart, and made a beeline straight to Letty who was in her office.

I walked straight up to her desk.

She greeted me cheerfully.

"Hey Boss. What can I do for you?"

"Miguel. Restaurant in West Hollywood. What do you know about it?" I snapped.

"Miguel has been saving his entire paycheck for years. He's got something like a hundred eighty thousand saved up, and the rest is from his friend, his long-time boyfriend that he only sees on his day off. They've got everything planned. Uncle Miguel has been working on the plan for years."

Letty looked up at me, the old Letty, the one I miss. I don't know what she saw in my face, but it must have gotten to her. She came out of her chair and put her arms around me and gave me a hug. She gives the best hugs. She whispered in my ear.

"Boss, it's going to be all right."

I don't know how long we stood there like that. I didn't want to break the moment. I knew it was going to end, but I was storing it up, like a battery.

"Melina will find you a new cook," she said.

It's not just a cook, I wanted to say. *First, I lose you and Tangles, and now, Miguel. Fuck, what is going on?* But, of course, I did not say any of that. Breaking down would be unmanly. I would have to soldier on.

And then the intercom buzzed. I wanted to smash it so I could hang on to the moment. Letty's body jumped at the sound. She released me and connected with Andrea who had a client on the line.

I slipped out of the room. I don't know if Letty even noticed. But I took her advice and reached out to Melina.

Years before, Melina found Miguel and Letty for me. Miguel had gone to one of her markets for a job and she sent him to me. I hired him, and his niece was part of the package. We didn't know what Letty was going to do when I hired her, so she did, well, everything. Best deal I ever made.

Melina to the rescue. She picked up the phone on the first ring, surprised to hear from me, but seemed glad I had called. I explained the situation.

"He's going to open a restaurant," I told Melina, "I'm not even sure I need a chef."

"You're running your kitchen through the business like everything else so it's almost free. You need a chef."

"Are you okay, baby? I miss you."

"I'm going to a therapist twice a week. Actually, he comes to me for one-hour sessions. I'm doing it to please Ronnie."

"Does it help?"

"I'll never get over losing the baby, therapy or not."

It had been years since Melina and I were close. It saddened me, not just that she had lost a baby, but also that we'd missed so much of each others lives.

"When we were an item, you always leveled with me about fucking the butcher or whoever it was at one of your markets. In other words, you always talked about just doing it and we'd laugh about it. Was it true?"

"Cuz, are you asking me if I was telling the truth about sponta-neously fucking other men?"

"Exactly, yes, that's what I'm asking."

"I can't remember them all but if I said I did something, it was true. Why?"

I thought about Letty and Tangles fucking around. If it didn't bother me when Melina was doing it, why was I jealous now? I tried to remember if I had been jealous when Melina did it. I probably was but was too proud to admit it.

"No reason," I replied. "It's complicated." I remembered she had even fucked a school friend of mine, thinking she could get something done in prison where our mutual friend Pélon was incarcerated. I bruised my fists on him. A story for another day.

"Did you ever tell Ronnie how you and I fucked day and night?"

"Cuz, I didn't hear that," she teased. Then she said, "I always figured if you didn't marry Olga, you would marry Letty. Maybe you should have, Cuz."

Silence.

"I don't need to get married," I said. "Maybe it is time for Letty and Tangles to spring away," I said, feeling like I was lying.

"Cuz, is it me or you that always says that nothing is forever?"

"I forget who," I said. "But it's true. No question."

I turned the subject back to Miguel.

"If you think of someone for the position, buzz me. I mean, buzz me anyway, anytime."

Olga had the same idea as Melina. "I figured you and Letty would get married," she said. "She was like a wife. She probably got burned out. The way I see it, you got burned out on each other just as if you were married."

I had the feeling that Olga was happy Letty and Tangles had left Casa Luna. Olga said she didn't care, but she had a jealous streak a mile wide.

Niley and Jo called when they heard that Letty moved out. They were on the speaker at their office.

"Did you show her the door or something?"

"Of course not," I said. "Why?"

"She said she would never leave you unless you showed her the door," Jo said.

"She didn't leave me, guys. She moved, that's it."

Even Pixie on location somewhere in South America heard Letty had moved out.

"I know Letty," she said. "If she moved, she didn't move far."

I didn't ask her how she'd heard. She had her own opinion of who could cook for me after Miguel.

"Use my chef," she said. "The fucker just sits around watching television. I'm never there. Boss, do it, take him, at least until you find someone."

I would have taken her up on that, but by then, the first iron in the fire paid off. Melina called.

"I have a cook for you. A woman, thirty-nine, divorced, no kids. She's from Phoenix, Arizona, and attended one year of culinary school in Arizona. For the kind of food you like, she can absolutely do it."

"You like her?"

"I like her. I can hire here for one of my markets, but she'd flip to work in a private home with lodging included. Want to check her out?"

Melina had her driven to the house, and she arrived just as I got home at five in the afternoon. Miguel was off that day. I sent Melina's driver on his way.

I hired Emma, not because she had a nice body or because she had a beautiful face or because I liked the way she talked Spanish, her first language (though all three were true.) I hired her because she told me she needed a job. I asked her how much she was looking to make.

"Whatever you want to pay me," she said.

Her gray sleeveless shirt was so threadbare, I could clearly see the black bra underneath. The shirt was knotted at her waist. One of the sleeves drooped down over her shoulder, and she kept putting it back up. Her ragged striped shorts had a parrot in the design, and at some time in its history had been washed with something red. Her tennis shoes had seen better days. A piece of suede was tied around her left wrist like a bracelet. Black purse, black eyebrows, black hair, black nail polish, but not goth, just Mexican. I don't think she'd been missing any meals, but I could see she could afford make-up. She was wearing a lot of it. Big cleft in her chin. She was standing with an attitude. She looked more like a street girl than a chef.

I told her she could have a trial run, and had Storm drive her to her place to get her things. She moved into one of the apartments in the back house that my staff lives in. All the units back there have kitchenettes and private bathrooms, and downstairs there is a larger kitchen and public area, as well as all the washers and dryers for the main house.

"She seems very impressed by the staff house," Storm said. "She was staying at a by-the-week motel, and unless she's got stuff in storage some-where, all she has is a couple suitcases of clothes and a big box of cookware. Storm copied her driver's license and got her to fill out a payroll form and sent that to Mason.

Within twenty-four hours, Mason called me back.

"She is who she says she is. Her husband was a pile of shit. He's doing fifteen years in New Mexico for night burglaries. She's clean."

"Even if she wasn't clean, I already hired her. I just don't want her to be a cop," I said, remembering Lola.

"She's not a cop, but you never know," Mason said.

I disliked that last crack from Mason covering his ass. He should know. He's paid to know. That's his job.

Miguel met Emma late on the night she arrived. I don't know the details, but they ran into each other in the staff house while she was moving in. He was in the process of gradually moving out. He spent the next three days showing her what he did, where he ordered food, where he shopped personally, how he had the walk-in organized, things like that. He introduced her to his contact person at Marron Markets, and when Storm confirmed Emma had a valid Arizona license, he gave her the keys to the station wagon we kept for going shopping.

Before the entire staff grouped to say goodbye to Miguel, I handed him a check for $100,000 dollars.

"I can't accept this."

"Yeah, you can," I said. "I'm bigger than you." I hugged him. "Love you."

When I hired Letty and Miguel, they had been down and out. Miguel had been an itinerant chef moving from job to job and had missed out on a permanent job working at one of Melina's markets. Luckily Melina had sent him my way. Letty had been part of the hiring package. We thought, at first, they were a couple, and then cousins, and learned eventually that he was her uncle. Letty had sneaked into my bed one night and told me in secret that they had robbed a liquor store, and she was in the get away car. They had promised never to do so again and had kept their word. Miguel was a wonderful chef. I have come a long way, too. And Letty, she had become a prosperous businesswoman.

I told Emma, "You don't need to look like a chef. Wear whatever makes you happy."

"Thank you, Boss," Emma said. "I want to wear black uniforms with a white jacket."

Storm ordered them from the uniform company on a list of vendors Casa Luna used.

"Who told you to call me Boss?"

"Miguel. Everyone calls you Boss. Is it okay?" She looked worried.

"Boss is fine." I smiled.

June 4, 1993 (Friday)
Pasadena
Niley

He answered on third ring.

"Hey Boss. Want company?" I heard traffic noises in the background.

"Are you home?"

"You sound like you're in the car. I can call you back."

"Storm and I are headed to Ontario Airport and then to San Francisco. Come with us."

"I'd love to go, Boss. Are you sure I won't be in the way?"

The way that he laughed, I could tell he wanted me to come along. He wasn't just blowing smoke.

An hour so later, I was on the plane with him and his young chick, Storm.

"Change in flight plans," Boss said. "We're going to have dinner in New Orleans."

I prefer New Orleans to San Francisco anyway.

"Woohoo! You are amazing, Boss."

"I keep finding that out. New Orleans, here we come," Storm said. "I've never been before." She turned to me and said, "I can open a bottle of wine before we go wheels up."

"Red, if that's good for you."

"I'm good with whatever you and Storm want."

"Boss, I like her already," Storm said.

"You better. I love this girl more than you can imagine."

Storm joked around but she was no Pixie or Letty.

"Uh oh. I have competition."

I laughed.

Storm headed to the bar in our cabin. The stewardess, Paula, got to the bar at the same time.

"I'll get what you need, dear. Go sit and relax."

"Red wine all around," Storm said.

"You got it."

When the plane lifted off, Paula was out of sight.

I was concerned about breaking the ice. I had, after all, crashed the party at the last minute. I wondered if things were going to be awkward.

The three of us were sipping slow. I could not get over the size of the plane. We were in club seats in a grouping of six with a table between us. For convenience, Storm and I dumped our purses on two of the three empty seats though there were plenty of storage places. The plane seemed bigger than the one we crashed in.

The pilot announced we had leveled off at 31,000 feet.

Storm unbuckled, got up and said, "Boss, we got three hours plus to our destination. Let me give you a relaxing massage. What do you say?"

Storm pulled the duvet off and covered the sheets with a decorative cloth from her bag. I flung my clothes off and jumped on the bed. Storm freaked out, picked up each thing I'd tossed, and folded it carefully like it was made of solid gold. I think the shorts were from those years in Italy, but she even handled my discount Neiman Marcus underwear like it was important. Boss and I lay naked with two huge monogrammed GAL towels covering us.

"It's chilly," I said.

"That's what the towel is for. Everything smells so new in this plane. It's a turn on," Storm said, working Boss.

"It is new," Mario said. "Made over from the inside out."

"It didn't used to look this good," Storm said, dropping hints that she had been on this plane before.

Storm was a talker, but I don't think she'd be talking so much if Letty and Tangles were with us, or if Pixie was along for the ride. I liked her hands and the lavender oil we chose from the selection in her bag.

Boss and I, we lay face down, our skin touching. I adjusted so I could face him, and we kissed. I didn't think about Storm or how she might feel about Boss. It didn't matter how any of us felt about him. He never plays for keeps, not even when he was engaged to Melina or Olga.

"It's not fair. We got massages, but what about you?" I asked.

Storm said, "It was my pleasure, Niley."

Before we landed, I massaged Storm, and didn't hold back. She had massaged my breasts and my coochie, and I did the same for her. I've known Boss a long time. He likes to watch, and I am okay with giving him something to see. Thirty minutes from landing, we all took showers.

When Boss came out, I said, "Come on. Let's shower together. Water has to be limited up here."

Boss said, "We're good. I had two tanks put in."

It was a fast shower and slightly erotic. It was very close quarters for two. I would have liked to try it with the three of us. It wasn't even close to my first time with a woman. It was going to be a nice trip.

The ice was broken between us.

When we were drying off, Storm said in a low voice, "I'm glad you are here. I know you two go back a long time. He's been kind of down since the girls left the house. I don't have what it takes to fix it for him. You do."

June 4, 1993
New Orleans
Storm

I have no starry-eyed blue-sky expectations for me and him, but I love living at Casa Luna, and being treated like I belong there is the bomb. I'm clearing five hundred a week. I'm getting good at filing. I read a lot of what I file since no one is rushing me. Sometimes Boss talks to me about working in leasing.

I'm not working for Boss because I'm good at filing. I'm good at other stuff, but I'm not Letty.

I'm trying hard to assist him the way Letty always did. She was into everything. She's still at work every day, anyway.

He checked us in at the Ritz Carlton in the French Quarter. We stood in the lobby some distance away when he was talking to check-in. I got a thrill looking at him, and knowing we were together. I bet all the other women around were jealous as hell. The clerk handed Boss a card, and when it fell off the countertop, I was going to rush in and pick it up for him. Niley leaned close and stopped me. She was dressed so well. Even her shorts and short blouse were designer, and her sandals were Steve Madden. Mine were from K Mart.

"Don't try so hard."

I bit my lip and whispered back, "I'm so embarrassed."

"Don't feel bad. Jo used to forget he wasn't one of her kids and sometimes used to cut up his meat. We all used to butter his biscuits."

I glanced at Boss's backside, wondering what she meant.

I giggled.

"No, that wasn't a sexual reference," she said. "We actually did butter his bread. But really, you don't need to go overboard. He's big boy. Sometimes he wants to do stuff himself. He's not shy. If he wants you to do something, he'll ask you. Ease up."

"Thanks, Niley."

Dinner was at Emeril's.

Niley had on a collar that looked like it was made of hammered gold. I noticed Boss touched it when we were being escorted to the table. Niley smiled at him, and it seemed a very personal moment. I looked at her and touched my neck.

She touched hers, and realized I was asking about the choker.

"Christmas 1990, I think it was," she said, smiling. "We all got one."

We ate a delicious meal at Emeril's Restaurant, and no one buttered Boss's bread. I've never seen so much food. They kept removing our plates and bringing us more savory dishes to sample. Niley didn't eat all the food. She concentrated just on the crawfish, but she sure put away a lot of crawfish. It would take about a million of them to fill me up. Boss really liked the steak of course, and my favorite was the softshell crab with crawfish sauce. We all ate the hell out of this banana cream pie they served. It had real bananas in some kind of custard, whipped cream on top and caramel and shaved chocolate on top of that. It was incredible. And the wine was amazing.

I'm not an experienced wine drinker. I have drunk more wine with him in the past few weeks than I have in my entire life. The wine they served us was exciting to drink, not boring. I can't explain but each wine somehow fit the food it was served with. No one cared that the three of us were in the same clothes we had worn on the plane, not that they could know. There were fancy people in formal clothes and slouchy tourists in Hawaiian shirts. Niley and I were in shorts with blouses that bared our stomachs and belly buttons. I stood next to Niley and tried acting like my blue light special shorts were designer like Niley's, as if the designer status could rub off on me. She even has on fancy lingerie. I hid my ratty underwear when I undressed. I hope no one noticed it. Boss wore jeans, a t-shirt, and tennis shoes, all looking brand new.

It was sticky hot even at night, but I didn't care.

I'm glad we walked around the French Quarter to burn off the big meal. There were so many shops. It was midnight and New Orleans was still open. I don't mean just the bars. Everything was open. We walked through two art galleries. Boss is really into art.

"I know very little about famous artists," he said. "If I like a painting and I know I want it, then it's about negotiating the price. Most of my paintings at home were purchased that way. I'm turned on by the work of the artist, not necessarily the artist."

Boss bought a framed oil painting of a blue dog. I wouldn't have bought it, but he loved the blue dog, and there were a number of them on display. He paid $3,000 dollars [4] for it. The price tag was double that. He got a receipt, and they delivered it to the hotel.

---

[4] Adjusted for inflation, $3,000.00 in 1993 is equal to $5,311.48 in 2019.

We got back to our two bedroom suite about three Sunday morning.

I showered and went to bed. I could hear the other shower, and every so often I could hear laughter and Boss and Niley in the other bedroom. I don't think I was jealous. I was happy that Boss was distracted. He had been so down in the dumps, even when we get it on pretty good.

I didn't mind being alone. I thought of the other night when I had been trying so hard to cheer him up. He seemed almost despondent. Nothing I did could make him smile. He was trying to get me to work the leasing phones, insisting I could do it because I'm not shy.

We were in the wine room, getting slightly stoned and washing it down with little sips of wine. Not as good as the wine at Emeril's, but far better than the two dollar bottles of Ripple I'd had before I knew him.

I got up and stripped to my bare skin. He wasn't smiling, but he was paying attention.

I poured what was left in the wine bottle, mostly into his glass and the rest into mine. I put the neck of the bottle in my mouth and when it was wet, I got up on the table and slowly inserted the wet end into my awaiting pussy.

"I'm not shy, Boss," I said.

The next thing I knew, he had snatched me up in his arms and was running up the stairs all the way to his fourth floor bedroom.

"You are so nasty," he said as he put down on his bed. "I love it."

"I can do other nasty things."

Boss said, "One at a time baby." Then he was on top of me.

We made enough heat that night that I sure don't begrudge Niley her night with him.

The New Orleans thing was a short trip, but fun. We landed in Ontario a little past midnight. Niley said her goodbyes and drove away. Boss and I got in the Rolls, and he drove us home. I sat right next to him with my hand on his thigh.

He was up at five in the gym, at the kitchen counter with Emma and me at seven, and in the car on the way to the office at ten till nine. Another Monday.

"I hope you had a good time on our little trip?" Boss said from the back seat. I heard the pages of his LA Times rattle as he turned to another section.

"Boss, I told you a zillion times, I loved the trip, and I love you for taking me along."

"I didn't know Niley would call last minute like she did," he said.

"Boss, I dug seeing you happy. I mean, yeah, happy-like."

"Are you saying I don't look happy?"

It took me a minute to figure out how to answer. "Boss, ever since the girls split, you look sad sometimes."

"Storm, you're wrong. I'm not sad."

"Great, Boss, I don't want you sad. I'd do anything to keep you from being sad."

"Storm, you're good people."

"Thank you, Boss."

June 7, 1993 (Monday)
GAL office, Pasadena
Letty

I beat Storm getting his coffee this morning and caught him alone in his office just settling in. I set the fifteen-year-old *World's Best Boss* mug within his reach but not too close. He's been known to spill it. I walked around, leaned over him, and gave him a kiss.

"Morning, Boss."

"Morning. How was your weekend?"

He pushed a big box of files my way.

"Nothing to write home about. How was yours?"

I sat across from him on the chair to his right.

"I took a fast trip to New Orleans. Spur of the moment."

"Gee whiz, how neat is that? Did you call to invite me, and I missed the call?"

Boss picked up an envelope from his inbox and slashed it open with the letter opener from the Italian leather desk set I gave him on his birthday four years ago. He took a sip of his hot coffee.

"I didn't think you'd want to go."

"Oh Boss, how mean is that?"

"Mean?" His eyes flickered from the letter to me and back to the letter. He gave a really good impression of being absorbed, but I saw the distinct orange envelope and the sender—some shyster start-up sending free vacation tickets to a seminar in Boca Raton marketing bad investments to suckers. I've been getting the same promo for weeks. They wine and dine you, fill you with cheap chicken casserole, out-of-season fruit, and mediocre wine, wait till you're seduced by the tropical breezes, then when you've relaxed your guard, start selling their lame shit.

"Never mind," I said. "Did you have a good time?"

"I did, but it was fast. I flew down, ate at Emeril's, bought some art, crashed at the Ritz Carlton in the French Quarter, flew back. Niley and Storm came along."

His eyes didn't return to me until he mentioned Niley and Storm, and then only for a second.

"A trio, nice."

Boss smiled. "Are you done interrogating me?"

"Are we going to Boca?"

"What?" He looked up, mystified.

Ha. I knew he wasn't reading. I picked up the envelope from his desk and read the sender. "Millionaire Investments Incorporated?"

He snatched the envelope, chucked it in his trash, and said sharply, "I'll let you know." He leaned forward and pushed the big box in my direction again.

I shrugged. The box was his signal that it was time for me to go. I got up and picked up the big box of files. My short skirt was hiked up, and my hands were on the box. I did a little shimmy to get the hem properly in place.

"I miss you, Boss."

"I miss you too," Boss said. His voice broke a little, but I know him. He didn't want to leave me with the impression that he cares as much as he does, so he had to knock me down with the next punch. Except for when we would be sparring in the gym, that's not who he is. But these months I've been moved out, he digs at me. "Are you putting on weight?"

I didn't answer but heard him chuckle as I walked out. Fucker.

Leaving his office, I ran into Storm. She was wearing a hot pink Lycra body shirt so tight I could see her nipples right through her bra. It's the kind of clothes Boss would have nixed when we were meeting family members. Even when we were working with randy widowers, we had to be more subtle than that, so it ought to be a no go for office wear, right?

"Did you fuck him to death in New Orleans?" I wanted to take a bite out of her, and not because she looked like a big pink cupcake.

Apparently, Storm was not bothered by my nosy question. Her smile never budged. "Actually, I did not, and if I had, I wouldn't be under any obligation to tell you. I don't need to go to New Orleans to fuck him."

"You're a slut."

She laughed. "Tell me something I don't know," she said.

After she disappeared down the hall, I checked myself out in the full length bathroom mirror. If anything, I had lost weight. I haven't made cookies once since we moved. Still, when Tangles asked me where I wanted to go for lunch, I told her I wasn't hungry, had a cup of black coffee, and spent my lunch hour in sweats running the stairs in this high rise building, damn him.

June 7, 1993
GAL office, Los Angeles
Tangles

I found Storm in the file room at a small round table behind a crate of folders she was sorting. She looked up when I walked in.

"Morning," she said.

I ignored the greeting. "Did you have a blast with him in New Orleans?"

"Hey, I just got the same shit from Letty."

"Don't hey me, bitch."

Storm got up. "What are you going to do, go Ninja on me? I'm not afraid of you. Don't call me a bitch, bitch."

I poked her in the chest, and she poked me right back. She's right that I could go ninja on her and leave her in pieces on the floor without messing my hair. I could have blocked her, but I don't need to show off.

"You left the house, and now all of a sudden you two are jealous? Give me a fucking break."

"Oh, so now it's your house?"

"What are you talking about, my house?"

"You wasted no time. We moved out, and you took over."

"You been gone since November of last year. That's eight months. Why are we having this conversation now? Is it the trip to New Orleans that got you and Letty all rowdy? Did you and Letty give Niley a hard time, too, or did you both get out of the wrong side of the kennel this morning? You shouldn't have abandoned him. At least Niley didn't. Niley is cool."

I looked her up and down, trying to look down my nose at her when we're about the same height.

"We're worried about Niley. Letty suggested that Niley get out more and take time to hang out with Boss. They go way back to when Pixie was first learning the ropes, and when Boss's good friend Tanis—who happened to be Niley's sister—died. She raised her sister's babies along with her own kids, all on her own. She deserves a break, and she and Boss have a connection. But you—you're a tramp."

"And what are you?"

It was a silly schoolgirl squabble that made no sense. I felt like laughing, felt like hugging Storm. I dig how she stands up for herself, and that she clicked with Niley. Letty refuses to admit she's jealous, but I know better.

As for me, fucking-a. I am jealous.

"I bet the trip was cozy with Niley along in his new plane with that big king size bed."

"Get up to speed," Storm said, cocky as all hell. "Two beds into one. Recliners."

"Smart fuck," I growled.

Storm made a fuck you face, punctuating it with a fuck you finger on both hands.

A clerk walked in, and that's when I split.

June 8, 1993 (Tuesday)
Pasadena
Letty

I can't stand being away from him. Sure, I feel the loss of being gone from Casa Luna, but it's just a house. It is Mario I miss. Even when I wasn't sleeping with him, it a comfort to know we were in the same house. Most nights we did sleep together. Many of those nights, Tangles had been with us in that spectacular bed with the beveled ceiling mirror.

When I worked out with Tangles in the gym, I knew it was his gym. His scent was there. I miss his scent, and not just because it was an aphrodisiac. It was just him.

We are in the same office every day, but I don't always see him. I go sometimes for long hours without catching sight of him. If I miss him when he leaves, I must wait until the next morning. Sometimes all I get is a glimpse.

He's busy. I barge into his office when I want, but he doesn't give me his entire attention like before. I'm so full of so much emotion. I don't know if he's just playing it cool. Maybe moving out was a mistake. Maybe making a big deal out of the condom shit was a mistake. Maybe the sex in Rio was a mistake. If we die from some sex disease, we die, right? So it goes.

I can get laid whenever I want, so I don't have to. It's just like having to prove yourself in the gym. I know I can, so I'm over it. I get so many calls from guys. I get invited everywhere. If doing it is just going through the motions, if it just for kicks, why even bother? I go with a guy, and in the end, he's not Mario. Even if the sex is ok, and I go off like a string of firecrackers, I end up feeling worse than before. If it doesn't compare to what I had, it's just stupid to do it just to do it. But I couldn't say something like that to Tangles. She'd think I was being critical of her. But I swear I'm not. She goes for stranger sex like athletes go for championship titles. If we're both free spirits, we're free to be who we are, and we're really very different people.

Tangles works hard at the office and plays hard after hours. She works harder at playing than I do. I pretend to be more wild, pretend to be upbeat so I don't bring her down, but truth is, I spend more time missing what was than I do exercising the freedom of what is. Once in a while one of us—mostly Tangles—brings a date over to the place we share, but we clear it with each other beforehand. If we're going to interact with a guy, the dude better have the bread to rent a high-end hotel. We really don't have that many top notch hotels in Los Angeles.

Then, at the office:

"I'm going to tour the Airbus plant in Toulouse, France. If you and Tangles want to join Storm and me, you're welcome to."

"Boss, thanks for the invite. I've seen all the Airbus plant videos. I'm totally up to speed with their planes."

"Good," he said. "I want to start leasing some of their planes. Be sure you are up to speed."

"I'll ask Tangles if she wants to go," I said. He didn't urge me to say

I'd go, so I had second thoughts.

"Sure, find out fast. We leave tomorrow. Be sure Andrea has you two on the manifest."

I smiled. It was a real smile, because he gave me an in. Maybe he wasn't as cool as he pretended. "Thanks, Boss. I'll get Tangles take on it."

I gave him a thumbs up that he didn't see because his attention was back to the work on his desk. I stood there like a dummy for a minute. He never looked up. I sure fucked this up.

As bad as I wanted to be with him, I didn't go to France. Neither did Tangles. There was something off-putting in this new cold attitude of his.

His saying we could "join him and Storm" was a deliberate slap in the face. All of a sudden Storm is in every portrait. Her clothes have gotten an upgrade. She didn't get years of lessons from Melina. Sure, it is about time that Storm dressed her part, but it irritates me to see her in designer stuff like ours. It's like we're so easily replaced. All he needs is next year's model, and he's good, and we're yesterday's news. I've counted three different outfits so far. Everything about Storm makes me feel bitchy. I don't hate Storm. I'm just fucking jealous!

June 8, 1993 (Tuesday)
GAL office
Mario

At the office, there was a message from Juan in Puerto Rico. I hadn't heard from him in a while. We played phone tag for a few hours, then I finally caught him.

"Good to hear from you Boss," he said.

"Is anything up?"

"Nothing going on here, Boss. Just touching base with you."

I promised to visit him at the first opportunity. It would be an easy thing to add Puerto Rico to the return trip from the Airbus factory.

The day before our departure to France, I walked into the office Storm was now using. She covered the mouthpiece with one hand.

"Butch from the Agency," she whispered.

I nodded and sat across from her. I figured eventually I'd have Storm working on plane leases. Andrea knew I expected her to help groom Storm. It had taken a while just to get her in her own office.

"To be clear, Butch, it's no different from when Andrea sets it up. Always send flight attendants that are female and lookers. Of course, only you and I and the fencepost know this is a requirement."

I didn't hear Butch, but I was sure he agreed with her. The customer is always right. I shook my head over this 'requirement' being spoken aloud over the phone. For many years, I've been careful about what I say over a phone line, where there is no such thing as privacy. You can call me paranoid if you wish, but there is a world out there full of invisible Masons and Lolas whose job it is to ferret out every time you step on a crack.

Andrea normally worked with Butch, but I had Storm learning the process. I didn't hold a mistake against her. She's still in training. Butch was a pal. He knew who to send.

My pilots work for GAL and were checked out on a number of air-craft. I didn't have permanent flight attendants, but the agency we used went overboard to fill our request for a particular person if we requested her. Rachel and Peggy were two new-to-us flight attendants.

As the plane lifted off the runway, Storm buried her nose in the wing of the seat and took a deep breath.

"Love that new plane smell, Boss."

I smiled and restrained myself from doing the same thing.

When seat belt light went off, we got up and walked to the bedroom with our bottled cokes that we had just opened. Peggy intercepted us.

She snagged the bottles.

"I'll bring them to you," she said. "Would you like anything else?"

"Assorted nuts," I said. "Storm?"

"Nuts are fine," she said. "Thanks."

It was a thirteen hour flight. I planned to take it easy so when we landed tomorrow at nine, we'd be fresh.

In the bedroom, I was in my undershorts and t-shirt. Storm was in baby doll lingerie with a thong panty. When she gave me a massage, she tended to slip off the top and leave on the bottom—what there was of it. Storm, still in her babydoll, thumbed through the DVDs for a movie. She read off titles that caught her eye, waiting for me to stop her when I heard one that I wanted.

"These are some of the new ones released last year: *The Bodyguard. Lethal Weapon 3. Sister Act. Beethoven.*"

"Beethoven the composer?" I asked.

"The dog," she said. She looked up from the videos. "We could do some prep for work and watch a plane video. We have a whole stack of Airbus demo videos."

"Nah," I said. "We're about to see plenty of those in person."

"I'm surprised Letty and Tangles didn't come with us," Storm said.

"They've seen all the videos of the plants and planes," I said. "And they've been on the Airbus tour before."

"They probably didn't want to come because I was coming along."

I recalled the times we had been together in bed.

"Baby, no," I said. "Why do you say that? You guys are buddies."

"We are, but since they moved, I don't know."

"I don't want any friction for you," I said.

"Boss, there is no friction. Chill. How about *Godfather*?"

I snatched the movie that was in her hand and tossed it aside. We play-wrestled for a minute and I let her play victor and sit on top of me. I could never have done that so easily with Letty. Letty and I, we'd be flipping each other on the bed until we were laughing too hard to continue.

She giggled, leaned over and kissed my lips.

"I got you all to myself. Is that lucky or what?" she said.

I put my hands on her ass and squeezed gently.

"I got you to myself as well."

As much as I loved Storm's company, I missed Letty.

Storm's face was about six inches from mine.

"Boss, since we're not watching a movie anytime soon, what would you like me to do to you?" she asked and proceeded to please my body. Letty wasn't going anywhere. She lived in my mind.

Storm joined me in an entire day at the Airbus plant. The assembly areas are huge and breathtaking. Two salespeople attended to us. We ate a VIP lunch in their VIP lounge. When we were finished, we hitched a ride to my jet that was parked at one of their hangers on the property.

We were at Airbus in Toulouse France. It reminded me of the time that Camila and I had been wined and courted at Boeing. She had flown there in her jet, and I had flown there in another jet. Remembering the experience really made me miss Camila.

We sat in the main cabin before lift-off. I looked at my watch: six-thirty. The sun was setting when we took off. My turbulent emotions had me craving a hit or two of a joint. Storm made it happen. She only smokes around me when I want to participate.

"Thank you for bringing me, Boss," Storm said, sitting across the table from me. "I thought I was going to hang out in the plane while you were in meetings. I didn't know you would be taking me inside like a VIP."

"You are a VIP," I said. "Airbus clearly thinks so, or they wouldn't have provided lunch and the VIP lounge."

That came out like a joke and made her giggle.

"Thanks for coming with me."

"Boss, I love working for you."

Peggy poured us a red. I didn't want food as Airbus had fed us at every turn. Peggy stowed away a boatload of Airbus-provided goodies for the long flight home. I know Airbus doesn't do catering, but whatever division handles the VIP lounge food must have a degree in French cooking. I told Peggy that she and Rachel could have the snails if they wanted.

"I love working with you," I told Storm "That makes the two of us very happy campers."

The pilot came on to tell us we were at ten thousand feet, headed for thirty-one thousand. Storm unbuckled, kissed me, took off my tie, unbuttoned my top button, and knelt to take my shoes off. I patted my thigh.

She sat on my lap. We hugged.

She held my face between her palms and kissed me. The kisses escalated to a crescendo. If there had been a camera on board, we would have faded to black, and the next shot of us would have been smoking.

Later while flying over the Atlantic, I revealed my surprise.

"We're going to divert to Puerto Rico," I said. "Wahoo! It's a long flight. Almost seventeen hours."

"Boss, why?"

"I want to see two friends who live there, Juan and Valita. Juan is an investigator who worked with me in the past as my advance team on foreign plane crashes. His wife, Valita, is a special friend of mine. Juan called me the other day, and I told him I'd drop in."

Storm clapped her hands. "I dig it, Boss."

"When I first went into aviation, I had a case where one of the crash victims had lived in Puerto Rico. The long distance operator gave me a few numbers of local private investigators. Juan was able to find the victim's family in San Juan. I flew over and met with the family. The widow of the deceased signed the retainer I took with me, thus becoming the client of the attorney I was sending my cases to. After that, I used Juan a lot. He would go wherever I asked him to go, as my advance team. He would ferret out details about the crash I was interested in, details about the family, locate the hotel where the airlines were putting up the family members, work with my team to get us in a conveniently-located hotel, and once we were there, he'd help out when he could in other ways. He made it easier to do our work when we arrived. I'm not doing cases anymore, so I have nothing for him to do, but I love him. He's a good friend."

"And Valita?"

I could not help smiling at the memory. "I met Valita before Juan did."

"Did you fuck her before Juan?"

"You sound like Letty," I teased.

"Oh, Boss, I won't interrupt. Tell me about Valita. The name is hot."

"She is hot," I said. "I met her years ago while on a case in Venezuela when I was kidnapped."

She looked shocked and put her hand to her mouth to keep herself from interrupting. I could see she was dying to.

"My kidnappers were actually my competition, lawyers in Venezuela. We were all working to get retainers signed. My team and I did too good a job and pissed off a couple of small-time local lawyers who were little more than hoods. I was drugged and taken to a warehouse in a jungle far away from Caracas. Our captors were quite a pair. They were married to sisters, as

I recall, though I never saw their wives or families. There were two mansions on the property, a plantation far from where I was being held. Valita, like many of the locals who were there, was practically a slave, cleaning the main house and providing personal services to one of the patrons when he flew in by helicopter. In addition to being bad lawyers in Venezuela, and growing coffee, the lawyers engaged in the local money-making pastime of holding people for ransom. The lawyers would kidnap their victims, and when the ransom was paid, they'd kill off the victims. Dirty shit."

"If you weren't the one telling me this story, I'd think it was made-up," Storm said.

I said, "Shh," picked up her hand by two fingers, and put them back over her lips. "Not a lie," I said. "Holding people for ransom is quite common down there. Anyway, Valita and a young boy named Ratón brought me my meals. I was constantly under guard locked up in a warehouse, and even I could see they were both pretty much abused by their Venezuelan patrons. The warehouse was my 'cell', but even more than the warehouse, the jungle was my prison. Valita and Ratón couldn't help themselves, much less help me escape because there was no where to go but jungle. Eventually, after I was rescued, Valita was taken in a sweep of the plantation and ended up in a horrible jail in Caracas. Juan was there when I helped her get released and took her with him to Puerto Rico. The coffee plantation burned down."

I did not mention Pepe's involvement. Jack and my lawyer Oscar had been concerned about my disappearance and had contacted Pepe to help with my release. This was actually the incident that led to my meeting Pepe. Pepe had a lot of shady connections. Better to let those sleeping dogs lie. I did not mention Pepe or his friend, the general.

"And did you see her after that?"

"A number of times. Juan brought her with him on some cases we handled. She was good at speaking Spanish with our families."

I took her hand and pulled it down to rest on the table.

"Boss, you could write a book or a movie about that."

I shook my head. "There are so many kidnappings in that part of the world, it's not even news. I'm just lucky to be alive. I owe my life to Ratón and Valita."

"Who rescued you?"

I was not going to mention him, but her question deserved an answer.

"It was a group effort. A lawyer I worked with named Oscar, an aviation lawyer named Tom, Camila's brother Pepe. A general Pepe knew. I think all of them are dead now but Tom."

"It all sounds awful, and terrible and dangerous. I am so glad you survived it."

"It was touch and go for a while," I said, "But by the time the cavalry got there, I was already halfway out the door."

I thought about what would have happened if the helicopter had not shown up when it did. I bet Valita, Raton, and I would have braved the jungles on foot, until we got to civilization and could make a phone call. That would have been a whole other kind of adventure. Everything is so much easier now that there are cell phones.

I was somewhere in my head when Storm flung her arms around my neck and started furiously kissing and hugging me.

"I don't know where I would be if you hadn't survived. Still living hand to mouth, giving massages with Betty. But Betty only needed me because you were helping her get so much business. No telling where I'd be without you. I owe you my life."

I pulled back a little. "You're a smart girl," I said. "You land on your feet. You don't owe me half of what you think you do," I said.

She shook her head stubbornly. "I know I'd never have another chance like you. There's nobody else like you. They made you and broke the mold."

She would have kept on hugging, but Peg came out with a fancy paper menu detailing the meal catered by Airbus's VIP lounge. It was all very French, four pages of little bits of this and that in fancy sauces. I'm not all that crazy about food I don't recognize in elaborate sauces, but I think Storm was very impressed. Anyway, instead of sleeping during the seventeen hour flight, Storm had me talking about my experience in Venezuela until we landed. We napped in the plane, and late Friday afternoon, I called Juan to let him know we'd arrived. Storm was excited to meet them. Juan called me when they got to the executive hanger at the International Airport where my plane landed.

"Wait here," I told Storm. "I'll ask them up here for a drink, then we'll split for a couple hours to have dinner or something."

I ran down the stairs and hugged my two friends.

Juan looked the same as when I'd seen him last. Valita had blossomed. She was gorgeous, and her English was vastly improved. She still had a strong face with high cheekbones, dark flashing eyes, endless long hair, and a body that didn't quit.

"Let's have a drink," I said, "Then we can go have dinner. I only have about four hours."

"Why so little time?" Valita asked.

"I'm late getting back, but I needed to see you."

I introduced them to Storm.

"The girls told me to say hello to both of you," I said. It was a lie; I hadn't told the girls I was making this stop. I don't think they knew Tangles at all, but they knew Pixie, Jo, Letty and Niley.

"Jo and Niley are managing my rentals, Pixie is out in the world singing for her supper, and Letty is busy leasing planes now."

Juan said his private investigator business was like always before, slow, barely making it. Valita worked as head housekeeper, director of all the maids in a two hundred room hotel.

We got in Juan's Chevrolet station wagon and drove to the International Hotel, a fancy high-end place.

"We once had a case here in Puerto Rico where a hotel burned horribly. We stayed at the International for about a month," I said for Storm's sake.

"Oh, how terrible," she said.

"More than terrible," Valita said. "Very sad. Mario work very sad. I happy he's doing something else now."

I smiled at Valita. I could not look at her without remembering the times we'd had sex. She always affected me like that. She's not only a stunner, but also a very uninhibited woman.

On the way to the main dining room, we passed through the hotel casino which was bustling with activity. Halfway there, we passed a long bar on my right. I wasn't really looking, only noticing that compared to the casino, it was almost empty. Something caught my eye. I saw the back of her. She moved. I saw the side of her face, her unmistakable profile. My heart raced. I'm too conditioned for that, but I still had an adrenaline rush when I recognized her, and I must have excreted a gallon of adrenaline. My heart leapt. I didn't want to be seen but snuck another look. That second look was enough to confirm a positive ID.

It was Lola.

She wasn't dead.

The part of me that shared her bed wanted to run over, swing her around, hug her, and congratulate her in general for not being six feet under, but if there's one thing I'm not, it's impulsive. The rest of me wanted to duck out of sight. My mind was running in circles on itself.

I was worked up. I maneuvered my group out of view of the bar. I put my arms around them all, and we stood in a huddle.

"Juan, listen carefully. I have some work for you. There is a woman, an ex-cop, a very savvy woman sitting at the bar. She's the only one wearing a cap."

Juan came alive. "What do you need, Boss?"

"I need you to stay with her, no matter what. I want to know everything. Where she is staying, where she is visiting from, everything about her. If she leaves, follow her. I will send you money. Remember, she's very smart. You can't get found out."

"Boss, don't worry."

I reached in my pocket, kept a hundred for myself, and gave him the rest, a wad of hundreds, about three thousand dollars.

"Take this," I said. "Spend whatever it takes. Report to me by phone every day until I tell you to stop."

"You got it, Boss."

"Valita, you look gorgeous. You too, Juan. Rain check on dinner. This is too important."

"Boss, do not worry," Juan said.

"We saw you fast, but we saw you," Valita said and kissed me. It was a good Valita kiss and made Storm's jaw drop and every part of me to stand at attention. Juan just grinned at me and shook my hand. Storm said her goodbyes.

"I'm going to split and take a taxi back to the plane," I told Juan. "I don't want her to see me."

"I'll be at the bar in seconds and stay with her," Juan said.

"I'll wait until you leave, then I'll go home," Valita said.

Juan and I exchanged a bear hug.

I figured the pompous-looking overdressed guy watching us suspiciously from the restaurant had to be the maître d'.

I handed him the hundred. No problem. I always kept spending money on the plane.

"We were planning to have dinner here, but something came up. Is there an exit close by?"

The restaurant had a street entrance, and we left that way. Very stealthy. Caught a taxi.

Soon we were wheels up on the seven hour flight to Los Angeles. We would be getting to LA by nine or ten pm.

"You don't need to explain, Boss," Storm said.

I was anxious. I am truly happy Lola isn't dead, but I did not know if she was friend or foe, or if she had been involved in Camila's death. I always suspected her connections of Camila's death, but up to this moment, had not considered she could have been involved. I mean, she was dead at the time. Now, it turned out she was alive. It changed everything.

I had convinced Camila to pay Lola a million dollars in compensation, though I don't think she ever quite admitted she was responsible for

Lola being shot. I had a video of that transaction in my office at Casa Luna. I had promised if she broke her word to me, I'd kill her myself. Lola promised that if she got paid, she'd never go after Camila or Olga. I tended to believe Lola because—as she once reminded me—she wasn't one of the bad guys. That was before I found out she faked her death. But I can understand her faking her death. Camila had tried to kill her before. It is likely she would have tried until she succeeded.

I wondered if the espionage team Lola had been working with had committed Camila's murder—with or without Camila, or if they had been involved at all. Camila had inherited plenty of enemies and made quite a few on her own.

Juan is good at his job. I would find out where she was living. Maybe she lived here. Maybe she was on vacation in Puerto Rico and living in Florida. Before she'd 'died' when her car blew up, she'd mentioned her family in Florida.

I could barely get my head around the idea that her car blowing up in the garage of a hotel in Beverly Hills had been a ruse. Now that I knew she was breathing, I was elated. I had been infatuated with her. At times Letty had been ready to take Lola's head off, but she'd also been on the verge of becoming friends. I couldn't wait to tell Letty.

Should I tell Letty?

I was jazzed over the discovery. I needn't do anything too soon. I could wait for Juan's first report. He'd have some answers for me, at last.

That night we made it home to Casa Luna. Emma greeted us as we came by the kitchen.

"Boss, what would you like for dinner?"

I kissed her cheek.

"I ate so much on the plane. I'll pass on dinner."

"Me too, Emma," Storm said.

"Saturday, you can cook up a storm for us," I said.

"No way," Storm said. "I nix that menu. I am not on tomorrow's menu."

Emma laughed, but looked worried. "Boss, I feel bad. I have nothing to do."

"Sure, you do. Do you bake?"

She almost looked offended at the question. "Of course."

"Bake what you like. Pies, cookies, food, whatever. If we're not here to eat, put it out. The staff will eat it."

"Are you sure?"

"The kitchen is yours. Yes, I'm sure."

I checked out the uniform she had on. Emma had a fine ass.

"You look hot," I said. "No offense."

"None taken, Boss."

We took the elevator with our luggage. Storm got off on the third floor, kissed me and said, "Call me if you need anything, Boss." She kissed me again, the second time on the lips. "Thank you for taking me with you."

"I'm going to shower, maybe hit the steam," I said. "I'll check on you in a little while."

She stood there smiling until the elevator door closed.

The next morning, I was in my gym at five working out. I finished off with three hundred sit-ups and fifty chin-ups.

At six-thirty, my mouth was watering. I followed the fragrance to the kitchen which smelled like a bakery, cinnamon and yeast in the air.

"You're up early, Boss," Emma said. "I was waiting till I saw you to start it so your coffee would be fresh." She pushed the button on coffeemaker and went back to what she was doing.

Emma wasn't lying that she could bake. Hot from the oven, three different kinds of Danish were waiting on a platter—one of them with peanut butter. Emma nodded at me when I walked through to the breakfast room but didn't pause what she was doing. She had her hands full. In passing, I saw a tray of raw doughnuts to her left. With tongs, she retrieved some from the fryer and put them on a metal grate, dropped more in the fryer, dipped the cooked ones in various bowls and stacked them high on a serving platter, eventually covering them with a big glass dome.

"Gotta wait till they cool," she said. "Cover them too soon, the steam gets trapped, and they get soggy."

I sat in the breakfast room overlooking the garden and opened the paper. I was still on page one of the LA Times when Emma placed a big plate in front of me: Denver omelet, six pieces of crisp bacon, three link sausages almost burned, the way I like them. A short stack of pancakes was on a separate plate.

"Emma, that looks great. Thanks."

"The house smells great," Storm said as she walked in, leaned over and kissed my cheek.

I looked up at her, and she kissed my lips.

"Want company?" she asked.

"For sure," I said, still reading. "Emma will fix you up."

"I'm good with one of these Danish. It's the best thing, ever," Storm said, sipping the cup of coffee that Emma brought her.

"I'm glad you said that, Storm," Emma said, putting a white card-board box on the table between us. "I put some of the Danish in here so you can take them to Letty and Tangles. Miguel said he always sent care packages." She turned to me. "Boss, I told Caro I put doughnuts and biscuits and stuff on the buffet, and they're for everybody. I also put some bacon out there, and told them if they want eggs, I can fix them to order."

"Good deal," I said.

It's a good thing I work out. I took the stairs up to the office. Storm took the elevator. By the time I got to my floor, breakfast had settled. I left a message with Andrea to have Letty and Tangles come to my office.

I parked Storm to sit to my left on my side of the desk. We had been gone from the office Thursday and Friday, and hadn't seen them Saturday or Sunday, so everyone exchanged kisses when Letty and Tangles came in. If the greeting was just for my benefit, I'd find out eventually.

"You know I trust and love you and that's why I will share this secret. You cannot talk about it, not in person, not on the phone, not with anyone. Walls have ears."

"Fuck me," Letty said in her usual manner. "What's up, Boss?"

"On our return from France, we stopped to see Juan and Valita. On the way to eat, I saw Lola."

Their jaws fell to the floor. Whatever they expected me to say, this was not it. I gave them the blow by blow of what happened.

"I knew the bitch was not dead," Tangles said.

"I thought she was dead. Are you sure, Boss?" Letty asked.

"It was her."

"Juan will find everything," Letty said. "He's good at this."

"Yes, he is," I agreed.

"So now what?" Tangles asked.

"I want to know what she's doing before I make plans," I said.

"Why not just let her remain dead, Boss?" Letty asked. "You don't need her. No telling who she might be hiding from since she stopped the cop biz."

"I don't know what the plan will be," I said. "I don't need her. I'd like to know if she killed Camila. If she didn't, I want her feedback on who she thinks did."

"Oh Boss, do you really think you'd get the truth from her?"

"Tangles, don't be negative. I didn't have to bring you in on this," I said.

"Storm didn't even know Lola. Why is she here?" Tangles snapped.

"Fuck off, Tangles," Letty said. "Boss's office. Boss's rules. He can have whoever the fuck he wants in here."

Storm stared directly at Tangles. "I didn't need to be in here, but I was invited."

"Stop the nonsense," I looked at Tangles. "I don't give a shit if you argue among yourselves, but an alliance against Storm better not be for real."

"Got it, Boss," Storm said first.

"No arguments," Tangles said.

Letty said nothing and got to her feet. Everyone stood up.

"I love you all very much."

I said I loved them all, but I was looking at Letty. She's never been good at hiding her emotions. The room was quiet for maybe ten, fifteen seconds. We were all looking at Letty. Letty was looking at me, those deep brown eyes of hers huge and mournful. They filled with tears, but none of them fell. She looked like a Margaret Keane painting, all that sadness trapped in those big eyes.

Melina used to say that Keane paintings are not art. They are trailer park. Now, I've said I'm no art expert, but I have learned a lot about legal cases. I think everyone in California knows about when Walter Keane got sued in the seventies for claiming he painted his ex-wife's big-eyed paintings. Nobs like Melina might not think Margaret Keane's work is art, but those big-eyed kitchy paintings could move me to cry.

Everyone in the room was perfectly still, perfectly quiet. All I could see or hear, or feel was the love in those big sad eyes.

Letty was suddenly in my lap, those sad eyes inches from my face. I had not noticed when my arms opened, but now they closed around her. I had a huge knot in my throat. My arms had been so empty without her, and now this instant, were finally full. She kissed my forehead, my chin, my lips., My face was wet from her tears. My tears too, I have to admit. And I was kissing her back.

She whispered in my ear, "Mario, I love you. I can't stand it. I can't stand not being at home with you. I'm sick at myself for leaving. Mario, I want to come back. Can I come home? Home is with you, and I—"

"Shaddup," I said. It was all I could get out of my mouth. I held her tight. No words. All choked up. Closed my eyes. It was just the two of us. I don't know how long. It was a while. I was lost in all the hugs of my life wrapped up in this one and tied with a bow.

I heard a sniffle. I heard someone yank tissues from the holder on my desk. I opened my eyes. Tangles and Storm were holding hands like a couple of little girls. Their eyes were streaming tears, tissues wadded in their free hands, but they were smiling.

I got my words back, or some of them.

"I love you. Always have. I miss you. Your bedroom is still yours."

It was hugs all around all over again. I had one arm slung over Letty's shoulder and turned to face Tangles.

"Your room is still yours, too," I said.

"Oh Boss."

Tangles made a flying leap for Letty and me.

I asked Olga if I could use the apartment in New York.

"Amor, you do not need to ask. What is mine is yours."

"I love you," I said. "Thanks."

"Amor, repeat after me: Whatever Olga owns is mine, too."

I laughed.

"Amor, I want to hear you."

She sounded so sincere. I humored her.

"Whatever Olga owns is mine, too," I said. "Thank you, Olga."

"I still love it when you call me by my name, Amor."

For a fraction of a second, I wanted to tell her that I had found Lola. How stupid would that have been? It would also put Lola's life in dangerous territory.

That night, I took my beautiful GAL airplane and my three beautiful ladies to New York for a short weekend.

June 12, 1993 (Saturday)
In Flight
Storm

Letty and Tangles are moving back in. For the eight months that they have been away, I kept thinking they'd be back. The question was when. Letty and Tangles have gone totally overboard apologizing for the chips on their shoulders.

"Bounced right off me," I said.

It was a lie. I gave them lip each time so it's not like I was a punching bag, but when it was happening, it hurt.

Letty said she loves Boss. We all love Boss. He loves us.

On the New York flight, we had one stewardess primarily for the cockpit crew, and one, Ginger, for us. Early on, Letty had told Ginger to take it easy until we called her.

All the way to New York, Boss and Letty were like a couple of teenagers, the way she cuddled him, sat on his lap. Boss's hands were all over her.

Tangles and I were in side-by-side bucket seats, a table between us and them. Letty's seat was empty because they were both in Mario's.

Tangles and I clicked glasses, sipped wine, watched Boss's antics, and were all smiles. I'm relieved that we're tight again. Tangles and me, we got in on the romancey stuff too. She leaned in with her glass and I with mine, and we each sipped each other's wine.

Tangles put down her glass and took my free hand. She kissed my fingertips and sucked on my index finger, looking deeply in my eyes while she was doing it. I felt it all the way to my pussy. Unexpected. Fuck, what a thrill.

Letty's back was to us. Boss is so tall his head should have been showing, but it wasn't. Then Boss surfaced for a moment.

"Hey, that looks like fun," he volunteered, looking at my finger in Tangles' mouth.

Letty turned around as I pulled my finger free.

"I'm already wet as sin," Letty said, licking her lips. "Hot stuff. Boss, we should all go to bed."

"I'll go turn down your bed," I said. "Give me five minutes."

Tangles was looking at me when she said, "Boss, you and Letty take the big bed. Storm and I can take the flat seats over there." She pointed to four seats near the windows.

I heard no objections.

I passed Boss and Letty again wrapped together on the one chair. From this angle, I could see what was going on, though I tried not to stare. He was kissing her breasts. Letty was moaning.

When I announced that the bed was ready, Boss wasted no time. He got up with her in his arms, and a moment later, they were gone.

I found Ginger in a jump seat outside the cockpit playing double solitaire with the pilot's stewardess on their dinner trays. They were both wearing some generic white stewardess suit. They looked like they had come from church.

"Can you make up two of the flatbed seats for us?" I asked.

She smiled, stacked her cards and gave them to the other attendant.

"Can do!" she said brightly and hopped to her feet.

When she was done, she offered to do more, but we sent her away. She dimmed the cabin lights.

Tangles and I were on our sides facing each other, a soft comforter covering us, a couple of larger-than-usual pillows that we shared. We kissed. Except for our shoes, we were dressed. The skimpy summer playwear we had on was no obstacle. Our hands worked each other. Releasing a couple of buttons gave us entry to each other's wetness.

"This is better than being naked," Tangles said, exploring with her hands, her lips on mine.

I agreed, my fingers working her.

We had shared Boss's bed a number of times but not each other like this. We were alone. It was dark enough. Planes are always cold, but our bodies were steaming.

Tangles pressed her mouth on my face.

"Three fingers," she whispered with passion. "Like this." She demonstrated with her own three fingers inside me.

I lost count of the orgasms.

Thoughts of Boss and Letty crossed my mind. I'd seen them together before, plenty of times, before or after a massage. The thoughts and pictures in my head made me more aggressive with my mate Tangles.

I knew Tangles and Letty were lovers, but everyone at Casa Luna that shares Boss's bed is lovers.

"I'm glad you're moving back to the house," I said, whispering, our lips two inches away from each other.

"Going to be fun, I promise," Tangles said, squeezing my ass with both hands.

"This is nothing to what I'm going to do to you when you move in," I said, adding coal to the fire.

"Promise?"

I squeezed her ass hard, one hand on each cheek. "Promise," I said.

"Letty is going to keep Boss busy in bed for some time," Tangles whispered.

"I want him to be happy," I said and meant it.

Tangles said, "Boss is happy, believe me. I know him very well."

If Letty is the answer to curing Boss's doldrums, fantastic. I hope I can stay at Casa Luna. If he asks me one more time about getting involved in leasing, I'm still saying no.

June 12, 1993 (Saturday night)
New York City
Mario

The driver of our rented SUV picked us up at the airport, and when he got to the apartment building, pulled up at the curb and stopped. Traffic was heavy. It had rained before our arrival, and rainwater was steaming off the hot pavement when we all slid to the sidewalk-side of the car and stepped out. Although tenants in this building pay millions for their apartment, if they are coming home in a car, curbside is the only way you can access the entry. I find the differences between New York and Los Angeles amazing. In LA, you couldn't even consider building an apartment building unless you have parking on the property. No such thing in the city that never sleeps.

"The plan is to shower, then go out and eat, right?" I asked.

Four yesses chimed in, as we pulled to a stop. They started talking about potential restaurants. The doorman moved quickly to take our luggage in his cart. I shook hands with him.

"Welcome," he said. "I'm Pete. Ms. Camacho told me to be on the lookout for you. The housekeepers left an hour ago. Everything is ready for you."

He handed me a key.

"I'll see you upstairs," I said. "Thank you."

Usually there have been at least six security people between the lobby and the twenty-fourth floor. Whenever Olga and Camila had both been here, a dozen guards would be here too.

Thanks to my history of receiving hair-raising threats, and a few attempts on my life, during our engagement, Olga had insisted on security for me. I no longer have security people monitoring my every move when I am out of the house.

The girls chattered getting into the elevator and were still at it when we got to the twenty-fourth floor.

"Wait till you see this place," Letty said to Storm. "It makes the Hilton look like a crack shack."

I put the key in the lock and opened the door.

"Out of sight," Tangles said.

"Do you miss the guards?" Letty asked, taking my hand.

"Not a chance," I said.

The lights and air-conditioning were on. We walked through three bedrooms, four bathrooms and a guest bathroom. The place was furnished spectacularly, and different every time I was here. Priceless art hung all over, investments all.

The double door refrigerator was packed with cheeses, pickles and all sorts of dips. Two under counter beverage refrigerators were loaded with soda and beer. The wine fridge was filled to capacity.

Storm stared into the depths of the full refrigerator. "This much food—it's almost hypnotic. Who ordered all this?"

"From wherever she is, Olga controls what goes on in this apartment," Letty said. "Same goes for all of her homes."

"Fuck," Storm said. "Can I have a coke, or do I have to sign something?"

Everyone laughed.

"No signature needed," Letty said. "Grab one."

"Have you decided where you want to eat?" I asked.

Letty turned her back to me, staring at drawers in the kitchen. She rubbed her chin like she was thinking.

"I think it's..."

She reached toward a drawer, but before she opened it, switched to the one under the wall phone. She opened it, and squealed with delight, pulling out a ring binder full of menus. "I hit paydirt. Let's order in," Letty said. "It's hot out there."

"You guys decide and order. I'm hitting the shower," I said.

I don't like sharing bathrooms. I took over one I'd claimed the last time I was here, a large one with a roomy shower enclosure and multiple shower heads, a separate extra-sized jacuzzi tub and a velvet tufted chaise. I tossed my clothes on the chaise, and waited till the water was at the perfect temperature before I got in.

I was under the running water when the shower's glass door opened. Letty walked in, and behind her, Tangles and Storm, all of them as naked as the day they were born. It's happened before, though I'd have to think real hard to pin down the last time I showered with three women. It had probably been in my spa at home. One of the gym showers has multiple shower heads with room for a soccer team to take a shower in simultaneously. I'm not a soccer fan. I'm just recalling a conversation I had a long time ago with Jo's builder-husband, when we put in the first version of that shower in Casa

Luna.

"When it's done, you'll be able to fit a whole soccer team in here,"
TJ had said.

"How many is that?" I asked.

"Eleven, if you're not playing shorthanded." Not that TJ is a soccer
fan. He's a former surfer, turned builder. Anyway, this shower of Olga's had
more than enough room for the four of us.

I was surrounded by naked, soapy women. Naturally, my thing reacted by growing hard and prominent as we soaped each other in a sensual
water dance of soap, and hands, and mouths.

We never got around to ordering dinner, but we all enjoyed the
shower at least once. The bathrooms were stocked with an abundance of light
terry robes that we lounged around in. After the shower, we went to the living
room, then to the master bedroom. All of the rooms had electronic shades
with remote controls. Once the lights were off inside, I used the remote to
open the shades, and we could see the New York City skyscape in all its night-
lit splendor. Twenty-four floors is pretty huge for LA, but here in New York,
the skyscrapers rose far above twenty-four floors.

In bed in the dark, Tangles lit up a joint.

We passed it around and got a bit stoned. When the second joint
went around, there was enough smoke in the room to get high on. We were
wasted, lying in the dark, wrapped around each other.

I knew I was forgetting something, then it struck me.

"I don't have condoms. What now?"

"We'll fuck like we did on the plane. Fuck rubbers. I mean, fuck
without the rubbers. I mean—"

"Right-on," Tangles chimed in. "Fuck rubber-fucking. Let's fuck rubber-free. Rubber-free dick for everybody!"

"I've said that all along," Storm said.

I wasn't about to complain.

I was up half the night. And when I say up, I mean up. Eventually after everyone came to stunning conclusions, I shut the blinds so we could sleep in.

When I woke in the morning, it was just Letty and me on the bed.

I hugged her and she moaned in her sleep. I whispered in her ear, "I love you, Letty."

She turned toward me, gave me her sleepy face. Her smile is so beautiful. Letty just keeps getting prettier.

"I love you, Mario."

We kissed.

"Where are Tangles and Storm?" she asked.

"Somewhere else," I said.

She gave me a look.

"Probably in their own beds or sharing," I said.

Letty giggled. "Is it okay if I call you Mario from now on?"

"I'd like that, boss," I said.

She giggled again. "Thanks, Mario."

But then she put her serious face on.

"Don't feel stressed when you hear this," she said.

I didn't know what to expect.

"I'm not expecting anything from you," she said. "But I only want to be with you," she said.

I kissed her.

"I love you, Letty. I missed you so much. Even with you being in the office every day, it wasn't the same, coming home to a house without you in it."

"I'm not leaving until you show me the door."

"Jo said that. I mean, she said that about you," I told her.

"Well, I always said that. That's how it is, and you know it."

I kissed her again.

"In that case, you'll always be with me."

Letty and I tiptoed down the hallway to the second bedroom where the door was open. The same blackout drapes as were in the other bedroom made it dark, but there was enough light from the hall to make out two bodies on the bed.

"I'm so hungry," I whispered. "Should we wake them up and go eat?"

Letty gave me a look, and pounced on the bed, yelling, "Reveille! Reveille! Wake up! We are starving."

She made a noise like a kazoo playing reveille and kept bouncing on the bed like it was a trampoline until Storm and Tangles yelled for her to stop.

I stood by the door, laughing.

This time, everyone showered on their own.

The girls were in sunglasses, short-shorts, skimpy tops and sandals, all designer wear. I was in faded jeans, a Versace t-shirt and Versace sandals.

Henry, the day doorman wanted to hail a taxi for us, but I handed him a twenty and told him to stay in the lobby where it was cool. That was a mistake. On the sidewalk, the girls got rowdy trying to flag down cab drivers and yelling at the taxis who passed us. Their laughter was contagious. I kept my mouth shut, and they did their thing, and in short order, we were in a taxi headed to the Ritz for breakfast. It was ten thirty in the morning.

I rode in front with the cabbie. The ladies were in the back seat. They were stone cold sober, but being loud, and rowdy, and everything was funny to them. I think the cab driver was as entertained by them as I was. We were all laughing.

The fare was about ten bucks. I gave the cabbie a fifty.

The hotel had no problem with our casual dress or with our appetites.

I sat across from Storm, and between Letty and Tangles. Letty reached for my hand. She did it while we were waiting for coffee, then as we were waiting for our food. Every chance there was, she touched me. Just as she used to do, she buttered my toast. Once Tangles dabbed at my lip with a napkin. Maybe I had a crumb or something. I looked at Storm to figure out her response to all this. She noticed my stare and blew me a kiss, which Letty pretended to intercept. Then Letty giggled and got up from her chair to deliver Storm's kiss to me with her lips.

We went shopping at Saks. Storm and Tangles went off to some other portion of the store. Letty and I were walking around menswear, looking at what there was in the tall department. Nothing there for me. Letty grabbed a trench coat and put it on. She pretended to flash me, then put her sunglasses low on her face, and looked at me over the rims.

"Do I look like a spy?" she asked.

"Sure, Lola," I said to Letty.

She hit me with her little purse. Not a girly little hit. She whacked me square on the jaw. It made me break out into laughter. Served me right for not bringing up you-know-who.

"Bastard," she laughed at the way I was rubbing my jaw. She grabbed my hand and kissed it. "When you decide to meet up with Lola, are you going to get it on with her again?"

"Who thinks that far ahead? Do I get brownie points if you're in the bed too?"

Her eyebrows raised like she had never considered that possibility.

"Mario, she's a trouble magnet where Olga is concerned."

I put my arm around her.

"Let's go find the two rascals and see what they are buying." I stepped back and looked at her high heeled sandals. "You got your shopping shoes on. Better get busy doing some buying too."

The girls were being assisted by a shopper's helper whose job it was to collect the items. When the girls were all shopped out, the helper was to page me to pay. Under no circumstances were they to pay for it themselves.

I put my hand on my waist and offered my elbow to Letty. She squeezed my bicep and took my arm.

Sunday night, we went to the Majestic to see *Phantom of the Opera* then had dinner at Sardis. The girls were dressed to kill in their new stuff from Saks. I wore a new suit that had been tailor-made in Milan. Wide collar shirt, no tie.

"I loved that fucking show," Tangles said as we exited.

"Why fucking if you liked it?" Storm asked.

"Oh hush, bitch," Letty said. "Who are you, the grammar police? The show was bitching."

"Me, bitch?" Storm said. "I will slap you silly."

Tangles rolled her eyes and said, "Only if the queen bitch gives you bitch-slapping lessons."

The three ladies laughed.

I had instant messaging on my laptop that I wanted to trust because the technology seems complicated. How could anyone breach it? I got the idea from Olga when it was known as something else, but now it was OLM messages—on-line messages. I had the software on my laptop, and so did Juan.

On Sunday when it was time to go home, the girls were packing and getting ready, and I sat in the living room with my laptop open, exchanging OLM with Juan. We kept the sentences short. The idea was to type slow because I was told that on-line-messages sent a character at a time to the person you were writing.

I learned Lola lived in Puerto Rico. I couldn't believe the luck of running into her like that.

"Does she have a job?" I typed.

"I don't think so," he typed back.

"Does she rent?"

"Her place was purchased this year by a Nina Caputo."

"Allegedly her real name. Does she have a car?"

"No, she rides a bus or takes a taxi."

"Are you taking pictures?"

"Many."

"Any roommates?"

"She lives alone so far."

"I will Western Union you in the morning."

"Sure, it's okay. Thank you for the work, Boss."

I'd have to let him know as we messaged more that I didn't want him to use words like boss or anything personal. The technology was new, but some whiz would inevitably break it. In reality, the only people I wanted to keep Letty's continued survival secret from was Olga, her organization, and Mason. I would hang Mason out to dry if I ever found out he was spying on me. The excuse that he was watching me to catch whoever was after me has been a dead argument for a long time, and if he pulled it on me again, he would be a dead man.

On the way back to Los Angeles, we hung out in the main cabin, drank wine, and kept it light. We sampled some good dips, intending to leave room for a big Mexican dinner at Casa Luna.

When we were over Oklahoma, I had Letty call Niley on a plane phone. She handed me the receiver but kept her head close, so she was in on the conversation.

"How mean you are. Boss, you didn't take me," Niley said.

"Next time," Letty said.

"We missed you," Storm yelled from where she was sitting. I doubt Niley heard Tangles or Storm, given the bad static connections of a plane phone, and all the engine noise.

She did hear me.

"I missed you. Next time I call you for sure," I said.

"Can't wait, Boss."

"Boss, you got a crush on Niley." Letty elbowed me.

"I love that girl," I said. I kissed Letty. "Love you more."

Letty blushed.

"We're watching you know," Storm said.

Tangles had her shades on, and pulled them over her eyes, leaning forward like she was looking particularly closely.

We laughed.

"We're a real fruity group," Letty said, laughing.

Tangles couldn't let that go. "Fuck you with a banana, you fucking fruit salad."

"My puss is too sore, or I'd let you, bitch," Letty said.

"Boss, you get how nasty she is?" Tangles said, ignoring how she was egging her on.

"Vulgar," Storm said, pretending offence in a fake pretentious voice.

"Fuck you, Storm."

"Letty, it's a date," Storm said. "When and where?"

We mellowed out after a joint made the rounds.

It was still daylight when we landed in Ontario. That left us the rest of Sunday to enjoy ourselves at Casa Luna. Raul picked us up at the airport.

"Miss Letty, Miss Tangles, am I taking you to Casa Luna?"

Tangles looked at me. "Boss, we're staying at your house tonight. Is that cool?"

I did a thumbs up. "Great."

"You heard the man, Raul," Letty said. "Casa Luna it is."

As usual, I tried to tip Raul, but he refused it.

"Can't take your money Boss."

Not once had he accepted the money, whether it was a hundred dollars or five hundred.

"Pixie will kill me if she finds out," he said. Kidding, of course.

"Well don't tell her, fool." Letty tried to set him straight, but he wouldn't take the money from her either.

"When're you guys moving in? Need help?" Storm asked.

"We got enough new stuff to tide us over," Letty said. "We'll do it little by little, starting tomorrow."

"That's bitching," Storm said.

They high-fived. I had to dodge all the hands.

When we went inside, Caro and Memo handled the luggage. Letty and I went straight to the spa. The girls went to their own rooms to unwind.

I turned on the sauna and steam before we jumped into the indoor swimming pool for a skinny dip. It's a big enough pool we could get some real exercise in, so we swam laps for a long time. By the time we got to it, the steam was so thick, we could barely see each other, even though we were sitting face to face on towels. Our legs were crossed, Indian style.

"Letty, I've had this strange feeling about you."

"Strange? How?" Letty asked.

"I feel so close to you somehow."

Letty reached out to me with her right hand but didn't say anything.

"What's strange is that it took you being away for me to realize how important you are to me."

"Way too nice," she said. "You are important to me too. I'm here, Mario, and there's no strings."

It was my turn to say, "That's way too nice."

We dove into the ice-cold small pool to cool off and stayed till we were chilled before we went into the sauna where we could see each other. We put fresh towels on the benches, and lay back as the heat sank in. I was on the higher bench, but we were on our sides facing each other. She poured a little water on the lava rocks, and they hissed, but it didn't cloud up like the steam room. She rearranged her towels and lay down again. We were both beginning to sweat but the hundred-sixty degree temperature wasn't bothering either of us.

"Mario, if I tell you something, do you promise not to take it the wrong way or think badly of me?"

"The last time you said that, you promised you wouldn't leave till I showed you the door. You're not changing your mind, are you?"

"I haven't changed my mind," Letty said.

"Good. Then you can tell me anything." I took her hand.

She looked very serious.

"If you ever want to make a baby, I can make it happen."

I didn't waver, eyes on hers. The only time I ever thought seriously about what it would mean to be a father is when Melina tragically lost her child.

"I thought I was too old," I said.

"You are not too old. Would you like a child?"

"I don't know," I said. "Not sure I'd be a good father."

"I always thought I wouldn't be a good mother either."

"Wow, you grounded me."

"You are too strong to be grounded that easy," Letty said.

"What if the baby turns out to be a girl?" That was dumb, but it was too late. I said it.

Letty laughed so hard that it made me laugh.

"No pressure, Mario. I would be honored to be the mother of your child, boy or girl. I'm not looking for anything. I have everything I need. Thanks to you I have a good position at work, and I'm making oodles of money. I'm not looking for marriage either."

I kissed her. Our teeth touched, then our tongues.

All these years and now, today, Letty offers this.

I love her more. I don't ever want to lose her.

We had dinner in the dining room at the table for twenty-four. The four of us sat on one end. Emma, Memo and Caro brought out platters of food: refried pinto beans topped with melted jalapeno cheese, chile rellenos, chicken enchiladas, steak picado made with filet mignon, a green salad, tortilla chips, flour tortillas and corn tortillas.

Both shelves of the dessert cart were packed with goodies. I saw a bunch of pastries, a couple of fruit pies, and one cheesecake, but no Danishes, and no doughnuts.

"Boss, I have some beautiful steaks that will cook fast if you would prefer a steak."

"This is great," I said.

During dinner, Letty said, "I have a suggestion."

She looked at me, then at the girls. "Let's pick out a great movie and kick back in the media room, eat popcorn, ice cream, cokes, whatever. No booze, no smoke. Is that too saintly?"

"Works for me," I said.

Did Letty want to clean up her act for the sake of a baby? But that would be nonsense. We hadn't really discussed it. We didn't agree on a baby.

Tangles said, "I dig it."

"I would love to do that. Thanks for including me," Storm said.

Letty looked from me to Storm and said, "You will always be included."

After dinner, the girls showered Emma with thanks and appreciation. Tangles wanted her to take a bow. Letty yelled, "Speech! Speech!" Emma turned bright pink from all the attention.

Letty got up to help carry in the dishes, but Memo and Caro pushed her back into her chair, and I stealth-fed her a bite of cheesecake.

After a movie and a half, we decided to call it a night.

I stood, ready to go to bed, Letty and me in my bedroom, Tangles and Storm somewhere else.

"I'm going to start getting jealous if you two keep sleeping together," Letty said with a Pixie-like giggle. Well, no one has a giggle like Pixie, but it was close.

"Suffer," Storm fired back. "You got Boss."

Tangles said, "Night-night."

She winked, licked her lips, and headed up the stairs with Storm trailing six inches behind her.

Letty moved to follow them up, but I charged her, and swept her off her feet.

"Make way!" I yelled, running up the steps with Letty giggling madly in my arms. Tangles and Storm flattened themselves against the wall and I thundered past, taking the stairs two at a time.

June 19, 1993 (Saturday night)
San Juan, Puerto Rico
Lola

I've had a feeling that someone is tailing me. It's just a feeling. I don't have proof, but my instinct is pretty well-honed. I know every tailing trick there is, and if someone was using them on me, I'd spot it in a heartbeat. I'm too smart a tracker myself to get followed. I find myself pulling some easy tricks like walking, minding my own business while on the way somewhere, then jumping on a bus last second. It hasn't revealed anyone suspicious, but I can't shake the feeling. I see no one. I never see a car with anyone in it parked anywhere close to my condo. Why would anyone be following me? I'm a nobody in Puerto Rico, a transient who wandered in, and moved into a condo. I've got no mortgage. I've got no car. I dress like everyone else here, lightweight casual, which is practically naked. There's no place to hide a gun, so I carry a big handbag. I'm like Teddy Roosevelt, walk softly and carry an Uzi in your purse.

It's not really an Uzi, but I've got one.

I'm on edge because of my invisible tail. Maybe I'm just getting paranoid, but I don't think so. I looked out of the window. This is a ground floor condo, which also makes me nervous. I hate first floor anything. I didn't want to buy the condo because of it being ground level, but the broker arranged the seller to give me a price reduction on top of the already reduced price and I had gone for it.

I had to unwind. I hit Miles up, and while waiting for his expensive services to arrive, went hunting for a joint. I don't usually get high unless the dude I'm with has it. I don't buy it. Nothing to do with me being an ex-cop. My team members on the Camacho case burned a hell of a lot more dope than I do now that I live alone and am out of service. If I need to get tanked, it's a little booze or a lot of booze, depending on how tanked I need to be. I found a joint in my dresser drawer, probably from Miles the last time he was here. I lit it up. I needed to lighten up. I was horny.

"Don't come over unless I call you," I had told Miles the first time around. Well, I called a second time. And a third.

"I never forget a voice," he said.

"I never forget a cock," I said. "I want you to come over."

"I let you slide for fifty. Now it's a hundred."

"Hundred it is."

I was so ready for him, I ached. This was his fourth house call.

I put on a teddy, something from my Lola days, which gave me fond memories of Mario. There wasn't much to it. Sheer black lace tied at the back of my neck, plunging neckline to the barely there skirt, which was all in front, and almost covered my crotch. There was no back to it except for a bit of a thong. I left the door unlocked for Miles, who knew to let himself in and lock the door. I'm just paranoid enough that my trusty gun-toting big purse was in reach of the bed, also the sawed off shotgun loaded for bear in case the imaginary spy following me decided to be flesh and blood. I folded the comforter, and lay down on the cotton sheets, cool crisp percale. Cool and crisp is priceless in Puerto Rico. I screwed in a blue bulb and turned on the bedside lamp. The bulb had more ambiance than light. It enhanced the action.

I heard Miles's car pull up. He gunned the engine before he cut it off, and I recognized his footsteps, his shave-and-a-haircut knock at the door. He came wordlessly to my bedroom door and looked me over. He had a certain proud and challenging expression on his face as he stripped down for me. And it was a striptease. The man enjoys every aspect of his work. He's no Mario, but his body is hard and beautiful to me.

The blue light adds something. I enjoyed the action as we did it the first round, or I should say, as he did it to me. Miles could wait and wait until I'd tell him enough, and then he asked me if it was okay to cum. Sometimes I said no, till I had had a second round, or a third. There is a sub in him that gets off on doing my bidding, the harder the better. I had a feeling that if I played it really mean to him, he'd pay me. It gave me a hint of the old rush I had being Lola.

I was on top, planning on going another hour. I heard a creak of something through the open window. It was dark, no question, but when I rolled on to my back with my eyes on the open screened window, I saw movement. A peeping Tom or the creep following me—I don't know which. I heard a camera click. No flash but I caught a glimmer of blue light reflecting back. I didn't go for the handgun in my purse, but reached under the pillow, shoved Miles to the side, and fired my sawed-off shotgun. The window is far enough away that the shotgun blast of pellets would take him down, but not do anything serious. My screen exploded. The bang was deafening. The acrid, sulfuric stink of gunpowder permeated my bedroom.

I heard someone scream.

"What the fuck?" Miles said. He leapt to his feet on the opposite side of the bed.

Only the blue light was on, and it wasn't giving me much detail.

I ran to the window.

My flimsy robe was on a chair. I bypassed it, and shrugged into a thigh-long shirt, and hit the lights. I left the purse, grabbed the forty-five, and buttoned one button.

Miles and I tangled, stumbling into each other as he was pulling on his shorts with difficulty. His flagpole hadn't gone down. He blocked the door, facing me for one second.

"I'm outta here," he said.

"Hey mother fucker, I ain't paying you. You ain't done."

He looked at me like I was good and crazy and took off for parts unknown. I was out the door before he got his engine gunned.

I laughed at my own words, but I was pissed, not at Miles either.

I ran around to the business side of the condo where the peeping tom had to be. I almost stumbled on the man who was curled up in pain.

"Who the fuck are you?" I yelled at him. Like the cop that I used to be, I leaned over and flipped him face down. My hand was on autopilot, and went to my pocket, but there was no pocket, no pants, and no handcuffs either.

The light was skimpy, but I knew he was Puerto Rican.

My neighbor came out, a tall fucker named Tomas. He put his big bare foot on the intruder's back.

"Stay down," he said loudly.

The cops showed up minutes later with paramedics and an ambulance. Some great job I was doing of lying low. But I blamed it on the intruder.

I grabbed the guy's camera and cell phone and stashed them inside.

The cops arrived and took him away. They wanted the shotgun I had used.

"The guy is not going to die," I said like I knew, and I did know. He was just hit in the chest with a bunch of pellets. It was all superficial.

I knew a sawed-off shotgun would be illegal, but I didn't resist, and gave them the gun. The cops frowned. They'd noticed the forty-five, too.

With two guns at the scene, the cops wanted identification. I let two of them in my living room. Another two cops were working the scene outside the window.

I had no intention of pulling the agent card, but one of the cops opened my wardrobe. The problem was that it wasn't a wardrobe. It was a gun cabinet. There was enough armament inside it to take down a small country, end a riot, start a war, or defend yourself against any Camachos who turned up in the neighborhood. I mean…Look, I have a million bucks in the bank, minus the cost of a cheap-ass Puerto Rican condo. I had to have my toys, even if I can't really use them anymore.

"Holy fuck," one of them said, turning his gun on me. Both of them turned their guns on me. The two cops who were outside, ran in, and turned their guns on me too.

"Guys," I said, with a little laugh, hoping none of them had an itchy trigger finger. I handed the lead cop my passport.

I put my hands up. And walked toward the gun cabinet. They weren't letting me close.

"Ma'am," the biggest one said, "You have great legs, but if you touch anything in there, I'm blowing you to kingdom come."

"I hope not."

I reached for my purse. "May I?"

He nodded.

I handed him my badge.

He lowered his gun and flashed my badge to the three other cops.

"I never met an FBI agent before," the lead cop said.

The whole atmosphere in the room changed as the badge went around the room. The cops went from being out for blood to fanboys. The badge says I'm retired, so I don't know what the big deal was.

I offered them a beer. They opted for coffee. I brewed it in the kitchen while they finished up the report. We exchanged names. The lead cop was called Ángel Baez. I suppose I could have put on pants, but at the moment, I felt like the bare skin was giving me an advantage. Ángel liked my legs almost as much as he liked my badge.

My bedroom smelled of sex and gunpowder, which at least covered up the scent of the pot I had smoked earlier.

"What were you doing when you saw the man?"

"A guy and me, we were fooling around." I didn't mention the camera. "I didn't see a man. I saw a shadow at the window. I heard him."

"Where is the guy?"

"He ran away scared to death," I laughed. "He didn't know I keep a shotgun under my pillow." I l laughed some more.

"Need his name and contact information."

"Don't have it. I picked him up at a bar."

Ángel put down his coffee, and asked, "What do you mean, picked him up—what for?"

"Sex," I said.

The cops exchanged looks.

"Is that what you want in the report?"

"I don't care. I just brought him home for sex."

After a very long time, the cops left.

Ángel was the last one out the door. He left me his card and told me to call if I thought of anything else. Anything at all. Anything, really.

They drove away. I went to my gun cabinet and closed it, locked it about seven different ways, turned off the lights, and flopped down on an overstuffed chair.

"Fuck," I said, though there was no one there but me. "What next?"

I didn't bother to change the bedding.

I hit the bed. The forty-five pistol went under my pillow, and I went out like a candle in the wind.

At seven ten in the morning, my cell phone rang.

It was Miles.

"What the fuck was all that shooting about?"

"I nailed a guy at the window watching you nail me," I said.

"No shit," Miles said.

"The cops carried him off. I'm going to find out if it was a peeping tom or what," I said. "You ran out of here like you didn't have a job to do."

"Are you alright?" Miles asked.

Nice of him to ask. He could have asked last night before he high-tailed it, but I guess he was in too much of a hurry.

"I'm good," I said.

"You owe me a hundred."

"You owe me a job. Come over tonight, and I'll pay you, but you got to finish what you started."

"I ain't coming over if you going to start shooting."

"No shooting. I promise." No shooting as long as nobody came snooping at the window after midnight, taking pictures of us bumping uglies.

I called my brother and left him a message.

When he called me back, I told him what happened.

"I need you to find out who this bastard is, and what the fuck he wants from me, or is it simply a peeping tom."

"I'll find out who he is but after that you need to do the rest. I'm here and you're there, and this is off the books, not federal."

"Okay, bro. Call me back."

I took a look at the guy's thirty-five millimeter. It was a pretty weighty device, kind of beat up, cracked lens cap. The heavy duty leather neck strap was supple, like it had been well used, well cared for, and like it could support a hundred pounds of camera. Heavy black metal and aluminum, and the lens was about a foot long and probably weighed all of fifty pounds. A brand name camera, a Canon. I bet he had a bunch of lenses for it. The lens had a zoom range, high speed film that was fairly light sensitive. With the right film, he wouldn't need a flash, but he would have to stand still a long time for there to be a good shot, and even then, the color would be distorted from my blue light. I pulled the cartridge of film out of the back and put it in my pocket along with the guy's cell phone. I walked to a photoshop that does overnight developing.

At a phone shop, I picked up a battery charger for the guy's phone. I took it home and put it on to charge.

My brother called me back.

The peeping tom was a licensed private investigator named Juan from San Juan. I wrote down the name and contact number my brother gave me.

"He told police he's on assignment for a local client who claims to be your fiancée."

"That's a crock of shit," I said, getting pissed.

"He's being discharged from the hospital tomorrow. The district attorney is considering no charges since it's just trespassing on private property. Sis, you better have insurance. He may sue you. Shooting a silhouette at a window is hardly within the law."

"Rat shit," I said. "If I saw him point a gun, I had the right to shoot."

"You didn't mention a gun to the police."

A soon as my brother hung up, I called Miles.

"What if you come over now instead of tonight?" I said, "And bring some smokes. I'm uptight and I don't want to drink."

"Day rates are $125. Plus, the cost of the weed," Miles said.

"Get your ass over here with your cock and the joints."

I took a shower and put on a babydoll with nothing under it. I checked the phone that was charging. It took a while to figure out where the phone book was, but I hit pay dirt. A hundred and seven contacts. I arrowed down, skimming the names of people, local companies. When I got to L, there was Letty. Pasadena area code.

What the fuck?

Arrowed down to M.

Mario Luna.

I slammed his phone across the room. It landed harmlessly on the bed.

"Fuck!" Actually, it was a whole mouthful of fucks.

I hoped I was fucking dreaming.

I got my phone and his phone and compared Mario's number.

Same.

What the fuck?

I arrowed to Mario's old team: Pixie, Niley, Letty. No mistaking it.

I set his phone down to finish charging and crashed into a chair beside my bed. I closed my eyes. How did he find me? Was he fucking with me?

My eyes snapped open. I bolted to the charging cell phone and looked for an entry for Camila, or Olga.

Their names were not there. Olga has that know-it-all Mason who doesn't know jack shit. I don't think he would have hired Mario's PI in Puerto Rico.

I looked for an entry for Mason.

No Mason in the phone book.

June 20, 1993 (Sunday morning)
Pasadena
Mario

The girls and I spent Saturday night at my little beach house in Santa Monica. Jo and Niley had their own keys but had not joined us on this spur of the moment thing. Emma stayed at the main house, so we went down to check out the vendors on the pier to eat a bad breakfast, gawk at the tourists and take in the local color. It was the first time Storm had ever been. Letty and Tangles were like fanatics, dragging Storm from hot spot to hot spot.

They were some distance away getting palatas when Valita called my cell.

"Nina shot Juan last night, but he's ok. I just learned about it. He's okay. He's in custody in the hospital."

"How bad is he hurt? What do you mean, custody?"

"Ambulance took him to the hospital. Buckshot from a distance, not life threatening. But the police were there. They called it trespassing or something."

"I'm flying over there right now," I said.

"Boss, no. He is friends with police. They will let him go, I sure."

She convinced me that flying over there would accomplish nothing.

"I got to see him for five minutes after they dug out the buckshot. He whispers he so sorry he mess up the mission for you."

"Valita, fuck the mission. He's already sent all I need. I kept him on it to learn more and to keep him busy. I am so sorry this happened."

"Boss, it is okay. Juan is in good spirits. I will let you know more when I see him later tonight."

I had warned him that she was smart and savvy.

The corn dog I'd had for breakfast wasn't sitting well on my stomach, and this development didn't help. I looked down the boardwalk where the girls were barefoot in bikinis, looking like co-eds, standing in line behind a whole family of pineapple-shirted tourists waiting for fruit popsicles. They were looking well-rested but pale. I know Tangles had wanted to spend some time relaxing on the beach, and Letty said the forecast was sunny skies. If I couldn't help Juan with a visit, I'd still find a way to do something nice.

"I'll send you money by Western Union," I said.

"We are good, Boss. You already sent him plenty."

"I'll send more. Storm will call you with the details."

Later, the girls were looking rosy from the sun and were still dressed in shorts and bikini tops and smelling of piña coladas and coconut oil.

"Boss, I'm still your driver. I drove us here, let me drive you home," Storm said.

I said I wanted to drive, and that started up Letty and Tangles who also offered to drive the twenty-six miles home. It was late Sunday afternoon, and we'd already given Emma notice we'd be home for dinner. I don't know about the girls, but as for me, I'd had enough of amusement park food to last me a while and was looking forward to the steak fajitas that Emma was going to start when Quito announced us at the gate.

Storm drove us back to Casa Luna.

"Did you call Lola?" Letty asked.

"I'm not ready to. Not sure I can do it on phone."

I looked to my left, at Tangles.

"If you go in person you may get all entangled, Boss," Tangles said. "Just my big mouth offering an opinion."

I looked to my right at Letty. She just shrugged.

"I am not craving Lola for sex. I want to know why she faked her death. I want to ask if she had anything to do with Camila's murder."

"No one tells me anything about this Lola so I can't say anything either way, Boss," Storm said from the front seat.

"That's good bitch. Keep your eyes on the freeway," Tangles said, pretending malice.

"Here bitch," Storm said, raising her right middle finger high enough to be seen from the back seat. "Sit on it."

"I'll move to the passenger seat so you can do it, bitch."

"Enough," Letty said. "I can't hear myself think."

Storm laughed. "Hear yourself think. What is that?"

Letty and Tangles went on and on all the way home, background noise to my memories of Lola, lying on various hotel beds, under the mirrors of my bed at home, on my private conference table naked at the office. We'd done it every which way on that table, then I ordered a lunch which was served on the same table. Lola was daring, unpredictable and different. Olga was too. I was infatuated with both. They were powerful women. Strong women are a turn on for me.

Olga is strong, a loose cannon, and after being raised as a Camacho, I really didn't know when she'd go off. Camila Camacho had been gunning for Lola, and I never knew if Olga had been on board that train, or against it.

A federal agent had to be smart to get the job. Lola was a looker but looks don't get you that job. I had relatively little knowledge of Lola's role as a fed, except that she'd been assigned to watch the Camacho family. I know firsthand that she plays the part of a prostitute with convincing gusto. She lied to me, but her strength is a turn on.

Maybe I am just attracted to women who are no angels. Before Olga and Lola, I had been mesmerized by Sami and Melina. Both came across as proper ladies, but only if you got close to them did you discover that they walked on the wild side. Sami liked orgies. Melina would have sex on the fly if it helped her get her way, or to blow off steam. She'd slept with a sheriff for a gun license. More than once when Melina needed a credit line from her bank, she claimed to have laid the banker. She'd also wanted to put out a contract on her father's killer and paid the middleman with money and sex. I found out about it in time to squash the contract, saving her from being the target of blackmail. I almost married her, more than once.

Lola had faked her death. I wanted to know why. Was it a routine end to a federal undercover assignment? Was it to keep the Camachos from killing her? Was it to free her up so she could go after Camila Camacho?

As Valita predicted, Juan had not been detained or booked. It was not just that Juan got special treatment for being a private investigator and having friends in high places. Nina dropped the trespassing charges. Juan refused to file charges against her.

"She gave me back my cell and camera. The roll of film in the camera was gone, but I still have hundreds of pictures for you, Boss."

"I'm just grateful you are alive, my friend."

"She mentioned you, Boss."

"Oh?"

I had wondered if she might recognize Juan. She'd said many times that she'd been surveilling me for years. At one point in time in the past, she probably knew every friend I had, and everyone I ever worked with, and had dossiers on each one of them, with pictures and life stories.

"It was dark, and I doubt she got much of a look at me, but Boss, when she gave me back my phone, she said she knew you sent me. She didn't expect me to admit you sent me—and I didn't admit it. She said if you wanted to find out about her, why you didn't ask for yourself, in person, instead of...what did she call it... all this 007 shit? I told her I didn't know any Mario Luna. She called me a liar, and threatened to shoot me. Did you get the information packet I faxed with the first pictures? Her phone number is in there. I mailed to you, but I don't expect the package is there yet."

"Don't follow her again. I'll call her on that number you faxed me. The text worked great. Pictures don't come out well on fax. I will be on lookout for the mail. How are you set for cash? I might have more work to send you."

"Boss, you sent me too much money."

"Spend it in good health my friend. I will send you more."

"Boss, no, not necessary. I will be fine in another week."

I hung up the cell and pulled out the number I'd scribbled on the back of one of my cards. I looked at the card for a few minutes, thinking. Letty had asked a couple of times what I was going to do when I finally talked to Lola. I had no idea, but this would not be the first or the last time that I've had to wing a situation.

The girls had all gone out for salads for lunch. Now was as good a time as any to make contact without any helpful interference.

Why hadn't I just walked up to her and said, "Hi Lola. Glad you're not dead."

Or should I call her Nina? I just don't know.

I picked up the office phone and dialed Lola.

June 28, 1993 (Monday morning)
Puerto Rico
Lola

At five pm, I was on a bus headed to the Hard Rock Café. My cell rang.

"Yes."

"I guess you didn't die in Beverly Hills that afternoon."

My heart jumped to hear Mario's voice, even though I'd halfway been expecting him. After the private detective fiasco, I had figured he would call or show up at my door. I used to show up at his office without advance notice.

February 19, 1991, I had officially died in a Los Angeles parking lot. A lifetime ago. I've been here almost two and a half years.

"You should not talk on phones," I said. "If you want to see me, jump on a plane. You know where I am."

There was a moment of silence, though I could tell he was on the line. Then we were disconnected. I wasn't sure if it was a reception issue or if he hung up. He didn't call back.

At the Hard Rock, I had a burger at a table, then moved to the bar.

It was an early crowd, too soon for Miles. I was getting pretty good at detecting the difference between regular locals and tourists. Tourists were always an extreme, either way too dressed up, way too casual, or looking wiped out by the heat.

It was early in the evening, and families were sitting at the tables. I looked around the bar for likely candidates, and spotted an animal eyeing me. Animal was one of the overdressed tourists. Shoes, socks, business suit. His clothes didn't fit him that well. It looked like there were muscles under all those clothes. Most muscled men don't look good in suits unless they can afford really good tailors. I decided that he'd do for the night if his biceps passed the squeeze test. I let him catch me looking at him, stared straight at him over the rim of my wine glass as he gave me the once over.

Animal got up from the too-small table where he'd been sitting and brought his mixed drink with him. I watched him walk over. He had most of his hair and looked like he was in his thirties. He did not have a Latin look. Nothing on his walk over chased the name Animal from my head.

"Whiskey sour," he told the bartender, and shoved the glass in his direction along with a twenty.

Sebastian the bartender snatched the twenty, the glass, the cocktail napkin under it, and glanced at me to see if I wanted a refill of my white wine. I put my hand over my glass, and he gave me a nod, before he flamboyantly mixed the drink, presented it, with change on a small plastic tray sporting a Hard Rock Café logo.

Close up, Animal had too little stubble to pass for a beard, but too much to be called stubble. He put a bill in his pocket and shoved a five back to Sebastian.

He looked me over, and asked, "How much?"

Sebastian had moved a foot down the bar, and I saw his eyebrows raise at the question. He turned his back, and walked to the corner, giving us a degree of privacy. I felt like laughing, and, though the situation was completely different, it reminded of when I had played the hooker to get in good with Mario.

Anybody else would have been pissed off. I went along with it.

"Two hundred in your hotel room, but it can't be a dump. You get one shot for that."

He put his hand out. I checked out his hard bicep before I took his hand. We shook. He didn't try to squeeze my hand to death.

"You got a deal," he said. "Name's Duke. What's your name?"

I didn't hesitate. "Lola," I said.

He peeled off his clothes to advantage, but Duke only cared about Duke. He came twice. I charged him four hundred.

"Give me some time, and I can do it again," he said.

"No more rubbers. Only had those two. Sorry."

I took a shower before I left. I laughed all the way home. Took a taxi. Whoring is easy if you like to fuck. I'd done it for the hell of it, but it wasn't my thing.

When I was fucking Mario and getting paid for it, I loved it. But that was Mario.

I got home and soaked in the tub until the water got chilled. Whoring really isn't my thing. I guess I need to call the shots. It was still pretty early. At ten, I called Miles.

"This asshole left me hanging. Want to come over?"

"Long as I don't have to see a shotgun, Calamity Jane," he said.

I closed my eyes and fantasized it was Mario pumping into me. My imagination put me in the back seat of Mario's Rolls. Who the hell knows why? The car wasn't parked. Letty was driving. She was just window-dressing, not involved in the action, maybe because Letty was the one who had driven me home a couple times, after dates with Mario. But it was Miles in my body and Mario in my mind who made sure I had as many orgasms as I wanted.

Miles stayed the night. The air conditioning was set to freezing, and it felt good to snuggle next to a warm body. Miles was in my bed but not my heart.

I don't know if it was the phone call, the memories, the confrontation with the private eye, or the sex in my imagination that had me thinking so much about Mario. I'd thought I was over him. Mario and me, we'd been on the phone right before my car blew up. I had wanted to say goodbye to him, and I practically told him what was going on. Mario would show, eventually. I wondered if we would fuck or if he would be confrontational.

July 13, 1993 (Tuesday)
San Diego
Mario

As the taxi took me to the hotel, I remembered years ago, the team and I were here in San Diego working on a horrifying plane crash. It's bad enough when innocent victims are in the plane, and doubly horrifying when the victims include innocent people on the ground.

Fortunately, I'm not dealing with plane crashes any longer.

I had checked into the Taluka Lake Hotel, not intending to stay the night. When my plans changed, the front desk clerk upgraded me to a suite with far more room than I needed. I wasn't looking forward to eating alone.

I turned to the bellman for advice.

"I need a beautiful masseuse to come up and give me a massage. Any ideas?"

He knew some call girls. That wasn't what I wanted, so he provided a newspaper, and I picked someone out of the classified ads.

July 13, 1993 (Tuesday)
Pasadena
Letty

Boss went to San Diego to close an eight-plane deal with Budget-DiegoAir, an operator that was new to us and picking up speed in its growth. Boss never chased business outside his office. The agreement was all but set in stone, but the airline's board asked him to go over the deal at one of their meetings.

He called home to tell us about a change in plans. We took the call on the speaker phone in the upstairs office.

"The CEO got sick and asked me to hang around here for a meeting tomorrow. If you guys weren't so busy with your own clients, I would have asked you to come with me," he said. "Now I have to suffer through finding someone interested in having dinner with me."

"Some suffering," I said, laughing. "Any or all of us could drive over there in a flash."

"Next time," he said.

No doubt he had something lined up already. I'd have to get used to it again but that's the deal. I'm as free as he is. That's the deal, too.

With Boss not at home, Tangles and I told Emma to fix whatever she wanted. The sky was the limit. She surprised us with plates of pork chops smothered in mango sauce, brown rice with pine nuts, a large bowl of guacamole, and homemade tortilla chips still warm to touch. She brought us two pitchers of Tamarindo water to drink.

"You can spike it with hard liquor," Emma said.

"It's perfect. Tamarindo is a treat. Thank you," I said.

Storm was first to bite into the oversized pork chop on her plate. Her eyes practically rolled back in her head.

I laughed at her reaction. "Pixie would be screaming, 'I'm coming.'" I looked at Tangles and pointed my fork toward Storm whose eyes were closed, with a sexual look on her face. "That was definitely an orgasm." I carved and took a bite. "Mmmm."

Tangles scooped a hefty amount of guacamole on her side plate and started eating the green stuff with chips. She used her teaspoon to move the mango sauce around the pork chop and cut the meat into smaller and smaller bits.

"You aren't eating the chop?" Storm asked. "It's delicious."

"I don't eat most pork or lamb. No reason why."

"I can tell Emma to make you something else," Storm said, getting up.

"Sit," Tangles said. "I'm totally okay with this. The mango stuff is to die for." She scooped it on a chip and crunched happily.

I coughed hard when Tangles lit the joint and passed it to me. I passed it on to Storm.

"You don't want it?"

"I think I'm coming down with something," I lied. "No reason you need to hold back though."

My offer to have Mario's baby is probably forgotten by now. His mind has moved on to another problem like how to approach Lola and when. I meant it when I offered and I'll do it, if it happens. If it happens, it will be a baby raised by nannies because its parents are too busy. It hadn't seemed to hurt Lainie.

"Did you ever have another guy on a bed with Boss?" Storm asked.

"You were with him over six months. Did he ever have a guy there with you?" Tangles asked, being a sarcastic ass.

"No way. Just asking. Sorry." Storm looked worried for about five seconds.

"Storm, you don't need to be sorry about anything you say. Got it?" I said. "I've been with Boss for years. Never another guy on his bed."

"Right," Tangles said, pointing at me. "What Letty said."

"Did you ever tell him you wanted another guy in the bed?" Storm asked.

"I never wanted another guy on the bed, but that's a good point. I never asked," I said, looking from Storm to Tangles.

"No, I never mentioned it," Tangles said. "I came close to asking before. I personally never heard anyone mention it, and I sure as hell am not bringing it up."

"You done it with more than one dude at a time?" I asked Storm.

"Uh-huh." Storm took a drag and passed it on. "Uh-huh," she repeated.

"Did you dig it?" I asked.

Storm exhaled some smoke, smiled, and said, "Uh-huh."

Tangles was focused on Storm, looking at her closely. She ran a hand over her hair, smoothing back the bangs that had fallen over her eyes. "Storm, you so gorgeous."

Storm giggled. "Thanks, Tangles. You so gorgeous, too."

"You two are going to make me jealous," I teased them.

Tangles flung her arms around me and said, "Join us, and I'll make you come first!"

"Give me a hit of that joint," I said, snatching it from Tangles. I took a deep drag and held for long time.

"What were we talking about?" Storm asked. I knew she couldn't be that high. We smoked too much to get smacked with half a joint.

"Boss," I said. "We were talking about Boss."

Storm remembered. "About Boss. About Mario Luna allowing a dude on his bed."

Tangles said, "I like threesomes. Two on one." She pointed at me. "You know it." She looked from me to Storm. "We had a couple of three-somes when we were sharing our apartment."

At the apartment, Tangles had talked me into it twice. Tangles and me and our dates had smoked a lot, squeezed into Tangles's bed, and traded guys on one date. The next time it happened, it was the same guys. Her date fucked me while Tangles kissed him and me. Then my date fucked her, while I returned the favor. That night we tried the two guys one girl thing, too. I watched while they did it to Tangles, then she watched while they did it to me. It was hot because we were so high it was like a dream. The guys wanted a repeat engagement, but I passed.

Storm wasn't shocked. "Back in massage school, I worked three or four orgies. It was a fucking mad house. I mean, I was hired to do massages, but...." Her voice faded away. She had a wicked smile on her face.

"Was it good?" Tangles asked. "They wanted you to jump in the dog pile?" She laughed at her own joke.

"It was good," Storm said.

"That's before this AIDS shit, I bet," I said.

"I don't remember exactly when it was, but you are right that I wouldn't do it now."

"How about with rubbers?" Tangles asked.

Storm laughed. "How do rubbers work in an orgy?"

"Boss went to orgies in London with Sami. Pixie and him, they went to local ones, too,"

"He told you?" Storm asked.

I nodded. Before Olga, he used to tell me everything.

"Rubbers kill the fun," Tangles said.

"Mario Luna is never going to have a man in his bed," I said.

"You never know unless you ask."

"No way," Tangles said. "He's a one man show."

I liked the freedom and the control I had after I moved out, but if there's anything I learned from that whole experience, it was that I want Mario. I want to be near him, to live under his roof, even if I can't have him for myself alone.

Being with Mario means keeping the option open if I want to fuck someone else, but I'm not fooling myself. Mario is my home.

July 13, 1993 (Tuesday evening)
San Diego
Mario

Maggie the massage therapist wasn't beautiful or even that good with her hands, but she showed up at my door promptly with her portable table and everything in a rolling bag. It took her five minutes to set up, linens, oil, the whole shebang. She did not remove her sweats during the massage. Her body was okay. She wasn't a raving beauty, but she couldn't be more than thirty and when she smiled, I saw pretty teeth. She didn't smile or talk much. For a while, I watched her during the massage. No makeup, light green eyes. Her hair was dark and cut boyishly short. Her lips were narrow, her eyebrows and lashes weren't noticeable. Something about her reminded me of someone. I laughed aloud when I realized who it was, then finally shut my eyes.

"Sorry," she said. "Are you ticklish?"

"No, just you remind me of someone."

"Okay," she said.

I shut my eyes. I thought it best not to tell her she reminded me of Archie Bunker.

When my ninety minutes were up, I pulled on a t-shirt and briefs, then handed her a hundred for the massage, and twenty for a tip.

"I'm tired," I said. "The massage made me sleepy. I think I'll turn in. Thanks for the massage. It was great."

Maggie was standing there with her table folded up, ready to leave.

"Are you sure you don't need anything else?"

"What will a hundred do for me?" I said like a fool, figuring I'd give her another hundred.

"A hundred will do," she said. "What do you want for it?"

My instincts were that she was pushing too hard. It just didn't feel right.

"A fast fuck?" I asked. I felt like I was making a joke, but she was egging me on. Maybe she really needed that next hundred.

This so-called therapist, a least a foot shorter than me, arrested me for soliciting an act of prostitution. I emptied my pockets. My personal belongings, money, wallet, credit cards, watch, and gold religious medal were put in a plastic bag. She had me cuffed with my hands behind me and standing there like a dummy. Two plainclothes cops walked in and waved their IDs. They were vice. They uncuffed me long enough to put my jeans on.

What a sucker I was. Stupid dumb sucker.

"We were just talking," I said. "It was conversation. Why did you spend ninety minutes giving me a massage then spring this shit on me? At the very least, you should give me that tip back."

I got the silent treatment.

"It was a nothing massage," I said.

"What you better do is shut up," Maggie said, like it was a threat.

I wasn't experienced in this type of case, but I was talking away. Rarely am I at a loss for words. Then I was in a patrol car in the back seat, my head touching the patrol car's roof, and still talking away. The cops ignored me. One of them called me a real chatterbox, and I shut up.

The holding cell—they called it the bullpen—already had eleven males and no seating. By then, I wasn't talking. The only place to sit was the floor. A payphone was in the cell too, and a guy was on it. An operator assisted in placing collect calls only, but I got pulled before I could make a call to Jack Fino.

I was taken out of the bullpen and waited behind four or five other studs to get mug shot and fingerprinted. It was the second time in my life that I'd been arrested. The first time around, I was already working for a lawyer, was barely an adult, had pled guilty to a tax charge, and though the judge technically sent me to federal prison, I had only been locked up for something like a week, and the arrest ended up getting me a raise, and a position with another lawyer. Everyone who knew me well had heard that story. That arrest on my record prevented me from having a gun permit like the girls. Not that the lack of a gun matters much to me. I have martial arts. I don't need a gun.

A story for another day.

"Your bail is $1,000," the officer told me.

"I have that much in my personal property," I said, feeling some excitement.

"You look sober," the officer said.

"I haven't had a drink," I said. "I'm sober as a judge."

I walked out of the San Diego Police Department an hour later with a signed promise to appear in court on the charge Maggie shoved up my ass. I had thirty days to figure that out.

A block from the jail, I caught a taxi to Talukagate.

The front desk said I had been checked out. Their policy was to boot out anyone who got arrested at the hotel.

I figured I'd have my day in court with them. I wasn't going to duke it out with a flunkey at the front desk. I got my small bag from my friend the bell captain who seemed as upset as I was that the police had hauled me off.

I got in a taxi and asked the cabby to take me to some five star hotel close by. I ended up on the top floor of the Marriott. It was not close, nor was it convenient to my business with BudgetDiegoAir, but at least it was on the beach and I was in the penthouse.

Fuck, what a mess.

It was after midnight when I called Letty and told her what had happened.

"I'll drive right over," Letty said.

"No, I'm going to bed. I have that meeting at ten tomorrow morning. I'm sorry to wake you. I just needed to tell someone about how stupid I was."

"I wasn't asleep," Letty said, "but of course you can call me any time. Sounds like entrapment. I've heard that in the movies."

"I know what it is, but it's complicated. I'll ask Jack Fino to take the case."

I should have called him and not Letty. Jack was the solution to the problem, but it was Letty I wanted to talk to.

"Tomorrow is another day, Mario. I'm sorry this happened. Now you have a record."

"Baby, I had a record all of my adult life."

"Boss, I bet that juvenile thing was expunged," Letty argued.

I don't know if she'd picked up the terminology from the movies, or from the work we used to do for lawyers. "Why do you use your energy to go back and forth? It's not worth—"

"You're right, Boss," Letty said. "It's late, and I don't want to distract you from what business you've got tomorrow with BudgetDiegoAir."

I hung up, and then took an hour pampering myself, trying to relax in the posh suite. Hotels are great, but I'm not in love with being alone. I thought it would take me forever to fall asleep, but I lay there in a familiar situation. I've gone to sleep in thousands of hotel rooms, listening to the distant muffled noises, the hum of the hotel's air conditioning system. I dropped off easily to a dreamless night.

I checked out of the Marriot that morning, left my carry-on in the SUV. My hired driver got me to the board meeting ten minutes early. We were on the 20th floor. In San Diego, that's considered high. Sixteen people and I sat around a huge oval table. I faced a wall of windows that provided a sweeping city view. The room wasn't much larger than the table, but at my back, the wall separating this room from the reception area was glass and made everything feel more spacious. The uncarpeted office space in this new building was spotless and as no-frills as the airline itself but didn't come off as cheap. I had been escorted straight to this room, bypassing the hard modular seating in the reception area that looked uncomfortable and modern.

I hadn't seen the CEO, Liam Lopez, in person, but Storm had compiled magazine and newspaper articles on him, so I recognized him as the medium-tall guy standing by the head of the table. I knew a few things about him and his airline. He was a former military pilot turned commercial pilot. He had told an interviewer that he couldn't find an airline he enjoyed working for, so he'd decided to start one himself. Nothing is ever that simple though. Letty's research revealed that he'd married money, which had gotten him some initial financial backing. The airline's hub was in San Diego, and it flew short no-frill hops. He also had some kind of hiring/profit-sharing arrangement with military pilots coming off of active duty.

Liam walked over to me. He was tall, but a few inches shorter than I am. We introduced ourselves and shook hands. Firm handshake. Warm brown eyes. Deep laugh lines around his mouth. He still had a military haircut, as did most of the people around the table.

"This is a big deal for us," Liam said, in a hoarse, cracking voice. Still standing, he drank from a teacup beside his chair. The receptionist must have been watching and immediately came in with a fresh cup of tea for him. She asked if anyone needed anything. No one did. A pitcher and a tray of a dozen or so glasses sat unused in the center of the table.

Liam took his seat at one end of the table. "We thank you for coming here, Mario."

"It's a pleasure being here," I said. "Let me know what questions you have for me."

All of the people around the table had name plates in front of them, and they all appeared to be vice presidents of various divisions. I wondered if having so many people on a board made agreements difficult. I wondered how many board members Olga had now that she was public.

"We've all read the lease agreement, and we're in," a woman, Cathy Echo, said. She had a military look. I wondered if all of the people around the table were pilots who had bought into the company. They all looked as vital and fit as you would expect ex military to be.

Liam coughed. I noticed that his face was flushed. He used a tissue and tossed it in the trash. Clearly, he had not been exaggerating when he'd claimed to be sick the day before. "We wanted to meet you in person, Mario Luna, and for you to meet us. The contracts are signed and sealed for you to take back with you."

I smiled. I got up and walked around the table to shake hands with everyone there. Afterwards, we went into a bigger room where a breakfast buffet had been catered. I ate, talked, and made friends with everyone there. I didn't mention my arrest the night before. At the close of breakfast, I exchanged cards, made my goodbyes, and gave my driver a call. He was waiting for me curbside.

"Airport," I said as I got in the car.

I dialed Andrea on her cell.

"I have everything signed. Done deal."

"Congratulations, Boss."

"I didn't do it alone," I said.

"You did. Don't be shy."

"Andrea, fix it so I fly to Puerto Rico from here. I'll be there for twenty-four hours then head back to LA."

"Are you flying alone?"

"Yep. Same way I got here."

I could tell she didn't know about my arrest. Letty was not a snitch, but she wouldn't consider telling Tangles to be snitching.

On the way to the airport, I called Letty on her cell.

"Are you okay?" she asked urgently.

"How did you know it was me?"

"Just." She heaved a sigh.

I thought I heard a quiver in her voice.

"I'm good." I said. "Listen, I got everything signed. Andrea juggled my flight plan. I'm headed to Puerto Rico for a day."

"Aw. I thought you were going to take me," she said.

I didn't know if I should take her seriously or not. Letty was strong. She was always sensitive to me but never touchy or demanding.

"It's a fast trip," I said. Thinking of Juan, I said, "Who knows? She may come out with guns blazing."

"Exactly why I should go. I can outgun her. Plus, I'm a woman. I can kick the shit out of her, and you won't."

She surprised a real belly laugh out of me, and I heard Letty laughing on her end.

"I miss you," she said softly, laughter still in her voice.

"I always miss you," I said. "Do you really want to leave whatever you have on your desk and fly with me?"

"There's nothing on my desk that Tangles can't handle. Pick me up, yes?"

"Baby, I do love you," I said. "Though I'm pretty sure you won't be needed to beat Lola's ass. You're coming because you're you, not because I need a security detail."

I heard a sniff.

"Tell Andrea I'm headed to LA to pick you up, and from there it's you and me to Puerto Rico."

"Thank you, Boss." She sniffed again.

Lola was going to be surprised not only to see me but to see me with Letty along. Fuck Lola. She has some explaining to do.

Ontario Airport is about 35 miles from Los Angeles and about under an hour from San Diego. It's up and right down, and we beat Letty. While we waited on the tarmac, the pilots did a walk around the plane, topped off the fuel tanks and did whatever they needed before we took off for San Juan. I spent the time on the phone over coffee. From the window where I was sitting, I saw a Ferrari pull up—Tangles delivering Letty. In the plane, I gave them both a bear hug. I felt a connection with Letty as I inhaled her scent. I felt the weight of her purse when we hugged. She was packing heavy. She put her purse on a seat, then kisses among the three of us went on as though I'd been gone for months. Our personal attendant for the flight, Lucia, walked toward the cockpit, leaving us alone.

"Have a blessed trip," Tangles said, kissing Letty and me goodbye. "I don't trust Lola bitch, Boss. I'm happy Letty's going to be there to watch your back."

Letty and I settled in the plane. I noticed she was in office clothes, and uncomfortable shoes. I reached down and slipped off her shoe.

"Where's your bag?"

"I didn't bring one," she said, pulling off her other shoe. "It would have taken too long to go back to the house."

"You need to buy clothes when we hit San Juan," I said. "I have this suit I'm wearing and jeans in the bag. We both need clothes."

"We can shop before we go find her," Letty said.

Thanks to the seat configuration, she was able to straddle my lap.

"Thanks for going out of your way to come and get me," she said. "It means so much to me. I have about seven hours to make it worth your while." She giggled, but there was more than laughter in her eyes.

It was at that very minute that I knew I wanted to spend the rest of my life with Letty.

"Boss, Miss Letty, wheels up in eleven minutes. Please fasten your seat belts."

Lucia checked us over, got us glasses of red wine and walked to the front of the plane to take her seat with the other flight attendant, Susan. We had three in the cockpit: two captains and one first officer.

Letty and I sat across from each other, a window for each of us and a table to share.

"Did Andrea ask what you had going in Puerto Rico?"

She didn't ask," I said.

"I know you love her, and I love her, too. She's done so much for me, but...."

"...but she's Olga's girl."

"Roger that," Letty said.

The cabin lights dimmed. We clicked glasses as the plane accelerated on the runway. An hour out, we showered together and put on the LAI designer robes. "I was suffocating in the suit," I said.

"You wear a suit every day."

"I know, but not on the plane."

Susan and Lucia were preparing to serve dinner.

Letty ignored them.

"I got a pussy just waiting for you," Letty said, licking her lips.

I played along.

"Should we hold dinner?"

Letty waited a second then looked up at Lucia.

"Hold our dinner till later, please."

We practically ran to the bedroom.

Letty's moans stroked my libido, from mews like a kitten to shrieks, even when all I did was turn her on her side. I just spooned her. I wasn't even inside her yet. I was confident the engine noise would drown out the noise we were making thrashing around on the bed. She writhed against me.

"You're the best," Letty moaned.

Her comment reminded me that she was comparing me to others and made me uncomfortable.

"Mario, harder, please," she begged. "I'm so hot, I'm on fire."

I brought her to a screaming completion twice before we broke apart for dinner, and the hour long stop in Miami.

Twenty-four hours ago, I went to jail for soliciting sex. If the masseuse had taken the second hundred and provided the fast fuck I had technically asked for, would I have fucked her? Yes, probably I would have. That makes two cops who have visited my life impersonating hookers.

We landed in San Juan at four-thirty in the morning. Letty and I were asleep when the pilots taxied to a hangar that rents by the day, asleep as ground crew hooked us up to local power. The customs officer did not come aboard till six a.m. By then, we had showered and dressed and were having coffee. As he stamped our passports, Lucia directed a catering delivery guy where to put supplies, and then I sent the flight crew to sleep at a hotel nearby. The door to the plane was closed and locked, the plane stairs in place.

The second that we were alone on the plane, Letty dropped her robe.

In her lingerie and a GAL steward's cap she found in the galley, she poured me seconds of coffee and gave me some kind of soft Puerto Rican sweet roll with powdered sugar on it.

"Would you care for cream and sugar Mr. Luna?" she asked.

I played along. "No thanks, Miss."

"Call me Lucia," Letty said, giggling.

"Have a seat and join me, Lucia," I said, patting the seat beside me. Letty sat, and automatically started buttering my bread.

I dialed Juan on my cell.

"Juan, I'm here for one day to meet with Lola. I prefer we meet in a public place."

"Boss, when I was watching her, she went out every night to a bar or a night club. I can check on her and let you know where she goes, usually before nine in the evening."

"You can't let her see you," I said.

"Boss, she never caught me following her. She caught me with my camera filming her through the window while she was having sex."

"If you need me, I'll be on the plane," I said.

Letty heard that and shook her head. She was hanging close so she could hear what Juan was saying.

"We need some clothes," Letty said.

"Who is that, Boss?"

"Letty is with me."

"Hi Juan," Letty said, waving as if he could see her in her mint green lace bra, and GAL steward cap. "Hugs to you and Valita."

"Thank you," Juan said. "Okay, Boss, I call you when I confirm she's at home, and call you when she's out of the house."

I hung up and wiped a smudge of powdered sugar off of Letty's lip with my forefinger. She caught me by the wrist and licked the sugar off me too.

I finished my sweet roll.

Letty said, "Why not call Lola and meet her at a restaurant or something? If she catches Juan again, she may kill him this time."

I laughed a little. "She won't catch him, and she's not going to kill him. She knows now that he's working for me."

I felt a yawn coming on, and there was no suppressing it.

"Let's go kick it in bed," I said, "I can use a catnap. If we sleep till noon, we can get in eight hours of shopping before Lola goes to the bar."

She giggled. "You just want to fuck me. Admit it."

"Okay, I admit it," I said.

I picked her up, slung her over my shoulder which made her giggle,, and made a mad run for the bedroom. Letty and I had been bed partners for years, lived together in the same house for years, and there is still this fire between us.

I never tire of her.

"This is just like camping," I said.

"I never went camping but always wanted to," Letty said as we lay beside each other, face to face.

"This is a big motorhome, parked on the tarmac. I hope a bear doesn't break in while we are doing it."

She giggled and hit my chest with her fist.

"Don't ruin the picture with a mean bear."

"Don't worry. It's a nice bear."

We laughed, and before either of us realized it, we zonked out.

Around noon, Juan confirmed that Lola was at home. I warned him again to be careful, and he promised not to stand at her window with a camera in broad daylight.

Letty called the car service we'd used years ago, and we left our make-believe camper where we'd been for hours. We stepped out into a blast of overwhelming humidity. Inside the hanger, we thought it was hot, until we stood in direct sunlight. A white Suburban pulled up to the hangar.

I was wearing the same heavy jeans and plain t-shirt I had gone to jail in. Letty wore a short-sleeved flowered blouse, her suit skirt and heels.

The driver got out to help us in.

"Our first stop is going to be a store where we can buy shorts for both of us," I said to the driver. Some services send drivers in uniform, but our shaggy-headed driver was in Puerto Rico casual: jeans, old tennis shoes, and a company t-shirt. He had a plastic tag pinned on his shirt that said 'Manolito.'

He looked past us and peered into the hanger we'd left, and his eyes got big.

"Wow, is that your plane back there?"

Letty ignored him. "Take us to Calle Loiza. We can get everything we need there."

We settled into the white Suburban's cool white interior. The driver returned to the wheel and put the vehicle in gear. Fortunately, the air conditioning was going full blast.

"Calle Loiza it is," he said. "Good choice. You been there before?"

"Yes," Letty replied. She looked at me. "Pixie and I shopped there before. So many shops."

"Yeah, I been there," I said. "I don't remember buying anything. Right now, I just need something for the day."

"Ditto," she said.

I stretched out and she laughed at me. "Look how you're sitting."

"I love these cars. Plenty of room for me to stretch my legs," I said. The seat in front of me was folded down and I drew my legs over it like an ottoman.

We shopped quickly. Within half an hour, our clothes were in a bag in the back of the Suburban, and we were in appropriate clothes. That didn't improve the weather.

"It's the humidity I have trouble with," I said, thankful I was not going to be spending weeks here on a case.

"I don't like it, but I can handle it," Letty said.

We stopped in a crowded little shop that boasted homemade gelato, took our place in line, and ordered a couple of cokes. The tiny shop was wall-papered with sprinkles and had a clashing industrial-style carpeting on the floor. There were no tables inside, and just a few seats near the window which is where we sat, but the air conditioning was splendid. We sipped our drinks and watched the steady stream of shoppers ordering frozen treats. A few went to the wooden benches outside, but most of them continued down the side-walk. I was soon bored with people-watching. It was going to be a long day if we were going to wait for Juan to give us an update on when Lola would be heading for the bars.

"I'm just going to call her," I said. "Fuck waiting."

Letty beamed. "About time."

I had already added her number to my cell phone book.

"Here goes nothing," I said.

I pressed her number and dialed.

Four rings.

Five rings.

She picked up.

"I have a feeling this is Mario Luna," she said.

"Once a cop, always a cop," I said.

"Did you get that line from a movie?"

"Probably."

"Are you in Puerto Rico?"

"I'm here with Letty. Leaving tonight. I want to talk."

"Why Letty?"

I ignored the question.

"Should we come over? Or do you prefer a particular location?"

"One hour from now, at the Hilton," Lola said. "There's a bar in the lobby."

"See you there," I said. "At the bar at the Hilton," I said aloud, for Letty's benefit, and hung up.

We arrived forty-five minutes later. Lola was already there in shorts and half of a shirt, no more dressed up than we were. Still, she looked great. She saw us walking in and pointed at a table off in the corner. She got up from her barstool and walked toward the corner. Letty ordered a carafe of iced sangria and three glasses from a passing waiter, and we arrived at the table around the same time. Lola opened her arms to hug both of us. We all exchanged light hugs and kisses on each cheek before sitting down.

"We watched the smoke of the explosion on television as it happened," Letty said. "Mario had just been talking to you, and when your call cut off, he believed you were the victim. I felt horrible. I figured the Camachos had gotten to you. I was pissed off because I thought they had done it. I see you now and I'm pissed, not that you aren't dead, but that you played me."

Lola said soberly, "I only remember you wanted me to bathe in bleach water to kill my cooties. I didn't believe you would care if I lived or died."

"Like Letty, I figured Camila and Olga had gotten to you and I felt guilty," I said. "I was a little uncertain because you had mentioned a rented car, and it was your car that blew up. I did hang on to a little hope that you had survived, but I don't think I said it aloud to anyone. It was a bad time for me."

Letty looked at me, surprise on her face.

Lola smiled.

"Were you crushed because you had just spent two days in bed with me at the Beverly Hills Hotel and you had fallen in love with me?" Lola said to me, a smile on her face. "I was sure infatuated with you."

"You're making fun, bitch," Letty said.

"Half the women in LA county are infatuated with your precious boss. Listen kid, not sure why he brought you, but keep your trap shut like a good girl," Lola said.

Letty sprang halfway across the table and slapped Lola, a loud smack that swept Lola off her seat and on to the floor.

I got out of my chair to help Lola up, but she was on her feet before I reached her. It had happened quickly, and no one in the bar had paid any attention except the waiter who was heading in our direction with sangria and three glasses. He put on a poker face and had the good sense to say nothing as he put icy glasses on the table. I handed him a couple of bills, waved him away, and we all sat down.

"Do that again and there'll be bloodshed," Lola said.

Letty and Tangles smack each other like that all the time and nothing happens because they are so fit, and accustomed to being punched when working out. I thought Lola took that slap well. Lola had probably had some kind of martial training though she neither jumped into action nor avoided the slap. She'd been a federal agent, and they are tough.

Letty poured herself some sangria, and put her hand was on the stem of the wine glass, spinning it. Letty could be hard as nails, but I'd never seen her do anything like this to anyone but Tangles. Her years of training include self-control. She had certainly showed no restraint when she slapped Lola.

"This is not why we came here," I said, looking at Letty. She was smirking.

She took a sip of sangria and nodded. She stood up.

"I'll go walk around. Call me when you are done," Letty said, taking her glass and the sangria carafe with her.

"Let's have a drink, Lola, and talk this out," I said.

Lola had a mirror out of her purse and was checking her face. She nodded curtly. There we were, the two of us alone at the table. The waiter returned.

"What can I get you?"

"A bottle of Santa Margarita, white," I said to the waiter.

"Right away, sir." He headed off, passing Letty sitting at the bar, her back to us.

I reached over and touched Lola's hand that was holding the mirror.

"There's no bruise. How do you expect Letty to act when she's been living with the lie that you were dead? She walked you out of my house with that million dollars and next thing she heard was that you died in a car explosion. She was as upset over your supposed death as I was."

"Fuck Letty and fuck you. What is it you want? I clearly stepped out of your life. I've been living here minding my own business, not bothering you or your clan. Why would you send a snoop to watch me?"

"I was here not long ago and saw you living and breathing. I should have walked up to you then and saved us all the drama, but I didn't know the circumstances. I had to find out what was going on before I came up to you. I made a mistake not doing that. I'm sorry."

"You weren't looking for me?"

"Absolutely not. I figured you were dead. If I hadn't seen you sitting at the bar that afternoon, I would still be thinking you were dead."

That seemed to cool Lola's jets just a bit.

The waiter arrived with the bottle and opened it. I waved off the tasting, and he poured us each a glass. I took a long drink. A second later, Lola did too.

"That cocksucker Letty has always had it in for me," she said in an angry voice.

"She didn't have it in for you when we thought you got killed that afternoon. And neither did Tangles."

"Slapping me like that. I should have shot her."

I swallowed more wine and chuckled. "You tried pulling a gun on her at my house, and she took it away from you before you knew what happened."

"Did you come to San Juan to talk about Letty?" she snapped.

"I gave you a million on your promise that you would never bother Camila or Olga again, and no harm would come to them by you or yours."

"Is that what I promised?" she said, a smart ass again. She poured more wine in her glass.

"I have a video of that conversation," I said.

"I should have known. I have a video or two of you and me fucking at the Beverly Hills Hotel," she said crisply. I didn't think she was drunk. Just very, very angry.

I knew it was stupid, but I had decided days ago to ask her straight out. "Did you have anything to do with Camila getting killed?"

She made no pretense that she was unaware of Camila's death.

"Fuck no. I was nowhere near Mexico City."

"Your death made you innocent of Camila's murder—until it turned out you're alive. When I saw you were alive, first thing that came to my mind was that you had it done," I said.

She sat back in the chair, shaking her head. "I don't murder people. Remember, I'm not the criminal."

"You threatened to do so if you didn't get compensated."

She leaned forward again, taking a sip of wine. "You have a video of that too?"

"Maybe I do, maybe I don't."

"If I did murder her or have her done, how stupid would I be to tell you, huh?"

"I've been reading people for decades. It was part of my training in martial arts. I'm pretty damn good at it. I asked you to see your reaction."

She chuckled softly, not a lot. "Did I pass?"

"You are practiced at deception. I can't say for sure. If I find out you had anything to do with her murder, you will not be happy." I was not kidding.

"Are you going to shoot me or beat me to death?"

"Lola, I gave you a million dollars of Camacho money. I told Camila and Olga that I believed you when you said your focus on them would end if they gave you that payment you demanded."

She nodded. "I had nothing to do with it. Go ask Olga, your fiancée."

She stared at me, her eyes dark and angry. She looked like she was telling the truth, like she believed every word she was saying. I looked down at the shining wine. Lola's image was reflected there, strangely bent. I took a sip, and the image of her fragmented and disappeared as I moved the glass and returned when I set it on the table.

"Is this one of your tell-all confessions?" I asked. "Like in the past when you said Pepe was my stalker?"

"Mario, you are an ungrateful bastard. Everything I told you is true. Pepe had your house burned the first time and had that asshole following you around and making your life miserable. Pepe was a sly bastard, always a step ahead of you."

I poured the last of the wine equally between our glasses. "Why should I ask Olga?"

"I bet you never put the question to her, did you?"

Lola was right.

I nodded. "Olga would not have killed Camila," I said.

She laughed softly, drank the last of what was in her glass, and stared at me. "If I were an agent investigating Camila's murder, the first suspect on the list would be Olga. If I were an agent on Pepe's murder, my first suspect on the list would be either Camila or Olga."

I knew details Lola didn't. I knew that Pepe had raped Olga more than once. Olga told me there were times when it was consensual. I doubt that even the FBI had dug up that fact. I had been in Paris with Olga and Camila when Pepe's plane blew up, so I knew neither of them had been on the scene when he died. Both Olga and Camila had been undone by the news of his death, or at least had convincingly appeared that way. Later, when I'd learned of the abuse, it gave me a rationale to excuse his murderer, whoever it was. Olga had assured me once that she was very certain that Pepe was dead. Her very certainty had been so chilling that I had managed to dismiss it from my mind. Sure, it was possible that she hired someone to do away with Pepe, but I could not imagine that she had killed Camila. Why would she? She already had more money than she could spend in a dozen lifetimes. I stared at the distorted image of Lola in my empty glass, then leaned forward and stared into her eyes. She leaned forward too, close enough that I could see candlelight reflecting in her eyes and feel her breath on my cheek.

"Why did you put on that show about getting killed?"

"It was my exit, my retirement."

"Just like that?"

"Yeah, just like that."

I reached across the table and touched her hand. "I'm glad you aren't dead."

At my touch, she shivered and closed her eyes. When she opened them again, her face was expressionless. "Thanks. I'm glad to be alive, too. Forget I'm here. I don't want to hurt or kill anyone who may come gunning for me. You understand that?"

"No one knows you are here. The PI is a good friend. I've known him for years. He's not going to say anything. Letty is not a snitch. And neither am I."

I got up. Lola remained seated.

"The other day I charged this guy four hundred big ones. Can I interest you in a quickie upstairs here in the hotel? Free of charge."

I looked at her, smiled, and shook my head. "Tempting, but I got a plane to catch."

"If you ever get the itch to see me, fly over here. Don't call. And don't bring that bitch with you."

"I got it," I said.

I leaned down. She looked up. Expressions flitted across her face. I saw no anger there any longer, no deceit. There was some mischief, and perhaps, a bit of sadness. I kissed her lips.

"Next time you are with your fiancée, ask her if she put Pepe and Camila six feet under. You know we investigators always follow the money." A grin sneaked across her face. "She's a billionaire now. Look how far she's come. Who else profited from Camila's death?"

Letty's seat at the bar was empty. I walked out into the hotel lobby and dialed Letty.

"Where are you?" I asked.

I heard a giggle. "I'm in a room getting laid by a dude that's almost as huge as you. I figured Lola would take you up to a room, so I picked me up this heavy."

Before I said anything stupid, I was poked in my lower back.

I turned and there was Letty, all smiles.

"Fooled you." She laughed.

I felt like picking her up and swinging her around, but the lobby was full of people. I had a sudden memory of Sami meeting me at Heathrow in London. I would pick her up and swing her around as she laughed away, people staring at us.

Fuck people.

I swooped Letty off her feet, and swung her around and around, till the room was a blur of lights and sound, and she laughed and clung to my neck.

"What do you say we go home?" I asked.

It took two hours before we went wheels up. The crew got snarled up in a traffic mess on the way to the airport, then we waited for catering to be delivered. Letty and I passed the wait talking on the big bed, a muted movie playing in the background.

"After you slapped her, she could have performed a citizen's arrest for assault and battery. You surprised me," I said.

"I'm sorry I did it in front of you, but I'm not sorry I did it. Besides, a blackmailer is not going to pull that shit on a law-abiding citizen like me." She giggled.

"Who knows what a blackmailer would do? But she's a cop. Letty, you know better. She's still a former cop. Don't do that to anyone who doesn't have it coming."

"She had it coming." Letty cuddled up to me. "Don't be mad at me."

The movie lit the space we were in. I spooned her, looking at Letty's bare back in the play of light coming off of the television. "I'm not mad at you. And what I saw is not you."

She moved up close and turned on her side to face me again.

"Okay, this sorry is for reals. I'll even call her and apologize. I can do it right now before we take off."

"She doesn't need to hear you apologize. She doesn't want phone calls from now on."

"From now on? Does that mean there's a plan in place to continue seeing her? Just a question."

"No such plan," I said.

The catering was worth the wait. In the air, our flight attendant served us steaming hot empanadas in the main cabin, where we were sitting across from each other as usual. We ate ground beef, crabmeat, chicken, fish. We passed on the octopus and conch. We drank a pitcher of lemonade and asked for a second one.

"I guess we won't have dinner in Miami," I said.

"That's for sure. We can go to South Beach and walk this off," Letty said.

"It's a hectic drive, but I'll do it if you want."

"Nah, let's head for home," she said.

The minute the dishes were cleared, I put my legs up on the table between us. Letty, still in her seat, massaged my stockinged feet.

"That feels good," I said. "Do you want me to return the favor?"

"I'm good," Letty said, poking one slipper-clad foot in the air and sneaking it back under the table. "What I really want is to know if you are going to tell me what you talked about? Or is it a secret?"

"I asked her if she had anything to do with Camila's murder."

"Did you expect a confession, Boss?"

"Hey, I like it when you call me Mario."

"Mario doesn't boss me around. Mario and I are equals. You just lay down the law about Lola, so Boss it is," she said, still working my feet.

I laughed. As if Letty had a submissive bone in her body. I told her everything.

"Please tell me you are not going to have this conversation with Olga about whether she killed Camila and Pepe," Letty said softly, worry creasing her forehead.

"That would be an awkward conversation. I don't think it will happen. I bought Lola's reaction that she had nothing to do with Camila's death. I weighed how misleading Lola can be, but she's not on the job any longer. I believe she is not lying. I think she had nothing to do with it."

"You were worried about your promise to Camila and Olga. Whether or not the compensation they paid at your recommendation actually did neutralize Lola as a threat," Letty said. "That means you are off the hook."

"You're right," I said.

"Now Pepe's death is in the picture again. Let someone else worry about who killed Camila and Pepe. Boss, stay out of it."

I smiled at Letty.

"What?"

"You were never this wordy before."

"Do you hate me to be wordy?"

"Wordy or not, Letty, I don't want to lose you. I know I'm being selfish."

Letty blushed. "You are never going to lose me. I love you way too much."

Full as we were, going to bed was not an option. Letty popped a DVD in the main cabin player and the picture appeared on the television.

We shared half a joint and mellowed out. No booze.

"If I hadn't been with you, would you have fucked her?"

"No," I lied.

"That's not true, Mario Luna," Letty said.

"Why are we still talking about Lola? We already did that."

We landed in Miami for customs check and to top off fuel. I advised the captain we would not be laying over for dinner and to get us back home as soon as possible.

I looked at my watch.

"We have three hours to landing. Hit it? Or another movie?"

"You better not call me Lola," Letty teased.

"I've never done that and never will."

Letty extended her hand to me. We went into the cabin.

Between moans, Letty said, "Eyes open. It's me. It's Letty."

It was a steaming moment, and I had closed my eyes. I had been fully in the moment, fully aware that Letty was on top of me, bouncing on my body, riding me. She changed positions, facing my feet, still riding me hard. I reached forward and caressed her. But at her words, in my mind's eye, I pictured Lola.

July 17, 1993 (Saturday)
Barcelona, Spain
Olga

I called the office to talk to Mario yesterday. Andrea told me he'd flown to Puerto Rico. It wasn't lease business that she knew of, and Letty was on the manifest.

There was a time when I talked to Mario twice or more each day. Now it was a call maybe once a week. How things have changed. I had thought we would be together for life, eventually married, husband and wife.

I do want him in my life for the rest of my life. I adore the man.

I caught him at the office today. Saturday noon in Los Angeles.

"Amor, you never call me. If I don't call you, we never talk," I said.

"Baby, I'm terrible about keeping up, but you know this. How are you? Where are you?"

"Barcelona," I said. "Leaving tomorrow for Rome for a few days. Want to meet for a night or two?"

"Baby, I have so many leases cooking right now. I'd love to see you, but the timing is bad."

"Have you done any traveling lately?" I asked, just to ask. What would he tell me about Puerto Rico?

"Too busy. I did go to San Diego to close the deal earlier this week, but that's not news to you. You know about it. That's it."

Had he forgotten about Puerto Rico, or is he lying?

I put the phone down. Riana brought me a cup of espresso and a cookie. Room service had left us a carafe and a wicker basket of fresh biscotti dipped in various chocolates and caramels.

"Penny for your thoughts?" she asked, sitting beside me on the flowered loveseat that faced the balcony.

"He just lied to me," I said. Was I jealous? Was I just curious? I don't know. I felt unsettled.

"Let him have his life just as he gives you the space to live yours," Riana lectured.

"Some help you are," I said.

"Let's go out again tonight," Riana said. "Don't sweat what Mario is doing or did. Be happy he's making a lot of money for everyone. You heard what my dad said about the consortium. Everyone is delighted with the returns from the plane leases. Mario's work is good."

"Amor, you're right. It's just he lied, and there's no reason to lie to me."

"Drop it, already."

Sometimes I think she's my only friend in the world.

"Okay, I'll shut up. Where are we going tonight? You're the Spaniard. Tell me."

Riana chattered on about our choices in Barcelona. I barely heard her, at a slow simmer over the lie. We dressed in short glittery clothes and took a car for a night out, traveling in an SUV to have room for the guards.

The SUV was rented, but Julio, one of the guards who, like Riana, was Spanish and familiar with the city, was driving. We were quickly on the road. Seated in back with two more of his men was my newest traveling head of security, Agosto. He was Colombian, thirty-six years old, and though his first language was Spanish, he spoke English fluently. He was a master of Brazilian Jiujitsu. I had cut back from a protection detail of six to four. Agosto and the men in back were silent, but I felt their presence.

I stared out the window at the night.

Riana took my hand and tugged it to get my attention.

"You don't own him," Riana said. "I can tell you are upset."

"I'm okay and you're right, I don't own him. It's not like before."

"Promise you are going to have a good time tonight."

"I promise," I said, meaning it.

People in Spain were complaining on the news of how bad the economy was, but, here at the Capri, the cover charge to walk in was seventy-five hundred pesetas, about fifty U.S. dollars. And it was packed, not the sign of a bad economy. The Capri Club was jamming. It was past midnight, and everything was just getting started.

Agosto was a fast mover and snapped his fingers a lot when he was giving orders. Riana and I waited in the thick of a crowd of people dancing, laughing, having fun. Agosto snapped his fingers and conducted the rapid work of his men and a couple of waiters to have a table with two chairs set up for us. The table's former occupants put up no argument. Agosto shook their hands, pointed us out to them, and told them the next round was on us. The pounding beat vibrated the air, shook the room, and made me feel like joining in the crowd of happy dancers. This disco reminded me of the clubs in Rio. I was happy I'd come. Mario faded from my mind. Today I had a Gucci Matelassé shoulder bag. I dropped it on the table beside Riana's clutch.

Our smiling waiter was a dark, slim young man. Slim looked good on him. Like the other waiters, he was in white shorts and a sleeveless v neck t-shirt.

"My name is Dani, and I have the honor of serving you tonight." He flashed an impressive set of white teeth. "What can I get you?"

"Vega Sicilia Unico," Riana said. "1991 or 1992 if you have it."

Dani bunched the fingers of his right hand and kissed them. "Magnifico."

I watched him walk away. "Magnifico is right."

The music was loud and getting louder. I spoke close to Riana's ear. "I like that kid. Bet he's not thirty yet."

"I think twenty-five," Riana said. "Take him home."

I smiled. I couldn't recall ever taking a waiter back with me, but there was a first time for everything. A couple of guys stopped at our table. We accepted their invitations to dance, finished the slow dance and two fast ones. When we were back at the table, Dani reappeared, showed us the label on the bottle, and got my okay to open it.

"Never had this before. It's great," I said after a taste. "Mario would love this."

"Stop thinking about him," Riana said, raising her glass for a second click.

"I'm not thinking of him. It's just he's so big on reds like this."

It was way too loud to talk. Riana danced with the same guy at least three times, a tall string bean of a man with shaggy black hair and a quick smile. Her actions told me she had him pegged. I played the field, accepting dance after dance from different men. I was escorted back to my table, and another man would ask. Two hours or so later, I had not turned anyone down or returned to the table. Our fantastic wine was still waiting. We were too busy to drink it, but I told Agosto to get a case for the road.

Riana signaled me. At the end of the dance, we headed through a crowd of people to the restroom. Agosto was right behind us, stopping outside the doors to wait until we came out. The three other guards were nearby, somewhere in the crowd.

"I'm having a blast," Riana said.

"Me too. I needed the distraction."

We walked past the brightly lit makeup area where several women were working on their faces or hair. The cubical walls and doors were maybe seven feet high, did not reach the high ceiling but were flush with the floor. Unlike public restrooms in the US, one could not see the feet of the occupant inside to tell if the stall was occupied. A woman against the far wall saw us come in and got up from her station. Uniformed in white like the waiters, the beefy female attendant opened a stall door for Riana. She gave me a nod but no smile. She had coarse features, yellow-lensed glasses, a dark complexion, and a thick head of bleached blonde hair. She motioned for me to follow her a few doors down to an empty stall.

"Gracias," I said in Spanish, turning my back to her as I entered the small cubicle.

Just as the door shut behind me, something slammed me in the back so hard that it shoved me into the wall. My purse hit the tile beside the commode's base, and I collapsed on top of the toilet. My knees hit the floor. The blow to my back took my breath, and I was gasping.

My attacker grabbed a handful of my hair and jerked my head back. I felt something cold and hard on my neck. A knife.

"If you scream, you are dead. If you raise your voice, you are dead. Understand?"

I choked out a rasping "Ok," between coughs. Every time I coughed, the knife pressed harder against my windpipe. "What do you want?"

"Sit."

She was right behind me. She had a broad build and felt all too substantial pressed close like a lover, with all the tension focused on the knife's edge on the intersection of my neck and collarbone. Her left hand came into view—stubby fingers, large bumpy knuckles, wide nails with stained cuticles—and she pointed at the toilet seat. She removed the knife from my throat and took a step back. I put my hand to my throat, covering the place the blade had been. No damage there, but my nerves still registered the hard pressure of the knife's dull edge. The feel of my own hand somehow helped dull the sensation. I leaned forward against the ceramic rim to get to my feet, and sat as she'd ordered, facing the blonde I'd assumed was an attendant, the one who had let Riana into the toilet and had walked me to this stall.

"Give me your jewelry and everything in your purse."

Her Spanish was not Castilian. The Spanish was good, but not native. I had on a necklace, earrings, and two rings. I reached with both hands to unclasp the necklace, but not fast enough to suit her.

"Let me help you," she hissed. She grabbed the necklace by the diamond and jerked hard. The clasp snapped off and pinged against the wall. She put the broken chain and the gem in her pocket.

I took off my two diamond rings and the diamond studs in my ears and handed them to her. As I reached for my purse, I saw her looking over the rings.

"Give me everything you got and maybe you won't bleed," she said.

"No argument from me."

I rested the purse at an angle on my lap and unzipped it with my left hand. I was breathing heavily but having a plan of action inoculated me against the fear. My eyes were on hers as I slid my hand in the opening. While she was pocketing my jewels, I was fingering the shapes inside the bag. My hand closed on the familiar cool metal. Entirely by touch, I switched off the safety, adjusted the angle, and fired the Walther PPK straight through the fabric. Once. Twice. The bullets went through her face. She jerked on impact, upright long enough for me to lurch out of the way. She fell forward against the toilet as if she were upchucking and I squeezed past.

Riana emerged white-faced from her stall. Agosto charged through the outer door.

"Oh my God, Olga," Riana said. "What is all that blood on you? What were those shots?"

Before I could answer, Agosto was beside me. I turned to face the wooden stall door behind me, which now had two bullet holes.

"The so-called bathroom attendant decided to rob me. She's dead." I was still laboring to breathe. With each breath I took, pain radiated through my back where she had hit me.

Women in various stages of inebriation had entered the bathroom and emerged from the stalls, some running in, some running out, and others gawking. One oblivious woman was still drunkenly applying mascara at a make up mirror.

"Agosto, she put my rings, necklace, and earrings in her pocket."

Agosto looked at my hand inside my purse. I took out my wallet and handed him my purse with the gun in it. He pulled out his walkie talkie and said, "Code four. *El servicio.*"

In a loud burst of static, the walkie-talkie responded. "Ten-four."

"Miss Olga, go with the guards outside. I will handle this," he said, his eyes flickering from the opening of my purse to the bullet holes in the stall door. "My men will take you to directly to the plane. Don't go back to the hotel."

I nodded.

When we came out, the music had stopped. Riana and I followed one of the guards toward the car. The other two followed discreetly behind. The live band and DJ were still there. The guards rushed us through an emergency exit so fast I didn't get a chance to see what the crowd was doing. The pain I was in consumed me, but all my attention was focused on the guard leading the way. The blood on me was drying, and I wanted to shower it from my face, hands, and hair.

Riana and I got in the middle seat of the Suburban. I handed my wallet to Riana, who put it in her purse as I called Eli in Milan. Since LAI had gone public, he handled personnel in all of my houses, and some of the plane assignments, just as I used to do that job when the houses belonged to Pepe and later on to Camila.

"I need my crew back at the plane immediately," I said. "Headed to Bogota."

"Consider it done," Eli said. "Are you aboard?"

"Be there in thirty minutes."

"Why Bogota?" Riana asked.

.   "I feel safe there."

"If it gets political, you can count on my dad," Riana said. "He knows everyone."

"Thank you, Amor." I would have kissed her, but I was still wheezing. She put her arm around me supportively.

"Maybe we should stop and see a doctor?" Riana asked.

"I'm okay. I just want to go home."

It wasn't dawn yet when we made it to the airport. My cough subsided some. My back burned with each breath like it was on fire.

The plane was still on local power in the hangar. Thanks to the circulating pump, I had instant hot water. I took the power shower I needed, soaping my body three times and shampooing twice. Riana insisted on getting in the shower with me to help, all the while keeping a conversation running about how quickly my back was bruising and making no secret of her hostility toward the attendant. I already had dark purple streaking across my knees where I'd struck the tile floor.

I was in a bathrobe when the crew arrived. Captain Martin was a Colombia-based crew member. I told him, "Be sure they top off the water tanks. I took a long shower."

I ordered hot tea from the flight attendant, Magda, a short red-head with a face full of freckles.

"Amor, I'm freezing. I feel like I'm coming down with something."

"Let's get you in bed," Riana said. She held my hand as we walked to the bedroom cabin.

My teeth were chattering.

"I think you have a fever," Riana said. "Maybe from the injury?"

Riana summoned one of the guards. "Fetch us a doctor. There's a hospital nearby." She took a wad of bills out of her purse. "Here are some dollars to entice him. If he asks what happened, tell him it was an assault. Give him no details. Understand?"

I shut my eyes as Riana gave the guard instructions. With difficulty I sat up against the pillows Riana arranged for me. She spiked my tea with Courvoisier. Even with the comforter and two blankets, I was cold. I sipped the brew. Cognac burned my throat with a promise to ease my chills.

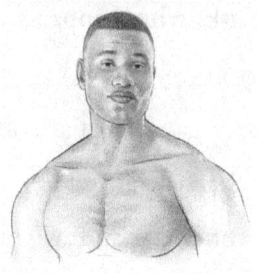

July 19, 1993
Barcelona, Spain
Dani

Manaus where I am from is a big city, the capital of Amazonas which is a state in Brazil. Manaus is different from Barcelona because it is in the heart of the Amazon rainforest, and the language is Portuguese. I was in a group of native dancers performing in a night club frequented by international tourists. I had no days off and was paid a pittance for dancing. Most of my income was tips from waiting tables after the dancing was done. As a waiter, I picked up a lot of English and Spanish. Sometimes a tourist invited me to visit her hotel room, and that I looked forward to. It was one of those tourist invitations that changed my life. I waited on a table with two American women, and at the request of one, made an appearance at her hotel room where I made her scream with pleasure. She invited me on her private plane, and I spent a week with her in a hotel in London. When she left for America, she gave me a thousand American dollars. Instead of going home, I found a room and a job. I stayed in London and got hired as a waiter at a club in Soho. I learned better English working almost a year in London. Foggy damp London is very different from tropical Manaus, and I grew to miss the sun. My first friend there was a Spaniard who waited tables at the Soho club. He showed me all the best deals to living in London, which can be pretty expensive if you go to the places where tourists go. He liked London, but all he could talk about was going home to his sunny Barcelona. Before going in to work, we would meet for lunch—usually fish and chips—and would then go work our shift. One day without warning, he quit coming to work, and moved out of his room. I assumed he went home. He was gone, but I kept going to the places he had shown me, and I often thought about the plentiful jobs he talked about, and the better weather. Eventually, after almost a year in London, I took a ferry across the channel and a train to Barcelona.

In Barcelona, it wasn't easy to get a visa, but it helped that I had a London stamp on my passport. I figured I would eventually go through the hoops to get legal. No one ever asked for my immigration status, so I didn't bother. My first job there was waiting tables at a club on the beach, and I shared a room with one of the club's waitresses. The room got smaller and smaller, and the waitress more and more possessive. After a few months, I got hired on at the Capri. Waiting tables at the Capri paid a small salary, but the tips were good enough to liberate me from my roommate, and cover rent for my own apartment.

The Capri was good to me, and I preferred the climate in Barcelona to that of London. There were plenty of tourists who gave me their hotel keys. I had developed an instinct about which of my tables was going to invite me in. I had some chemistry with a woman on the night of the shooting, and expected something would happen with her, but I guess she got scared away.

The next night, a man came to see me on her behalf. He introduced himself as Agosto. I recognized him as the one who had bought a case of wine last night, and who had paid the tab of the woman I had failed to connect with. He said she was going home to Bogota and got my contact information.

I did not think much of it.

Agosto returned to the Capri a few days later.

"Miss Camacho's flight home was delayed," he said. "But she will be back home in a few days. She might be interested in hiring you. I can't guarantee you a job, but she wants to see you in Bogota."

I laughed at what the bodyguard had said. I stopped laughing when he handed me a business card with a phone number and two thousand U.S. dollars.

"If she likes you and hires you, you will travel the world with her and her companion. This is an opportunity. Buy a ticket to Bogota and when you arrive, call that number."

I took the money. I won't lie. I was dazzled by the money. This was more money than I'd ever had at one time.

"What if I don't make it to Bogota?"

Agosto was a big, intimidating man. He frowned, and it made me nervous.

"I'm not saying I'm not interested. It's possible I won't be able to get a visa. My passport is Brazilian."

"Don't disappoint me," he said, poking my chest with his index finger.

"I'll get there one way or another," I said. "Why me?"

He looked down at me, making me feel about an inch high.

"I have the same question," he said, and he was gone.

I took the cash home and it sat in the top drawer of my dresser for a few days.

The tips at the Capri were good enough to cover living expenses, but I spent everything on rent, transportation and food. I'd been in Barcelona for three years and was still living week to week. My rent was paid till the end of July. I booked a flight to Bogota and sublet my place to a guy I worked with, with the understanding that I might not be coming back. I had left South America with nothing but a suitcase, and now I would be going back with the same.

July 21, 1993 (Wednesday)
Pasadena
Mario

Tangles put the papers on the conference table and pushed them in my direction. Specs on the planes they'd found for Letty's Utah buyer.

"These Boeings need a little work, but not only are they exactly what FlyUtah wants, I got us a deal on the upgrade from passenger to medical facilities," Letty said. "It's the same group that upgraded your current plane, and they said for a plane to be used as an ambulance—," Letty cut off when my phone rang.

"Olga's in the hospital," Riana said on the phone. "We're in Barcelona."

"Olga's in the hospital?" I repeated for the girls' benefit. I stood up. Letty and Tangles got up and walked toward the conference room door, but I pointed to the chairs, and they returned to where they'd been sitting.

"I'm listening. Is it serious?"

Riana said that Olga had been assaulted Sunday morning.

"Afterwards, we were about to split for Colombia, but Olga was feeling bad. We had a doctor make a house call."

"I'm on my way," I said. "Barcelona, you say?"

She gave me the directions to the hospital, and I jotted them down. "It's the second best in the country. She hasn't asked me to call anyone other than Eli. Mario, she didn't ask me to call you."

"It's okay." I handed the hospital information to Letty, who nodded. "Letty will call you in a few to handle the logistics."

"Mario, thanks."

"For what?"

"For coming. She wants to be a warrior about everything, but I can tell she's hurting."

I could hear Riana crying on her end of the line.

"Baby, easy," I said, trying to comfort her. "Is she okay at this hospital? Should she fly to the best hospital in Spain, or go to France?"

Riana was from Spain. She knew the good and bad of her own country.

"This is a very good hospital," she assured me. "The best would be La Paz in Madrid, but this is a close second."

When Riana hung up, I reached for my coat.

Letty got on the line to Andrea. "Mario's flying to Barcelona ASAP. Line it up."

She also called Storm in.

"Coming?" I asked her.

Letty looked like she was on the fence.

Tangles said, "Boss, we're trying to close the Utah lease."

Storm walked in, and Letty put her hand on her shoulder, pointing her my way.

"Take Storm," Letty said decisively. "If you decide you want us, Tangles and I can join you in a heartbeat."

"I'm in," Storm volunteered.

"Get your name on the manifest," I told Storm, "And bring the car to the front in twenty minutes. We'll go home and pack."

I called Riana several times before we took off. On the way home, I learned that Olga was in and out of it on a pain drip. Doctors had not concluded anything yet. Before we took off, Riana said that doctors thought her lungs were inflamed.

"I'm glad she's in the hospital," Riana said, "but she is not happy. It hurts her to breathe, and she needs oxygen from time to time. She came to about an hour ago and is totally pissed. I did tell her you were flying over."

"What did she say about that?"

"She smiled."

En route to Barcelona, we ate a meal, and I brought Storm up to date. I still knew very little of what had happened to put Olga in this state.

"How about I give you a long massage?"

"You read my mind," I said.

We had a folding massage table aboard, but we always used the bed. I lay down on the blanket Storm brought to protect the bed linens and tried to lose myself in her massage. But I was thinking about the tentative diagnosis the doctors had made, something called pulmonary sarcoidosis. It sounded scary.

July 21, 1993 (Wednesday)
Barcelona
Riana

Even lying there sickly and pale, Olga was beautiful. She'd gotten a short haircut for the summer, and it made her look like a big-eyed waif.

Though the hospital room was small, and the building from the early nineteen hundreds, the equipment and facilities were up-to-date. This is a private teaching hospital, and the attending doctor was a teacher, not one of the interns. To me, Doctor Lugo looked more like a woodsman than a doctor. His dark hair and full beard were about a half-inch long, and his cologne was something that smelled woodsy. Maybe I was just fixated on the woodsman thing because the first time we saw him, he'd been wearing an out-of-season flannel shirt that looked like it belonged in the Pacific Northwest. Ever since, though, he'd been in standard hospital garb or scrubs. He arrived today all smiles with only one student following him around.

Olga's hello ended in a coughing fit that lasted more than a minute. The doctor had the intern put down his clipboard and turn on Olga's oxygen mask for a few minutes.

"Try not to talk very much until your breathing is back to normal, and the cough is totally gone."

Doctor Lugo was bearing happy news. He explained that the blow had been in close proximity to her left lung, and that the MRI showed no sign that a rib damaged the tissue. The blow had caused inflammation which was affecting her breathing.

"You are going to be just fine, Senorita." He smiled at her, then at me.

"Can I leave?"

Dr. Lugo shook his head but kept the smile. "That would be unwise. Here you have everything you may need, attention, and oxygen. And if fluid accumulates in your lungs, we can easily remove it."

"Mario is on his way," I reminded her.

"Doctor, I do not want to go under with drips," she said. "And only enough pain medication to make the pain endurable."

"As you wish, Senorita."

Olga flashed him a smile. I figured Dr. Lugo was attracted to her. His visit was done, and he continued making conversation, even though it was obvious he had pressing concerns to move on. The intern kept looking at his watch and trying to get them to finish the rounds. Eventually he left.

"I want to know what happened at the club," Olga said. "I wonder what happened to the mess we ran away from."

"Agosto has been waiting out there for hours," I said.

Agosto is a burly, brawny guy, not the kind of person you expect to see with tears in his eyes, but he saw Olga on the hospital bed and teared up. She reached out with one hand and he kissed her on the tops of her knuckles.

"This was not your fault," Olga told him. "And I didn't give you my hand to kiss it. I'm not the Pope." Her laugh was interrupted by repeated coughs.

"Olga wants to know what happened after she left," I said. I opened a mineral water and handed it over to Olga to sip.

Olga nodded and gestured for Agosto to begin.

"Your jewelry is on the plane. It needs cleaning, but I don't know how to do that. Sorry."

Olga gestured impatiently for him to go on.

"There is no video surveillance at the Capri," Agosto said softly. "The purse was burned to ash, and the gun smashed into pieces and dumped in a iron urn. Your injuries here are listed as being from an assault. The hospital has no details."

"You didn't have to talk to police?"

"No. No one saw anything. I'm sure your attacker has a record a kilometer long. I doubt she will be missed, but if she is, the investigation will run into a dead end. The lights were so low on the dance floor, no one would have noticed anything out of sorts. I wiped down stall's handle, and there are probably a million fingerprints. I was ready to make a report but the police and later two detectives came in without asking for me. The coroner took the body."

"This shooting may just slide by," I said, but was surprised at the negligence that Agosto described. Spanish cops are as good at what they do as those in any modern country. I wondered if money had exchanged hands somewhere along the line.

"I tipped your waiter, told him you got a headache and left, and I paid the bill," Agosto said.

"Find that waiter. I want to see him when I am fit again."

"As you wish."

"I will take good care of you for handling this like you did," Olga said.

"Please no. I am ashamed that this happened to you when I was just outside the bathroom door."

"It was not your fault. End of story," Olga raised her voice a little, and it started up another series of hacking coughs. When she was in control, there was silence.

Agosto was unconvinced. I could see how terrible he felt about causing more distress.

"Miss Olga, you are the personification of kindness."

The Camacho family had a brutal history. In the old days, and even the not so old days, guards and their families were killed for such blunders. Being Colombian and employed by Camacho, Agosto had to know this. It had not been that long since Olga's crew had hijacked us for possession of a non-existent drug cargo. The hijackers had paid with their lives by Olga's own hand; and their families had died at Camila's command. Consequences hold no lesson if they are secret, so among Camacho staff, it was no secret. I was probably the only living soul who knew that Camila's merciless edict had caused a rift between Olga and Camila. Agosto would have no idea that Olga didn't condone brutality that extended to family members and children. Camila had always warned Olga that letting the children live would cost Olga her life.

The hospital was closer to the airport than the hotel where we had been staying. I decided to stay on the plane. Eli arranged for Magda and a new hire I hadn't met before to work back-to-back 12-hour shifts, so the plane was always ready, provided with food, utilities, and the bed made with fresh linens after each use. Agosto posted round-the-clock guards outside the plane and outside Olga's room. Four guards from the rest of his team flew here in a Learjet.

July 22, 1993 (Thursday)
Hospital
Barcelona
Olga

"I have been here since Monday. There is nothing they are doing to me here that I couldn't get done on my own plane, or at home once I get to Bogota. It's time to leave," I said.

"Not till the doctor gives his permission," Riana argued, repeating the doctor word for word. "You know a plane flight will cause your healing lungs undue stress."

That's when Mario walked in. Seeing him is the best medicine.

"Amor, Amor, my breath probably sucks but come kiss me. Amor, you do love me. You came all this way to see your Olga."

"Of course. I love you, and I love your breath."

We kissed. Mario's arms came around me tightly. I fought off a coughing fit.

"Careful, don't press on her," Riana said, pointing to the soft sponge mat on top of the sheets. "The injury is on her back."

"Amor, I haven't washed my pussy in three days, or I'd ask you to fuck me right here and now." I'm so bad.

Mario laughed. His eyes had a worried look, but his words were light.

"I guess I can go home. You look fine to me."

"My knees are all bruised, and I have to tell you about the dead bitch who posed as a bathroom attendant to rob me and hit me so hard that she damaged my left lung."

"It could have been a lot worse. I'm glad we got out of there alive. She had a huge knife," Riana said, making a gun with her fingers and firing into her own forehead. "But Olga gave her some forehead ventilation."

"Hush," I said. "Let me have my drama."

"It was drama alright if the villain ended up dead," Mario said.

"Villainess," Riana said.

I beckoned him closer and whispered into his ear. "No one knows what happened or where," I whispered. "Guns in Spain can be a problem, but I think I'm good. My security guy handled it well."

Mario was leaning over me, so I didn't see the doctor when he came through the door. I just heard his voice.

"Excuse me," Dr Lugo said. "I'll come back."

"Doctor, no. Please come in."

Mario stood, and moved so I could see who I was speaking to.

"Dr Lugo, let me introduce you to an associate of mine. Mario Luna."

I was silent as they shook hands, exchanged a few words and sized each other up. Mario had several inches on the good doctor, but I've rarely come across a man as tall as he is.

"Doctor, I have a question. How was I able to get away from the attacker in the parking lot and take a shower? I hurt more now than I did then."

"It's the inflammation. Inflammation in your lung is part of the healing process. Swelling is the body's normal reaction to an injury. Sometimes the body goes overboard, and the swelling response is excessive. In an injury to another part of the body, we can use compression, but not with your lungs. But it is the swelling and inflammation that you're feeling."

"Doctor, I need you to release me. I will go directly to my plane and fly home where a doctor can stay at my home and duplicate there whatever you are doing here. You've done a fabulous job for me. I haven't had oxygen in at least a day. I really think I'm ready."

"I will release you if you promise me to follow my written instructions. When you get home, you must give your doctor the copy of your chart."

"Deal," I said, shaking the doctor's hand, and grimacing because when I moved, it hurt so bad.

"Are you sure you want to leave?" Mario asked. "It's a long flight to Bogota."

I took a look around the small white-walled hospital room. Nothing here but white paint, the lame hospital bed, and the small chair where Riana was sitting. There was no cabinetry, only a tiny closet built into the wall, a window with a pull-down shade hiding an ugly view of the hospital parking lot, an iv stand, and a collapsible table with some medical machines I was wired into.

"I'm certain." I would not miss this place.

"I am not getting in a wheelchair!"

I must have said it a hundred times, but Doctor Lugo refused to release me unless I agreed to the wheelchair and returned to the plane the same way I had arrived at the hospital, in an ambulance.

Eli filled the list of items I needed on board, including the wheelchair and a registered nurse to fly with me to Bogota.

Mario sent his plane home. He, Riana, and Storm rode with me. The security team was somewhere aboard. I was in the bedroom, and complained all the way, but I was happy to be out of the hospital.

The Spanish nurse's name was Iria. She was small, efficient, and so quiet that I often forgot she was there. A number of times during the flight I asked her for oxygen because it seemed to clear my head and I felt it was good for my lungs. Oxygen treatments were on the instruction list from the doctor.

I warned Riana at least a dozen times not to light up a joint even if the oxygen wasn't flowing. It scared me to death to think we'd blow up. Magda served paella from the oldest restaurant in Barcelona, but I didn't want food. I told her to give it to the crew.

Mario was gentle as never before. He lay facing me on the bed as the nurse gently rubbed my back with arnica.

"Amor, thank you for dropping everything to be with me. I will never forget this."

We smiled at each other.

I didn't know if Iria spoke anything but Spanish, but I switched to English.

"You are so kind. Just think, we could have been married by now and had children."

"We could have but we are better like we are. I love you more than you imagine."

"And I adore you. Always will, Amor."

Iria helped me sit up for a few minutes. She coaxed me into drinking some broth in a cup, made sure I drank it, and opened a mineral water so I could swallow a lightweight sleeping pill. She offered me the use of a bedpan, but instead, I let Mario carry me to and from the bathroom. When I got back, the bed had fresh sheets. Iria gave me a sponge bath with Mario watching. The plane was chilly, but I declined putting on the GAL sweats. There was a seat in the bedroom where Iria could sit to attend me, but finally, she left me alone with Mario.

I rolled to my stomach, turning my head on the pillow to face him.

"I wish you could fuck me," I said.

"No way am I going to take a chance of hurting you."

He pulled the covers over us, and he rubbed my ass.

Our lips touched.

"Your cough is getting better," he said.

"Having you with me is why I am getting better."

"You had the same type of injury when you were hit by that big truck outside my house," Mario recalled.

At least this time there were no broken bones or sprains to deal with. "Fuck, that was horrible. You're right. I remember I had pleurisy. The cough wasn't exactly the same, but it hurt to breathe. Don't remind me."

"Baby, I'm sorry I brought it up," Mario said.

We kissed again. He kept rubbing, moving from my ass to explore lower, caressing. I felt one of his fingers move inside, and then he was still.

"Amor, if you stop now, I'll never forgive you," I said breathlessly.

He laughed softly, and his fingers began moving again, driving me to a feverish pitch. I closed my eyes and melted into the soft sheets with all points of my attention focused on the exquisite movement of his hand. What he was doing felt heavenly. I came more than once and lay there bonelessly in heaven.

"Amor, I should return the favor at least once or twice," I said.

"Just lie there and heal," he said.

The cabin light was dimmed, but I could see the ridge of his erection under the covers.

"There is no need for you to go without," I said. "Storm and Riana are here." I was drowsy, floating on the edge of sleep.

"Both of them?" Mario whispered as if we had company.

"Amor, si, especially Riana. She's been through hell with me at the hospital."

July 23, 1993 (Friday)
Somewhere over the Atlantic
Storm

I shouldn't have told Boss it was my first time in Barcelona. I would have been happy to sit in the waiting room, but Boss chased me off.

"Letty hired the driver who picked us up at the airport. Make him earn his keep and get a tour of Barcelona or shop or whatever you want," he said, just before walking into Olga's room. "Give me a call every couple hours, and I'll let you know what the plans are."

I missed Boss, but I got to see a little of Barcelona that wasn't the inside of an airport or hospital. The driver was a hoot. He could have been my Grampa, and he kept pointing out places in the city where he grew up, or where he lived when he was first married back in the stone age. I called Boss from the Four Cat Café and told him the pumpkin gazpacho here wasn't half as good as Miguel's.

When the driver took me back to the hospital, I peeked into Olga's room, gave her a kiss and hugged Riana.

"As you can see, I'm back. I'll be in the waiting room."

When plans were made for Olga to leave, Boss handed me a couple of business cards with the airport addresses. He said, "Move our luggage to Olga's plane. Have her crew get you settled in and wait for me there."

"Right away Boss."

I took the liberty of bringing my portable massage gear too. Never know when it will come in handy. I didn't even ask him where we were headed. I was in the main cabin when Olga arrived by ambulance. Medics brought her inside and put her to bed. I walked behind the medics and greeted her.

"Welcome to your plane," I said with a kiss. "You're so beautiful, Olga."

Boss and the nurse rode in the ambulance. Magda, Riana and Olga's security guys came in a couple of SUV's with enough luggage to sink a barge.

I am as proud as can be at myself. I've been very well-mannered. Being part of Mario's team, I have had so much freedom, but it is not like I have forgotten how to be as accommodating as any masseuse should be.

The second time I offered a foot massage, Olga accepted. I worked her feet with lavender oil for an hour, and then I worked her legs.

"This is so nice of you, Storm," she said.

"My pleasure. Please let me know if you want me again. Stimulation is good for your blood circulation and distracts your brain from the pain."

Olga drifted to sleep. I covered her and shut down the lights..

"I'm afraid to roll over and run into her," Boss said, as if he needed to explain. He moved to the main cabin, and I fetched him a snack. Before I went to my seat, I found where Iria was sitting with the stewards beside the cockpit. I picked her brain about massage therapies for Olga's injury. While we were talking, I mentioned that Boss had gone to his seat.

"Miss Camacho is alone?" Iria asked.

I nodded.

Iria rushed to the bedroom to sit with her as she slept.

I went to my seat. Magda, who had joined us on Olga's plane, alerted me when Olga woke up and was asking for me. She wanted me to massage her neck.

I got arnica from Iria and worked the bruise.

"This stuff is working. Your bruising is getting lighter," I said.

Olga seemed delighted with the news.

"Storm, please put more of that stuff on me."

I left Boss and Olga alone, and went to my seat in a small media room off the main cabin and amused myself examining the little cubbies and hiding places all around, all stuffed with exotic European packaged snacks and canned drinks, toiletries and whatnot. The seat was the kind that folded flat into a bed, and I had more than enough room to stretch out. While I had been off massaging Olga, Magda made the bed for me. It looked inviting, with the corner folded back and a wrapped chocolate on the full-sized pillow. The seat spurred some memories, and I wished that Tangles was aboard.

Riana had the same kind of seat beside a window in the main cabin. Boss had one beside her but only sat there when Olga was asleep. The security guys were invisible in some other compartment on this huge plane.

When the main cabin lights went out, I dimmed my lights. My stomach was growling, and I regretted turning down the paella that Magda had offered me earlier. My Cousin Vinny was playing on my console. Although

I'd seen it a couple of times since it came out last year, I didn't want to miss anything. I stopped the tape and started for the galley. To get there, I needed to go through the main cabin. I turned down the aisle and froze.

Riana was glowing in the emergency lighting. Her bare breasts shimmered in the light, and two big hands moved on them. I recognized those hands, even in the dark. She moaned softly. I didn't need to be a genius to know she was riding Boss in his bed. Our eyes met, and Riana smiled at me. I stood there like a wind-up doll that had run out of juice. My eyes were used to the dark, so I could see when Riana's eyebrows went up. If I passed them, would I be invited to join them, or would I be intruding? I didn't know how I felt about that. I did a little wave like they do on parade floats. Riana waved back. I went back to my seat, turned on the movie, opened a package of pistachios, and a can of coke, and fell asleep before the end of My Cousin Vinny.

Two hours before landing in Bogota, I gave Iria a break. She went to the front of the plane, and I gave Olga a frontal massage with very little pressure.

"My back feels better," Olga said. "Thank you, Storm for being so sweet."

"It's my pleasure, Olga. I'm here for you."

I massaged her shoulders, her breasts. She loved the breast massage. I used so much oil that my hands were slick, and I had to towel off the excess. Boss walked in when I reached her stomach.

"She's ten times better than Betty," Olga told Mario.

I winked at Boss but who knows if he caught it in the dim light. I wonder if Riana had told him I walked in on them. Probably. He left the room, and I continued the massage below her abdomen. I knew this whole flight was about Olga, and that I was to do anything I could that made her feel better. When I touched her, I could tell she was needy. She moaned and moved her hands on top of mine. I remembered everything I had ever learned from Letty and Tangles and Boss. I did my best to give her a massage she would never forget.

July 24, 1993 (Saturday)
Colombia
Mario

Colombia in July is hot. I put on a sleeveless shirt just before we landed at the international airport, not the military base where Olga usually landed. Her assistant Eli met us at the airport with three helicopters. I kissed Olga just before she was transferred to the gurney by the medical team Eli had ordered.

"See you at my house, Amor," Olga said. "Colombia at last."

She was still pale but looked happy to be almost home. Technically, we said our temporary goodbyes on the tarmac, in front of the six medics, two security guards, Riana, and Olga's physician, all of whom accompanied Olga on the medical bird on her flight home. I watched them load her in and saw when Riana gave the doctor the medical records Dr. Lugo had sent. Storm and I rode in the smallest chopper, and there was another one for the rest of the security guards.

After two days at home, Olga was tottering around like a two year old, slow, but on her own. Whatever duty nurse was on the clock dutifully followed her around pushing the much-detested wheelchair. Iria had gone home, but she had been replaced by three nurses who worked eight-hour shifts. Of course, Olga's personal maid and regular household staff was there too. Everyone was constantly monitoring her and asking her if she needed anything. She complained about being mothered, but I think she loved the extra attention. I took meals with her, and was there most of the day, but at night, only the night nurse attended Olga.

During breakfast I asked about borrowing the Learjet for the ride home. Olga disagreed.

"Amor, you are taking my plane. No argument."

Olga sat with us during a breakfast of Colombian coffee, fruit and breads. The delicate antique side chair she usually used was against the wall, replaced by a massive solid throne of a chair big enough to pack in numerous cushions. She looked radiant at the head of the table, like a queen. The rest of us, including Riana and Storm, were in the regular antique chairs. I was always a little anxious sitting at this table, sure that one of these days I was going to collapse the chair while squeezing in or out of it.

With a mischievous grin, Olga handed Storm a black velvet box.

"Amor, thank you for helping me so much through a rough time. I love you. Wear it in good health."

Storm's eyes got big, and she flushed pink.

I had seen Olga give out expensive gifts before. I leaned forward to see.

"No gift is necessary, really," Storm protested.

"Open it already," Riana said, laughing.

"I can't accept this," Storm said, eyes still wide.

"Yes, you can, Amor. Riana will put it on you."

Carefully, Storm lifted the top of the velvet box, revealing a diamond block bracelet that looked to me like platinum and diamonds all the way around. I'd say a half carat each, about ten carats total.

"This is gorgeous," Storm said, not touching it.

Riana laughed at Storm's reaction, lifted the bracelet out of the box, and clasped it on Storm's right wrist. Storm held her arm up for a good minute, turning her wrist this way and that, and admiring the gift, then pushed away from the table and went through an awkward dance trying to find a way to hug Olga without causing any distress.

While these thanks were going on, I was reminded how Olga could be so generous.

Lola had urged me to ask Olga what she'd had to do with Camila and Pepe's murders. That was never going to happen. I would never insult her with that kind of question, even if I would always think about it. I wished Lola had never told me that story. I believe that if Lola had tangible proof, she would have offered to sell it to me.

My cell phone rang while Storm and I were boarding.

I ignored it until we were inside, when it rang again.

"Hello?"

I heard a hoarse voice but recognized it immediately.

"Hey Tiger. Remember that video you said you had? Well, I got it now. Oh, and I took the liberty of taking twenty thousand as compensation for your pet guard dog knocking me off my chair."

The voice was strained and fake, but I recognized it as Lola.

"I thought you don't like phones," I said.

"I don't. Have a good flight."

I hung up the phone, sure that the timing of the call was no accident.

The more I thought of the call, the angrier I got, not so much over the words as the timing. It's like she calls just to let me know she's watching. But how?

Storm was about to take her seat across from me but had stopped moving and was staring at me with an odd expression on her face.

"Boss, are you okay? Your face is as red as a tomato."

"I'm fine," I said, taking a few deep breaths. "Get us a bottle of wine."

Storm nodded. I watched her head for the galley.

I wasn't certain Lola was telling the truth. To get into Casa Luna, she'd have to breach my heavy twenty-four hour security, and deal with my big safes. To get the video, she'd have to break into one huge, impregnable safe, and for cash, she'd have to deal with an even bigger one. I had far more cash on hand than that but didn't believe she took it. I believed she knew I was on a plane ready to fly out somewhere. The call was so much like the teasing ones she made while she was a cop that I wondered if she was really retired.

Before I touched the wine that Storm had just served, I called Quito, head of house security.

"I have reason to believe that someone got in the main residence and broke into my safes."

"Not possible, Boss."

"I'm just leaving Colombia. I want you to personally check all the surveillance videos for the past five days. I will check your results when I get home."

"Yes, Boss, of course."

Storm said, "So who broke in?"

"Lola. At least, that's what she claims."

"Boss, how could anyone get past all the security? She must be pulling your leg."

I raised my glass and clicked hers before she sat at her seat and buckled up.

"Tangles and I watched the surveillance tapes with Quito," Letty said, passing Storm the steak sauce. "There was no sign of anyone breaching security."

Storm poured steak sauce on her burger. She and I were barefoot but still in the shorts and tees we'd worn on the plane. Tangles and Letty had gotten home from work close to six pm Monday just as we had arrived from the airport, and after a quick greeting, changed from jeans to swimsuits to dine alfresco by the pool. Tangles's hair was pulled back in a short ponytail. Letty's was drying close to her head, still wet from the outdoor pool. She and I had swum a few laps—yes, me in my shorts—while waiting for the outdoor grill to heat. Emma brought us serving bowls of French fries, tall glasses of ice, and an ice bucket with cans of coke and diet coke chilling inside.

As I polished off my hamburger, I told Letty and Tangles about Lola's call.

"I figured something like that," Letty said. "When Quito said you wanted him to review the tapes, Lola was the first thing I thought of."

"She's a lying bitch. She's bluffing," Tangles said.

"Probably," I said, pushing my plate aside, and standing up. I could not linger over the meal but had to see for myself. "Stay and finish your dinner. I'm going to check the safes," I said, heading to the room that housed them on the spa and pool level.

Tangles, Letty, and Storm trailed after me. Storm still eating her burger.

I opened safe number one.

Right away I saw the sealed envelope where I had put the video. I handed the envelope to Letty. "Play a minute of it and see if this is the tape."

She nodded. She and Tangles went to the closest player, the one in the spa.

Storm finished her burger, wiped her face on the napkin she'd brought with her, and crumpled it into the trash as I opened the other safe.

I remembered when I had given Lola a million dollars out of this safe, payment to Lola on behalf of Camila. It had been 'compensation' for Lola's pain and suffering after the Camacho's enforcer had put Lola in the hospital. The million that was in the safe now was the cash that Camila had sent to reimburse me. I looked at the bundles of cash. It was exactly as it had been when I had put it in the safe.

"I'm not counting this," I said. "She was lying."

Storm snorted. "Ain't that a pill."

Letty and Tangles came back to the room.

Letty handed the envelope back to me. "Boss, this tape recorded when you gave her the million upstairs in your office. She promised not to ever bother or harm Camila or Olga."

"It's untouched," I said, pointing to the million in the safe, and locking it away. I put the video back in the other safe, and locked it, too.

I turned my back to the safes and faced the girls.

"You know what I need now?" I asked.

"A massage," Storm said.

"An ice cream sundae," Tangles said.

"Your bed," Letty said.

"You're all correct," I said "But first, steam."

Storm looked sad. She clutched the bracelet.

"What's wrong?" Letty asked.

"I don't want to take it off," Storm said. "But is steam good for jewelry?"

"Well, it could heat up and burn you," Letty said. "You have to pay attention you don't burn yourself. And things expand in the heat, and contract in the cold, so—"

"Diamonds and platinum can handle the wear," I interrupted, "As long as you don't knock it around and loosen the stones, it should be okay."

I was in dire need of a steam bath after the trip from Colombia, and apparently it was contagious. We spent the next two hours in the spa, in the sauna, steam bath, ice dip, and showers. Tangles and Letty took the opportunity to ask a million questions about the trip.

"I wasn't sure if I should be worried about her or not," I said. "Ended up, I just went along for the ride."

They asked about Olga's injuries, the hospital, the medical care, the flight from Barcelona to Bogota, Iria, and then about the couple of days we'd spent at Olga's place. Storm and I ended up alternating with little anecdotes.

"How's Riana?" Tangles asked.

"Riana was lonely on the flight back. I paid her some...personal attention," I said, grinning at Storm when she blushed. "Storm could have joined us, but I think she was shy."

"I was not shy," Storm said, pouting. "I was watching My Cousin Vinny. Then I got hungry, but I thought it was rude for me to walk past you and Riana to the galley while you guys were so busy."

Tangles laughed her head off at the way Storm had said 'busy.'

"Busy must mean fucking," Tangles hooted.

Then she asked Storm about when Olga gave her the bracelet.

"We had an early breakfast this morning before we left, and that's when she gave it to me," Storm said. She described the moment in more detail until Tangles finally left her alone.

The discussion turned to food. We ate a lot of paella in Barcelona. Olga traveled with many servants. We joked that they must have spent the whole trip scouring Barcelona for restaurants that served paella they could take it to Olga at the hospital. Finally, all their questions were answered, and Letty and Tangles told their stories about office events we'd missed. Apparently, Andrea had spent a lot of time on the phone with Eli.

"I should have had Betty here for massage," Letty said, as we dried each other off, and put on the house robes. "I can call her later."

"No need to call. I volunteer," Storm said, with a wicked grin. "But just for thirty minutes each. The spa wiped me out, almost."

I declined the massage but watched as Storm went to town on the girls on the permanent massage tables down in the spa.

"I am dreadfully jealous about the bracelet," Letty said, when she was on the table. She kept turning her head to watch the bracelet. Storm kept repositioning Letty's head face down, then working Letty's back. Storm had worn it in the spa, all through the sauna, steam, ice and shower. I'm pretty sure she hadn't taken it off since Riana put it on her.

I could see Letty was having a great time teasing Storm.

She winked at me when Storm wasn't paying attention and turned her head again to watch the bracelet. "So jealous," Letty said.

"Ditto," Tangles said.

Tangles took the spot on the table. She followed Letty's lead, and watched the bracelet too.

"No sweat. We can take turns wearing it," Storm said, pausing the massage and lifting her arm to show it off again.

"My bracelet's not as flashy as yours is, but it's expensive. I won't put it through what you do."

"Me neither," Letty said, "Storm loves her bling. That's all."

"No lie. I love my bling. I never had such blingy bling before."

They were all laughing. I was glad to see everyone so happy, but the week in Colombia had taken its toll on me. They ganged up on me and tried to drag me to the massage table.

"I'm good," I said, "I'm going to have that sundae Tangles mentioned, and hit the bed. I'm worn out. All this medical shit was hectic and exhausting."

I thought about calling Lola but that would just be opening up a can of worms. If I called her, I felt sure her secret would come out, and everyone would know Lola didn't die, including Mason and Olga. Maybe she was just reminding me that she'd promised to leave the Camachos alone. I don't know what was in her mind. I bet she will break her own ban on phone calls and eventually be unable to resist poking fun that she had me on the run with her lie about the video and cash.

Emma fixed us enormous sundaes with three scoops of home made vanilla with our choice of every possible topping including peanut butter, fudge, marshmallow, whipped cream, nuts, fruit, and sprinkles. We ate them at the kitchen counter, then we all went our own way.

I stopped in my home office to check the mail. I sat at my desk, looked through a dozen envelopes that appeared to be bills. That was when I found it.

I was getting up. I looked on top of the credenza that sits behind my desk and found a polaroid. It was a picture of Lola seated on the chair I had just got up from. It wasn't a good picture because she took it herself. It was close, but it was definitely her. I tried to remember if I had ever brought her in this room or had taken a picture of her in that chair.

She wanted me to know she'd been in my house.

I called the girls to come to my office.

They filed in and looked at me expectantly.

"Sit down," I said.

I showed them what I found.

I handed them the photo. Silently they passed it around and handed it back.

"There were no strangers in the videos we checked," Tangles said.

"Let's look at those surveillance videos again," Letty said. She got up from the couch.

"Don't bother, I'll have Quito do it tomorrow."

"She needs to get a life," Letty said, shaking her head.

I looked at the image again and tried to make out if it was a current picture, or if it was one she'd taken on one of her earlier visits. Maybe someone working for me had planted an old picture for her. I did not want to think badly of any of my staff, but my home suddenly felt as secure as a house of cards.

July 27, 1993 (Tuesday)
Hawaii
Pixie

My call caught Mario at home before dinner. I was bursting with news and skipped the usual hellos.

"Mario, guess what?"

"Pix, what a pleasant surprise."

"Mario, you haven't guessed."

"It's Pixie of course. I know your voice. No guess needed."

"I didn't say guess who. I said guess what."

"Guess what, then?"

"All right, you don't want to guess. I got married to Felipe Guzman."

He quit talking for at least ten seconds. I heard the sound of a television commercial playing in the background, and the clink of glasses and silverware.

"Baby, I just want to know, are you happy?"

"I'm fucking happy, yes."

"Congratulations, Pix. I wish you were here. I'd carry you piggyback through the halls."

I giggled at the thought.

"Who is this Felipe Guzman you married?"

I heard Letty squeal in the background, yelling her congratulations and telling Mario that Filipe was a big shot entertainer.

He shushed her and asked me again who Felipe is. Mario can be a dummy. I could hear Letty in the background listing some of his big hits.

"Felipe Guzman is a singer. He never put out a record that sold less than three million and he packs concerts to capacity. Just one problem."

"Which is?"

"He's eight years younger than me."

"Melina would think so," he said. "Not me. It can't be a problem if you married him and he said I do. In a marriage, all that matters is how the two of you feel about it."

"Fuck it. I look great and I know it." I can say anything to Mario, my oldest friend on earth, my once-time boss, my lover, my family.

"Fuck him if all he married is your beautiful face," Mario said. "Baby, I know I'm going to be jealous. It just hasn't hit me yet."

"Boss, we can still fuck. There's ways," I giggled.

"Who knows? Maybe Letty and I can throw you a big celebration."

"Keep a lid on it for a minute. You're the first to know. Lainie knows we been getting serious, but I haven't told her yet."

"Where are you?"

I pushed open the sliding doors and stepped out on the lanai. The salty breeze swept through the white picket fence, blowing over my bare skin as I looked through a scatter of palm trees and beach to the waves crashing on the sand. The distant water was a brilliant blue, reflecting the kaleidoscope of hues that were the sunset. Like me, Felipe has been living in his bathing suit. He was asleep on a chaise, a straw hat tilted over his face.

"In paradise," I said. "Hawaii. We're at Olga's Hawaii house."

"Does Olga know you got married?"

"Nope, not yet, Mario."

"Baby, I'm touched you called me first."

"You will always be first in my life. Always have been. I'm calling Aunt Carmen next."

"I love you, Pix."

Mario handed the phone to Letty. She congratulated me like mad, and I swore her to silence. Letty gave me a pinky swear, and handed the phone to Tangles, and then Tangles to Storm, who serenaded me with 'congratulations to you' sung to the tune of Happy Birthday.

After he hung up, I realized I hadn't told him that Olga stepped aside as Lainie's and my manager. She hired the best team to be her replacement, the Los Angeles firm that represents Felipe and works all over the world and are the top dogs in concerts. Olga is too busy with her business to mess with me any longer. I know I made her a lot of money, but I know it wasn't the money. I was her ticket to get her name out there in the entertainment business, and she was my ticket in. And Lainie's too, of course.

Olga and I finalized a deal on the house that's across the street from Mario. I wired three million to Olga as full payment for the house and the contents. The house is worth twice that much. Once it had been Melina's house, back when Melina and Mario were on the edge of committing to each other. Jealous of Melina, Olga paid Melina six million for the house, furniture and personnel, then let me live in it as part of my representation arrangement. I've always had an option to purchase, but we never put a price on it.

"If you push it," Olga said, "I will deed it to you free."

I love that lady, no question.

I've come a long way since I was a kid hooking on 4th Street in East Los Angeles for whatever the traffic could bear. My signature wasn't worth the paper it was written on. These days, all it takes is a phone call for my banker to wire Olga three million, and the amount doesn't even dent my balance.

When we have time off, Felipe and I will have my house in Pasadena as our West Coast residence, and his beach house on South Beach, Miami, on the East coast If you can stand the weather, the house is to die for.

I could have gone all my life just singing for family if Olga hadn't got me my first audition and taken charge of my career. What did I ever do in my lifetime to deserve all this?

August 2, 1993 (Tuesday)
Pasadena
Letty

It's silly to drive two Ferraris to work every morning, so now Tangles and I take turns, one day my car, one day hers. I hold my breath on the days Tangles drives. She weaves around traffic like they're giving out trophies to the first car to the next light. Today we passed car after car, then caught a light, and all the stragglers we'd passed came to a stop beside us, blowing all her effort and risk. Without turning to look at me, Tangles adjusted her sunglasses. She looked sleek with her hair gelled back, big gold earrings, and sixties-style eyeliner. We'd already stopped off at the dry cleaner. A couple of Mario's spare summer suits were lying flat in their plastic wrapping on the back seat, destined for his office closet.

Storm was chauffeuring Mario in his Rolls. Last night, he'd brought up the subject of giving Storm a car next December, if she hit a sales goal. I don't know her taste in cars, but he suggested something midrange now that she's begun to take more of an interest in selling.

"You and Boss were getting so lovey. Is something brewing?"

"Did you think we'd get married?"

"I did think that."

Tangles was right but I wasn't going to agree. If somebody is going to make a public declaration, it won't be me.

"I think he likes Storm," I said.

We were on hold at a long light. Beside us were the usual random crowds, people of all shapes, sizes, and ages off to work. The cars around us were of all types, but we didn't come across other Ferraris all that often. The temperature in the car was temperate, but the windows were up and the ac blasting barely filtered air. Outside, smog hung in the atmosphere.

"He likes all of us," Tangles said, stating the obvious. "That's just him. How about you?"

"I love him," I admitted. "You know that."

"I love him, too, "Tangles said. "What's the difference?"

I shrugged. "You willing to put up with his nonsense?"

"So, it's nonsense he plays?"

I knew Tangles didn't put him ahead of herself. "Hey, concentrate on the road," I said. "Stop with the third degree. What's next, matchsticks under the fingernails?"

The light turned green again. Tangles gunned the engine, and left rubber, racing to the tail end of the traffic ahead of us, weaving around stragglers to get to the front of the line.

"Fuck you," Tangles said, punching me with her right fist, bypassing an Audi, a Volkswagen, and three Fords.

"Pull over and you can fuck me. Come on." I unbuttoned my top two buttons and did a little shoulder shimmy in her direction. Her eyes faced front, but she adjusted the mirror. I'm pretty sure she was reflecting on my cleavage.

She laughed.

"I love you, Letty."

I poked her shoulder. She stomped the brake, and pretended pain, still laughing. Her engine raced again, and we passed a Toyota, another Ford, and a little foreign convertible with some idiot driving with his top down in the open smog. He'd be a mummy by the time he got where he was going. We merged on to the freeway and got jammed in a forest of massive semis blocking the view of everything except of the vehicles in our immediate vicinity. Tangles groaned aloud at being boxed in.

"I love you too," I said. "I'd French kiss you if I wasn't strapped in."

August 6, 1993 (Friday)
Los Angeles
Mario

I lost count of how many times I started to call Lola, and it wasn't just to talk about the picture I found on my desk. I stared at the impish expression she was wearing—and the unbuttoned shirt—and felt it in my gut that she, herself, placed that picture there after sneaking in, sitting on my chair behind my desk, and snapping the Polaroid. It didn't matter that the surveillance cameras had not caught her at it. She had the same snarky, sarcastic sense of humor as Letty, and took pleasure in lying about the money and video. She couldn't resist the useless challenge of showing me she could get in my house.

I should have left her dead instead of infringing on her secret private life. I let the lion out of her cage. What a dumb fuck I am. What a dumb fuck I am to want to see her and do what we did before.

I'm not calling her.

"Your lunch is here," Andrea said on the intercom, before sending the delivery kid to the conference room. It wasn't anything fancy, just a club sandwich and fries for me, and a filet and asparagus for Letty. Tangles and Storm were wining and dining a potential client somewhere in Los Angeles. Letty opened my office door, and followed the kid in, handing him a couple of bills.

"Thanks, Skip."

We sat shoulder to shoulder facing the gray view outside, each of us with half-frozen diet cokes from the office fridge. As I opened the paper package revealing my sandwich, Letty flipped her steak from the carton to a paper plate.

We had a tab running at the greasy spoon downstairs.

I offered her a fry.

"No thanks," she said. "I'm saving my carbs for Emma's homemade ice cream tonight."

We ate quietly for a few minutes.

"Quito told me he went over the tapes again, and still didn't see anything," Letty said.

I told Letty that my take was that Lola got in the house somehow.

"I agree. You don't employ anyone who would have snuck a picture in for her."

"She snuck in and planted the picture," I said, watching Letty's expression. "Just as you would have done if I had challenged you to do it."

She gave me a surprised look. "You challenged her?"

"Not on purpose," I said. "I think it is just knowing that she's dead to us, and can't do it that would make her sneak in."

Letty nodded, reluctantly. "I can almost understand that. If it bothers you, you could add surveillance cameras inside." She finished off her steak, and only ate the tips of the asparagus.

"No indoor cameras. It's bad enough I have security guards like I'm somebody important."

Letty dumped our plates in the trash and came over to sit on my lap. She kissed me.

"You *are* somebody important."

That night, before dinner, Tangles kissed me and Letty in the foyer. She was dressed for clubbing.

"I'm out on a date, and after, I'm staying at the apartment. Back tomorrow."

I gave her a thumbs up and stuck a bottle of red in her shoulder bag. "Thanks Boss."

The wine had been one of two bottles that were going to the kitchen for Emma's take on spaghetti sauce, but all was good. She'd only asked for one, anyway.

In the breakfast room, Letty, Storm and I ate angel hair in red wine marinara, marinated artichoke hearts, antipasto, and garlic bread, and gorged on Emma's ice cream. Storm and I had seconds, and Letty went down to the gym for an hour on the treadmill. After her workout, she joined me in a robe in the wine room to laugh over a badly dubbed karate movie.

"Storm's in her room, earphones on," Letty said. "She's burning out her ears on heavy metal."

We ended up playing at copying the very badly choreographed fight scenes that involved lots of impossible flying around the room. I gave Letty a little toss on the couch, and she flipped over on top of me, pretending to pin me down.

"Letty, no date?" I heard myself say. "You aren't under any obligation to hang around with me."

"Yes Mario," she laughed at me. "You're so hard to take." She sat up. "I'm cool right where I am," she said, giving a little wiggle, still straddling me. She reached for my wine glass and took a sip from it before holding it for me. Wine drinking while (almost) flat on your back is a learned skill.

Eventually Letty and I went to bed naked as we usually did, eyes on the mirror above. We slept that way, most nights. We turned the temp down on the ac, and the covers up.

"Remember you told me you'd have my baby?" I said.

"I meant it when I said it, but I'm so into work. A baby needs a mom and a dad. I don't think I'd make a good mom. Selfish of me." She turned so that we were face to face.

"When I think of what you said, I feel flattered."

We kissed.

"I felt flattered when you told me you never wanted to lose me," she said.

"I meant that. That's pretty selfish, too."

We kissed.

We embraced.

We spent the night in a long slow hug, our bodies at each other, our mouths on each other like there was no tomorrow. We went over and out that way and I loved it. I think she did too.

"This is good," I said, into her mouth.

Letty whispered back. "Yes, it is," she said, her lips moving on mine as she spoke.

August 6, 1993 (Friday night)
Los Angeles
Tangles

Mark Sosa is a Ferrari and Lamborghini salesman I met when Boss gave Letty and me Ferraris. He charmed my ass off when we went to the dealer to pick up the cars. When he takes me out, he drives a brand new company car, a Ferrari. That's a lot of car to give a salesman. When he picked me up that night, he talked about how Fiat had just bought out Maserati, big news in his world.

"I have a waiting list of buyers waiting for delivery. That's how good I am."

"How good are you?" I asked.

"I'm so good, I could sell a Ferrari to the CEO of Fiat."

He was something of a braggart but a funny one. I liked him. He was a big guy, almost as tall as Boss. He kept me laughing, was at least an eight in bed, and didn't mind wearing a condom. He had a car salesman's gift of gab. Mark was smart and had an answer for everything. I figured it was part of what he was, a salesman.

We had dinner, danced in a packed crowd at the disco on Olympic

Boulevard in downtown L.A. then headed to my apartment in Pasadena, the one in the building that Letty and I owned together.

"Nice place," he said when I opened the door. It wasn't his first time over.

"Thanks," I said. "Letty and I got the building for a steal. It's paying for itself."

He poured me a glass of Boss's red wine that I'd just opened.

"Tangles, get me in with your boss. I would lease so many planes he'd beg me to stop taking orders."

"Ask him yourself. He bought cars from you. He knows who you are."

"I may do that," he said, sitting next to me on the couch.

"You got this beauty sitting unused, and I'm suffering in a one bedroom on Sunset Boulevard," he said.

"You know Letty and I live at Mario's."

"I know, I'm just putting my nose where it doesn't belong," he said.

"It's okay, Markey. Put your nose anywhere you want, you big beast."

"That's Mr. Sexy Beast, to you," he said.

"Are you done dancing?" I asked, putting on an old slow dance record, some New Orleans jazzy thing that Pixie had given me a few Christmases ago. We polished off our glasses of wine, and danced our way around the den, then headed down the hall dropping our clothes along the way. When we got to the bed, we were both naked. I yanked the comforter off and a minute later, Mr. Sexy Beast was on top of me, pushing himself deep inside. We orgasmed ourselves through the night.

It wasn't until till morning I realized we had not used a condom. It wasn't the first time for that either. Dawn peeked its way through my curtains around six a.m., and I woke sore, sated and pissed off.

I whacked his chest hard.

"Hey, some thanks are in order," he chuckled.

He got up, and stretched, filling the room. "You got coffee in this joint?" he asked, kissing the hand that had whacked him, and heading bare-assed for the kitchen.

"We have to use rubbers, Mark. No shit."

"Your fault lady. You were too ready." He walked down the hall, re-trieved his pants, and returned to the bedroom. He shook his pants out over the bed.

His wallet fell out on the rumpled sheets, then his keys, then at least a dozen condoms.

"I came prepared," he said.

"I came about a hundred times," I said. "But you better not get me fucking sick," I said, tossing the condoms in the drawer beside the bed.

We had coffee on the little dinette.

"I better never learn you are married," I warned.

"Me? Married? I'm not even close to that," he said. "Next time we go to my place, you can go over it with a fine-toothed comb, looking for this wife you imagine."

Ever since I dumped the married lawyer, I go through a whole number with any man who asks me out. Men lie, though I was pretty sure Mark was not lying. His apartment was in a nice building, and it was most definitely a bachelor pad. His kitchen trash was full of tv dinners, his refrig-erator empty, his laundry in big plastic bags in his closets, his sheets smelled like sweaty clothes hanging on a line, and if he had a housekeeper come in, she needed to be fired. I prefer my apartment.

"I don't understand the relationship you and your friend Letty have with Luna," he said. "You both live with him, you both work for him, he buys you each a Ferrari, and they're not a birthday gift or special occasion."

"Consider the cars a work bonus," I said. "We're a team," I said, trying to think of a way to make him understand. "We love him."

"Care to explain?" His eyes were full of curiosity, affection and humor, but I'm not a mind reader. I don't know if he was jealous.

I accepted the relationship, but I didn't think I could explain it. I knew I couldn't explain Storm being there too. Luckily, I was under no obligation to satisfy his curiosity.

"Mark, is this an interrogation? Because I don't like interrogations."

He raised his hands in surrender and flashed me a big smile.

At seven, we kissed at the door, and he left. I douched and showered and took a short nap on Letty's bed where the linen was nice and fresh. By nine, I was in the car on the way to Mario's, dressed in a summery sundress that had been hanging in my closet, last night's clothes were in my trunk in a laundry bag, and I'd left a note for the housekeeper's weekly visit, telling her she could have the half-finished bottle of excellent Merlot I had left on the counter.

At Casa Luna, I checked with Emma.

"Boss and Letty are still in bed," she said. "Can I make you breakfast?"

"Bed? I don't believe it. It's almost ten."

"It's Saturday," Emma said with a wink.

"He never stays in bed this late. Is he sick?"

I didn't wait for a reply but ran up the stairs to the fourth floor to knock on the door.

"Come in," Letty said.

Two candles and the television were the only lights in the room when I walked in. It was dark enough that Boss and Letty were anonymous shapes on the bed. The AC was blasting December air and I was dressed for August.

"Are you okay?" I asked.

"We're just fine," Letty said, sitting up, stretching like a cat, and flopping back on a stack of pillows. The blackout draperies were pulled tight, but my eyes were getting accustomed.

"Did you fuck all night?" I asked.

"Did you?" Letty asked, rolling over on to Boss like he was a giant body pillow.

"I did, but I am as clean as a virgin. Want to check?"

Mario laughed.

I kicked off my shoes and sat on the bed fully dressed.

"You never stay in bed this late," I said.

"It's Saturday," Mario said.

"Yeah, that's what Emma said. But you never sleep late."

"Who said we were sleeping?"

We laughed.

"It sure doesn't smell like you were sleeping. Smells like sex in here," I said.

"No rush today, no office, no business. An easy day in Casa Luna."

They were facing each other under a heavy gold comforter. I climbed on top and straddled them both. Letty scooted back and lifted the cover for me.

"You smell delicious," she said. "Get in bed with us."

"I thought you'd never ask," I said.

I stood on the bed and tossed my clothes item by item on to the couch before I got between them.

"Polyamory."

"I didn't know what it was," Boss said, his big arm on my chest, his hand reaching for Letty on my left.

"What is it?"

"What we got," Letty said. "Multiple consensual non-monogamous relationships. If it's a couple plus one, the plus is called the unicorn."

"Unicorn?" I laughed. "Where did you hear that?"

"I read it in Boss's Playboy," Letty said.

Mark had banged me so many times that I should be exhausted, but here I was wet with heat and need.

"It's good to be home," I said. It was at times like this when all I needed was to be near Mario and Letty.

"I love you guys," I said, snuggling in.

August 10, 1993
Puerto Rico
Lola

"I hate Puerto Rico. Besides, I got found out," I said. "I'm out of here," I told Alex.

I paid cash for the place, too much money to keep in Puerto Rico in a condo with shit resale value. I am more than ready to pull up stakes.

I'm not in witness protection, but it is similar in some ways. My handler Alex is my official contact to the outside world. Like witness protection, I can call it quits any time I wish. I didn't tell him everything—not who found me, nor how, and especially not that I had just returned from Los Angeles recently and how it killed me to return here.

Alex tried to convince me that leaving Puerto Rico was unwise. So did my brother Nico, who is still in the FBI.

"Why should I spend the rest of my life in hiding? I'm not living in find me alive. I'm not afraid of Olga, and she's the last one standing."

"Why do you want to leave Puerto Rico? What are you not telling me?" Nico asked. "I worry, even if you don't. Especially if you don't."

"I promise to let the bureau know where I'll be," I said, ignoring his

George Hatcher

question. My brothers are a pain in the ass.

"You better if you want to continue getting your monthly retirement checks," Nico said.

To avoid an argument, I agreed. It's not like the checks come to my mailbox. They go directly into a bank account that I have no need to touch. Except for the cash I put down on my place, I've barely touched my nest egg, a safety deposit box filled with cash.

The broker who sold me the condo said that the market was depressed. "I can rent it for you," he said, "especially if you plan to leave the furniture."

"Will renters leave any of the contents?"

"I'll find you a nice family, to rent or buy. Want to list it?"

"I'll let you know."

I called the broker with the biggest ad in the yellow pages. He came out. I gave him the ten dollar tour. I didn't open the gun wardrobe.

"I can sell this easy," he said, no doubt lying to get the listing.

"I'll give you the listing for two percent," I said.

Commissions are normally six percent.

"Three percent," he said.

"Deal."

If the place doesn't sell in six months, I'll be back to burn it and collect the insurance.

When the broker left, I dropped on the bed to take a twenty-minute power nap. I went to sleep and woke up laughing. I guess I had Pasadena on the brain, because I dreamed of my recent adventure sneaking into Casa Luna through the servant's entrance in my telephone repairman get up.

In real life, my little adventure had been a lark, but I bet that Mario must have been in an uproar when he found the picture on the credenza. If anyone had seen me, I doubt they recognized me from when I used to visit Mario. Hooker Lola certainly never visited in fake eyeglasses, coveralls, hard hat and tool belt with all sorts of telephone gadgets.

The fucker never called me after I hung up on him. No doubt he went through his safe with a fine-toothed comb, looking for a sign that I had gotten in, trying to see if the video or money was missing.

I rolled over, face up. Instead of the ceiling, I saw his face.

I bet I blew his mind.

I bet he still likes me.

I bet he remembers all those things I did to him. All the things he did to me.

Once I settle down, I'll find an excuse to meet up with him again. As for Olga, I'm not going looking for her. If she finds out I'm still breathing and decides to come after me, I'll ace her before she gets to me. She'd have to be psycho to come after me. The Camacho family is dead, its illegal corpse buried in Latin American industries, which went public as a giant solid gold nest egg in Olga's bottomless wallet.

Beside, why would she go after me? Over the million? That was compensation. I didn't steal it. Over Camila's death? I didn't do it. I was dead.

The power nap and thoughts of Mario made me restless. I called Miles.

"I got a hundred for you. I've got an itch for you to scratch."

He arrived fast, I always asked him if I was his only client.

I wasted no time. I got on top and fucked him. I called him Mario. When he got on top and fucked me, I called him Boss, like all his disciples do.

August 25, 1993
Bogota
Olga

Riana and I had breakfast on a balcony facing the sunrise. It was simple: Arepas stuffed with banana cream and coffee. The morning was lovely, and I was feeling good. The bruising was gone. The pain was gone. I was ambulatory, mostly because I'd had the treadmill carried into my bedroom and walked it every day for at least thirty minutes. I chased my coffee with a thirty minute walk.

Nothing in my home gym was ever used. There was a second treadmill gathering dust there, and I had it moved to Riana's room because she liked the idea of working out when we were staying at this house. At least in the bedroom, these things got used, for some reason. We slept together most nights, but she split to her own bedroom in the mornings to shower and get ready, and now, to get on the treadmill.

Before I hit the treadmill, Agosto called.

"The young man is in Bogota."

"What young man?"

"Dani from the night club in Barcelona."

"Get him picked up and bring him over."

I hung up. I know Riana must have been curious about the huge smile on my face.

"Who is it?" she asked.

I reminded her.

I heard the knock on the door, sat behind my desk and gave a nod to Riana. We'd had our showers and had dressed for business before we came downstairs to the office in this manor. It was a comfortable room with a massive antique desk, lots of oriental carpets, bookcases full of art, Brazilwood furnishings and several new comfortable leather chairs. I am guilty of frequently rearranging and redecorating.

"Come in," Riana said.

Agosto led the young man in. As he walked in, I remembered him, tall, leaner, younger, darker. I dismissed Agosto right away, and Dani turned as if to follow him out. Riana laughed aloud.

"She means for him to go and you to stay," she said.

He hesitated. I saw the uncertainty cross his face.

"Come. Sit."

I was behind my desk and pointed to one of the leather chairs. He came closer and sat.

"Want a root beer? Coke? Pepsi?" Riana asked.

"A coke would be fine," he said.

I saw him swallow nervously. I could see his Adam's apple as he swallowed.

Riana pulled a glass bottle from the drink refrigerator, opened it and handed it to him before she sat beside him in a chair identical to his.

"Don't be nervous," she said.

He accepted the coke but hadn't taken a single swallow.

"I understand you're from Brazil. I have two homes there," I said this in Portuguese. Dani's eyes opened wide and showed us his pretty white teeth. "What language do you prefer?"

"I had no idea you spoke my first language," he said in Portuguese. "I can speak Spanish and English, and I understand, little bit, other languages. Waiting tables educated me a little bit."

He was wearing a white cotton shirt tucked into long, tightly fitted black pants. The shirt did not look new, but it was well made, and fit him like a second skin. He had the body of a dancer. I could see long lean muscles straining the soft fabric. He met my eyes, palmed his head, running his hand over his hair, but it was a flirtatious gesture more than grooming. His eyebrows raised and he gave me a smile, and then Riana. Flirting, but with a theatrical sense of his surroundings.

He stood, reached across the desk for my hand and kissed it, and then did the same with Riana. He gave a bow that looked like a dance move, sat down again and delivered a unique smile to me, and then one to Riana, the expressions somehow completely different, personal.

I smiled back and so did Riana.

"Well, he's not shy," Riana said, in English.

"No, I'm not," he agreed, in English.

"Tell me about yourself," I said.

His story took about ten minutes. He mentioned one relative, his mother in Manaus, then talked about dancing in Brazil, a female friend who traveled with him to London, waiting tables in London, and three years in Barcelona.

"Are you curious why I asked you to come see me in Colombia?"

"Yes, madam."

I grimaced. "Miss Olga is good enough, and Miss Riana."

"Yes, I understand."

"When we met, I liked your looks, your manners, and your knowledge of wine. Are you interested in employment?"

"Whatever job you have, I take it with pleasure, Miss Olga."

"Did you leave anyone behind, Dani? I don't want to be separating you from your loved ones," I said.

"There is only my mother in Manaus," he said. "And she is much closer now than she was when I was in Spain."

He talked comfortably, said a few things that made us laugh, and charmed us both.

I looked at Riana and she nodded. She liked him.

"When he visited me in Barcelona, Agosto mentioned a job," he said, looking at me expectantly. "But he did not mention details." The expression on his face was intense, and his eyes were glued to mine. I could feel his eagerness, his high energy.

"Ah, the job. I am not sure of the details. I have homes in many countries, and I employ a full staff in each house. I have a personal maid wherever I go, and I have security personnel that are nearby wherever I am. I need someone I can trust. At the moment, I don't know exactly what you would be doing. Chores as needed, I suppose. Handling whatever comes up. You will travel with me. With Riana and me on a private plane."

"Dani, you will be looking out for Olga. Filling her private needs," Riana said.

"Wrong," I said. "You will be filling both our private needs."

His demeanor didn't change, but I could tell he was interested in all possible aspects of the job.

"Miss Olga, I am flattered and grateful that you are considering me."

"Do you want to be our personal assistant?" I asked.

"I would love to be your personal assistant."

"I have a question," Riana said. "What did you do for the nameless American lady that dropped you off in London?"

"I gave her sexual satisfaction."

He had no smile on his face or expression to go along with what he had just said. He had not let slip the woman's name, so technically, he was not breaching her privacy. He might need encouragement to keep him trustworthy.

"Would you mind taking your clothes off?" Riana asked Dani.

He looked at me, expressionless.

I nodded and said, "Not if you don't want to."

"I have nothing to hide," he said. He got up, fastened his eyes on mine, and dropped his pants, his undershorts and his button-down shirt. He was lean, and the muscles hinted at by his tight clothes were impressive without being bulky. His smooth hairless body was black and strong. He wasn't erect, and it hung like a long thick sausage.

"Where did you get all that strength, Dani?" I asked.

"I dance," he said. "Native dancing requires a man to lift a woman high overhead and hold her for minutes at a time."

"I can see why your lady friend took you to London with her," Riana said.

The corner of Dani's lip curled up. He wasn't at all embarrassed. He was amused and trying to look sober and dignified.

"What I can't see is why she left without him," I said.

Riana laughed. Dani's half smile got a little bigger.

"I like you, Dani," I said.

"Thank you, Miss Olga."

"We can discuss money later. I can provide accommodations. But there are a couple things you should never forget," I said. "Never cross me," I said in Portuguese. "Don't ever lie to me, and don't ever talk about me to anyone, ever."

"I see nothing. I hear nothing, Miss Olga." He looked at me then over to Riana. "Miss Riana, you can trust me too."

I picked up the phone and dialed Elisa. When she came to my office, I introduced them.

"Dani, this is Elisa Sarmiento, a member of my house staff. She manages international office duties in my place when I am not here. Elisa, give him a guest room, and let the housekeepers know. Elisa, this is Daniel who prefers to be called Dani. He will be a live-in personal assistant."

"Yes, Miss Olga. Should he follow me as he is, or should he get dressed?" Elisa asked.

I looked at Dani, still standing there nonchalantly as if his clothes weren't piled around his ankles. He finally drank the Coke, swallowing it in one long pull on the bottle, and then putting the glass on a coaster on my desk as if he were wearing royal robes, not standing bare-assed in a room with three women staring at him. The guy had no shy bones in his body.

"Get dressed Dani. We're going to get you some new clothes and get you comfortable and situated. Elisa will send a cell phone to your room. That's how I will reach you when I need you."

As I called my personal physician Carlos, Riana poured two glasses of red wine, Vega Sicilia Único from the case we got in Barcelona.

"I need you to come over and check a new employee named Dani Silva. Blood, everything. I want to be sure he is healthy, and I want to be especially sure that he is not AIDS infected."

I hung up the phone.

"What do you think?" I asked Riana.

"He's a hunk, especially what's between his legs."

"Yes, he's good looking. I want him to shadow us as an assistant who is always around."

I was actually happy. I felt confident his medical would be okay. If not okay, I'd put him on a plane back to Barcelona or Manaus.

"All the dudes we have sex with, we don't test them before. Why Dani?"

"Amor, he's going to be living with us."

"He's the picture of health," Riana said.

"If you don't want to wait, go for it," I said.

"I'll tell the doctor to rush the test results."

My attorney in Switzerland had cut a deal with the candidate I wanted as CEO of LAI. He was the founder and former CEO of a technology company that had sold to Intel. Ted McGuire had been the architect of the sale, a multi-billion-dollar deal.

"A million a year plus all sorts of fringes and stock options," Riana said. "Is he really worth all that?"

"Amor, he is the best candidate. LAI needs a hard ass to run the company. He's exactly what we need to give us the cachet I'm dreaming of for

LAI."

"You're a genius," Riana said. "I never question you on business matters."

"Thanks, Amor. This will free me up. We can find new things to do, challenges to conquer. I don't want a single day of my life to be boring."

"I agree. Let's make each day special. But I can pay my way. No need for you to pay for everything. I have money and you know it."

I kissed my best friend, her lips flavored with wine.

"Your money is no good around me," I teased. "Besides, I have money enough for a zillion lifetimes."

We toasted each other with a smile.

August 27, 1993
Hawaii
Pixie

It wasn't like my husband Felipe and I didn't do it before we got married. We probably did it several hundred times before we said I do, but Felipe had never acted like a psychopath. Here's the setting: it was the middle of the night, and the glass doors to the lanai were open. The mysterious bird calls, the sound of the waves, the ocean breezes were in the bedroom with us. With all the palms and green things growing inside, plus the rattan, and grass cloth, it was like making love on the beach without the bother of sand and gawkers. I was on my back with pillows propping up key body parts, and Felipe was on top braced by his elbows missionary style, but then he sat up and moved his hands around my neck. I wondered what he was doing but didn't say anything; at first his grip was gentle, then his hands were a vice, choking me almost to passing out. His nails dug hard into my neck. I'd waited too late. With the room spinning and my consciousness swirling down the drain, didn't think I could snap a finger to break his grip. In my head, I thanked Letty and Mario for being my sparring partners for years. I popped him on his side, then his kidney, then threw him off me. He went flying off the bed, smacked the wall, and hit the floor. I jumped off the bed directly on top of him and pinned him flat with my right elbow in his neck.

"What the fuck was that?" I asked.

His eyes were wide like he was looking at a stranger. His eyes were dilated, like he was on something. For sure he was dumbfounded that I had lunged him off me with such strength. I made no secret of my black belts, but he had never seen me in action. That little toss was child's play, nothing compared to what I could do.

"I don't know what happened," he said in Spanish, shaking his head.

I let him sit up on the carpeted floor.

"Pixie, forgive me."

I said nothing.

I went to the ensuite bathroom to put a closed door between us. I'm no delicate snowflake. I was ready to kill him when I saw the bruising on my neck. In karate workouts I have been tossed around, knocked black and blue. I've gotten bruised, but not by my fucking husband.

I found him in the bedroom, lying in bed like nothing had happened. I turned on the light, grabbed him by his long hair and yanked him into a sitting position at the edge of the bed.

"Look at this," I said, pointing to my neck. Red marks now, but they would soon be blue.

He did and started to cry.

"You even think of doing this to me again, I'll kill you."

"I'm sorry, Pixie. I'm sorry."

I went back to the bathroom, got in the shower and didn't come out until I knew he was asleep. I went down the hall to a guest room and went to bed alone. I locked the door behind me.

I cried like a baby.

The first bastard I thought I was going to marry dropped me and got engaged to my daughter Lainie, then he killed himself because he'd been caught out as an embezzler. Now, this famous Felipe that women adore turns out to be a psycho sadist. I have fucked a ton of men, and I never had one of them try to choke me. What if I'd passed out? What would he have done if I was at his mercy, unconscious and helpless? Kill me?

The next afternoon, we were on his plane headed to Mexico City. We hardly exchanged a word. I slept in the reclining seat to avoid him. I was still boiling inside. This fucked up the honeymoon for sure. We'd been in Hawaii a month. I'd told Mario that we were married exactly thirty days ago.

On arrival in Mexico City, I couldn't take it anymore. Being near him made my skin crawl.

"Felipe, I'm going to fly home. I'll be in touch."

"Pixie, this is home."

"My home is Pasadena, remember? Your home is Miami. Mexico City is not home. It's just a house you own."

My plane was parked at the airport in a hanger. I spent three hours in the plane, alone, sitting on a sofa with my guitar, singing, drinking wine, waiting for my crew to arrive. I called Letty and told her what happened.

"You aren't going to dump him, are you?"

"Ask me that when I take the makeup off my neck in four hours."

"Pix, I'm sorry," Letty said. "All of us were so happy on your behalf. I love you girl. Do you want me to kill him for you?"

"Kick his ass maybe. No, not really. I'll do any ass kicking for myself.

Don't tell Mario. No telling what he'd do," I said. "I'm embarrassed that I let it happen. I could have kicked the shit out of him the moment he put his hands on my neck, but my guard was down. I mean, we were fucking, right?"

"Don't fret, Pix. Hurry home. Safe flight. I love you."

"I love you too," Tangles chimed in.

Lainie was on tour in Argentina. I didn't call her because she would not keep her mouth shut or mind her own business. She'd find a way to hurt Felipe, probably using the media. I wasn't interested in hurting his public image.

I was deeply afraid of what I would do to him by reflex if he tried this shit again. Maybe I should just call it quits. The love I thought I had for him was driven out by my not knowing what he would have done to me if I hadn't defended myself. The bruising would go away, but the wound would not.

August 28, 1993 (Saturday)
New York City
Lola

I rented an unfurnished studio apartment in Manhattan's East Village, which I knew well. At six in the afternoon, I was in a mattress store buying a nice velvet-tufted headboard, queen size frame and mattress. Two hours later, the delivery guys set everything up for me. It being Saturday, I had already cruised a garage sale and picked up a couple of things including 12-drawer dresser that the owner let me have for cheap. At Barney's, I found linens that matched the headboard, a beautiful wine color, a Bordeaux if you were to pour the wine in a good light.

Except for what I shipped, I had left my household stuff behind, so I bought two televisions, a wood stand, a leather couch and a chair to match. By the time I squeezed in the coffee table and two end tables, it was a little crunched, but it was cool. The stove was a foot away from the living room. I didn't outfit the kitchen for cooking, but I had to have my coffee maker and a flatware set because I needed the spoons. I didn't plan on cooking. The apartment was tiny, but the location was bitchin'.

The bathroom was all tile, even the ceilings and walls, and the ancient bathtub was cast iron, without a nick in sight. The toilet was brand new. I could span the width of the room with my arms outstretched, and although the length was a bit longer than I could reach, it was still miniscule. My condo in Puerto Rico was much bigger, but here I felt free.

Four days after I arrived, I was settled. I started calling United Parcel Service General Delivery to check on the package I had sent to myself from Puerto Rico. The package took a week to arrive. I got home and unpacked. I had carefully packed some kitchen pans and even a waffle maker. In the center of the box was seven hundred thousand I had left from the million that I gotten from Camacho. I had taken a chance by sending the money like that, but life is a chance. Everything you plan for tomorrow is up in the air because who knows if you'll be around? I opened an account in the bank across the street, and got a safety deposit box to put the money in.

Inside of two weeks, I was feeling at home in the big city. I had a bank account, a safety deposit box, and cable service for both my television sets.

The place was pretty much a big rectangle, with the kitchen at one end, the living room in the middle and the bedroom at the far end, with the windows all along one side, the floor entirely carpeted except for the tiled kitchen. The bedroom was open to the living room but having a TV there I didn't have to move the bigger set so I could see it from my bed.

I sent my brothers my contact information first, then notified the retirement division of the FBI with the information they needed to get my monthly payments deposited to my new account.

Camila had an apartment in Manhattan, no doubt taken over by Olga, but she rarely came to New York. There's hardly any chance she'd run into me here, and she's never seen me in person. I don't know if she's seen a picture of me. Camila probably had a picture of me from when she sent her assassins after me.

Mario said all along that Olga had nothing to do with it. Who knows for sure? Only Olga.

Prestige Resources was a private investigation firm that apparently reached across the globe. I didn't know anyone there, but my brother Nico said that when he retired, he probably would hook up with one of their offices.

"Speak up. I can barely hear you," Nico said.

I was downstairs in my building, drinking coffee in a booth in the small greasy spoon that was open to the public. I wasn't interested in cooking, so it was convenient that they were there, and open twenty-four hours. It wasn't anything special, but there were a dozen booths against the glass, an aisle, and a counter with a bunch of stools. There were usually three or four people working: one cook, and the rest handling tables. Nothing in Puerto Rico was open twenty-four hours a day.

Gina the waitress brought me my regular toasted bagel with cream cheese and refilled my coffee.

"I'm not ready to work," I said louder, on the phone with my brother Nico.

"Prestige Resources is loaded with retired FBI, and they are constantly recruiting. You don't really work for them. They refer cases, for a percentage. It's like working for yourself," Nico said.

"I'm not ready to work," I said for the third time.

"When you are, hit them up. They have a big office in New York."

"Thanks for telling me about them."

"When you have time," Nico continued, only now he laughed. "All you have is time. When you feel like it, get your PI license. It will be a breeze for you to get it. You will need it if you connect with Prestige or anyone in the business."

"Will do, Bro. Thanks for looking out for me."

Compared to Puerto Rico, New York is expensive. I'd lived there before, and in spite of the expense, returned for the pluses. Good public transportation. No need for a car. Plenty of clubs. Lots to do, and all of it at a faster pace than Puerto Rico.

No doubt there were plenty of gigolos and escorts here, but no one appealed to me. I doubted I'd find a Miles for a hundred. I cruised night clubs and got offers, but no one turned me on. I bought a vibrator at an adult toy store, went home and put it to work. The next time I was out, I dressed up and went to a night club with a fifty dollar cover. I had a plan. The fifty was an investment at this place where fifty barely covered the cost of two drinks. I sat at the bar. In no time, I had plenty of offers wanting to buy me a drink. I already had a drink in front of me and smiled the offers away.

A good looking man came shoulder to shoulder with me at the bar. He looked fiftyish, strong and pleasant.

"I'm Art," he said. "Fill up your drink?" He glanced down at my glass as he ordered his first drink from the bartender.

Something about him struck me. I nodded. The bartender performed, provided the drinks, and left us alone. We talked for a while, and before long, he had me laughing. Along the way, in response to something he said, I said, "I'm not cheap, but I can be had."

"How much?" he asked.

"Five hundred for two hours," I replied, eyes on him.

"I was thinking all night," he said.

"A thou."

We walked two blocks to his hotel, the swanky St. Regis that reminded me of the hotel in Beverly Hills where I met Mario several times. It was ironic that I'd bombed finding a date until I went out as a hooker, and then nailed a big spender. I had a feeling he was going to be a good. I needed a fuck at least as good as what Miles gave me in Puerto Rico. Mario didn't just give me a good fuck; it was great sex all around. I didn't expect that from a trick who was going to pay me a grand for the night. Only Mario gave me that kind of sex.

In the morning, I was still there. I might have gotten three hours of sleep, but I wouldn't bet on it.

"Art, you are a tiger," I said as I got up. Before we went to sleep, I kept asking him what he took to stay hard for so long, but he just laughed.

"Don't leave. Stay. I'll give you more money."

Actually, I'd forgotten about the money. I had not asked for payment in advance, and his offer took me by surprise. I was so satisfied I thought about telling him to forget the money, but I had already carried the fantasy of being a hooker this far. Why back off now? Last night, he didn't get drunk or sloppy. He was too busy fucking me.

I leaned over and kissed him. He liked Scotch. The Chivas in his breath and on his lips was an aphrodisiac. I felt close to this guy.

"It's not the money," I said.

"What is it then?"

"I will need a walker to get out of here. You wore me out."

"You probably say that to everyone," he said good humoredly.

"Not true."

I took a hot shower, switched it to cold and felt revived.

When I came out, he was out of bed. "You look wonderful," he said.

I gave him a smile.

"Here's the thousand and five hundred," he said, handing me the money.

I heard myself say, "I should be paying you. I lost count of my orgasms."

I had told him my name was Vivian, like Julia Roberts in Pretty Woman.

"Give me your number," he said. "I get to New York often."

I intended to write out a fake number, but that's not what came out on the hotel pad. I handed to him.

"Stay in touch, Tiger," I said.

We kissed soft and fast, then he hugged me. We kissed again, long and slow and deep, like we had during sex. This was not me. I was going to take the train home, but I figured a taxi would be faster. When I closed my eyes, I dozed off. We got stuck in traffic, and I woke remembering how Art had drummed into me, almost made me come again in the back seat of the taxi. He could have picked up someone and not had to pay a dime. He had a good look about him, clean cut, someone you could cuddle up to.

I didn't even know this man.

I didn't even ask him when he's coming back.

I don't know why I didn't stick around. I had no reason to rush back to my empty apartment.

September 4, 1993 (Saturday)
New York City
Art Hughes

"I think she likes me," I said into my cell phone.

"You're halfway home if she does."

"My plan was to hit on her. I didn't realize she was hooking."

"Not a chance. She's not a hooker."

I laughed. "She took my fifteen hundred."

"I don't believe it. She doesn't need money."

"She didn't hesitate. Took my hundreds. Didn't say thanks, either."

"Are you sure you got the right person?"

"I don't make mistakes," I said. "I'll be back to you."

September 4, 1993 (Saturday)
Pasadena
Mario

"I'm home from Hawaii," Pixie said on the phone. "I'll be over in a sec for breakfast."

"Is your hubby with you?"

"No," she said abruptly.

There was something in the tone of her voice.

We walked down to breakfast.

"Emma, hold off for a bit," I said. "Pixie's coming over to join us."

Letty and Tangles exchanged glances and whispers like they were sitting on a rocket about to go off.

"What's up?"

Letty still looked about to explode but shook her head at Tangles. Tangles didn't listen. She swore me to secrecy then said what was going on with Pixie and her husband. I got pissed off. If I'd been in Hawaii when it happened, I would've beaten the guy to a pulp. I know Pixie can take care of herself—a special ops pro doesn't have the fighting skills she has—but it irks me that the jerk married her and went after her like that. A total sicko.

I kept my promise and didn't let on that I knew. Five minutes after we sat down for breakfast, Pixie revealed the bruises on her neck and told the story I had heard from Tangles. Emma brought out a tray of waffles covered with a tortilla cover, and bowls of fruit compote, whipped cream and assorted toppings.

"You want me to fly over and have a 'talk' with him?"

"I can handle him," Pixie said. "If he tries it again, he'll be smashing his balls on my knee." She let out a little giggle.

"Maybe he was on something," Letty said. "You must have loved him. Why would you marry a guy who would do that?"

"I do love him. I'm afraid if he does that again, I may hurt him. I don't want to hurt him."

"If he does that again, kill him," Tangles growled.

"I've watched his music videos," Letty said. "He seems so fucking suave and fantastic. Maybe he took something? Did you ask him why he did it or what he was on?"

"Fuck no, I didn't ask. I was fuming."

Pixie and I had grown up together. Now she is an international celebrity sitting in my breakfast room, sharing her feelings with us while munching away at a big waffle smothered with strawberries and whipped cream.

Life has bumps. Pixie is strong, and I knew she could handle this and a lot more. Still, I felt bad for her. I wanted happiness for her, the real thing.

Maybe he was sick.

"Tell him he has to see a shrink," I said.

"The media would find out," Pixie said.

"If you let him fuck you again, you are on top, no exceptions," Letty said.

Pixie laughed.

"I'm not letting him fuck me for a long time, if ever."

"Stay tonight. Sleep with us," Tangles said. "We'll help you get over it."

Pixie hung out at my house all day. It was just like old times, with Letty and Tangles and me, watching movies in the media room, hitting the pool, doing the spa, and ending up in the wine room. I was on the recliner, Letty, Pixie and Tangles were on the couch. Storm was up in her room with cramps and a heating pad. There we were with the wineglasses out, and Tangles stood up and toasted Pixie.

The toast went down. Tangles cuddled with Pixie.

"We're going to have a girls' night out," she said. "Girl therapy. My room."

Letty, Tangles, and Pixie all stood up at once, a human tripod. They wobbled a little bit when Letty stopped abruptly. Letty looked in my direction.

"Boss?" she asked.

"I'm good," I said softly. "You go make Pixie better."

I watched the three of them stagger out of the room.

After a few minutes, the wine room was too quiet. I cut off the lights and headed up to the third floor, passing Tangles's closed door that didn't muffle the giggles behind it. I had insisted I was just fine, but I wasn't. Storm's door was open, and from her position curled up on the bed, she saw me standing in the hall.

"Hey Boss," she said. "Come in."

She looked miserable, curled up in a ball on top of the covers, an electric heating pad on her stomach.

I sat on the side of her bed.

"How you doin' kiddo?"

She let out the whimper of a wounded puppy. "I hate this time of the month," she groaned.

"Would snuggling up with me tonight help?"

Five minutes later, Storm was in my room, under the covers.

'Thank you, Storm."

"Boss, no. Thank you for asking me."

We lay quietly in the dark, and I rubbed her stomach.

"That feels so good," she said in a low voice.

She rolled over, her back to me. I spooned her, one hand caressing her belly. I pressed against her we soon found sleep.

Sunday morning, Storm joined us for breakfast.

"Did you ladies have a relaxing evening?" I asked.

"I feel great," Pixie said. "I'm leaving for Mexico City today."

"So soon?"

"Can't stop a tour."

Pixie's plane was due to lift off at five minutes past noon.

"I love you, Boss," she said over the phone. "I'm wheels up any minute. Wish I had spent more time with you. I'll be back to see you before you know it."

"Call me if you need my help with him. I'll be there in a flash, no matter where you are."

I heard a sigh. "I love you," she said.

Reception was bad, got worse, and we lost connection. She didn't call back. I stared at my cell phone, remembering my first time. Since I was ten, my friend Carson and I had scoped out adult magazines he swiped from his stepdad. Pixie had always been my pal. It never mattered to me that instead of having a mother, an auntie like mine, or a regular family, she was growing up in a cathouse. We were tight, and I didn't care she was a corner girl, though I didn't have much of a concept of what that meant. When we were both about thirteen, she unzipped my khaki pants. Of course, I thought she was a good bit older than thirteen, but what the hell did I know.

"Let's see if you get a boner."

I let her pull it out. It grew in her hands as she stroked it up and down.

I already knew it worked because it often got big at night and before I got up in the morning.

I worked after school, but sometimes Pixie and I met up at my place while my aunt was at her job. I explored Pixie's body and she did the same to me. Our bodies were not like the adults in dirty magazines, but it was exciting. Pixie got me off for the very first time of my life.

Pixie was my friend, my pal, my lover for decades.

All along, I'd thought Pixie was older than me, rather than a couple of months younger. Anyway, her Nana died, the cathouse where she lived changed hands, and she was suddenly homeless and pregnant. I took her home to my Aunt Carmen, and Aunt Carmen took her under her wing. I was working to get clients for one lawyer, then another one, and my business got so good, I got Pixie to start working for me. She never much went to school, and I always took for granted how musical she was, always singing, or playing an instrument. Pixie was one of my team for years, until Olga heard her sing English and Mexican songs at a party I was having and was inspired to get Pixie her first audition.

She deserves every morsel of success. She oozes with talent. There isn't a music instrument she can't play by ear, and her voice is addictive. More than half of her hit songs she wrote herself. Thinking about her made me feel maudlin. I went to my stereo and put on some of her albums.

"Boss, where are you?" Tangles yelled.

"In here," I yelled back. I was sitting on a lounge chair in front of the indoor swimming pool. The acoustics in the pool room are fantastic. I was about halfway through hearing the stack of songs.

She handed me a glass of wine.

"The whole house rings of Pixie," she said. "It's like she never left."

"I was thinking of Pixie, of when we were kids."

"Boss, from the look on your face, I thought you were having a wet dream."

"If it was a Pixie dream, it was a wet dream, for sure. I've heard stories about these two," Letty said, laughing.

"Why didn't you marry her?" Tangles asked.

"We never talked about marriage." I drank from my glass. "I don't think she considered marriage back then, after being a corner girl."

"Like her big hit song, Corner Girl?" Storm said. "It was so brave of her to come out about her life like that."

"She didn't have a choice," I said. "The studio wanted to keep it quiet, but Pixie was sure it was going to come out eventually and scare off her fans. So, she wrote a bunch of songs about her young life. Instead of being a liability, her secrets became her asset."

"So, you didn't ask Pixie to marry you. Who else have you not married?"

"Too many to count." I laughed.

"You should count Melina," Letty said. "You almost married her."

I nodded. "I love her. She loved me, but I don't think either one of us really wanted to get married. We already had each other. We never lived together. It would have been a battle figuring whether we'd live at Casa Luna, or her house across the street."

"Did you not marry anybody else?"

"Olga, I loved her like you wouldn't believe, but we weren't really wanting to get married. It was this thing, a custom."

"Are you saying you will never get married?" Storm asked.

I drank and thought for a moment. I looked at Letty.

"If Letty was going to leave me unless I married her, I'd do it, hands down."

Letty covered her mouth and laughed.

"Boss, you don't mean that."

"I mean it. Don't look so surprised. We talked about it before."

It took a minute for Letty to speak. "You know I'm never leaving unless you show me the door."

We were probably supposed to laugh but didn't. Tangles looked from Letty to me, back and forth like a tennis match.

"If you two go through with it, can we do a polyamory thing, so I'm included?" Tangles asked.

We laughed. Neither of us answered the question.

"More wine," I said.

September 6, 1993 (Monday)
Pasadena
Tangles

Before going home for dinner, I headed for the apartment building that Letty and I owned and where we kept an apartment that we were not using. Once a week I picked up the mail. Sometimes when I drove with Letty to the office, we'd swing by and check the apartment and mail together. Today I was alone.

The plan was to get the mail and drive on to Casa Luna. It was still pretty early, broad daylight, but I was starved. Mario had had lunch but at lunchtime, Letty and I had been on a conference call with an operator in France looking to lease eight planes. I wanted to get in and out quick because I knew Letty was starving too, but she was going to hold dinner till I got there. I parked my Ferrari in my space. An unfamiliar car—a boss looking Buick was in Letty's designated spot. It made me grouchy, because as a landlord, I should do something about it. The sign was clear: Private Parking. The lot wasn't full, and the three spots for guest parking were empty. I scribbled down the license plate number before I opened the mailbox.

I pulled out my key and jiggled the box lock. My stomach growled painfully, and I gaffed off checking up on the apartment. I headed back to my car, barely paying attention to the area, flipping through the stack of mail as I walked. I used my key, got in the car, and dropped the mail on the seat.

I reached for the door to close it. A woman was maybe fifteen feet from me, walking in my direction. I would not have noticed her except that she was holding a twenty-two, and it was pointed at me.

"Whore, I warned you to stay away from my husband, and you didn't listen."

I didn't recognize her, and I don't fool around with married guys. Not knowingly, anyway. This had to be the wife of fucking Matt, the fuckhead lawyer whose office was in the same building as GAL. I had been seeing him two years ago, but I ended it when I got the wake-up call from the ball and chain herself that he was married. I hadn't been out with him since. If I saw him in the lobby or elevator, I ignored him like he was a ghost with leprosy.

"I haven't been with your loser husband for two years," I yelled out the window. "Fuck off lady. I don't want to hurt you."

She fired a round.

I kicked off my heels, dove out the passenger side, and rolled out on the driveway, handgun in hand. I took cover behind the rear wheel.

"Lady, scram," I yelled.

The twenty-two cracked twice more, and two shots whizzed by.

I didn't fire, but my handgun was out. I remembered my gun coach telling us—Pixie, Letty, and me—to take serious aim if our lives were in danger. Sure, it was a twenty-two and lethal, but this woman couldn't hit the broad side of a barn. I scooted around the back of my car, as fast as I could. To my advantage, the lady was crying, trying and failing to feed more shells in, shaking so hard she couldn't manage. I saw her drop two shells, and bend down to pick them up, sobbing her heart out. As pissed as I was, I felt sorry for her. I would sure as hell hate to be married to that lying jerkoff that she called husband. She was bent over when I lunged in her direction. I took her down like some Hall of Fame football jock. I yanked the twenty-two out of her grip and slung it to the grassy knoll before I pinned her down.

"Listen, Mrs. Martinez, I cut all ties with your dead-beat old man the day you called me two years ago. You're shooting up the wrong bimbo."

I sat up straddling her stomach as she sobbed softly and put her hands over her face. She didn't say anything.

"That jerkoff you're married to is not worth this. Any moment the cops will be here. Do you want to go to jail?"

She moved her hands and stared at me with bloodshot eyes, her lip wobbling like some kid who got coal for Christmas.

I got off her, took her hand, and yanked her to a standing position.

"Go," I said. "Get the fuck out of here. I got no intention of making your kids' mama into a jailbird." I pointed to the car in Letty's parking spot that had to be hers.

She mumbled something between gasps and rushed to her car. She was sorry.

No doubt.

She burnt rubber getting out of there.

I found myself in the apartment and tossed the rifle on the floor of the linen closet. I could see that the housekeeper had done her usual bang-up job cleaning up and airing things out. The dinette was set for dinner, looking like a spread out of House and Garden, fresh candles in all the sconces, fresh flowers in all the vases, but it didn't seem very important noe.

My right knee was skinned, my suit looked like I'd slept in it, grass clippings were in my hair, and my handgun had a scratch from grinding into the pavement, but I didn't have any wounds. My car wasn't so lucky. It had two holes in the driver's door. Shells hitting a Ferrari make a distinctive sound.

I hung out in the apartment hiding my face behind the curtains like some neighborhood gossip, gazing out toward the car, but no cops showed up. No tenants came out to see what was going on. On one hand, I felt I lucked out not having to deal with cops and all the red tape. On the other hand, I wondered where everyone was. What is this world coming to when the shoot-out at OK corral is in your front yard, and no one even bothers to dial a phone?

I was still standing by the window when my phone rang. I glanced at the time and saw an hour had passed.

"Where the fuck are you? We're going to start eating already."

"I'm on my way, Letty," I said. "I got held up. I'll tell you about it when I get there."

I ran a brush through my hair. The rest of me was too wrecked to fix fast. I locked up and hit the road.

When I walked in and they saw what shape I was in, it took ten minutes for Boss and Letty to settle down. They saw my skinned knees, rumpled, grass-stained clothes, and I showed them the scratch on my handgun. After I told them what happened, I ran up to my room, took a shower, and put on shorts and a blouse. That's what I was wearing when I came into the wine room to join them for dinner. Finally.

"She could have killed you," Mario said, very upset. "I'm not pleased that cops were not summoned. When she finds the broad her husband is seeing, what's going to happen?"

"I took the twenty-two," I said. "She was scared shitless and broken-hearted. I don't think she'll try that again."

"She'll get another gun."

"I felt bad for her. I'm not going to snitch her out. She's got it bad enough married to the jerk-off. She was wailing."

"We would be wailing if you had been hurt," Boss said.

I couldn't take the way Boss and Letty were looking at me. "I thought we were all starving," I said.

Food went around. Fruit salad, baked mac and cheese, short ribs, yeasty rolls. We started eating.

"You should have popped out of the car and gone for her from the start," Letty said. "Grab the offensive."

"She came up pointing the twenty-two at me when I was sitting in my car. I played it by ear. My gun was in my purse on the seat. I rolled out the passenger side with the gun in my hand and took cover behind the tire till she bent down to pick up the ammo she dropped. Then I tackled her."

"You did good," Boss said. "You are here with us." He raised his wine glass, gestured like a toast, and took a sip. "Call that prick husband of hers and tell him what happened. He needs to know."

"I plan to call him. He doesn't know it yet, but he's paying whatever I get charged to fix my car. I think there are two holes. Maybe more. I didn't look that close."

After dinner, I called Matt. He answered his cell and was unaccountably happy to hear from me.

I nipped that in the bud.

"Listen up. You need to keep that thing of yours in your pants. You're a menace."

I told him what happened. "I let her go because no one deserves the grief of being married to you. It's on you if she goes on the hunt for the bimbo you're seeing. It's your fault there's a target on her back. And Matt, I will send you a bill for the repairs to my car."

"I'm speechless," Matt said. "I'm still at the office."

I could clearly hear a restaurant in the background. I'd bet a million bucks his bimbo was sitting at the table with him. I wonder if she knew he was married. "Sure, you are."

"I'm going home," he said. "She must be there. The kids will be back from school by now."

"No doubt," I said. "It's past seven."

"I'm sorry, Tangles."

"Yeah, that's what she said after I disarmed her. She could have fucking killed me. If she kills your bimbo, it's on your head."

"This is a nightmare. I'm sorry," he said.

I hung up with no further comment.

After the call, I went back to the wine room.

"Boss, do you mind if I light up a stick? I'm a little tense."

"Good idea."

"Let's go to the bedroom and get comfy," Letty said. "We can smoke, drink, have ice cream later."

"We just ate," Boss said. "I don't want to go to sleep yet. Do you?"

"Who said anything about sleep?" Letty said.

Boss was the first to get up. We took the elevator together, and Letty immediately lit candles and incense. I excused myself and took a detour to my room to soak in the tub. I was beginning to hurt. In karate, you learn to take some heavy hits, but when you go down, it's on a mat, not concrete. The hot water stung then soothed my skinned knees. I didn't linger though. I'd already kept Boss and Letty waiting too long tonight. I put on a baggy tee over my underwear.

While I was in the tub, Boss had changed into sweatpants and a tee. Letty and I stripped down to our panties and bra. Boss's bedroom was made for relaxing. There used to be his-and-her sitting rooms until one of them had been made over for closet space, but there were still lots of comfortable places to sit and lay back. The TV was on mute as always, and I put on some of Lainie's music.

The drapes were open, the sky painted with the color of the setting sun. The grounds were gorgeous. We sat out on the balcony and watched the play of the landscape lights. The outdoor pool lit up, changing colors every couple of minutes, the Koi pond bubbled, the waterfall cascaded.

September 7, 1993 (Tuesday night)
Pasadena
Mario

We were just arriving home from work when Olga called. I went straight to the breakfast room and sat down. Storm disappeared upstairs, Tangles disappeared downstairs, and Letty ducked into the kitchen to ask Emma if she had any hors d'oeuvres.

"Amor, I just now learned what happened to Pixie," Olga said. "She said you know. Why didn't you call me?"

"Baby, first off, it's good to hear your voice. You never call anymore."

"Amor, I'm sorry for getting right to the point. I'm upset that I didn't hear about this sooner."

"Yes, I understand how you feel. Apparently, she told Letty and Tangles first, and swore them to secrecy; and when she told me, she made me swear to keep quiet about it."

"Now that I don't manage her or Lainie, I speak less and less with her. Maybe I should have stuck it out with her. I love her so much."

"She was only here one night, and then went on to Mexico. She says she still loves him. I offered to kick the shit out of him, but she turned me down. You know she's a warrior and can more than defend herself."

"Amor, we're family. Please let me know about these things. She just begged me not to do anything to him."

I laughed.

"What's so funny, Amor?"

"Just the way you said that. You talk like a Camacho."

Olga laughed. "I'm not really a Camacho, you know that. My roots are just as bad though. He should be shown the error of his ways, and what is in store for him when he messes with one of ours."

"Baby, let it go. Pixie will put everything back in order. I hear she catapulted him off the bed in a double-gainer with a half twist. He was a little surprised."

I handed the phone to Letty to say hello then Tangles got it from her. I got it back to say goodbye.

"Love you, Olga," I said.

"I adore you Mario Luna."

September 7, 1993 (Tuesday night)
Bogota
Dani

First, I was a general assistant, then a valet, and now I am Olga and Riana's personal butler. I love the job, whatever they call it. I'm with them all the time, like a shadow. I don't get to drink or smoke or dine with them, but I still get to live in luxury, am never hungry or broke, and have no bills.

We haven't traveled yet, and that is coming soon. I gave Miss Olga's lawyer my passport, and he is fixing it. I will not have a problem entering any country she goes to. I have four suits tailored for me.

"You may need nice clothes where we go," Miss Olga said.

The tailor came to the house.

I have a dozen walking shorts, a dozen short sleeve shirts, a dozen long sleeve shirts, and six dress shirts for my suits. Miss Olga says I will never have to use a tie, but I have a collection of them now.

I heard her tell a guy on the phone that she adored him. How lucky for him. I never heard her say that to anyone but Riana. One day when I am deep inside her, I will make it so good for her, she will tell me that.

Normally I go to my room at night, unless she asks me to stay on the sofa until she falls asleep. Tonight, she and Riana were in bed, and she asked me to join them.

"Dani, come lie with me please."

She reaches out. Touches me. I grow hard.

"Get in bed. Take it all off."

"Yes, Miss Olga."

"Use a rubber," Miss Riana says.

I put it on.

"No rubber," Miss Olga says.

Miss Riana disagrees.

I hesitate. Miss Olga does not wait for me to remove it, lifts the covers, and I get in beside her.

"Let me show you how I want you to fuck me," she says.

I move beside her on my side, facing her, my right hand cupping the right cheek of her ass, left hand on the other cheek.

She spreads wide and guides me in.

"Now on top," she says. She rolls on her back. I roll with her on top, cock and hands in place.

"Fuck me deep as you can. Squeeze my ass. Understand?"

"Of course, Miss Olga."

Riana sits up on the bed.

"Olga you just got your back to stop hurting from that attack on you. Let him take it easy," Riana says, catching my eye.

I try to indicate that I hear her. I have no intention of hurting her, but of course I am going to follow her direction.

"Dani, fuck me. Lie on me, but don't kiss me."

I had fucked Miss Olga before but not with her guidance.

My hands cup her ass, and my index finger teases her back door. She moans in pleasure. I fuck as deep as she wants, not lying flat because I have to make room for Miss Riana who moves close. I see them kissing as I pump hard into her. When Riana is kissing, I sneak a pinch to myself once or twice to keep in control.

"Mario," she moans.

She calls me Mario four times.

"Mario, she likes to hear your body slamming against her pussy," Riana says.

I do as she asks.

The night rings with the wet slap of flesh on flesh.

She comes furiously.

"Come now," she says.

My body obeys. In my head, she is mistress in all things.

The blankets, spread, comforter, and linens were on the floor. The sheets were a mess.

Miss Olga stood up, naked. The light was dim, and in it, she looked like a goddess. If Miss Riana had not been there, I would have told her so.

"Dani, while I bathe, please change the bedding, everything."

"Yes, Miss Olga."

She disappeared into the bathroom.

When she was gone, I tossed the rubber in a trash can. I changed the sheets for her, still naked, found fresh blankets, comforter, and spread. Doing her bidding was so arousing, I was half erect by the time I had it perfect. I remembered the day that Elisa had asked Miss Olga if I was to follow her through the house naked. I did not dress. I did not leave.

She came out of the bathroom in a robe. The overhead lights blazed in the bedroom. I had turned them on to do the bed.

"Dani, turn those off for me and get dressed."

She was in bed when I asked her if she needed anything else.

"Riana is sleeping in her room tonight. See if she needs anything."

"Yes, Miss Olga. Sweet dreams."

In total darkness, I started for the door.

"Dani, you did good. Thanks."

"Thank you, Miss Olga."

I crossed the hall to Riana's suite. She opened the door before I knocked and pulled me in by my shirt.

"I should shower first, Miss Riana."

"You're just fine like you are."

I followed her to the bed. In the light of the bedside lamp, she was beautiful. She had insisted I wear a rubber with Miss Olga, but she herself did not want one.

"Kiss," she said.

She liked to start off with her on top. It was three in the morning when I went to my room.

There is nothing not to love in my job. I love the work, if you could call it that. I love the accommodations. Compared to my place in Barcelona, this is palace. Well, it may be an actual palace. My bathroom is bigger than the two bedroom apartment I shared in London.

September 11, 1993 (Saturday)
New York City
Lola

"Hey Vivian."

I felt a little shock hearing his voice on the phone. It had been a week since Art gave me fifteen hundred to spend the night with him. He had said he came to New York often, but I didn't think he'd be back this soon.

"What a surprise. I didn't think you were going to call me, ever."

He laughed. "I told you I would. I'm hooked."

"Sure, you are."

"I would love to see you tonight."

"That would be nice," I said. He turned me on, this man.

I met him in the lobby bar of the Peninsula Hotel, across the street from the St. Regis where he said he was staying.

"I like this bar better," he said, "I hope it's okay."

I looked around, absorbing the grandeur. I was glad I had dressed up. Black sequined halter dress, black sequined purse too big, fashion-wise for dress-up. Butter-soft black leather stiletto boots. I should have brought a clutch, but I opted for the larger shoulder bag my gun fits in. At least it was black and sequined but not a true match. Old habits die hard. Besides, the mink covered the bag.

He kissed me lightly on the lips and we sat at a table for two, an open bottle of wine in the bucket. The waiter asked if I wanted something from the bar or wine.

"Wine," I said, my eyes on Art.

The candle centerpiece illuminated his handsome face.

"You're so beautiful," he said.

"I'm not beautiful," I said with a little laugh.

"Wrong," he said. "Are you hungry? Want dinner?"

"Are we going back to your room?" I asked.

"Of course. Want your money now?"

"What I meant is that if we're going to play, I'll skip dinner, but I'm in if you want to eat."

Art reached for my hand.

I let him hold it. He squeezed it lovingly, if there is such a thing.

I don't know what was up with me, or why he affected me so. I went with cops for so long, maybe I forgot what gentleness is, if I ever knew. Mario wasn't gentle either. He got right to business. Sure, he made sure I was satisfied, but there wasn't a lot of necking or holding hands while enjoying a drink or just sitting, talking. I'd watched Mario for so long, I fell in love with him. The sex with him was blinding.

Art is different.

He thinks I'm a call girl. Maybe he's being nice because that's how he treats high-class call girls.

I had two glasses of wine and was feeling good.

"I have a confession," I said. "I'm not a hooker."

Art's expression did not change, or maybe the candlelight was cloaking his reaction.

"I have a confession too," he said. "I didn't think you were."

"I took your fifteen hundred," I laughed. "I can give it back."

"No, it's yours."

"A few nights before you, I was on the hunt for a one-nighter and bombed out. So when you thought I was, I just ran with it."

Art laughed.

"Now you know," I said. "Are you okay with that?"

Art nodded, his face curiously serious. "I'm okay. I want you. I have an idea. Let's take off. Let's fly somewhere. You know I have my own plane," he said. "We can go anywhere you want."

"You must be doing some kind of business to afford a plane. What kind of plane?"

"A Falcon. It's a baby, only three years old."

"I'm impressed," I said. "Do you push drugs or something?"

Art laughed. "Or something. I'm in real estate. I buy and sell. Always hunting good deals. Nothing huge. It's just me, no partners. So where are we going? Anywhere in the world."

"Gee, I didn't bring my passport," I said. "Maybe next time."

"I want you now," Art said. "Let's walk across the street."

By two thirty in the morning, I'd had so much sex, champagne and so many chocolate-dipped strawberries that I was considering abstinence.

"Art, I'm going home. I'm spent."

I sat up on the corner of the bed and looked around the for my clothes. They were around the vicinity of a chair, pretty much everywhere except on it. It wasn't that much. Panties, a fancy halter dress. Heels. A black mink for the chilly night. I dropped the dress over my head and tugged it in place.

"Please stay. We can sleep. In the morning, we can plan something to do," Art said.

"I'm so wiped out that I'm not going to shower. You're a prince."

I continued to get dressed. Adjusted the girls in my dress. Pulled up my panties.

He rolled out of bed and put my shoes on for me.

"Thanks," I said, surprisingly touched by the gesture.

"I'll get your money," he said.

I laughed.

"No money, Art. I told you, I'm not a hooker."

He kissed me all the way to the door of his suite. I took the elevator to the lobby. The taxi driver had to wake me when he pulled up to my building. Champagne does that to me, especially if I mix it with wine.

I hung the mink in my closet.

I dropped the rest of my clothes on the floor and collapsed into bed. New York was getting chilly at night, a far cry from Pasadena and Puerto Rico. That was fine with me. I burrowed into my delicious bedding and was over and out.

In the morning, I felt good. No hangover. With a clear head, I went down to the coffee shop and had coffee and a scone, then went back to my apartment. I bagged the little sequined number for the dry cleaners and picked up my mess from last night.

I dug out my fingerprint kit and latex gloves and tossed them on my kitchen dinette.

I opened my purse and unpacked it: gun, wallet, makeup, keys, cloth napkin. Inside the napkin was the flute I had swiped.

I mailed an envelope to my brother Nico.

"Nico," I said on the phone, "I'm sending a print to run for me." I told him what I mailed. "I like him, and everything seems so perfect. I need to know who he is."

"I can get in trouble," Nico reminded me.

"Oh please. Just do it for your sister."

Of course, he would do it. Nico always looked out for me.

September 12, 1993 (Sunday)
New York City
Art

When I got up in the morning, I called.

"She owned up to it. She's not a hooker."

"I told you."

"I tried to pay her for last night. She said no."

"Don't mess it up. She's smart."

"I'm taking my time."

"I know you're good. Finish this when the time is right."

"When I get her on the plane," I said.

"I don't want to know how, after."

"I'll be in touch."

September 13, 1993 (Monday)
Pasadena
Letty

Boss left for the office with Storm. I followed Tangles to the dealership where Boss had bought the cars for us. Mark Sosa, the salesperson that handled the sale, was Tangles's boyfriend. He told her to leave the car and he would have a top notch body shop handle it.

I got out and observed the interaction between Tangles and Mark. Dark hair. Brown eyes. He was not as big as Mario, but he was big. He was not as fit as Mario, but he was fit. I didn't need to be a mind-reader to tell how much he liked Tangles.

"Are you sure you aren't hurt?" he asked.

"Do I look hurt?"

She denied it, but I snitched her out, laughing.

"She put makeup on her knees. She got hurt."

On the way to the office, I said, "He's a hunk."

"You didn't say that when you met him the first time," Tangles said.

"I checked him out while you two were talking."

"Yeah, I like him, but only like," Tangles said. "He's not as tall as Boss."

"Is that criteria for you? Tall as Boss? You never said if he's good in bed."

"He holds his own. He doesn't have the abs Boss has."

"What is all the flattery about Mario?" I asked.

"Eyes on the road," Tangles said, pretending to reach for the steering wheel.

"My eyes are on the road," I said, looking at her.

We laughed.

"You are so jealous," Tangles said.

"You know I'm not."

"Are too."

"Not."

"I wish you two got married, and I was part of the family."

"You said that before," I said. "You mean that, huh?"

"Fucking A. I love both of you."

"That's fucking awesome," I said, my eyes back on the road, my fingers on the steering wheel.

"You dig it, for reals?" Tangles asked.

"I want to be with him the rest of my life, I don't care if there's a marriage certificate and a wedding ring. I'd say yeah in a split second if he asked."

"And what about me?"

"If I'm in, you're in, or no deal."

"Want me to finger you?" Tangles was laughing.

"Should have asked before we were a half block from office, bitch."

September 13, 1993 (Monday)
Pasadena
Mario

"Nothing lasts forever," I told Olga. "I have an operator who wants six new Boeing 747s. Boeing manufactures the planes and now they are pushing financing. I'm looking at a written proposal they gave this operator. He shared with me hoping I'd drop the price. If I match this price, we lose millions."

She sighed. "Pass, of course. You may want to consider flying to France to talk to the heavies at Airbus. You went there before to check the plant."

"I can do that though I hear they are starting to do the same financing. They pick and choose. They beat us to a pulp with what they are willing to do to move their planes."

"Are you saying we need to close shop?"

"I'm saying we need to change focus. Andrea told us from the beginning that the money was in used planes. We shifted the focus to new planes, but I think we should emphasize used for the time being. We've bagged millions doing what we do."

"Amor, I trust you. Do as you think is best."

I thought about the insurance company that had sent a rep to talk about buying out the company. I reminded Olga.

"I'm the one that sent them to you last year. Amor, I'm not interested in selling. GAL is a gold mine. Make it work. I'll back any play you make. You know you have the consortium backing right where you want them. That's a lot of bread you got behind you."

"Thanks for the vote of confidence. I am double-checking every deal. We're not rushing to say yes to any new plane deal unless it's small aircraft."

There was a hesitation on the line, then she said, "I miss you, Amor."

"I miss you, too."

Another hesitation. "I got Riana and me a butler."

"A butler? Like you need a new employee."

"Not that kind of butler," she said.

"What other kind of butler is there?" I said, then figured out what she meant. "Oh."

"No one is as good as you, Amor."

"I get it," I said.

"Amor, get in the plane and surprise me one of these days."

"Whenever you say," I said.

"I'm going to Europe; I'll be in touch."

I hung up. Letty and Tangles were in their office working on a deal. Storm was scoping the field for second-hand planes on the wish list of potential buyers. I felt like calling someone in with me, but I wasn't going to interrupt work. Our half hour conversation got personal for under a minute, but that minute had more impact than the rest.

I pictured this new butler Olga had hired. How could I blame her? I thought about how empty my home would be without Letty, Tangles, and Storm.

Before we went home, I briefed Andrea, Letty and Tangles that the focus was going to be used planes again. We would still do new plane deals, but probably only with operators that couldn't get preferred financing. Prime operators would certainly go for the better interest rates that the factory offered.

"We have some inventory, and we can buy more. The leases are less money but if you put a pencil to the numbers, you'll find that the returns are great. It's less risk than fronting millions on new planes. And this way, we aren't in competition with the factories."

GAL and the consortium of banks had their money invested in leases collateralized by the planes. If an operator failed to pay, we repossessed the plane just like banks repo cars. If we repossess a plane, it doesn't sit around. We lease it out again ASAP. Everything worked out, at least everything did for everyone but the poor schnook whose airline went belly up.

I could count with one hand how many times we had to repossess a plane.

Betty had cancelled on us several times in a row, until we took matters into our own hands and had her over for dinner one night. Emma pulled out all the stops, though we just ate in the breakfast room.

Wine. Empanadas, falafel, peanut butter ice cream. It was all delicious and served family style.

Betty brought us up-to-date. She had a man in her life.

"I don't want to give up my clients, but I keep cancelling appointments."

"I know," Tangles said. "Boy, do I know."

"Not just you," Betty said. "All my clients. I'm afraid I'll lose them. And if I don't spend time with Sam, I might lose him."

"Everyone has the right to settle down, if that's what they want," I said. It was easy to tell she liked this Sam. Every other sentence out of her mouth was "Sam says..." or "Sam wants..."

She promised to let us know how things worked out.

We would have invited Betty to stay but she got a call from the new man and cut the evening short.

Tangles had a date with Mark, and Storm was going out to a movie. Letty and I had the night to ourselves. I may be showing my age by saying this, but I didn't mind. A night with Letty is just what I needed.

So, we have a routine with the bed, folding down the top cover, me on one side of the bed, Letty on the other. I had just taken hold of my top corner when Letty spoke.

"Miguel's restaurant is not doing well," Letty said. "He thinks his partner is stealing money. Miguel is not that good with money."

Letty fluffed her pillows. It was already perfect, but I adjusted mine.

"If he needs a loan, I'm in."

"Boss, you gave him a hundred thousand. Not a chance he's coming for a loan. His heart is set on being successful and paying you back."

"You know I love him."

"He knows and I know."

Letty slipped out of her robe and under the sheet. I turned out the lights and joined her.

The next night for dinner, it was the girls and me. We ate in the wine room. Taco night, a regular thing.

We decided that the next time we scheduled a masseuse, Letty would call a service.

"Let's not get personal with anyone they send," I said.

"Why not?" Letty asked.

Perhaps it was because of my bad experience with the hotel masseuse who had been a cop.

"I don't have the fortitude or the energy to start the trust thing all over again with someone new."

"Who knows if the next masseuse could be another Lola," Tangles said. "Boss hire a full-time masseuse."

Storm waved her hand meekly. "I'm a masseuse."

You should have seen the face Tangles made. Her jaw dropped, her eyes popped, and she turned three shades of pink.

"So am I." She put her hands on her hips emphatically. "Are you telling me you want to take a pay cut and demotion go back to that?"

"Not really," Storm said. "I like the money, and I'm starting to dig the office, and the office wear, and the respect I get."

"I rest my case," Tangles said, turning from Storm to face me. "So, hire a masseuse, put her on payroll and write off her salary."

I laughed. "I can tell you been talking to your CPA."

"My CPA is your CPA, Boss. He says we've got to try and write off everything."

"I'm saving all my clothes receipts," Letty said. "I buy to dress nice for work."

"I'm doing the same," Tangles said.

"Good for you," I said. I still had the same CPA that I started with. He was getting old, and now he also had the girls to protect.

I put the five a.m. karate workout habit to rest. It was my eighth day of jogging in the morning instead of going the usual martial arts routine. I didn't start my jog until six in the morning. I enjoyed the morning run. I hadn't jogged since first moving into the neighborhood. The run was six miles in forty-five minutes, certainly not a record. My body needed to get used to it.

"Are you going to hang up your regular workout?" Letty asked at breakfast, after a week of me not hitting the gym.

"Taking a break. I like the outdoors. Running, I feel I get to sort out everything. I can't do that so much in the gym."

"What do you sort out?" Tangles asked. She had a green moustache from the strange smoothie she often drank for breakfast.

I reached across the table, pinched her nose, and wiped some of the green from her upper lip. "I got to think of you and Letty."

Letty handed Tangles a napkin.

Storm pretended hurt. "Hey Boss, do you ever sort me out?"

"I wish I could marry the three of you," I said.

"You can marry one of us. Why should anything else change? We're a family." Letty said, intent on her scrambled eggs and bacon.

Storm handed me a sourdough toast buttered up the way I like.

"Letty, are you serious? Knowing me, you'd marry me?" I asked.

She looked in my direction and put her fork down. Her elbows went on the table, her chin resting on her hands. She looked thoughtful, then she grinned at me.

"Sure, I'd marry you, Mario Luna."

"Fuck, this is serious," Tangles said. "Aren't you supposed to kneel or something?"

"Shh," Storm said to Tangles. "This is getting interesting. Don't interrupt."

"Are you two for real?" Tangles asked.

Letty stared, a big smile on her face. "Boss and I, we're just joshing. Right Boss?"

Bless her heart. She was giving me an out. I didn't touch the joshing. I took a sip of coffee. Smiled at Letty. Bit toast.

"Damn," Tangles said.

"I'll get the car," Storm said, getting to her feet.

What the fuck just happened in there?

The safes had once been hidden in my office, much to my contractor TJ's grief. On the remodel, we'd moved the safes to their own tiny room on the ground floor, where their weight is better handled. I went to the safes before leaving for work. From one, I took five bundles of cash, packages of twenty thousand dollars in hundreds. I put the money in a small Louis V zipper bag. I opened the other safe and retrieved what I really had come to get. I put that in the cash bag, too.

The safe room had its own tiny office with a little desk, chair, phone, intercom, and an old computer that used to be upstairs. I used the phone to call Andrea.

"I'm running late. I want you to handle something for me but not a word to anyone."

"Sure, Boss."

I gave her instructions and headed out of the house. Storm was in front waiting in the car, a tabloid open across the steering wheel. The girls were in Letty's car, probably at the office already.

"Sorry it took so long," I said to Storm.

"It's good, Boss. I caught up on the news. Look!" She turned the tabloid to me, and I saw her version of news was a picture of Kate Moss standing on a table. "Kate Moss, dancing on the table at the Brasserie Lipp. Have you ever been to that restaurant in Paris? I think her shirt is see-through. Models can do anything."

"Never been there, not that I recall."

She folded up the tabloid noisily and jammed it in the door pocket. "No sweat, Boss. Radio or no?"

"How about a CD? An oldie like Neil Diamond." I immediately thought of Melina. "Axe Neil. You choose anything you want."

Was this is what I want or what I need? Both. I don't want to find myself alone and have to hire a lady 'butler' to service me. It might be fun, but it would be a sad thing.

What about Olga?

Fuck Olga.

She was on her own. On her own, but not alone. She was with Riana and her butler. Wonder where he's from? I felt curiosity but nothing else.

Olga was history. Melina was married. Jo was happily married to TJ. Pixie was married, unhappily to her psychotic rock star. Niley had a whole different life. What Lola was doing was anybody's guess, but she wasn't doing it with me. History told me that even when I love my girls, and they love me, they left.

I didn't want them to leave me again.

Especially not Letty.

I got to the office at ten, with less than two hours to straighten out pending business that needed my attention. Andrea was in my office two minutes after I sat in my chair.

"Everything is set, Boss."

"Thanks, baby. What do you need from me before I leave? Anything other than what I have on my desk?"

"Boss, relax. Everything is going to be fine. We both have phones."

Andrea came around my desk. I got up, and we hugged. We stood there for a long time. I kissed the top of her head.

"Remember when you asked me if I did anal?" I asked.

She swatted my butt with one hand.

"I never said that."

"Yeah, you did." I said, remembering our trysts before she got married. I kissed her on the lips. "You are so special to me," I said. "I love you."

"I love you more," she said.

Melina had always said that to me.

Olga would respond with "I adore you."

My mind is crowded with memories.

I took a deep breath, walked into Letty's office, and closed the door.

She looked up. "Hey Boss. Are we going to do it? I heard the lock."

I approached her desk. She got up and met me halfway. I lifted her by the waist and sat her on the desk. I sat in her chair and rolled it to face her, almost eye to eye. Letty's dark hair was cut short, and she had a waifish look.

"Boss, what's going on?"

"I'm not dramatic, and I'm kind of clumsy about some things."

She swatted my chest. "You are not clumsy."

"Okay, let me just get it out," I said. My heart raced. I could run for an hour and not get my heart pumping this hard. I don't know why I would be nervous, especially after this morning.

"Are you firing me or something?"

I laughed.

"Far from it. I'm not firing you." I coughed. Cleared my throat. I reached in my coat pocket and pulled out the ring hidden in my closed fist.

"I'm trying to find a way to tell you that I want us to be together for the rest of our lives," I said. I opened my hand and held out the ring.

Her head straightened. Her cheeks got pink, and her eyes glistened.

My eyes filled. I'm the guy that killed four guys in self-defense, a master in karate and judo with so many tournament awards I can't even count, and here I was, crying. Letty caught my arm and dabbed at my face with a tissue.

"I told you, I'm never leaving."

"Letty, I love you with all my heart, with all of my being. Will you take a chance and marry me?"

She hugged me. My mouth found hers. Our tongues and our teeth rubbed.

"I'm sorry for not being romantic like—"

"My heart is about to fly out of my chest," she said, tears rolling down her face. "You don't need to marry me to keep me."

"You don't get it," I said. "You are what I want. I want you for my wife. I don't need a housekeeper or a baby maker or a trophy. I don't need a grocer, or a rock star or a mob princess. I need you."

"Yes, I'll marry you, Mario Luna."

We got lost in an embrace, I don't know how long. But I was still holding the ring. I wasn't sure what that meant.

"It was Sami's intent that I give this to my bride, but if you don't want it, I can buy you another ring."

"This is too much, Mario. Just a plain wedding band, Mario."

I took her left hand and slipped the ring on. Olga had said the rock on this ring was worth a million dollars. I didn't like that Letty felt it was too much.

"It was meant for you. Look how it fits," I said.

It had always been a little tight on Olga. Seeing that ring on her finger had me rubbing my eyes again.

Letty grabbed a fresh tissue, wiped my face and eyes, then her own.

"Letty, it doesn't have to be an open marriage. I'll can try to be a textbook husband."

She laughed a little.

"We can talk about that."

"Later," I said, looking at my watch. "On the chance that you would accept, I made arrangements for a trip. We need to split from here at noon."

"Where are we going?" Letty asked, excitement shining from her like a light.

"Paris. I included Tangles and Storm on the manifest, if it's okay."

"Of course, it is okay." She looked at her hand with the ring on it. "It's so heavy. Oh my God, is this for real?"

I picked her up, cradled her in my arms, kissed her and carried her next door to Tangles's office.

"We're going to Paris," I said, "Get your purse."

"Oh my God," Tangles said, looking at the rock.

"That's what Letty said. Let's get Storm and split."

Storm was not in her office. Andrea found her in the atrium watering something.

I stood Letty on her feet in front of the elevators. Tangles and Storm gathered around, waiting for the light to hit our floor.

"What's going on?" Storm asked.

"We're going to Paris," I said. "All of us. Right now."

Letty raised her left hand to show off her ring.

"Oh my God!" Tangles said again, and Storm said simultaneously.

Andrea had arranged our chopper ride to Ontario Airport where my plane and crew awaited our arrival, and she came along to see us off. We all put on microphone headsets that muffled the noise of the chopper and allowed us to speak normally and hear each other.

"I will love you for the rest of my life," Letty said as we took off.

The pilot raised his hand with a thumb up.

"Such a beautiful moment," Storm sighed.

"I love you both, so much," Tangles said.

In the helicopter, all the way to the airport, Andrea, Tangles and Storm congratulated Letty and me.

Outside the hanger, Andrea waved goodbye.

We were lined up, getting aboard, and Tangles said, "Does everyone realize we have no luggage?"

"Paris," I said. "Shopping."

"Am I dreaming?" Storm said, excited.

We met our three pilots and three flight attendants inside, and sat at a round table, Letty on my lap.

"First things first," I said. "Storm, please check the strongbox in the bedroom and make sure all passports are in there. I have mine."

"They are," Letty said. "I made sure last time we were here."

Storm confirmed.

"Okay, we're set to go," I said.

"I want to hear how Boss popped the question," Tangles said.

"Letty, spill. Come on."

Letty laughed. "You had to say it that way," She jumped off my lap. "I been wanting to pee for an hour. Be right back."

"Are you happy, Boss?" Storm asked.

"Yes, I'm happy."

"I'm so happy for you both," Tangles said.

Letty and I were belted into seats in the bedroom, at the foot of the bed. The room was dark except for a few built-in night lights along the floor line.

"Where do you want the service?" I asked.

"Anywhere," Letty said. "It's Paris, the city of love. How could we go wrong?"

I wanted our marriage to be strong.

"A Catholic church and a Catholic priest," I said.

"That way there's no divorce," she said. She touched my hand in the dark. "I'm not leaving you, Mario, as long as you want me. Are you that sure you want it to be for keeps?"

"I am if you are," I said. "How about Notre Dame, if we can swing it on such short notice?"

"I'm in, any way that you want," Letty said. "Notre Dame would be heavenly, but it could be a preacher in a store front on the Champs Elyse. It won't be getting married by the Catholic church that keeps us together. What keeps us together will be us."

"I agree," I said.

"That was a big one," Letty said, as turbulence rocked the plane. She clutched my hand.

"We'll be through this soon. Then nothing but smooth sailing ahead."

"Speaking of smooth sailing, let's talk this out," Letty said. "We don't need rules to be married, and I already said I will never leave you. Still, we need to talk."

"I agree rules suck," I said. "I will do my best to be a good husband."

"Mario, I'm okay with open marriage. I only get bent out of shape if you go find strange pussy and don't take care of yourself. I don't mind you fucking those we both love. I love Tangles. If could marry her legally, I already would have. Thing is, I love you more. Married, we can keep on doing what we do. But what's sauce for you is sauce for me. One day I may see some dude that turns me on. What if I want to fuck him without you getting bent? I don't want him for ever, just for a minute, and then, done? But I still want you forever."

"Are you serious?"

"I told you, we don't need to marry to keep together. I don't want the 'I do' to make you feel imprisoned. No imprisonment for either of us."

"But you want to get married?"

She raised her hand with the ring.

"Only if you do. I love you, and I know what this ring means, but really, I'd be happy with a plain wedding band."

"But you do love the ring?"

Letty kissed the diamond and kissed my hand.

"I love this ring because it came from you, and because I know how much it means to you."

"I love you," I said. "What else do you want to discuss?"

"I want to keep working. I love what I'm doing. I never thought I could do it and now that I'm in it, I love it. Even if we have a kid, I want to work."

"You got it," I said. "Besides, I'm too old to be a dad. I'll be at least sixty-five when my kid is nineteen or twenty, too old."

"That's not old. Don't worry, I'm not going to give you a child unless you want me to. If one happens by accident, you can pull the plug on it. Do you have a problem with Tangles and Storm living with us?"

"No problem."

"You are such a womanizer," she said, "but so am I." She giggled. "It's okay, as long as I know. No hiding. You do that for me, and I will always do the same. I will never lie to you. I don't know if I can handle you and Lola. There's just something about her that troubles me. Thing is, I saw what promising to stay away from her did to you and Olga. It would be crazy to say yes to every woman on the face of the earth except for Lola. Really, I saw what Olga's demands about Melina and Lola did to you. So, do what you do, just tell me the truth."

I kissed her.

"Thanks, baby," she said.

"You never called me baby before."

"We can both use baby. What'cha think?"

"Deal," I said. "I love you." I unbuckled my seat belt and moved a few feet to her. I sat on the plane's carpeted floor, put my arms around her, and my head on her lap.

"I love you, too," she said.

"I could have done a lot better when I proposed," I said.

"You took my breath away. You could not have done it any better."

She leaned down and kissed the back of my neck. My face pressed against her stomach. I could feel her warmth, and her scent was a turn on.

"You are getting me excited," she said softly, her hands in my hair.

I moved my hand against the warmth of her stomach and blew air against her skin. She twisted a little to unbuckle her seat belt. We slipped on to the bed, still dressed. That changed rapidly. The plane was chilly, Letty's nipples were tight points, her skin was goose bumps, and I could feel her shiver.

"Let's put on the GAL sweats," I said. "We got years to be naked. Let's get warm."

I hit the lights from a bedside switch. Letty was already headed to the dresser. She pulled out two shrink-wrapped packages and tossed me one. Years ago, the Camachos had provided tailored sweats in a size that I could use, and I had a stock of them available on every plane since. Comfy is good.

We landed in Paris at eleven thirty in the morning. All of us had gathered in the main cabin. The plane worked its way to the hangar as I called Olga, and Letty called Miguel.

Olga answered after four rings.

"Baby," I said. "I have news."

"Let me guess. You're in Paris to marry Letty."

"Aw, that's not fair, stealing my thunder."

I suppose I need not be surprised. After all, Olga signs Andrea's paycheck.

"Amor, do you want me to pretend I don't know? I can do that."

"It's just that I wanted to tell you myself. You're right. We're in Paris. Just landed."

"It's good news, Amor."

Olga's voice was too calm. She was hiding her true feelings. I was pissed at Andrea for flapping her lips. "You're right," I said.

"Amor, congratulations." She sounded anything but excited.

"Thank you, Olga. It means a lot to me that you are wishing us well."

"Amor, you're my best friend. Letty is good for you. I thought all along that one day you would marry her."

"There was no planning," I said. "Tangles and Storm are with us. That's it."

"Amor, I will call Letty when I get back home. Tell her I'm extremely happy for her, and know that it goes for you, too."

From the lackluster tone of her voice, my best guess is that Olga was not happy.

If Olga is not happy, fuck her.

I got off the phone. Letty was still talking to Miguel. He was so excited that I could hear him crowing on the phone. He yelled 'congratulations boss!' at least once that I heard for myself. Letty saw I was done and said a quick goodbye.

"Tio said if he can't cater the wedding dinner, he must fix a feast for when we return, and he is proud he didn't have to pull out the shotgun on us," she laughed. "What did Olga say?"

"She will call to congratulate you. She's landing or taking off. Not sure which."

Letty unfastened her seat belt, sat on my lap, and put her arms around my neck.

"She was pissed off, wasn't she? No doubt she's pissed. Fuck her if she is," Letty said.

I put my arms around her. Does it mean someone is perfect for you when they say the thoughts you are thinking?

"Right on," Tangles said.

"Can't please everyone," Storm said.

The interior of the plane felt cool until we stepped out into the hanger where it was freezing. At least our car was heated. I'd brought a good coat, but the girls hadn't been forewarned. On the way to the Louis V, the shiny white Rolls Royce we got in made a stop at Anastassios Tallidis, a great store for trying on fur.

"I have a lovely mink at home," Letty reminded me.

"I know, but you can use another. It's chilly here."

Letty was trying on a full length black sable, spinning around in front of the mirror. This one was more fitted than the one in her closet. Tangles was twirling in brown, Storm in a coat dyed two shades of pink not found in nature, standing still, transfixed at her mirror image, and very focused on stroking the lapel.

"You can't do this, Boss. It's too much money," Tangles protested.

"Are you telling me no?" I laughed.

Storm's jaw dropped. "We're just window-shopping, aren't we? Oh, Boss, is this for real? You're buying us all mink coats?" She ditched the pink fast and put on beige.

When we left, they were all wearing the full-length minks they had tried on, with hats to match. As we waited, the in-house tailor embroidered their names on the inner lining. The store owner gifted beautifully crafted matching kidskin gloves.

At the Four Seasons Hotel, I made friends with the concierge, Michel Renard, and had help from him paving the way for the wedding. The Catholic church requires proof that both parties are Catholic and have been baptized. The priest waived that after Letty and I assured the priest through the concierge that we didn't have the documents, but we were baptized Catholic, had made our first holy communion and were confirmed. We agreed to a hefty donation to tidy it up.

At noon the next day on a green lawn a stone's throw from the Eifel Tower, I proposed again to Letty in front of Michel Renard's friend, a photographer, and put the ring on her finger.

The white Rolls delivered us to Notre Dame. Letty opted to wear her mink coat instead of a wedding dress, as did Tangles and Storm. The cathedral was packed with tourists, but we were oblivious to the crowds. Thanks again to Michel Renard, we met Father John minutes after we entered the church. He had outdone himself getting the church authority to agree to marry us. I handed a sealed envelope to Father John with the agreed donation. It was Friday, the first of October, 1993, and in minutes we were joined.

We were pronounced husband and wife with no tears from either of us, but lots of hugs and kisses. Tangles and Storm were red-eyed when we walked out into the sunlight. I don't know or care if anyone was paying attention, but Letty gave Tangles a meaningful look, a full-on kiss on the mouth and they embraced. She did the same with Storm.

In the car on our way back to the hotel, we called my Aunt Carmen who was thrilled to hear the church was involved and congratulated us. We got to the hotel room, andmade a list: Pixie, Lainie, Jo and TJ, Niley, my friend Jack Fino, Valita and Juan. The list went on till we pooled our phone books. Some calls could wait—like the one to my childhood friend Pélon, who was in prison. Betty made the call list. The vindictive widow of one of my lawyer friends did not. We started dialing. The next call was to Melina. In the old days, we would call different markets not knowing where she was working. With a cell phone, she was easy to catch.

I was waiting for my phone to ring Jack, when I looked over to where Letty was talking animatedly to someone, probably Pixie. The mink had been hung up, and she was wearing a white suit, I think Chanel, that the girls had picked up from the lobby store. We were in the honeymoon suite, and the soft light through the white window sheers touched her face. I felt so full of love for her, so choked up that for several seconds I failed to register Jack had picked up and had said hello at least twice.Letty looked over at me without breaking her conversation and smiled. I felt all at once that everything was going to be all right.

How many newlyweds spend the hours after their vows shopping? We followed Letty's lead, changed into clothes from the George V's lobby stores and took off for familiar turf, Les Galeries LaFayette, the largest mall in Paris, depending on who is doing the telling. Letty and Tangles had been there before with me and Olga. Storm was overwhelmed with enthusiasm and excitement, and that made me feel good.

I gave Tangles and Storm five thousand each, and Letty, double that amount.

"There is a currency exchange on the first floor," I told them.

"They accept dollars," Letty said. "This is a lot of money to give us."

"Yeah," Tangles agreed.

Storm just smiled.

"Hush," I said softly. "Let me have my fun. Spend the cash and stop bitching."

There was no resistance once I told them to go have fun and to let me try to find some clothes that fit me, always a problem, no matter where I shop.

Letty kissed me with a gentle bite on my lips.

"Ouch," I said.

Letty kissed me again.

"Better," I said. Shoppers walked around us. We got smiles and laughs.

The girls were together. We made a test call to make sure the phones worked inside, then I wandered toward the menswear. The plan was to stay in touch by cell.

October 1, 1993 (Friday)
Paris
Letty

I never gave much thought to marrying Mario. I figured he'd tie the knot with Pixie, then Melina, then Olga. As long as I could live with them, I was happy with that. When Mario and Olga broke up, I figured Mario Luna was never going to be married. I hoped that he would want me around. After I moved out, I went to sleep wondering how I was going to get back into Casa Luna without losing face.

Now I'm the one with the ring. I'm married to him, by the Catholic church no less.

The twenty minute ceremony with Father John was beautiful, touching and emotional. That's how I felt, and I believe it was the same for him.

He really loves me. I feel it, and the feeling is beautiful.

October 1, 1993 (Friday)
Paris
Storm

Gobs of strangers were around us, taking pictures of the church and of themselves and there we were, taking up valuable space. I watched Letty kiss Tangles and felt a rush. I had seen them before at home and even the office, but this was Notre Dame in Paris, France. Letty came out of the church and hugged and kissed Tangles. Lightning heat shot through my body.

"You are my sister going forward," she said to Tangles, then to me.

"Congratulations, Mrs. Boss. I love you."

Then we hugged and kissed without a care in the world over who might be watching. If it was hot to watch, it was ten times as hot to experience. I felt like I was made of wax, hollow, and as she kissed me, the warmth shot through, and all of me melted. It's a wonder I didn't end up as a puddle on the ground. Letty is gutsy. I love what she does. I looked up to find our photographer snapping away. He took pictures in and outside the church, until we got in the Rolls and drove away. The happy couple climbed in and took one seat. Tangles and I sat across from them, holding hands. To me, it felt like we'd all gotten married.

October 1, 1993 (Friday)
Paris
Mario

The presidential suite had three bedrooms and five bathrooms. A half-bathroom for guests was near the entry. The grand living room had a grand piano and wet bar. The bathroom count was perfect because I insist on having my own bathroom on a trip. It doesn't always happen, but I scored in Paris. On our first night when Letty and I finally were alone in the master bedroom, my bride had news for me.

"Baby, I started my period a few hours ago. I'm so sorry."

Letty and I had a history of great sex going back a very long time, and I brushed the news off.

"It's my fault for not letting you in the planning. I'm the sorry one."

Still dressed, we lay face up on the bed, holding hands.

"It's our wedding night," Letty said, "Level with me. Are you pissed?"

"No," I said. "Are you?"

"Of course."

"We can cuddle," I said.

Letty got up went to the bathroom. When she returned, she was in a beautiful nightie.

I was in bed, sitting up. The television was on when she came out. I did a wolf whistle. No matter what she wears, she's lovely, but her night-clothes were out of a fantasy.

"I found some lingerie at Les Galeries LaFayette. You like this?"

"I love it."

She climbed in bed next to me.

"I'm going to hit the shower and put on the pajamas you bought me," I said. "I can't remember wearing pajamas, even as a kid."

"You didn't own any. Now you have two pairs and I know they fit."

I showered and put on the two pieces of soft black flannel sleepwear. I glanced in the mirror before exiting the bathroom and whistled at my reflection. The PJs were nice: soft cloth, oyster buttons, and a button fly. I'd never fucked with PJs, but I had with sweatpants that had a similar fly.

When I went back to the bedroom, the lights were on. I was caught by surprise seeing Letty in bed sandwiched between Storm on her left and Tangles on her right. They were propped up by a bunch of pillows.

"Baby," Letty said, laughing at the look on my face, "if the four of us didn't know each other so well, this would not be happening. I'm going to watch while they seduce you."

I stood by the bed, uncertain what to think.

"We don't need to do this," I said.

"Baby, if we hadn't gotten married today, the four of us would be in this bed, and nothing would be said about it," Letty said. "Come on. In bed with you. It's okay."

I wondered what Father John or my Aunt Carmen or our friends would say. On my wedding night I went to bed with my bride—and two other women.

"Boss don't be reluctant. We've fucked a million times," Tangles said.

"And me, Boss. Not a million times, but a bunch," Storm said. "Come and get it."

"Are you okay with this?" I asked Letty, again.

"Totally, Baby. It was my idea. I know you love me."

I didn't need any more persuasion.

I got under the covers next to Letty and kissed her passionately. I felt a body pressing against my back, lips kissing the back of my neck. I opened my eyes and saw Tangles inches from my face, kissing Letty, her hands in my hair. It was like one of those dance marathons there used to be, with the crowded dance floor, all the bodies touching, moving, on and on. It was a marathon, but all through the night, Letty and me, we were always skin to skin. It was all laughter and giggles.

In the morning, Letty and I were alone on the bed. I don't know when the others slipped away.

"I love you, Mario," my princess said as she stretched like a cat atop the covers.

I smothered her with kisses.

She wrapped her legs around my waist and squeezed.

"You don't know your strength," I teased.

"Yeah, I do." She squeezed harder.

The next thing I knew, we were wrestling. It was going to be a challenge to get on top. I'd better not entirely quit my karate workouts.

It was one in the afternoon when the four of us went down to the lobby restaurant.

"I am so starved," Letty said.

"Ditto," I said.

The restaurant is set up like a huge living room with heavy cushioned gold and red velvet armchairs, black glass tables with gold legs, and a thick textured gold and red Persian rug underfoot. When we arrived, they whipped out a fresh linen for the two tables they set us up with. We ate. The girls all had fancy salads. I had steak in a rich truffle sauce, very fancy, and they had peanuts for me for dessert. They were in a bitter dark chocolate that went well with the French red wine they served. We were there for a long time, very comfortable, all teasing Tangles for taking a very long time to eat. Then Letty got a call on her cell. She walked towards the lobby to talk. The place was not full yet, but it was noisy. I could see Letty from where I stood, and just looking at her, I felt a rush of possessiveness. That was not just Letty. She was my wife. She turned to face me, smiling, and finally hung up her phone and returned to the table.

I got up and pulled out her chair for her.

"It was Olga."

"Oh, what did she say?"

"She congratulated us. She is thinking of giving us a spectacular gift. She's been going through Camila's safes for months and keeps coming up with gorgeous little treasures."

"Sounds nice," Tangles said.

"Too nice. She asked if we plan to stay here, and for how long. She offered any house to spend time in. She mentioned the Rome house is just an hour from here, and always ready."

"That was nice of her," I said.

"I didn't commit. I told her I'd tell you." She looked at me.

"That would be so neat," Storm said. "Rome, fuck."

"The Rome house is okay but it ain't no Casa Luna," Tangles said. "All you think about is fucking."

"All you think about is getting head," Storm shot back.

"You give fabulous head," Tangles said.

"Keep it down, waffles," Letty said.

"Waffles?" Tangles looked at Letty quizzically. "Are you implying I'm indecisive?"

"I'm implying your food is getting soggy," Letty said.

We all looked at the dessert Tangles had ordered, a tall structure of four fluffy waffles with some kind of brown mousse filling between them, dusted with powdered sugar, and topped with several inches of whipped cream. It was obviously not dessert for one, as it had been delivered with several extra plates, something the waiter may have tried to explain, but his English was, well, creative.

"If you finish that," I said, "I'm going to have to get you a bigger coat."

"If you finish that," Storm chortled, "I'm going to have to get you a bigger chair."

My phone rang.

I glanced at Letty, who nodded, then I got up and walked to the lobby. The restaurant was quite loud now.

"Amor," Olga said. "I told your bride that you would honor me if you honeymooned in any house I own. I know you just picked up and left without planning. What do you say, Amor?"

"Olga, that's very kind of you. We may take you up on it."

When I got back to the table, the towering construction in front of Tangles had been deconstructed on to four plates, with each of us getting a tier of waffle, mousse and a dab of whipped cream. Tangles had the top layer with no mousse, and the lion's share of the whipped cream. She had already done significant damage to it, and her moustache of the day was white.

I sat down to finish our feast.

"Chocolate peanut mousse," I said. It was delicious. The waffle was as good as Emma's but not as good as Miguel's.

"We don't need to stay at one of Olga's houses. I'll take you anywhere you'd like," I said. "I'm sorry I planned nothing."

"For not planning, you did good, baby, considering we got married in Paris at Notre Dame."

I smiled. "Yes."

"Baby, Rome will be delightful. We will have a ball in that house, unless you're in a hurry to get home."

"No hurry, baby."

"Olga surprised me. I'm glad she's not angry."

"Me too," I admitted.

The next morning, we were on my plane headed to Rome to the first Camacho house I ever visited back when Pepe was alive, back when and where I met Camila. It was a gorgeous mansion, fit for a royal family. One year, I met Pepe, Camila and Olga there and we went to Easter Sunday Mass with seats on the first or second row at St. Peter's Square where a million people behind us attended mass. The following year, Olga and I were supposed to attend Mass on Easter Sunday but instead we stayed in bed.

Tangles, Storm, Letty and I spent nine days in Rome at Olga's, formerly Pepe's. We all tagged along as the butler gave Storm the full tour of the house, from the attics to the wine cellar. Storm asked how many people it took to keep the house in the pristine shape it was in.

"Eighteen inside workers, including a chef and his staff of three, plus six outdoor workers," he said.

We were so pampered that it was embarrassing.

Olga did not join us but sent a messenger from Colombia with a note for us and wedding gifts.

> Dearest Mario and Letty,
> Congratulations! These little gifts came from the treasures that Camila left behind. She was a shopper. Letty, wear this in good health and remember I love you. Mario, I know you don't smoke cigars, but this will look fantastic on your desk.
> Love you both,
> Olga

The ornate humidor she gave me, lined with a padding that needed an occasional addition of water, was a work of art. The exterior was solid gold. I had never seen anything like it. She'd given Letty a Rolex watch on a platinum band with diamonds all around it, and a diamond bezel, more than fifteen carats.   Letty and I called Olga to thank her.

"She doesn't seem to be pissed off," Letty said after we hung up.

Was she upset that we'd had gotten married? "We'll never know unless she wants us to," I said.

October 2, 1993
Rio
Olga

"Olga let it go. You have a life of your own. You don't need him. Why second-guess yourself when you're the one who ended it?" Riana said, pouring me a glass of sangria. When I held the heart-shaped glass up to the lamp and squinted, the tears in my eyes made yellow spars of light that sparkled and speared straight through the wine, a drunken illusion, just like the illusion of a broken heart. I took a sip. Riana liked this wine. Mario would have hated it. Too sweet.

Riana was looking at me earnestly. I turned away from her to stare at the pretty crystal snifter.

Sangria is too sweet for Mario. So is Letty.

When it comes to Mario and the women who hang around him, I've always been jealous. I tried not to let on. When we first met years ago, he'd had a serious open relationship with his neighbor Melina Marron, a businesswoman who owned a chain of supermarkets. She kept busy, but not busy enough to stop her from seeing him every day. They had a routine—early before she left for work, late at night when she got off work, weekends, and, I bet, afternoon delights in her offices. It wasn't a secret that they almost got married a few times, except she had a thing about being ten years older. She felt the age difference would eventually cause a problem between them and never went through with the wedding. I gave her six million dollars for her house. She moved ten minutes away, but it gave me comfort she was no longer right across the street. Ten minutes away gave me plenty of room to move into his life.

I showed my colors that time. I said I wanted the house across the street from him for myself, but Mario didn't fall for it, and neither did anyone else. I never moved in. I rented the house to Pixie after she became a star and just recently, I made it easy for her to buy the property from me.

At one time, I was jealous of Pixie. She's known him since they were kids. She was living in his house and working with him in his business. I heard her sing and made a star out of her, a gold mine for her, and a gold mine for me as her manager, but it was never about money. The singing career pulled her away from him. Once, Mario was close to Pixie. It took the adoration of a whole world full of fans to take Mario's place. Now Pixie's always on tour, busy everywhere but in Pasadena. She married a rock star who turned out to be a nut. She's waiting for the annulment to be final. Poor Pixie.

Mario must have made a deal with Letty. I don't buy that the trip to Paris and the wedding was an impulse. Letty's so stupid that she would have gone along with any open marriage deal he proposed to her. I never considered her a threat.

"You're the one who ended it. I don't see why you're upset," Riana said, pouring me more sangria.

I finished it and held out the glass. She filled it again and settled back in the recliner. Well, maybe she didn't settle. She was perched on the edge of it, leaning in my direction.

"You read me wrong, Amor. I'm not upset. I just need to get used to it."

I denied it, but I felt the tears. Riana got up from her recliner and sat next to me on the loveseat. She hugged me.

"Mario's married now, but what does that matter? The thing you have with him has no boundaries. Don't feel hurt. Don't feel angry. Listen to me. He still works for you. Hell, Letty works for you too. And you always said you like Letty."

I screwed a smile on my face.

"I'm okay, Amor. I'm not going to do anything to mess up that relationship. He is responsible for how GAL rises to a new level every quarter. Like it or not, she is part of his team, as are Tangles and Storm."

"If the leasing company folded tomorrow, it wouldn't dent what you're worth."

"Amor, I know all this. But the money doesn't matter. You are right though. I'm going to let it go."

Riana took the glass out of my hand, set it on the console table, and kissed me. She kissed the tears I failed to wipe away, my wet cheeks, and my lips. I forgot a little about Mario, but she was still talking, damn it.

"It wouldn't dent your fortune but if it folded, the consortium my dad put together would get hurt. If anything happened to GAL, and if—"

"Amor, GAL is not going to fold," I interrupted. "And I'm not going to do anything to disturb Mario and how he runs the company. How do they say it these days? Chill, Amor."

Riana looked at me, her eyes flashing. She is Spanish, and sometimes hot-headed. She kissed me fiercely, like she was jealous of the idea of Mario, and wanted to put herself there in my heart instead of him. Her kisses were like the sangria, dark, and fruity, and very sweet. I felt better. Maybe all I'd needed was to cry a little. Mario's marriage had caught me off guard and kept catching me off guard each time I remembered it.

"Me, I can not chill when you are hurting," she said.

"Remember when Camila's guard said that she had been shot? I saw her abandoning me. This news of Mario's, it felt the same way. He was abandoning me."

"I see how you've been covering up your feelings ever since you talked to Andrea. It has festered in you for days. But this is nothing, a hiccup. He will still be your friend. He is not abandoning you," she said. "Some words in front of a priest won't change that."

"Amor, I love you so. I wish you were a man, and I could marry you. You are so perfect. I adore you."

"I can be a man whenever you want," she said, climbing on me and giving a little wiggle. She pushed my thighs wide and slid down my body and with her mouth and hands made me forget about Mario.

Even at the height of my relationship with Mario, I was never as close to him as I am with Riana. As much as I adored him, he was never warm. Not like Riana. Mario and I, we were always about how much sex we could get out of each other. Our talk was short. We were always in a rush. I was always hot to rush back to my plane to hit the next banker who didn't care where the cash was from.

"What are you thinking?"

"Amor, I'm sorry. My mind was wandering. Was I a fool to break off our engagement?"

"You were no fool," Riana said. "Remember how he took the news?

Like a whipped dog. He accepted what you said. He let you leave the next morning."

"I remember rounding everyone up, including you."

"I will be there for you. I would not give you up, not even if you chased me away," Riana said, her eyes steady on mine. "I would make you keep me. Forget him. You can count on me."

"Count on me as well, Amor, for eternity."

October 7, 1993 Thursday
NYC
Lola

Tomorrow I would be leaving for New Orleans for a weekend with Art. My brother Nico called.

"The prints you sent me came up with nothing," he said.

"No rap sheet. Good," I said.

"I should have pulled up something. I got nothing. If you're still curious, get me his driver's license or at least what state issued it."

"Thank you. I love you."

"I wouldn't do this if I didn't love you," he shot back.

He was too young to be as grouchy as he is, or maybe he is just that way with me.

"I'm going to New Orleans with him tomorrow. I'll memorize the tail number of the plane."

"Why see him at all if you have questions about him? Why date him, much less go to New Orleans with him?"

"I dig this man," I said. "You know how I am. If it's a good thing, I'm going to be skeptical. Why am I getting something good for a change?"

"You should see a shrink," he said. My brothers believed that the only sane people in this world were themselves.

"You know this business makes us skeptical. If that wasn't true, you wouldn't have looked him up, and it wouldn't be bugging you that you came up blank," I said.

Art was already there when I arrived in the car that he sent for me. Our task force team flew around in a federal executive jet, but it was utilitarian, nothing gorgeous like his plane. Wide white leather seats. White belts. Polished brass buckles. It must have cost six or seven million. Who was he that he could afford it? He said the plane was three years old. It still smelled like a new car. I passed two pilots and a flight attendant when I got aboard.

"I'd be lying if I said I'm not impressed."

As soon as I sat, the flight attendant poured red wine in my glass.

"I've always liked planes like this. It took a long time for me to afford it," Art said as the flight attendant filled his glass and slipped away.

We toasted, and our glasses met halfway.

"What are we going to do in New Orleans?" I asked.

The plane was seconds from liftoff, speeding down the runway.

"Eat," he said with a laugh. "Unless you have something else in mind."

"I love the food there."

"You been there?"

I replied, "I have." Several times, we'd been to New Orleans following a Camacho plane with Camila in it. Our interest was drugs, but we loved getting away from a boring stakeout.

"We're staying in the French Quarter at the Ritz Carlton. I hope you approve."

"I approve."

"There was a time when I couldn't buy a Hershey bar on credit," Art said. "Every day I strive to make up for lost time."

I drank a little and yawned.

"I like you, Art."

"I seem to be putting you to sleep." He laughed.

"Flying always makes me sleepy."

"I'm glad you like me," he said. "I'm crazy about you."

"You're so sweet, Art."

"I want you right now. Or should we wait?"

I emptied my glass. The wine was a little bitter. "Standing, sitting, or lying down?"

The plane had leveled off, and it was smooth flying so far. He took my hand, and we walked in a cabin. He slid the doors shut. We sat on one of two red velvet sofas that faced each other.

"These unfold into a bed," he said.

"Cool. But there's plenty of room as it is."

I was excited, but the thought of a catnap was also alluring. I turned on my side facing the sofa's back. I moved my hips as I felt my jeans being pulled off. I giggled. My eyes closed. So tired. I fought to stay awake. I felt him enter me. Moaned in pleasure. That is the last thing I remember.

"Wake up, Nina. You've been asleep for hours. Nina, wake up."

I tried to open my eyes, but they were heavy. I couldn't do it. I felt dizzy. The room was spinning, and my arm hurt.

The woman's voice was persistent, nagging. She shoved me, jostled me, kept repeating, "Nina, wake up."

Who called me Nina? Art called me Vivian. I'd named myself for Julia Roberts in *Pretty Woman*.

I was lying on my back, my arms rigidly pinned. I couldn't move them.

I opened my eyes. Focus. Focus. I saw only a dizzying blur, and I shut my eyes.

I tried to sit. My wrists were strapped. Zip ties for handcuffs. My eyes were like slits, barely open. I managed to focus on a burning pain in my right arm. My forearm came into focus, bruised, a needle taped to my skin. I was hooked up to an IV. I could not move my arms. Hospital?

Not a hospital. Hospitals don't zip tie your wrists.

"Where am I?"

My eyes were drooping, but my mind raced.

Had the plane crashed? Where was Art? Why was I restrained?

"Nina, I wanted to see with my own eyes that the car bomb in Beverly Hills didn't kill you."

I heard laughter. Who was talking to me? I managed to get in control of my head and turned towards the voice. My slitted eyes made out the shapes in the room. This was certainly not the Ritz Carlton in New Orleans. I knew that face. I was looking at Olga. Impossible. But that sure as hell was the voice I'd heard in thousands of hours of tapes.

"I can't see what Mario saw in you." It was Olga's voice. Hard. Mocking. "He should see you now. He should smell you now. You stink of urine and look like a street tramp."

"What the fuck am I doing here? Where is here?"

I looked at the I.V. and wondered what concoction was dripping into me. I was in a hospital bed, rails on each side. To my right was a big black car. Flat on my back, I was like a beached whale. I managed to turn my head to see a white four door Lincoln to my left. Overhead, numerous fluorescent lights hung, four long tubes in each fixture. A fixture hung above me, and one above each car.

I was in a spacious garage. Voices echoed. Women's voices. Men's voices. Olga wasn't alone. Behind her were two burly Hispanic men, and a woman I recognized from surveillance as Riana Carrera. I pictured her dossier. Olga's companion. Party girl. Rich father. Ties to Lisbon and Barcelona.

"You're awake. Good. I want you alive for your death." Olga laughed madly, very amused with herself.

I was less amused and felt more like throwing up than talking.

"I was beginning to worry that the fool may have overdosed you," Olga said. "And I wouldn't have a chance to speak with you."

The fool had to be Art.

"Art brought me here, didn't he?" It figured he was too good to be true.

"Art got you to Bogota. An ambulance and three medical techs got you here from the plane," Riana said.

"I ask the questions here, not you," Olga said like the snobby bitch she is.

"Get this IV off me and take the restraints off this minute, bitch."

Olga laughed.

"Threatening me in the position you're in? You're not very smart, are you? I see I will have no choice but to bury you in Colombia. Or do you prefer cremation?"

"If you had wanted me dead, you'd have saved yourself all this drama. Why go to the trouble of getting me here in person? That is, if I'm really in

Colombia."

"Oh, you're in Bogota all right."

"What do you want?"

She leaned over and got in my face. She looked different in person than in surveillance. She's a devil in disguise. Beautiful outside. Satan inside.

"I want to know if you killed Camila," she said.

"You know perfectly well that I did not kill Camila, nor did I have anything to do with her death. You killed her, not me."

"I killed her?"

As fucked up as I was, I caught mockery in her voice.

"Yeah, you killed her. Why this game?" I asked.

"I'll show you what kind of game this is when you are out of my house."

My mouth was dry as dust. I was dying of thirst.

"I need water."

She pointed at the IV. "You have all the water you need."

"Fuck the IV. I need water to drink. Get these ties off me. I'm not saying another word."

She thought about it. The silence dragged on for at least a minute.

"Marcos, cut the plastic off her. Fetch her water."

"Miss Olga, she may know martial arts. Are you sure?"

"If she does anything funny, I'll shoot her. Do as I say."

"Yes, Miss Olga."

Her puppet Marcos cut off the zip ties. My arms vibrated and trembled as circulation returned. I'd been pinned me down for who knows how long. I hated everyone there. I hated myself for falling for Art, walking right into hell when I boarded the plane. A fucking fool is what I am.

With tremendous effort, I sat up. It took two tries, but I pulled the IV tube out of the cannula attached to my arm. The effort made me dizzy. I was disappointed that the damn needle was still in my arm, but they'd wrapped the cannula with industrial strength tape. I wouldn't be able to pry it loose until my fingers were in working order. Marcos handed me a plastic glass half full of water. I took it with both hands and drank slowly.

I coughed.

"Drink slower," Marcos said.

"Let her choke," Camila said with continued mockery.

"You can't get her to talk if she's gone," Riana said.

"I need to use the bathroom."

Riana said, "Marcos, show her the way."

I saw Olga give Riana a dirty look.

I swung my legs over the gurney's side, and got to my feet, no thanks to the bastard. No help from him, even when I lost my balance and went down on one knee. I got up and continued to follow him barefoot on the cold concrete, passing ten or more cars.

It felt like a long walk, fifty feet or more from the hospital bed. At the door, I turned to look back. Olga, Riana, and another man were waiting for my return. If only I had a gun, I'd take them all down. It wouldn't matter if I was shot and killed as long as I took out everyone there. I was furious. Olga's puppet was blocking the bathroom's entrance. He looked at me mockingly.

"Stand outside," I said.

He raised his hand.

He slapped me, almost knocking me off my feet. The crack of flesh on flesh echoed through the garage. It sounded worse than it was. I'm not saying it didn't hurt. It stung, but it woke me up, too.

Olga's voice was loud, echoing in the rafters.

"Marcos, you do nothing unless I order it. Do you understand?"

"Yes, Miss Olga."

"Fucking brute. I curse you in the name of the devil, you bastard!" I said in Spanish.

He made the sign of the cross and backed away from the door.

"You're a dead man," I said.

It was like I was pushing it to be injured or killed. I had reached a point where I didn't give a fuck. I was humiliated by my stained clothes and smell. If I made it out of here alive, the first person I would punish for this would be Art.

When I find him, he's dead.

Inside the tiny bathroom, I relieved myself. I splashed my face with water and wiped away the raccoon eyes of my ruined makeup with paper towels. Marcos's red handprint stood out on my face. I stared at myself in the mirror and swore to survive this.

I was able to walk back a lot better than before.

"I hope you appreciate the break I just gave you," Olga said, still mocking.

Riana looked troubled. I looked past them to the bed.

The bed I'd been in had a fresh sheet and a pillow.

Riana and Olga, both of them, snakes, were waiting by the freshened bed. That's when I noticed the nicely dressed man near them. He avoided looking directly at me as he put on a white doctor's jacket. I figured he was too well-dressed to be a medic.

I slowed as I walked closer. Marcos was directly behind me, herding me forward like a sheep.

"She has to be lying down," the doctor said.

"Lie down," Olga ordered.

I stopped.

The second burly guy who until now had done nothing, moved to my side and took my elbow. Marcos took the other, and between them, they hefted me on to the bed. I was so tired, and so sick from whatever they'd dosed me with that I'd never have been able to get there on my own. The pillow felt good against my head and neck, but I wasn't about to be defeated by a pillow. My body still thrummed with adrenaline from the slap. I had the juice in me to resist—but if I fought back, they'd strap me down again. I gritted my teeth. I didn't resist. The man in the white jacket injected something into the cannula. I felt the burn of it go into my veins. God only knows how I kept from punching him in the face to keep him away. I was back on the IV. I just knew I was outnumbered. I didn't want to be pinned down again, strapped down as before.

I told myself that if Olga wanted to question me, she needed me alive. I closed my eyes. I heard them talking back and forth, Olga and the white jacket. It was hard to follow the conversation. Words and more words. Sodium pentothal. I recognized that much. In the middle of the roller coaster ride they'd put me on, I realized I was doped up, and no way to get off.

Just great. On top of whatever nightmare cocktail that they'd dosed me with, they were adding truth serum. Sodium pentothal does not always work. The drug burned through my veins. I tried opening my eyes, but it was impossible. I could hear Olga and Riana talking. My brain was awake, but my body felt heavy, slow, unwieldy.

"What is your name?" a man asked in Spanish.

"What's yours, honey?" I replied in Spanish, and yawned. My eyes were shut. Sleep was not far away.

Olga and Riana said something in the background. I couldn't make it out.

"What is your name?" white coat asked again. Persistent bastard.

"Nina Caputo."

"Is that your real name?"

"Yes."

"What does the name Lola signify?"

"It's just a name."

"Are you an agent with the FBI?"

"No."

"Are you telling the truth?"

"Yes."

"Were you ever FBI?"

"Yes."

"Why aren't you FBI now?"

"I took an early retirement due to medical conditions."

"What medical conditions?"

"I was shot and never fully recovered."

I heard Olga arguing with the white coat. She was questioning if the drug was working. He insisted it was working. She didn't like my answers. I didn't either. I didn't like not being in control of my mouth. She and the white coat went back and forth a few times.

"If you question her more than thirty minutes, I will have to inject her again."

"Did you kill Camila or have anything to do with her getting shot?" Olga asked.

I tried not to answer, but the drug was doing its job. I had no control. My forehead was beaded in sweat, and my hair felt damp, but the room was chilly. A big fan was circulating air.

"Did you kill Camila or have anything to do with her getting shot?"

"No."

"No what?"

"I had nothing to do with Camila's death."

"Do you know who killed her or ordered her death? Are we still being investigated?"

"No."

"Doctor, how do I know she's telling the truth?"

"This drug works, Miss Olga. Ask short questions."

"Are you still connected with the FBI?"

"No."

"Did you blow up your car?"

"Not me."

"If not you, who blew up your car?"

"The agency."

"Why did they bomb your car?"

"The agency did it to keep me safe."

"Safe from who?"

"Camachos."

"Did you kill Camila?"

"No."

"Do you know who did?"

"Olga killed Camila."

"Fucking bitch! I didn't kill my sister!"

"You don't want to wake her, Miss Olga," white coat said.

I heard Riana's mumble something.

"Who told you Olga had Camila killed?" Olga asked.

"The agency."

"You said you had no connection with the agency!"

"Ask her a question, Miss Olga."

"Exactly who told you?"

"My brother."

"Is your brother with the agency?"

"Yes."

"Is he active now?"

"Yes."

I felt my insides rumble, and overwhelming nausea. My head was killing me. The fucking drug was making me so sick. It was like a hangover, nausea, migraine, vertigo, all the shit rolled up into one. I puked up the water I'd had earlier. I felt myself dry heaving.

At least the damn voices were leaving me alone. I heard them, listened hard through the misery.

"Olga, she didn't kill Camila. I believe her," Riana said.

"Well, I didn't kill her," Olga said.

"Miss Olga, maybe the FBI believes you had it done. Doesn't mean they have proof," a man's voice said. Must be another person there. It wasn't the fucking white coat.

"They can't have any proof you idiot. I had nothing to do with it!"

"Of course, you didn't," the man said.

Olga asked another question. "Have you been in contact with Mario Luna since your fake death?"

I understood the question. I wanted to say no.

"Yes."

Olga's voice was not calm. "Did you speak with him on phone?"

"Yes."

"Did you see him in person?"

"Yes."

"Where did you see him?"

"Yes."

"Where did you see him?"

"No."

"Damn it, Nina, answer my question!"

"Yes, I am."

My eyes were closed but I knew it was Olga who hit me, more of a punch, very hard. I kept my eyes closed. I was so out of it, I'm not sure I could have opened them.

"Enough of this," Riana said. "I don't want to see this any longer."

"I'm not done!"

"Olga, for me, stop," Riana said.

Long silence. Mumbling voices.

"Will she remember this?"

"It will be like remembering a dream," white coat said. "She will remember everything up to getting on the plane thinking she was going to New Orleans. Everything after that, bits and pieces."

"Fucking shut up," Olga shouted, sounding frustrated. "I know that!"

I heard a clatter of things going on, noises like someone hit something or broke something.

"Why was I getting yes and no?" Olga was screaming.

"The serum is wearing off. I can inject her again if you wish."

"Enough of this! Doctor remove that thing from her arm, now," Riana said.

I felt a wrench to my arm. The cannula, I guess. Hurt. Sting of alcohol. Rip of tape. I tried to feel my forearm with my free hand, but I wasn't in control of my extremities.

"What are you doing?" Olga asked.

"She should be coming to soon," the doctor said.

I opened my hundred pound eyelids. Everything was a blur. Death had to be easier than this. I felt nasty, smelled nasty. The clothes clung to my skin. I stank of vomit, urine and sweat, my head was bursting, and I was still dry heaving. I could hear them arguing amongst themselves. If they were done interrogating me, I guessed I was about to die, and shut my eyes again.

"Hurry up and get it over with," I said between heaves. "Kill me and be done with it."

I felt myself being lifted off the bed. I glimpsed Marcos. He carried me through a door, into the quarters the garage was attached to.

I felt myself being lowered into a hard cold surface. A coffin? But I opened my eyes again and found myself lying in a dry ceramic tub in a lovely bathroom, with a dark haired girl standing over me holding a large pair of shears. Marcos was standing behind her barking orders.

"Take her clothes off and bathe her. Do not let her hurt herself. Understand, Luciana?"

The shears cut through the shirt. I could feel both of them staring at the huge tattoo covering awful scars left from my gunshot wounds.

"Si, I understand. Go. I will handle this," Luciana said.

Marcos left.

"*Pendejo*," she said, under her breath.

She pulled away the fabric in pieces and turned on the hot water. It felt wonderful and revived me somewhat.

"Thank you," I said, managing to sit up. "I need to use the toilet. I can do it myself."

At least Marcos was gone.

"Let me help you," Luciana said.

"No."

She was reluctant but agreed.

"I will be just outside the door."

I heard the door close, and managed to get to my feet, though I felt like I was on a rocking ship, and gravity was working at double-strength. Feeling like I was balancing on a ball, I stepped out, used the toilet, then returned to the tub. There were plenty of products on the side of the tub, American products with Portuguese labels. I scrubbed my hair in Prell, and let the hot water wash the sickness from me.

The large porcelain tub was beside a double sink set in a mahogany cabinet. Hand painted tiles lined the wall over the sink. The floor and wall tiles were terra cotta. The brass fixtures of the bathtub looked brand new. I relaxed in the water but struggled to keep hold of the memory.

"They asked me questions. They asked who killed Camila. They asked if I was FBI. They asked if I talked to Mario." I repeated this to myself, over and over. Already, I couldn't remember exactly what I said or exactly who I'd said it to.

"Are you okay?" Luciana asked through the door. "I have fresh clothes for you when you are ready."

"I'm okay," I said.

October 9, 1993 (Saturday)
Bogota Colombia
Riana

The sun was shining, the flowers were blooming like the garden of Eden, but I was filled with darkness. I knew Olga was furious at me, but I'd been sickened by the interrogation.

"Amor, if I didn't love you like I do, I'd shoot you for taking control in there," Olga said.

"Shoot me. Go ahead. Anything you want, just don't torture me like you did that woman."

"That was not torture."

"Olga, I've seen you kill people. You were my hero. It was a courageous act that saved our lives. I didn't have a drop of pity for any of them. They deserved what they got. This movie you directed using Art to lure her to a plane and entrap her here is not who you are. You just hate her because Mario had the hots for her."

"Oh stop, already."

"She said she'd talked to him, that she saw him. That bastard. He must have known that the bomb didn't kill her."

"Olga, I believe she was waking up. I don't believe what she said about Mario is true. Mario would have told you she hadn't died."

"The fuck he would. He would not tell me, and you know it!"

"Olga, stop doing this to yourself. Mario and you are friends. He doesn't own you, and you don't own him. He's married. I can't see him flying across the country to New York to visit with Lola who was just another fuck. Besides, Letty would no doubt have something to say about it. You see her as a yes man. She's not a pushover. I've studied her. Calm, cool and collected. Consumed by martial arts training. You've seen her in action. She's a weapon of mass destruction."

"Now you're a fan of Letty's?"

"That's irrelevant. The point is he's his own man. He and all of his... his little ninjas."

"His flock of ninjas as you call them, work for me. He works for me. I own him. I own them all."

"You're just talking nonsense, and you know it," I said. "Stop."

We walked out of the sunroom, and into the downstairs living room of the main house. I poured us each a healthy shot of Louis XIII into whisky glasses. I banged mine down. Olga joined me. I put my glass on a coaster and hugged her.

"I won't stop. I know you are after who killed Camila, but it wasn't Nina Caputo."

"If not her, who was it then? Mason hasn't found out who did it."

"I don't think Mason lives up to his reputation. I don't see him bringing any results, including the search for who killed Camila. Mason's hair would stand up if he knew what you had done to this woman."

Olga doesn't like criticism. She narrowed her eyes at me.

"You cut the interview short. I was thinking of giving her another dose and going at her for another half hour."

"I meant no disrespect. I couldn't take it anymore, watching her puking her guts up on that table. There were no more secrets there." I sat down on a padded bench beside the window and looked out. "I've never done anything like that before. If you are offended by me, I'll fly back to Spain."

Olga sat down beside me, and hugged. "Amor, I don't ever want you to leave me."

"You know I won't," I said. "But if you are mad at me, I can leave for a while."

"No," Olga said, hugging me tighter. "You're all I have."

I laughed. "You have whatever you want. You're a billionaire a hundred times over, unlike that pathetic creature recovering in your guest house."

"Amor, I believe the bitch. But why would anyone would think I had anything to do with Camila's death?"

"You know why. You inherited. People are bound to think you had her put down to take over the empire she left you."

"I suppose you're right," she said. "It's hard to let go of the idea that it was her."

"It wasn't her. Let her go."

"Let her go and she'll return with an army. She'll put us both away."

"What army? She has no proof. She's alone. She was in hiding from you. I think she will appreciate that you let her live. She won't risk getting you mad again. Think of it. All she had was Art, and you're the one who sent him."

"Art lived up to his reputation. He's long gone. I don't even know his real name. The plane was rented and untraceable," she said. "Let's have another Louie."

I filled the whisky glasses again. This time we sipped the brandy slowly like you're supposed to.

"Since she didn't kill Camila, you have no reason to kill her," I said, still fighting for Nina's life.

"We should have done a lie detector test."

"Doctor Dominguez said that a professional like Lola can beat a lie detector but can't beat truth serum."

"The Army uses Dominguez," she said. "He's not perfect, but the general trusts him. I suppose I should trust him. But I don't trust her. She took a million from us, threatened to kill me and Camila if we didn't pay."

"Olga, Mario said she wanted the million as compensation for Camila having her shot, putting her in a coma, injuring her so bad she took early retirement. A million is nothing. I'll give you a million myself. Just let her go. I hate to see you with unnecessary blood on your hands."

She gave me a little smile.

"You'd put up a million of your own money to free this bitch?"

"You know I would."

"It was stupid to bring her here. I thought she'd confess, I could end her, and it would be over."

"What if you let her escape?"

"I don't trust that bitch at all. She'll go to the cops or go rogue. I'll have an enemy out there looking to do me harm."

"She will get over it. She must be scared to death right now thinking that you are letting her clean up before you kill her."

Olga laughed. "I hope the bitch is scared to death. If not for her, I'd still be hooked up with Mario. Maybe not married but still as my fiancée."

I didn't know if that was true. I don't know what got into her head the day she suddenly called off her engagement, but it was entirely her doing. We all believed Lola was dead. How could a dead woman break up her engagement? I didn't remind her. She has a right to wear rose-colored glasses for hindsight.

"Mario is the big beef you have with this woman."

"And believing she killed Camila."

"Let's have a toke or two and put away the booze. We'll come up with something," I said.

Olga hesitated then nodded. "Okay."

I lit up a joint.

"If Camila was alive and Lola was here, she would have her butchered without a second thought."

I handed her the joint.

"You're not Camila."

October 11, 1993 Monday
NYC
Lola

I sat up in my bed wincing at the glare thanks to my blackout curtains standing wide open. I had a killer headache. Sunlight was blasting
straight through my skull. I staggered out of the bed, and the room spun. I
jerked the curtains closed. I felt a mess, my brain was foggy, and my guts
burned like I'd survived a night of bad sex. I squinted at the clock. Nine fifteen. I was naked except for black panties that weren't mine. Various parts
of me hurt terribly. My entire body was sore. I had handprints on my arms.
I sat on the edge of the bed and examined bruises ringing my wrists. A bandage stuck to my forearm was ringed by massive bruising, as if I'd had blood
taken by a ham-handed nurse.

I pictured the IV.

The memory felt like a dream. The bruises were real. I sat on the bed
staring at the damage to my arm, zip tie bruises on my wrists. How had I actually been with Olga who told me I was at her compound in Colombia?
How did I get there? How did I get back to my apartment?

I felt sick with fury. She had let me go, but how had I gotten there in the first place? I didn't remember the details. It had to be fucking Art.

New Orleans he said. Instead of the glorious New Orleans weekend he promised, he doped me up and delivered me to Olga in Colombia. I let my guard down and got totally fucked, kidnapped.

How the fuck did I get from Colombia to my own bed and in someone else's panties?

I shut my eyes. I clearly pictured the servant woman's face. I saw the bathtub I'd been lying in flat on my back, felt the cold hard surface. I remembered the woman with the shears, how she cut my clothes off of me, and turned on the hot water. I had gotten out, maybe even got dressed. Where are the clothes she gave me to wear?

I got up from the bed and looked around for laundry. Nothing on the floor, nothing in the hamper. Had I been delivered here wearing only panties? Probably not.

My overnight bag and purse were sitting on a chair. I checked them out. My makeup bag, my wallet, my house keys, my passport. Everything was in my purse as it should be, but when I paged through the passport, no stamp was there to indicate going through customs. I must have come through customs. Why no stamp? Impossible. A flight to and from Colombia and no entry stamp for US Customs? Could I have been in the states and told I was in Colombia? No matter where I'd been, the destination was not of my choice. I'd been kidnapped.

Did I imagine it? The bandage on my arm told me it was no dream. I had to check for evidence of what happened. The extra shoes, lingerie, everything was gone from my suitcase. Instead of my things, I found stacks of cash. Stacks of hundred-dollar bills with a rubber band around each stack. Fifty stacks of ten thousand dollars, each. I counted.

My clothes had been replaced by half a million dollars.

I dumped the cash back into the suitcase and shoved it under the bed. Too much to think about right now. I was overwhelmed.

I lay down, trembling, filled with anxiety. I never feel that way, never.

I shut my eyes, and what came to me were questions. Questions about Camila.

Had I killed her?

Had I had it done?

Did I know who had killed her?

Is that what the whole crazy spectacle had been about?

Planting Art?

Getting me to trust him?

Getting me aboard a plane and into Olga's clutches?

Why not just swoop me off the street?

I broke down. I cried and cried. At times I wailed. I was furious. I was heartbroken. I felt invaded and unsafe. My emotions were in upheaval. I went into the bathroom and took a shower to wash the nightmare from me, but all it did was bring up more memories. I did not remember having sex, but clearly it had happened. I scrubbed myself furiously, removing every trace. I was shaking from emotion. I stood there at the bathroom sink staring at my shaking hands and realized that I was probably in withdrawal from their concoctions, coming down from truth serum and who knows what else. I didn't feel any better, but realized, intellectually, that some of these crazy emotions would subside. I returned to the bed and cried myself to sleep.

October 15, 1993
Pasadena
Mario

After getting married in Paris, we spent nine days in Olga's Rome house. When we got back to Pasadena, the entire staff was there to congratulate us and greet us at the front door. The same thing had happened when I moved into the Milan house to run the leasing company. There were three times the staff I have at Casa Luna.

Married life did not mean much change for Letty. She stopped driving her Ferrari to work and rode with me, most of the time, with Storm driving and Tangles riding shotgun. Letty has shared my bed for years, though when I was engaged to Olga, she slept often in her own room. She'd been back in my bed for a long time. Now she moved her stuff to the closets connected to the ensuite bathroom that was just for her use. During breakfast our first day home, the staff relocated the contents of her closet. The things that had filled her third floor closet barely made a dent, even when she added the things from her apartment. The space was huge.

"I'll never have clothes to fill this," Letty said.

"Yeah you will."

"Mario, I don't need that much," she giggled.

"Yeah you do."

I felt a closeness to her like never before. As much as I had loved Olga, my feelings for Letty were deeper. Letty was uniquely mine, and special. I had trouble keeping my hands off her.

We'd been back for a month when Storm closed her first lease to an executive from Los Angeles. The client leased a new Falcon, a seven-million-dollar plane. He signed on the dotted line first thing Monday morning. My number two at the office, Andrea, made a big deal out of this and ordered lunch for the entire office.

Letty and Tangles pushed Storm to speak and she did.

Storm turned pink with pleasure from all the attention and stumbled over some words of thanks.

"I had the support of everyone on this and I know I owe you," she said. "Thank you very much for that. I've here for your payback anytime."

"Careful with the promises. Lots of dudes in here," Letty teased.

The conference room did not have enough seating for everyone but standing room was plentiful, and the food was served buffet-style.

Storm took a seat between Letty and me, and across from Tangles. We had all the assistants join us, the staff computer geek, everyone from reception, and even the boy who we used as a runner, the son of one of the office staff. Business was growing by leaps and bounds.

I had already heard what Storm said about the client as she repeated it to Andrea and those who could hear her at the table.

"He kept going back and forth. He wasn't sure it was a good deal I was giving him, then he wasn't sure it was a Falcon that he wanted, then he had trouble choosing between the extras in the decor. I didn't have to fuck him, but I would have."

Laughs.

"You'll fuck anyone," Tangles chimed in with that big smile of hers.

One thing is for sure. None of my trio have a shy bone in their body. Andrea who was sitting at the table with us, laughed at Storm's remark.

"Storm, you rock," I said. "You did it, and I'm not surprised."

"From now on, it will come easy," Letty said.

"I've heard you talking on the phone. You've really gotten to know the planes," Tangles said.

When everyone else was done and back to work, the girls, my wife, and I remained at the conference table. Three workers from the restaurant downstairs were picking up and placing everything in trays on two rolling carts.

I called Olga in Bogota.

"You're on speaker in the conference room," I said. "Storm closed her first lease."

Olga screamed like I remembered her doing when she was extremely excited. We all laughed.

"I just put you on speaker, too. Riana is with me."

Everyone said hi to Riana.

"Storm, I'm proud of you and I love you. It's wonderful. I'm going to send you something special," Olga said.

"Please, Olga, no, I'm getting paid so well. Thank you for the opportunity. Please no gift."

At her request, I made a second call to Olga, in private.

"Amor go ahead and match or beat the financing Boeing is offering.

Riana's father said the consortium is willing to be competitive and make less on the interest. He doesn't want to lose volume by turning away new plane leases. He said you should call him."

"Great news. Thank you for making it happen."

"Amor, you are doing a fantastic job. I'm here for whatever you need."

"Thank you," I said, ready to hang up. I thought we were done.

"Amor, do you think Lola died in that explosion?"

I did not know what to say. Seconds ticked past. My brain went blank. I said the first truth that popped into my mouth.

"You threw me off with that name," I said. "What brings this up?"

"Every once in a while, I think of how she fucked up what you and I had going."

"Olga, you head a worldwide empire. Be happy. Don't bring up names, events that stress you out."

"I agree. Answer my question, and I'll let you get back to work."

I came close to telling her she wasn't dead, but I feared for Lola's life.

"Yes, I think she's dead."

"Thank you, Amor."

That was the end of the call.

I stopped and started a dozen times, but finally dialed the number I had for Lola. It made a harsh tone, and a recording said that the number was disconnected. I was glad to hear that the number was no longer.

I asked Andrea to let the leasing specialists know that we would not slow down the new plane leases as we'd discussed. We were going to take a profit hit, but it was necessary to let Boeing know we were dead set on keeping our pace in the leasing market.

I called Letty to come into my office and I told her about Olga asking me about Lola. I had always confided in Letty with most of my secrets. It felt good to share everything with her now that she is my wife.

"She was fishing," Letty said.

"I almost told her Lola was alive, but I don't want anything to happen to Lola. I don't want to lie to Olga, but what choice is there?"

"She was jealous that you were hooked on the hooker, but not so jealous she'd kill her," Letty said. "I wasn't happy about Lola either."

I waved her to come around my desk. She sat on my lap, which is a good position for kissing, and not so good for ass-squeezing. I squeezed half of her ass.

"Want me to lock the door?" Letty whispered in my ear.

"I prefer leaving it unlocked and getting caught," I said.

The timer on her watch gave a little buzz. She got up, kissed me, squeezed my crotch and started for the door.

"Hey, where you are going?"

She stopped in the portal with the door half open, her hand on the knob, the timer on her watch buzzing again.

"Got two calls to make. Be right back."

She blew me a kiss.

"Before we married, you would have been raring to go. What's more important, the job or me?"

She gave me a hot look. She closed the door, put her back against it until it snapped shut. She stripped off the watch, sliding it down her arm, dropping it and its annoying buzzer on my desk.

She dropped her panties in my trash and straddled my lap with a little wiggle.

"You tell me," she whispered in my ear.

November 15, 1993 (Monday)
Pasadena
Pixie

I arrived in Pasadena a month after Mario and Letty returned from their honeymoon. Since everyone would be hard at work on a Monday, I hung out at the Van Nuys airport until my daughter's plane landed a few hours later. I had Raul waiting for my call to pick us up. He and Memo arrived in separate vehicles.

Lainie and I had a tearful reunion in the hanger. We kissed and hugged for a long time, so busy with each other that Raul had to come get us to say our stuff was packed up.

She is absolutely gorgeous. No wonder her fans love her. The record company told me they can't keep up with the demand for autographed photographs the fan club sends out on request. I had a fan club too, but no one ever told me they were having trouble keeping enough pictures to keep the fans happy.

We rode back in the limo with Raul. Our stuff rode back in the SUV that Memo drove. Memo works for Mario, but sometimes we trade staff. Truth is, I know Mario's staff better than my own. Other than Raul, I have a lot of turnover, since neither Lainie nor I are around much.

"You look fab, Mom."

"You are the one who looks fabulous," I said. "It's so good to see you. I miss you a hell of a lot."

"Mom, we talk on the phone at least three times a week."

"Good thing or I'd miss you more."

When we got home, the staff was lined up formally to greet us. Memo hung around just long enough for my crew to unload our baggage. By the time we showered and dressed, it was after six. We figured everybody would be home and walked across the street to Casa Luna. I told Mario's guard not to announce our arrival. It was a surprise. It's a lengthy walk to the house, which sits way back past the guard gate.

"He's probably already called the house to let him know we're coming," Lainie said.

"Of course. It will still be a surprise."

Mario and Letty were waiting for us at the front door. Letty was jumping up and down. We didn't even make it into the house, but stood outside, transfixed with kisses, hugs, and mutual congratulations chatter back and forth. Tangles and Storm came out, and the reunion continued until Letty, who was barefoot, made note that it was November, and we should come inside.

After two bottles of wine and the best nachos I have ever eaten, we sat down to dine in Mario's dining room. We heard about Storm's first successful plane lease, and the office luncheon in her honor. Emma fixed us a familiar meal, steaks and fixings. It was subtly different from Miguel's cooking but still excellent. Lainie and I both made utter pigs of ourselves but couldn't finish what was on our plates.

"All we need now is a little Mario or a little Letty. You better hurry, Boss," I said. "You're not getting any younger."

"Hey, I'm a kid at heart," Mario said, laughing and raising his wine glass up high for a toast.

"How many kids are you wanting?" Lainie asked.

I saw Letty quickly exchange looks with Mario with a smile. She said, "Actually, we're not sure about children just yet."

"What is there to be sure about? You have to have kids. At least six of them."

"Oh mom, stop it," Lainie said. "Letty, I'm sorry I asked."

"No don't be sorry," Mario said. "We're busy people. Letty wants to keep working, and I'm not planning on slowing down. Like Pixie said, I'm not getting any younger."

"You are the oldest, and not the one who will give birth. Letty is a youngster and can handle it," I reminded Mario.

"I want a child or two," Letty said. "I have to consider if we will be absentee parents. Will our lifestyle be good for a child? Do we want to give up what we have going? Are we ready for that kind of change?"

I knew she meant giving up the open relationship with Tangles and Storm and maybe others in the future.

"I admire you for thinking the way you do," I said, putting a lid on the topic. Tangles and Storm had not gotten in that exchange. They were eating and pretending to be deaf.

I'm happy for Mario. I'm happy for Letty. I'm happy for Tangles and Storm. Maybe I'm a little jealous that I'm not still living in Mario's house. I was there first, before Letty and Tangles and Storm, even before Jo and Niley. I've never been part of their plane sales. It's been a while since I was on the inside of team Mario. It's crazy how time flies.

We made it out of the living room to the disco on the first floor. A big table was set up just like in a nightclub. We had everything but a live band, with music blasting from the best sound system you can buy. The volume was loud enough to feel it and low enough so we could hear each other.

Lainie was grown and in show biz, so I wasn't surprised when she lit up a joint. She was next to me, took a long drag, and handed it over with a grin. I took a hit and passed it on to Letty. I lit one of my own, took another hit and handed it to Lainie. She accepted it with a grin, and the two joints made their way around our small group, going in opposite directions. It was a rare occasion when I smoked a joint with Lainie and probably the first time with more than just us smoking.

Truth is, I enjoyed sharing a joint with her. I was in a good mood because I was home and with people I love, but also because the annulment was approved and final. The press would hear the news in two days. My fans would love it because that's how fans are. My ex-husband's female fans would be thrilled that I was out of the picture. I did not make public why I decided to dump him. He is a sick puppy. I wasn't going to play nurse to a man who might kill me while I slept.

We were all buzzed.

"It's neato that you still have Tangles and Storm here with you. Is it like it looks?" she giggled.

"Yeah, we got something special," Letty said. "How Boss is that?"

Outspoken as always. Gotta love her.

"It's Boss, alright," Storm said.

"Letty makes it work," Mario said.

I've known Mario all my life. There's no question that he loves Letty. No doubt he loves Tangles and Storm too. He loves all of his women, but the ones he lets live in his house, he loves more.

"Hey, listen," Letty said with just a little bit of a slur from the wine. "We dig being together."

If I wasn't away all the time, I would still be in this life with Mario. Letty and I have a thing, as much as Mario and me.

"Do you do orgies, or what?" Lainie asked. "I mean, I always figured you did. I had to get away from home to find out it wasn't the thing for everybody to swim naked together, and shit like that."

"Oh, you poor innocent child," I kidded, lacing my hands over my eyes. She's always known I got together with Mario, no matter who else he was with. When she was younger, at the age when some of her friends had started getting divorced over things like infidelity, I'd had difficulty explaining the kind of jealousy that was in typical relationships. I think I'd said that some people think like Aunt Carmen, and some people don't. Other than that, I don't think we ever talked about it.

"Oh Mom," Lainie said, tugged one hand off my face, and holding it. "I'm not a kid anymore. I almost married Jason, whose ideas about sex were warped as shit. I've known all along there were a whole lot of goings-on over here. No big deal."

"We don't consider it an orgy if we're all in bed," Tangles said. "We consider it Wednesday. Or Saturday. Or any ordinary day of the week. It happens sometimes. It doesn't happen every single day."

"Yeah, we do it when we do it. That's all. Why does it need a name?" Storm asked.

Lainie took a hit from one of the joints making the rounds. "If I ever get married, it will have to be an open marriage. I'm jealous."

"You better not marry a rock star," I said, not specifically mentioning my recent experience. "They want to have their cake and eat it too. I mean, they fuck around, and do anything they want, but they won't want to extend you the same freedom."

"Mom, I totally agree."

Lainie and I don't agree often, but since we were both touring, we've been having many similar experiences.

"That's not me," Mario said. "I'm no rock star, but your mama taught me early on, it's stupid to be like unfair."

"Are you saying that if you fuck around, Letty can to?"

"For sure," Mario said.

Letty was smiling. The light was dim, but not so dim that I didn't see Letty blush.

"How can I get in this clique? I want some," Lainie said.

"You always want."

"Mom is impossible," Lainie said.

We called it a night. They invited us to stay but tomorrow was a big day. We planned to do some serious shopping for the newlyweds. One of Mario's security guards walked us across the street. I pointed out to Lainie where I had kicked the crap out of an attacker long ago, an unexpected lunatic who came after me while I was crossing the street from Mario's to go home. Cops had come and taken him away. I never knew if he had been trying to hurt me.

"I always felt bad that I turned the matter over to the cops," I said. On tour, I've had plenty of whackos that security and cops handled. Several times I've had to defend myself. Lainie has the same problem.

"He deserved it," Lainie said, her arm around my shoulders like we were pals coming home buzzed from a party.

The gates to my compound opened.

We said hello to my guards and good night to Mario's guard. Our gates shut, and Lainie stopped in the middle of the driveway with a horrified look on her face.

"Mom, we didn't give them any wedding presents."

"That's why we're going shopping tomorrow. What do you buy them? They have everything."

"Mom, we have to get them something special. Did you see the watch Olga gave Letty?"

"I'd have to be blind to miss it. Of course, I saw. It's gorgeous."

"Bottom line," Lainie said as we walked past the foyer in my house. "You copped out before that you had sex with him when you were young. Were you lovers after I was born?"

"Yes, we were lovers before and after. Are you happy now? It was hardly a secret."

Lainie laughed. "I was right."

I knew Mario had married Letty, but there was no reason to think that things had changed. Letty and Mario both were my lovers.

"Why didn't it go further?"

"Who knows? I love him more than anyone other than you. He always loved me. It was as far as we wanted it to go."

"I would have never let him go," Lainie said.

"Stop with the dreamy eyes," I said. "Mario is married and for all I know he may be your father."

"Mom, you and me, we've discussed this before, and you told me he was not my dad because you two had not had sex for more than two years before you got pregnant. If you thought then he was my dad, you should have told me."

My daughter is a royal pain in the ass.

"Lainie, he's not your dad but stop with your flirting and acting up like you do around him. Got it?"

"Got it," Lainie said.

"I'm going to bed," I said.

"Mom, we're not done talking."

"Yeah, we are," I said, walking upstairs.

I had always done my best to provide for Lainie. Her formative years had been spent with me at Aunt Carmen's. Mario had taken me there when I'd been pregnant and homeless at seventeen, and his aunt had welcomed me into their little family, and never once made me feel ashamed of being a 'corner girl.' She has been and will always be Lainie's abuela.

It was public knowledge that I had been raised in a cathouse and was a hooker until I was seventeen. I had made my fortune on songs of my childhood, partly because that is all I knew, and partly because I wasn't going to let my past become a big secret that would destroy my career. Mario has been my best friend, as far back as I can remember. I would never have gotten exclusive with Mario. I love him too much to do that to him. How could I burden him with an ex-hooker? I would never put him in that position. I had stood aside and watched him not marry Melina. For a long time, it had seemed that he would marry Olga.

I love Olga. How can I not love her? She got me my first record deal and became my agent. She made possible the life I have today. Lainie and I are living a dream thanks to Olga. Her ties to a family of power on the wrong side of the law have never mattered to me. But still, I'm happy it was my beloved Letty and not Olga that Mario finally married.

November 16, 1993
Pasadena
Letty

Before we got married, we never went to bed together without taking a shower first. Now, when we are too zonked to shower after a day of work, we go straight to bed—and in pajamas, no less. We do shower in the morning. It's not like we're slobs. After years of sleeping naked, he now says he likes wearing pajamas. Of course, it's November.

I only lit one candle, very unlike me.

So, we were clad in pajamas in our dark bedroom, my head on his chest, my leg across him, his hands on me. It was just the two of us. Tangles and Storm were off doing their own thing.

"What a wonderful surprise to see Pixie and Lainie. No one snitched them out and ruined the surprise."

"Except the guard who called and said they were walking in."

"It was still a big surprise."

"Indeed, it was."

"I love Pixie. And Lainie is a chip off the old block."

"Their talent made them famous," Mario said.

I thumped his chest. "I know, dummy."

"Ouch, that hurt."

"Sissy."

He grabbed my pussy. Is grab the right word? He put his hand between my legs, and I felt instant heat. My hormones sprang into action, intensified by the buzz.

"Who is a sissy?"

"Babe, how do I answer that so you don't remove your hand?"

We didn't have sex. It was like Mario no longer had to prove his manhood. We were still what a goody two-shoes would call sex freaks. We just did what we wanted when we wanted. There was nothing to prove. Some nights, it was enough to smile at each other in the overhead mirror that in the past had seen it all.

We were quiet for a long time. Mario's breathing was steady and rhythmic.

"Good night, my love," I said, thinking he was asleep.

He kissed the top of my head.

"Good night, Letty. I love you."

"I'm the happiest woman in the world with you. It's all a dream come true."

He pinched my ass, hard.

"Ouch!"

"See? You're not dreaming."

November 18, 1993 (Thursday)
Pasadena
Mario

The four of us rode together to the office, Storm behind the wheel of my Rolls.

"We should have stayed home today," Letty said. "Pixie and Lainie leave tomorrow."

"We're coming home early," I said. "I talked to Pixie when you were in the shower. They have something to do this morning. I told her we'd be back by two and to plan on lunch and dinner with us."

"I'll call home and let Emma know," Letty said. "You should have told me."

"I already told Emma, and now I'm telling you."

Letty squeezed my thigh. "Honey, thanks for taking care of it."

"I'm going to be black and blue with all the pinching," I said.

She punched my shoulder. "They're love taps," she laughed.

"That's what you get for having a black belt for a wife, Boss," Storm said.

"Eyes on the road, witch," Letty said.

"Hey, I went from bitch to witch. Fuck."

"You prefer bitch?"

"We're going to end up in a crash. Stop you two," Tangles said,

The bickering was a usual thing. I ignored them and dialed my secretary.

"Good morning," I said. "Whatever I need to get done, I need to be out of there by one, okay? And reschedule everything we have on Friday to Monday. We're not coming in on Friday."

"Sure, Boss, no problem."

When we got home that afternoon, Pixie and Lainie were already there, sitting at the counter in the kitchen while Emma was fixing lunch.

After a session of hugs and kisses as though we hadn't seen each other in a long time, Lainie said, "Come to the living room. We have surprises."

"I dig surprises," Letty said.

On the den's Persian rug were four bicycles. Beauties.

Three girl's bikes, one guy's bike.

"What is this?" I said.

"What do you think?" Letty said, laughing. "These two have been shopping."

"Hold your horses," Storm said. "Where are your bikes?"

"We have bikes at the house. If we happen to be here and you want to go riding with us, we can do it." Pixie giggled.

"That's not all," Lainie said. "Check this out."

She went to a stack of boxes piled in the corner and handed them out.

Storm, Tangles, Letty and I each pulled a skateboard out of our boxes. I held mine out, looking at the dragon painted on mine. It was a work of art.

"These are neatest ones you will ever find," Lainie said.

"Skateboards?" Letty said, laughing away.

Tangles and Storm did high fives with each other, and then with Pixie and Lainie.

I was too busy laughing.

"I don't even know how to ride a skateboard," Letty said.

"You think I do?" I asked, still laughing.

"I'll teach you," Storm said.

"I'm in. I think it will be fun."

Letty kissed Pixie and Lainie.

"Thank you!"

The hugs and kisses started again.

"Okay, and now the wedding gifts," Pixie said, picking up two small packages from the coffee table. "You two are fucking hard to shop for when we've been away from you so much." She giggled.

I have always loved Pixie's giggle.

In my box was a Corum Indian head gold coin watch with a gold band. It was beautiful and as flashy as my Rolex watches, Rolls Royce and my house.

"This is fantastic," I said. I dropped Olga's gift in my pocket and put on this one. The Indianhead coin was the actual face of the watch. "I've never seen anything like this."

"I've never seen anything so pretty," Letty said, putting on the watch they had given her. The girls circled Letty, admiring it.

"It's also a Corum like Mario's, only it's an ingot."

"I fucking love it," Letty said, hugging Pixie. The hugs and kisses started all over again.

We ate Mexican for lunch. Letty gave Emma a plan for dinner and then we went down to the indoor pool for a swim. It was a serious Olympic-sized pool, but over the years, we've improved it with water features that could be turned off and on. A fifteen-foot tower cascaded like a real waterfall. Spiral water jets were set at the bottom of the pool in one section, and splashed water beautifully.

A manicurist came in to work on the girls. I waited in the wine room after the swim and read the LA Times that I missed that morning. I always read the classified ads, especially the miscellaneous for sale ads and business opportunity ads.

Letty and the girls joined me in the wine room with the girls. Pixie and Lainie had changed into jeans and sweaters like the rest of us. I didn't know if they were borrowed, or if they'd sent someone across the street for fresh clothes. They showed off their nails.

"I travel with a hairdresser who does my nails. She's visiting her family in ELA," Pixie said, showing off long, bright talons. "Lainie has a girl who does her hair and a second girl who does her pedicures and manicures. They stayed in Mexico City."

Lainie said, "They needed a break. We've been on the road with back to back shows for three weeks."

"Mario, we should hire a massage therapist who does manicures and pedicures," Letty said. "And I'll buy couple of those new chairs to wash and massage the feet while you get a pedicure."

"Whatever happened to Betty?" Pixie asked.

"She's into some dude," Storm said. "I called to see if she could come over and she said she couldn't. I told her not to sweat it."

"Without Betty, we've been using a service," Letty said. "I want to be a good hostess. Want me to get some masseuses over here before dinner or after?"

Lainie said, "That will be so boss. After dinner for me. I'm not sharing. I want a long massage."

"Spoiled brat," Pixie said.

"Takes one to know one," Lainie shot back.

"Letty, I love the bidet you installed down here," Pixie said, changing the subject.

"Not just downstairs," Letty said.

"I had them in hotels," Pixie said. "Who was your plumber? I want them too."

"I'll have TJ send his guy," Letty said.

"Get them for all the bathrooms," I said. "That's what we did."

"The salesman who gets that order will be one happy mother," Storm said.

"The one I had in my suite in Japan had a blower to dry you after it washes you," Pixie said.

"Love it," I said, "We should upgrade. Where have I been? Not keeping up."

"I'll find them," Letty said.

After dinner was served in the dining room, we had massages in the spa.

We talked back and forth the whole time.

Lainie was turning into a joker.

"I want a full body massage. Is that what I'm going to get?"

"Yes ma'am," her masseur said. He was a young guy, so young that Lainie called him Opie, like the kid on Andy Griffith's tv show. She made a fuss over him being so cute. He was starstruck, overwhelmed that he was in Pixie and Lainie's proximity.

"Don't stress Opie out," Pixie said. "She doesn't bite."

"I won't stress, ma'am."

He kept his clothes on, and Lainie didn't get the works, though I bet if he and Lainie had been alone, anything could have happened.

"I must have known one day I would need all these massage tables at the same time," I said.

"I wish Melina had done the spa like you," Pixie said.

"Mom get it done. No big deal."

"Maybe I will, at that, now that I own the house. I can't believe I own that place. Fuck-me, it's been a crazy ride."

"Proud of you," I said.

After a while, we all went silent, mesmerized by the talented hands of our therapists. Letty and I were side by side on the massage tables, and we had masseuses. The rest of them had masseurs. I drifted off to a boneless, happy sleep.

Friday, we stayed home. Lainie had already flown out.

Pixie was leaving that afternoon. We all wanted to be with Pixie until she took off to the airport, like every minute was important, and it was.

After Pixie began her singing career, Letty had filled her loss with

Tangles. They were tight. As Pixie had once tutored Letty in karate, so Letty had taught Tangles. Practicing karate together bonded them even more. Storm and Tangles had boyfriends sometimes, but each other the rest of the time. It was clear that Letty loved them both. In the beginning, when Storm accompanied me on trips and had a lot of my attention, there had been friction. It was so bad that I stepped in and put a stop to the nonsense. Ever since, it appeared to me, it was like they were like sisters.

Rewind Two Years: September 1991
Puerto Rico
Lola

Something that smelled wonderful was blooming outside, and I'd left the window open. The air smelled like a fruit salad, like mangos and gardenias with a hint of sea air. Even in September, days warm up to the eighties here, and rarely fall below the mid-seventies at night. I spent the leisurely morning with warm breezes on my bare skin, lying alone on my bed in my condo in San Juan, watching shadows and lights on my ceiling. I was appreciating it all—the tropical breezes, the balmy sweet scent, my physical comfort, not needing to get in my car and drive to a day spent in surveillance. I had no plans other than to check out a couple of the tourist venues where I'd never been and perhaps visit one of the restaurants a neighbor recommended to me. I did not welcome the ringing phone. It rang half a dozen times, and I just let it ring. One of my brothers. It rang again, and I rolled on my side to answer.

"It's your dime," I said.

"Don't hang up," the voice said.

My ears knew the voice. It came out of the past, but it took a few seconds for recognition to register, and a few more seconds for the name to come to mind. By the time he said his name, I'd already figured it out—but with some disbelief. I shot upright on the bed and leapt to my feet, my heart racing.

"This is Mason from Pasadena," he said.

Mason had a public reputation of being a case solver, but he was a puppet belonging to the Camacho family, hiding in plain sight. Insurers, fences, and collectors who took risks hired him to recover expensive works of art. He was a psychiatrist and a lawyer, and though he was licensed to practice law in California, he applied his skills in a forensic manner, ostensibly in search of stolen art, but mostly in various capacities for the Camachos. The agency judged him to be a master at finding people using the same psychological techniques as the FBI. After all, he was a shrink.

"Don't hang up. I know you know who I am."

I didn't hang up. Maybe I should have done something else, pretended I didn't hear, or that it was a wrong number. How had he found me? His call was disturbing but no surprise. Sure, I covered my tracks but finding people is one of the things he is known for. Only my brothers had the number of this cell.

"What the fuck do you want? How the fuck did you know my number?" I shrugged into a t-shirt and shut my window. I felt like checking my doors. I grabbed my gun from inside my bedside table, then sat on the edge of the bed. For all I knew he could be calling from outside my house.

"That's not important right now. No one will know from me you are alive. You have my word."

"Your word? How good is your word? You're a Camacho errand boy."

"You must know I'm not an errand boy."

"Fuck you, Mason."

"I have a proposition for you. Big money. Five times more than you got before."

"Fuck you."

"Nina, Lola, don't lose it. Don't hang up."

"You could burn for this."

"I'm doing nothing wrong," he said.

"What the fuck do you want?"

"Come see me in California at my house," he said. "Have to see you in person."

"You're crazy, Mason."

"I am crazy, yes. There are no tricks to this call. Can't do anything on a phone. I can tell you are curious. I know you will be interested when I tell you what I want."

"Oh, you can tell. Is that the psychiatrist talking?"

"Yes," he said.

"Why would I travel all the way to California to listen to a proposal from someone I don't trust one damn bit?"

"I want you to come see me at my home. Come see me, and I will hand you fifty thousand in cash. I'm not stupid enough to let something happen to you in my residence."

"What's the catch?"

"You can't show up wired. You get the fifty after a strip search. If you don't like my proposition, you go back to where you are, and you take the fifty with you, no strings attached. It's up to you whether or not we strike a deal. When you're here, I'll explain how to get some more money."

"Are you bullshitting me?"

"I think you know I'm not, or you would have hung up by now."

"Who is behind this call? Camila? Olga?"

"No. They believe you are dead."

"How did you find me? Who else knows I'm here?"

"I'm good at what I do. No one knows. Only me."

I itched to hang up but couldn't do it. What the fuck did he want from me that would earn me five million dollars, or, for that matter, fifty just for showing up?

"Are you there?" he asked.

"Call me tomorrow and I'll let you know," I said. "If anything happens to me, my brothers will hang your ass. Since you know everything, you must know they are feds."

I thought I must be dreaming one of those realistic dreams where you realize you're dreaming. I paced my condo, digesting what had just happened, and going over every word he'd told me. He was not lying. He was up to something big. No matter what it was that he wanted, it had to be bad to cost him fifty thou just to tell me about it.

If he was up to no good, it could be anything. Maybe he already told her I'm alive, and she sent him to me. None of this made sense. The bitch would go into cardiac arrest if she found out I had not died in the explosion. Did she know?

If they knew, what good did it do to go through the charade of faking my death, settling in Puerto Rico hidden from the Camacho family and anyone I may have stepped on during my agency career? What good was all that shit if Mason was able to find me? He knows the phone number that no one in this world knows other than my brothers. Fuck!

The next day, his call took two minutes.

"Here's my cell number," he said. "Call and let me know a day before you come. I will make sure no one is at the house when you arrive. Any morning is okay. Eleven works for me."

"I have your address," I said. "I know where you live."

He chuckled. "I have your address, too."

I disconnected.

Fucking asshole!

He called back.

"You haven't changed your mind?" he asked.

"I'll be there."

As he'd requested, I gave Mason twenty-four hours notice that I was on the way.

I am an expert at changing my appearance, but I didn't go to the trouble of a disguise. I have a wall of wigs in my closet, bins of various make-up types, lenses and prosthetics that significantly change my features. Unless Mason was playing me, no one knew I was going to Los Angeles. I didn't feel like fucking around with a wig and everything else it takes to change my looks. After arriving late at night, I rented a car from Avis at LAX and drove straight to check into a Holiday Inn in Pasadena, a room where I could park outside my door. The parking lot entrance was easy entry and exit. It was a generic hotel room, beige-figured carpet, beige print bedspread, beige wallpaper. Holiday Inn plasterboard dressers, desk, end tables, all bolted to the walls. I walked in and collapsed on the bed. I lay for thirty seconds on the bed, being beiged to death. I'd had it with the sleeplessness, the anxiety, the worry in case something might go wrong. Fuck it. I needed sleep. Not that the beige-ness was keeping me awake. Simply, with tomorrow coming, I knew as soon as I was horizontal, sleep wasn't going to be my friend. I took a sleeping pill to put me under for at least seven hours, and it kicked in like gangbusters.

In the morning, I woke with time to kill. I showered, turned on the TV news, and brewed a pot of coffee in the machine that lived in the entrance to the bathroom. I drank the coffee and used the second package of Folgers to make more. I still had an hour to brood over what I might do to Mason if he was playing me. I watched the clock and put my Uzi in my purse. The old Uzi was a treasure, and just carrying it made me feel safe.

I was ten minutes from his house. I checked out, and at eleven sharp, I was parked across the street from his gates. The design of the ornamental ironwork blocked the view of his property. Tall gates, but baby gates compared to Casa Luna.

I hefted the strap of my massive bag over my shoulder, tested that I could easily and smoothly reach my weapon, and walked across the street to push the intercom button. The cul-de-sac was quiet with hardly any traffic.

A male voice said, "One gate is opening. Walk in."

In the countless hours of surveilling Pepe, Camila and Olga, countless hours of Mason were included when he happened to be around. He may have been the focus of another team, but for my team, he was not a person of interest. We never observed him break any laws. Our team had included FBI, DEA, ATF and Customs, and our target had been drug trafficking. If the Treasury Department had thrown in with our team, they probably would have caught the money laundering that my team eventually concluded was going on with the Camachos.

I had seen aerial views of the house, a rectangular two-story early

Mediterranean, red-tiled roof, stucco walls, wrought iron balconies, plenty of arches and interesting windows, too pretty to be hidden behind gates. It was not huge, but it was no small house either. I walked up a long driveway, my soft-soled shoes barely making a sound on the poured concrete. The yard looked like it was professionally landscaped, rock gardens, shrubs, ground-cover that was probably spectacular in the summer. He met me just as I got to the front door of his home, and we shook hands. I'd never met him in person. It's funny to me that when I saw him, I felt like I had met him before. Surveillance breeds familiarity like that. He was clean-shaven. A white guy, about fifty-two, he was stocky and square-built rather than tall, a plentiful thatch of white hair. Well under six feet. Very well-dressed.

"Thanks for showing up," he said. "Come in. No one else is home."

He opened the door for me. I was glad that the temperature inside was ten or fifteen degrees warmer than outside. Though I'd gotten accustomed to the weather in Puerto Rico, the chill I was feeling was from more than weather. I did not trust the guy.

"I'm not wired," I said. "I'm not here officially. I am no longer an agent with the FBI. I am packing. It's in my purse."

I lifted the Uzi out far enough for him to get a good look.

He gave a little laugh.

His home office was on the ground floor close to the front door, so I didn't see much of the house when he led me inside. I sat on a stiff leather couch and he sat across from me on a wing chair. I glanced around looking for something that could be a camera but didn't see anything out in the open. On the butler's table between us, I saw a brown paper bag. I wondered if it held the cash that he'd promised me.

"As I said on the phone, I need you to strip completely to confirm there are no wires."

I stood and unzipped my jacket. The purse was to my left, the Uzi in it in easy reach. The base of the jacket separated.

I remembered the time I'd filmed Mario and me going at it in a hotel bedroom purely for my own entertainment.

"Are you recording this by any means?" I asked, holding my zipper between my thumb and forefinger.

"I am not recording by audio or video, nor is anyone else on my behalf."

I had come dressed like a soccer mom—gray sweatpants, matching zippered jacket with a hoodie, white cotton blouse underneath, tennis shoes. I undressed quickly. He was watching every move I made. I'm not particularly an exhibitionist, but his close attention was a buzz that made stripping almost fun.

I made eye-contact.

"Are you sure this is for wires, and not to satisfy some kinky desire?"

Mason grimaced.

"Give me the clothes."

He fondled the clothes, feeling for a bug, his eyes no longer on mine. When he was satisfied the clothes were clean, he was back to checking out my body.

"Go on," he said.

"I'm obviously not wearing a wire," I said.

"All of it."

I had peeled down to the tamest lingerie in my wardrobe, but there wasn't much to it. I hesitated, but I didn't want to give the impression that he intimidated me. I pulled off the sports bra and plain bikini panties. Cold floor, cold room, but his eyes on me were hot. I fought a shiver, and wished my breasts were smaller.

He got up from the chair, walked to the thermostat and turned it up.

"I'll warm it up a little. Sorry about that."

He must have noticed the goose bumps and the prickling of my nipples.

The fucker came at me with a flashlight.

"Mason, come off this shit. I'm not being booked. You want to check my vagina and anus? What the fuck! A cavity search and a flashlight is overkill for looking for a wire."

"Not at all," he said. "You would do the same if you were me."

I stood there, hands at my sides. Until that moment, I had felt my tan was gorgeous, a warm golden brown. My bikini line was miniscule. I stood there too many seconds, embarrassed about the tan I'd gotten in Puerto Rico, and the contrast to the untanned skin. The private parts of me were too white, too exposed. The whiteness against the tan made me feel twice as naked. I wanted to pull out the Uzi and clunk him with it. He gave me a surprisingly personable grin and put his hand up as if he was surrendering the idea of a cavity search.

"Thank you," he said, after staring at me for too long with interest unrelated to any job. "Please get dressed. I had to do this. What I have to discuss with you is delicate."

I grabbed my clothes and put them on.

"Let's go to the kitchen," he said. "I have coffee going, and I bought a dozen donuts early this morning."

"You first," I said.

He walked to the door. "Take the bag," he said, pointing past me to the table. "It's yours. You can count it in the kitchen."

"I don't think you'd screw me with the count."

"You're right," he said. "You know, you have a beautiful body."

"Is that a pass? Are you making a pass at me?"

"Not at all. Call it a doctor's observation."

The kitchen was on the ground level. We passed through a den, and I was still so rattled that I barely paid attention to it. I'd known ahead of time that he was going to strip-search me. Why was I making such a big mental deal out it? I had a bag with fifty thousand, as promised. I would have fucked him for less. At least that thought made me feel better.

Mason sat me at a dinette in the kitchen. A folksy collection of mugs with doctor slogans was lined up on a shelf by the window. Very Norman Rockwell. He grabbed two and put them on the table.

Mine said 'The head shrink is IN.'

He poured coffee into the big mugs, and put cream and sugar out, with a couple of spoons. His cup said 'The Doctor is always right.'

The spacious table had four chairs, two more against the wall. The bay window beside us looked into a big back yard. One of his walls had pastoral wallpaper. I felt strange about his treating me like an honored guest. The homey setting was hardly something I would picture with Mason. He returned the percolator to the counter and sat across from me.

"Sugar? Cream?"

I took two spoons of each and stirred. I lifted the cup to my lips.

"I want you to take Camila out."

I jerked, spilling a few drops, and put down the cup undrunk.

"What did you say?"

"You heard me."

I looked at his deceptively nice face.

"What are you up to? This is some kind of trick, isn't it? The Camachos pull your strings, and you want to murder the boss?"

"Not a trick. You got the fifty. If you don't want to take the job, you can walk."

The agency expects you to keep a cool head under all circumstances. You're not supposed to be shocked by anything. I was shocked, but don't think I showed how much.

"Why? And why me?"

"I have my reasons. I picked you because you know how to get to her, and you are smart. The Uzi in your purse. At six hundred rounds per minute, you are ready for anything. I can hire professionals for a lot less money, but I would worry about all sorts of things. If you do it, you have as much to lose as I do. You'll do it and walk away, and no one will ever know who did it or who ordered it."

Mason pushed half a doughnut into his mouth. A crumb of glaze lodged in the corner of his mouth. Like a viper, he flicked his lips with his tongue. He polished off the rest in a single bite and swigged his coffee. Something about him, about this scenario reminded me of off-hours in the agency, how many coffee doughnut hours I'd spent off hours with team members.

"Olga wants her half-sister gone. Is that it? Is it for the money?"

"Who wants it is not important. Olga has nothing to do it. She will never know. She will drive me crazy when I can't come up with who did it."

"Five million."

"Yes, five million. Has to be a wire to a foreign bank account. The sender can never be traced."

"I don't have a foreign bank account."

"Fly somewhere and set one up."

"When is this supposed to happen?"

"Within forty days from today."

"How will I know where she is? I hope you don't think I'm going to use the agency."

"I will let you know when she is in different countries. You take it from there."

"What if she doesn't go anywhere in forty days?"

Mason laughed again. "That's impossible."

"Is there any connection to the last attempt on Camila's life?"

"We caught the party who did that. No connection."

"When do I get the money wired?"

"When it's done. You need to trust me."

"If I do this and you don't pay me, I will end you, Mason."

I took a bite of my donut.

"You will get paid, and your secret will always be safe with me. As for your secret, why are you in hiding? Why the car bomb?"

"Standard exit strategy," I said. "My team and I don't trust either of your bosses."

"I'm a hired contractor. They are not my bosses."

"Right, and my name is Richard Nixon."

He ignored my sarcasm. "I would know if Camila wanted you dead, that is, if it was known that you're alive. As for Olga, she doesn't give that kind of order. It's stupid for you to be hiding, unless you did some bad shit to someone other than the Camachos." He quirked his eyebrows at me, as if he was asking a question, but there was no question there.

"It would be stupid for me not to be in hiding. Camila ordered me dead. I'm alive now only because her assassins failed," I said, keeping a lid on my anger. "If one of them hadn't come too damn close, I wouldn't have that tattoo you were staring at five minutes ago."

"A good reason for you to take her out," Mason said. "You said that you would kill her and Olga unless you were paid a million in compensation."

"Talk is cheap." I finished the coffee. "I'm a fool to agree to this, but I'll do it."

"Only proves I was right. You're smart."

"Don't play me, Mason."

He didn't respond.

"I don't like cell calls," I said. "I need to be in touch with you. I need to get wire instructions to you. We need a way to communicate."

He told me he'd reach me at seven in the evening Puerto Rico time, directed me to use a particular brand of remote data and file transfer software, and gave me the phone number to send it to. He gave me a small box with a software disc. I put it in my purse with the bag of cash.

"I know how this software works. Safe, I don't know," I said.

"Safer than a cell phone," he said.

He walked me all the way to the gate, but he did not go outside his property.

As I drove to the airport, I found it hard to believe that Mason was now arranging kills. I wondered who would pay five million fifty thousand to turn off Camila's lights. I wondered how much Mason's cut was. No way was he the source of the promised five million.

My rolling suitcase was in the trunk. I stashed the cash and Uzi inside while I was still in front of Mason's house.

I returned my rented car and rode a shuttle to the American Airlines terminal. With no available non-stop flights to Puerto Rico, an agent at the counter had to juggle some shorter hops to get me there. It took three connections to get back home. The ride back was brutal, but the trip was worth it. Fifty big ones more than covered the stress of getting back to San Juan, Puerto Rico.

On the way, I reflected on Mason's interest in my body. All that said to me is that he's a man who hasn't lost his interest in strange pussy. The fifty thousand smoothed over whatever uneasiness I'd had since his initial call.

Two weeks after I met with Mason, with Mason's fifty thousand cash, I set up an account in the Cayman Islands. The bank didn't care about a name. It was a series of numbers.

I contacted Mason on my computer at seven in the evening his time.

"I have a number. Do you want it now or later?"

"Later."

"Are we a go?"

"Yes," he said. "I will let you know when."

The software provided a swift way to communicate, but planning the deed was impossible. I had to know where and when I could find her with enough wiggle room to set things up. Even the weapon depended on where. Mason and I never talked about what would happen if I get caught or I missed, or if I got shot. No plan B.

I did plenty of thinking alone in my condo.

The television would be on and I would be sitting there in front of it, but my head was on planning the kill and all the possibilities. I thought about the five million. I thought about the taxes in the event I did not declare the foreign account. The government would not care where the money came from, only that I pay the taxes. What would I do with the money? It was so much money. I was mostly at home, but once in a while, I would become frustrated with waiting. I went out to a night club to have some drinks, laughs and maybe get laid.

I waited thirty-one days exactly before I initiated another contact. At seven my time, I typed in his number. He was at home to answer.

"Anything?"

"Waiting. If it takes longer, the time frame gets extended."

I typed back, "Okay."

With my eavesdropping know-how, I figured this mode of conversation would be private, at least for a while. I'd never attempted to tap this kind of communication, but knowing the skill of my team, someone somewhere was going to crack it, sooner or later.

Fuck it. It's not like we were discussing details.

I went to a club. There's little for a local to do in Puerto Rico. Tourist traps to check out. The beach during the day. Drinking and dancing at night. I suppose if I had a job to pour my time into, the hours would pass faster.

I had too much time on my hands.

I never turned off my desktop computer. I stood near it at seven every evening. Mason had never contacted me on it. Each evening I gave it fifteen minutes. If I didn't hear the notification that sounded like a ringing phone, there was no call from Mason.

Close to the end of October, my brother Nico called. I remember exactly what I was doing. The phone rang after I dumped my to-go dinner on to a plate that I shoved into the microwave. His news put me off, and I ended up not eating. The food petrified in the oven until eventually I found its hardened remains a few days later.

"I just heard that Camila Camacho was shot in Mexico City. Thought you'd want to know."

"You heard what?" I asked, not in control of my voice.

"Camila Camacho was shot in Mexico City."

My knees turned to rubber. I sat down, shocked.

"Shot or killed?" I whispered, barely able to catch my breath.

I remembered the pain of my gunshot, the flashes of memory that came from the ride in the ambulance, the ER, the gurney rushing through the halls, the long path to recovery. She had been the one responsible for shooting me. It was symmetry that I would be able to shoot her. But that opportunity had been stolen from me.

"I only have it she was shot. I will let you know, when I know."

"She was shot at before and the shooter missed. This is old news."

"Sis, that's history. This happened an hour ago."

I looked at the clock. Afternoon in Los Angeles.

Damn.

Damn.

A few hours later, Nico notified me that Camila had died at a hospital in Mexico City. The killer was an unknown long range sniper at the airport.

Somehow, I made it to seven pm, when I rang Mason's computer.

He answered.

"What the fuck?" I typed.

"No idea."

"Are you playing me?" I typed.

"No."

"What now?"

"It's over," he said.

"Over like how?"

"There is nothing to do. I'll be in contact," he wrote.

The line disconnected.

Fuck.

Fuck.

Present day
November 18, 1993
New York City
Lola

I'd been home since October eleventh. It was past the middle of November, and I was still in bad shape. Everything hurt, still. I had to shop for food, something I could barely manage. When I slept, nightmares. Shopping meant going down a million stairs, walking three blocks, and pushing the groceries all the way back from the store—all of this when I could barely make it from the bedroom to my bathroom. Most of the time, I ate at the greasy spoon downstairs, or paid extra for a kid on my floor to make a grocery run.

My hate for Art grew. It was a nourishing emotion, a nuclear reaction, a hatred that kept me going. I started myself on a regimen of physical therapy. I struggled with light exercise and easy repetitions several times a day. Easy reps to start, but I had to start somewhere. I had always been good at athletics but getting up to speed was more difficult than I imagined it would be. Eventually I recovered physically.

I don't know if I'll ever get my head back. I don't know how to shake the hate inside me.

I could not make up my mind.

Before the interrogation, I was sure that Olga had been in on Camila's murder with Mason. He would not have had five million to offer me—unless he'd never had the money to begin with. But I believed he was caught off guard when he learned of the timing of Camila's murder.

I never talked to him again.

Olga's interrogation changed everything. I'd had weeks to think it through. Mason must not have hired Camila's murderer. Olga had to have had it done. Who was Mason representing when he gave me the proposal? If Olga had nothing to do with it at all, if she kidnapped me believing that I was the shooter, who had ordered the hit? I wondered if Mason knew. Had Mason just handed over the job to someone else instead of me? I didn't believe that. I don't think I believe that. He's good at finding things out. He's had two years to find the killer. Maybe he's known all along.

I keep thinking about the five hundred thousand Olga had given me. Why, why would Olga spare my life and send me home with a package of cash like that? Her friend Riana had stood up to Olga. I only remember bits and pieces, but I do remember her ordering the doctor to stop.

Riana. She saved my life.

I had my last egg for breakfast and cobbled together a sort of salad with wilting things from my refrigerator. After one rep of my exercises, I went down to the greasy spoon for a couple of bowls of stew and half a pie that would hold me for a couple of dinners, walked to a bookstore and picked up a bestseller just for the exercise, and to get out of the house. At least in New York City, everything is in walking distance.

So, there I was, sitting in front of the television with a bowl of beef stew steaming on the tray table, but my mind was not on the sad news that Bill Bixby died, or wondering about some brand-new thing called Food Network that was just born. No, I was brooding how, if not for Art, Olga's inquisition would never have happened. Why didn't I follow through checking him out? I'd suspected him. Nico had been suspicious. His dead end had meant something. I couldn't believe that neither of us had managed to figure out who Art was.

If Mason had given me up, that inquisition would have happened right away, not two years later. Why would he wait two years to double-cross me?

I blamed it on Art. I came to New York to get suckered by a bastard who plays it off like he cares for me. I tried reaching Mason on the computer and three times on his cell. Neither way was successful.

I was still waking up in a cold sweat in the middle of the night, unsure of where I was, terrified that I was in that garage under Olga's tender care, but by mid-December, I was in a normal range. I could manage walking and stairs. I'd started jogging again. I could make it through a yoga class at the Y without falling over or collapsing.

I needed answers.

The news came on. I dipped my spoon into the stew, but it had gone cold. I carried it to my microwave and warmed it up for the second or third time. While I was waiting, my mind went back to the issue at hand.

I need to find Art.

December 15, 1993
Pasadena
Mario

The Christmas tree I ordered, a twenty-five-foot noble, was delivered a week late.

"Finally, we can plant it when Christmas is done," Letty said. "I didn't know the container was going to be so big, or that it was going to delay the delivery for a week."

"I didn't think it would fit," Storm said.

"The tree always fits," Tangles said.

"Memo's going to plant it. It is a beauty. That barrel it's in is so huge, I don't know how they got it through the door. It's bigger than a hundred gallons, they said."

"Patrick says that for every tree they cut down, they plant a hundred trees," Tangles said.

"Patrick will say anything to keep selling us this size tree every year. And of course, they plant. They have a tree farm," Letty said. "If they didn't plant today, they'd have no trees tomorrow. This one was container grown. It's so root-bound, it's going to grow like mad when it can stretch out."

"Okay, are we going to decorate or what?" I said.

As usual, the staff pitched in to move the two skyscraper ladders around and unpack the decorations. Letty and I were on one, Storm and Tangles on the other.

Emma brought out four giant pizzas she'd made from scratch. Unbreakable plates and pizza were set up buffet style in reach of where we were decorating. It was fun eating, and messy. The whole staff ate with us. I loved it.

I kissed Letty every few minutes, when she hung a decoration, or I hung one.

We laughed a lot.

Tangles and Storm giggled constantly. Their laughter was contagious.

"I remember this time of year, a couple of years ago, when Pixie and I went out for ornaments and lights. We got accosted in the parking lot," Letty said. "Pixie and me, we beat their asses because we thought we were big shot karate bad-asses. We came home and didn't notice they followed us. They didn't get inside until after Betty came over, and she and boss went down to the spa. Boss figured out something was wrong, and when he caught those guys in the house, he wiped the floor with them."

I ended up killing one of the intruders and sending the other one to the hospital in handcuffs.

"I wish I'd seen it. Memo and Yoli were there, and so were Chete and Caro," Tangles said. "That was before my time. I know the story though, because Pixie tells me about it every Christmas."

"I wasn't here," Sunny said, blushing bright red. She was one of the housekeepers who started working at Casa Luna a few years later. She was tall, skinny, meek, and barely said a word. She picked up an empty pizza tray and crept silently into the kitchen. We all went back to decorating.

It felt good to know I could stop working and spend the rest of my life with Letty, using money I had put in the bank. If we burned through it, I had rental income I'd never touched from over two thousand rental units that Jo and Niley managed for me. But I didn't want to quit, and neither did Letty. We loved leasing planes. We loved working in the same office.

Letty started jogging with me in the mornings. Before long, Tangles and Storm joined us, although Tangles complained she preferred the rough stuff on the mat with Letty.

"You'll love running when you get good at it," I said.

Storm was a natural runner.

"Bitch, you probably jogged before you met us," Letty said.

On alternate days, we rode the bicycles Pixie and Lainie had gifted us. It was a good thing the neighborhood was practically empty at six in the morning. Where the street narrowed to two lanes, we rode side by side, taking up the entire street. It reminded me of that opening scene of the Monkees, when they were walking weird side by side. I mean, on bicycles, we balance okay, but we each cope with bicycles differently. Letty and I were a little wobbly, Tangles was loud and aggressive and would ride hard and tire out first, and Storm was always trying to out-do everyone else without calling attention to how hard she was working at making it look easy.

"This is not easy," I gasped when I had the breath for it after we ended up going uphill. My turn to complain.

"Sissy," Letty teased.

"Where did you learn?" Tangles asked Letty.

"I'm a natural, bitch."

"Are you going to talk like that when the baby gets here?" Storm asked, trying hard not to pant.

"Baby!" I was riding next to Letty. She smiled, shrugged.

"Storm is having a baby moment," Letty said, pumping fiercely so that she was in the lead.

"You better tell me if there is a baby on the way," Tangles said.

Tangles had been in the lead and had slowed to get even with us. Now she was dropping back and dripping with sweat.

It was so cold that the air was almost hard to breathe. Biking was going to be rough in the summer. Maybe by then we'd be back to karate. We were all sticky, sweaty, and warm in spite of the temperature.

"I'm the one who needs to know," I said.

Letty had promised not to spring a baby on us unless I wanted a baby. I knew there was no baby. If there was even a chance of one, she'd be telling me first.

"Can't take a joke," Storm said, laughing and peddling past Letty.

We had made it to the halfway point and were heading back.

"Last one in the pool is a rotten egg," I said.

Miraculously, we weren't late for work. If we were, it was no big deal since I am the boss. I can't speak for the girls. Somehow, I had loads of energy for the rest of the day.

I thought of Lola often.

I was curious if she was okay.

The idea of being married had mellowed me out, but not entirely. Life hadn't changed all that much from before, but, theoretically, I was not sure what I'd do if Lola was on a bed, naked, spread eagle and beckoning me.

She was worth fantasizing about but in reality, a moot point settled far away in Puerto Rico. Lola and her games. I still thought about the picture she'd left in my office. Letty had put it in a frame (not a nice one, just plastic) and left it on my desk. One day when she was mad over something, she didn't give any warning, but drew a red moustache on the frame. Cheeky gal, my Letty. She didn't even use permanent marker, and one of the housekeepers wiped it clean. Letty and the girls never gave Lola's breach of security a second thought. We talked about it for a while, but that was as far as it went.

Olga and I were frequently in touch because of the business. I didn't need to call her. She called me two or three times a week at the office. She always asked me how Letty and I were and how business was. I knew Andrea kept her updated, but Olga never mentioned Andrea.

Olga asked if I was truly happy and if I thought about her now that I was married. It was a regular thing.

"Olga, I will always love you, and yes, I'm happy."

"You and me, we could have been married."

"Olga, you're the one who canceled our engagement. Why would you want to be married? You're at the top of the world. I see your name in magazines, and newspapers, a celebrity. You're up there on the Forbes list with Warren Buffet, Bill Gates and that guy who owns the shopping network. I'm so proud of you."

She sniffed a little bit, and then asked if I was really proud.

Olga didn't have an insecure bone in her body. I figured she was putting on a show for me.

"Olga you are the smartest woman I ever met." That was a lie. She was one of the smartest. Melina was no dummy. She'd built up her chain of supermarkets from scratch, though from a money angle, no comparison to Olga's financial position.

Olga controlled a multi-billion-dollar global company and retained eleven percent of LAI stock. She was a billionaire in a world with few female billionaires. Olga, the woman who did sixty-nine with me, who knew every inch of my body as I knew hers, who could be in my bed at any time. It was incredible how Olga had ended up inheriting the Camacho fortune on top of the millions she'd earned laundering money for the Camachos.

Money sticks to money. I haven't done too bad myself.

December 15, 1993 (Wednesday)
Pasadena
Letty

I'm doing great at this plane leasing thing. My office is half the size of Mario's, but that's the way I want it. I don't need a couch or my own conference room. If I need a shower at work, I use his. For a wedding present, Mario allocated a chunk of LAI money for me to redecorate. I got the carpet removed, and the marble floor beneath it polished. My new bespoke cherry desk is beyond exquisite and topped with a piece of glass so it can't get damaged when I dump over my coffee, which I've been known to do. It sits on a beautiful circular wool rug we brought home from an open air market in Paris. I hung a tapestry, again from Paris, on the wall I face, and there was enough left in the budget to give Tangles and Storm new desks of their choice, too.

I just want somewhere I can get down to business. I just leased a used asset and one new Boeing 737 airliner to two customers. I can handle more than one or two deals at a time, and I do. Tangles had a good month leasing a new 737 with a promise from that operator of coming back for more, when the operator takes delivery of the leased plane in the new year. Storm is persistent. She needs polish, but she will get there. She's the coolest of cool. Everyone loves her. She's is kicking it. Now that Storm has found her place in the office, I told her we would be looking for someone else to drive. Mario wants to hire a driver.

"No, I dig driving," Storm said. "Don't waste the bread on some stranger."

So, I told Mario, "She's on the payroll and gets paid if she leases a plane. She's happy like she is. Let it be." It's what she wants.

Mario sprang it on me that he was flying to Zurich to meet up with Olga.

"Can I go?"

If he had said yes, I would have explained I'm too busy at the office unless he absolutely wanted me to go. Then of course, I would go.

"I should go alone," he said. "It's a fast trip. Olga says she wants to talk shop."

"Shop?"

"She's thinking that if the leasing company went public, it would give us unlimited capital."

We already have unlimited capital, pretty much.

"I won't be in the way," I said. I just wanted him to say, 'Sure, come with me.'

He kissed me. A fast kiss.

"Baby, I'm going alone."

"With all of her money, she can get her oil changed by thousands of takers wherever she is. Why you?"

He looked at me like I had punched him. Actually, I felt like punching him. When you're into karate as we are, we can punch each other, but I didn't.

Later he came into my office, went behind my chair and kissed the top of my head.

"Baby don't be pissed. What's the big deal? It's just Olga."

I was completely honest with him.

"If you had said, 'Of course you can go,' I would have told you I'm too busy here. But no, you said a firm no, and that, my friend, ticked me off. Oh, I'm good," I lied. "You have three pussies at home, and you need to high-tail it all the way to wherever she is to dick her and Riana. I don't understand."

"Ouch," he said, making a joke of what I said.

"Go do what you have to do. I'll do the same. I'll be here when you get back."

"I've never seen you like this. I thought we had an arrangement."

"You're right, Amor," I said, using Olga's favorite word. I got up and hugged him. He towers over me. "Sorry to be such a bitch."

I wasn't sorry.

"You're not sorry," he said. "You are putting me on." He hugged me tight.

My phone rang.

"I got to take this call. It's a client I was expecting."

He walked out of my office.

I kicked off my shoes and dug my feet into the soft pile of my new wedding rug. It didn't make me feel any better. Took me a while to get over it, and then I was pissed at myself for feeling jealous. I don't really care who he fucks, except for a couple exceptions: Olga and Lola.

Those two are a problem for me. I'm not jealous of Storm anymore. She doesn't want Mario for keeps. She's not looking to split Mario and me up. Olga is a different story. Lola, same.

I took the elevator with Mario to the top floor of our office building where a helicopter waited to take him to the Ontario Airport. Our goodbye kiss was passionate. I love him more than anything or anyone in the world. Jealousy was in my back pocket.

Before he got in the chopper, he said, "I'll be back for Christmas for sure." Actually, he did say something after. He was halfway in, and yelled at the top of his lungs, "I love you, Letty."

I watched him settle into the chopper. He looked at me through the window as the pilot was waiting for me to go back in the building. I opened the door to the penthouse floor, smiled at Mario and gave him the finger. The look on his face was priceless. I went inside laughing. As the door shut behind me and I headed to the elevator, I could still hear the roar of the engine, and feel it vibrating the floor, the walls, and rattling pictures in their frames.

I took a late lunch with Tangles and Storm in Mario's private conference room. I wondered how many women besides me he'd fucked on that table. I remembered Lola had visited him several times in his office, door locked. Probably Melina before that.

I knew all this before I agreed to marry him. We said I do. I have no regrets. It is okay.

I told Tangles and Storm about this bullshit trip. Olga calls him umpteen times a week.

"You signed up for this," Tangles said. "You knew going in."

Storm was smart enough not to comment. She just bit into her hamburger, enticing me to do the same. The burgers from Goonies are so juicy you need a bib when you eat them. Tangles complained she didn't have gloves like she used at home.

"Let's hit a club tonight," I said.

"We're not in Rio," Tangles reminded me. "LA is so dead."

"It's not," Storm said. "You just need to know where to go."

"If you're a guy, yeah," I said.

Mario had met Lola for the first time at Whiskey A Go Go. That was his go-to hot spot. Sometimes the Playboy club.

"We could have eaten lunch downstairs. Lots of dudes from the building down there."

"Think about it," I said. "I got to get back to work."

"Ditto," Tangles said.

"I'll pick up the mess," Storm said.

"Have the restaurant send someone to clean up." I took her hand. "Let's get back to work."

We didn't go out that night. We stayed home, skipped dinner, sipped a little wine and smoked some good weed. Olga was no longer our weed supplier. Storm found it locally. I wasn't a pot connoisseur. It was all the same to me. One joint is the same as another.

On a red velour round sectional sofa that I'd bought before the tree was delivered, we sat around the Christmas tree lit up with hundreds of twinkling lights. A pile of gifts was already accumulating beneath the branches, though none of them were mine. I'd been putting off shopping. We always held a lot back for the Christmas morning reveal. Wreaths were out all over the house, and mistletoe in key places, Christmas candles strategically placed, and the whole house smelled of pine. It pissed me off all the more that Mario was not there with me. With us.

Storm told us about a guy in Santa Monica who had a beach house. On Friday nights, the owner, Stone, hosted a high-end orgy. Admission for men was five hundred dollars, for women, a hundred.

"I thought all that had stopped after AIDS moved in."

"Used to be a lot of places to go like that. They all shut down but Stone, he has regulars."

We all went to bed that night in the master bedroom surrounded by twenty-seven candles, with incense flavoring the air. We played and watched each other in the huge ornate mirror on the ceiling. Women know exactly what to do to a woman. It was the kind of night Mario loves, and I was still pissed off he wasn't with us.

We were falling asleep. "We can back out if you want," Storm said.

"Are you kidding me? We're going," I said.

"That's a ditto," Tangles said, turning to Storm. "Are you chicken?"

"I'm not chicken. I told you, I used to go there. I hope it's still nice."

"If it's not nice, we'll split," I said. "Don't sweat it."

"I'm going to sleep if everyone shuts up," Tangles said.

My mind was not ready for sleep. I was quiet, lying on my stomach, my right leg draped over Tangles's legs, my left arm across Storm's belly. We did not have to be this close because the mattress was huge, but we were. That's what I mean about women. Mario would start off cuddling me, spooning me and before I knew it, he'd be across from me at the end of the bed.

Men.

I heard the soft white noise hum of the heater kicking in and listened to the soft regular rhythm of Tangles's and Storm's breathing. I felt Mario's absence keenly and tried not wondering if he missed me the same way.

Will I have any regrets after I go to this orgy?

Will I tell him?

Do I want to go?

Am I pissed off?

Yes, to everything.

Will I be as pissed after I attend the orgy?

No.

If he can go fuck Olga and Riana in Rio, Zurich, or Timbuktu, I can do some fucking of my own.

I haven't done any Christmas shopping. I was running out of time. It's on my list of things to do.

Another reason to be pissed at him. I thought we'd shop together.

It's okay. I got Tangles and Storm. We'll make a day of it, hit the malls here in Pasadena and LA, and shut down all the shops. Last year, we made a special holiday night of it at my Uncle Miguel's restaurant, but he had to shut it down this year, thanks to his chiseling lowlife of a partner. Okay, I don't know if the partner was a deliberate con, or if it was just a screw up, but the end result left Uncle Miguel sad, broke, and without his dream. Uncle Miguel's got a sad job as a line cook at one of the hotels, even though he made a big name for himself in the area. He's got to come for Christmas. As much as I love Emma, I don't have the heart to fire her, but I wish I could hire my Tio back. I'll help him out but he's so proud. Broke and proud.

I never cared about big money, but it sure comes in handy, like being able to help Uncle M. He'd saved his whole life, and lost it all when his place went down, including the hundred thousand Mario gave him when he quit working here. Mario and me, we'll have to put our heads together to figure out how to help my uncle in a way that won't crush his pride.

I've got to get to sleep. I have an orgy to go to, tomorrow.

December 17, 1993 (Friday)
Pasadena
Lola

I took a non-stop flight to Burbank, California, a flight that brought me closer to Pasadena than LAX and got me there in the wee hours. I rented a car and a room at the Hilton that was less than ten minutes from Mario's house and five minutes from Mason's house. Two years ago, I had stayed at Holiday Inn. The Hilton is a step up.

I checked into the hotel and slept until five in the morning. Once I was out of the shower, I felt alive and ready to rumble. I put the Berretta and my badge in my purse, in case I need to defend myself or explain my presence.

I picked up a copy of the LA times, parked across the street from Mason's house at six thirty in the morning and waited. Having done surveillance for so long, I found it to be a breeze. I don't smoke so I chewed gum and paged through a newspaper. Around noon, the gates opened for a VW driven by a woman in a blue housekeeper uniform.

I went back to the hotel for lunch in the dining room. At six the next morning before the sun rose, I parked my car in the same spot.

Just before seven, the gates opened. The sun was up by then, and I saw a car waiting for the gates to open. I wasn't sure Mason was driving, but I dashed across the street and made my presence known just as the Cadillac's tires rolled on to the street.

Luck was with me. I saw Mason at the wheel.

I pulled my Berretta, pointed at the empty passenger seat, and shot out the windshield. Two shots did it. The car door popped open, and Mason was out before it stopped rolling. He was freaked out, and showing it.

"What the fuck is wrong with you?" he yelled, "Are you out of your fucking gourd?"

"You haven't seen anything," I said. "Now that I have your attention, we need to talk."

"Look what you've done to my car!"

"Relax. Aren't you glad I didn't point this thing at you?"

"We can't talk here. There are people here. Let me back up and we can ride somewhere in your car."

"Sounds like a plan," I said, shoving my gun back in the purse.

"You are a bitch," he said as we walked across the street to my car.

"And what are you?" I snapped back. "I'd rather be a bitch than Olga's errand boy."

December 17, 1993 (Friday)
Pasadena
Storm

Friday at dawn, we jogged together. I love watching the sun rise over the city. Some days are gray, start to finish, but this morning the colors broke across the sky like melted crayons of blue, white and gold on a canvas of the palest pink. The streets are always empty this time of the morning, and it's like we have the whole world to ourselves. We split to hit the shower and met in the kitchen nook for breakfast at seven sharp. Without Mario, we ate light. I had a big glass of fresh-squeezed orange juice because I have a sweet tooth. Letty, the protein queen, had a hard boiled egg and two link sausages. Tangles had a glass of that horrible green slime she's always drinking. I'm surprised she doesn't glow lime green like the Grinch.

Everybody calls it a nook, but when you picture a nook, you think of a small area. This nook was as big as a dining room. Seems to me that sometimes a person, meaning me, misses what's staring me right in my face, day after day. Casa Luna is a freaking palace. Anyway, the nook is comfy and beautiful. Emma calls it the breakfast room.

"Seems so quiet," Letty said.

None of us mentioned him. but I know we are all missing Mario.

"Let's pencil in a day to do some Christmas shopping," Letty said. We all agreed.

I drove us to the office in the Rolls. Letty sat in the back seat, looking professional in a black and gray pinstriped suit. Calvin Klein. Tangles rode shotgun. She was dressed like a rainbow.

"We walk out of the office at two," Letty said. "Gets us home before three. I'm going to call the service to send three therapists to give us a massage at three fifteen. We can spa it after, swim, and get ready."

"Did you program any toilet time?" Tangles said, being a smart ass.

"Hush, bitch," Letty said.

"I don't want you pissed at me if Stone's operation isn't as cool as it was when I used to go there," I said.

"Stop worrying, already," Tangles said.

"We're going. If Tangles doesn't want to fuck or you don't want to fuck, it's okay. You can watch. Or wait in the car," Letty said, laughing. "Maybe I'll just watch. I'll play it by ear."

December 17, 1993 (Friday)
Pasadena
Letty

Before lunch in Los Angeles, nine at night in Zurich, my cell rang.

"Baby, are you okay?" Mario asked.

I said, "Amor, I miss you."

"I prefer you don't call me Amor."

"She calls you that."

"Baby, she calls everyone that. So did Camila."

"Okay, Amor, I won't call you, Amor."

He ignored me.

"Did you have a good night?"

"We did. The girls and I went wild on each other."

"Wish I had been there."

"You could have been. Not being there was your choice."

"What are you doing tonight?" he asked.

"Not sure yet. What about you?"

"We're going out to dinner with a banker."

"I see, okay, Amor. Don't be a stranger. Call me."

"You are being such a bitch," he said. He wasn't angry. His voice was good-humored.

"Not really, Amor."

We hung up.

I had seen him alone with Olga, with Olga and Riana, and with all four of us together many times. I never let it bother me before. It seems different now that my love for him is public and we signed on the dotted line. It's not a secret.

Olga would do anything to split us up. I know it. I feel it. How does he not see it?

Stone's house was on the boardwalk, on the sand. Storm had said it was Santa Monica, but I think it was Venice Beach. The neighborhood was practically wall-to-wall houses, charming in pastel colors, some of them. At this end of the beach, the houses were bigger, with a little more space between houses, though none of the space was wasted. The better view was from the beach, where you could see the balconies and glass walls open to the water view.

It is more of a statement to say you live in Santa Monica than to say Venice Beach. Mario's house in Santa Monica hugging the pier is now worth more than six times what he paid for it. At one point he thought of getting rid of it because he seldom uses it, but when I checked the property values, he changed his mind.

"I'll sit on it," he said.

Niley and Jo still have their own keys to Mario's beach house and spend weekends there with their families a lot during the summer.

Stone's house had to be more than double the size of Mario's beach house. I paid him three hundred dollars for our admission. It had a modern look, lots of glass, and steel, all sharp angles and beachy colors on the outside. Inside, you could see the bones of the house. I mean, you could tell which rooms had originally been meant to be public communal rooms, and which were private bedrooms. But the public areas had been dressed up very differently from a house a family would live in.

"It will come alive in an hour," Stone said. "Look around. There are no off-limits rooms. The four bedrooms go for extra. One of them is a master. Take a look and let me know."

He showed us other rooms. The living room and open spaces upstairs were wall-to-wall foam pads, silk sheets and tons of pillows. Throw pillows, bed pillows, floor pillows, every size, shape and color, scattered everywhere, and in neat piles along the walls. It looked how I thought a harem might look, with all the pillows and linens.

"Nice place," I said. "Why would I want a bedroom?"

The action would be on the foam pads, bodies entangled everywhere. No bodies were there yet.

December 17, 1993 (Friday)
Santa Monica
Tangles

It's been years since I went to an orgy, and it hadn't ever been in a top notch residence like this one. This place is head and shoulders above the dumps I used when I was down and out. Even on my best days, before I met Mario, I couldn't have afforded a place like this.

"If you tell Mario about going to an orgy, he's going to get pissed at me and Storm."

"Nonsense. He knows I have a mind of my own," Letty said.

"You do but now you're married."

"Why are you making a big deal out of this? In Rio we fucked someone new every night. Before I met Mario, I fucked when and where I wanted. If you don't want to go, don't go. I'm going."

"Who said I wasn't going? You crazy or something?"

Truth is, I know Letty had been exclusive with Mario for a long time. Our free days in Rio followed years she wouldn't think of fucking a man other than Mario. She was always there for him. Girls are another story—she's been with most of the girls Mario ever brought around, except maybe

Lola. There's more to Letty than being the boss's appendage. She also has karate. She toughed out strenuous workouts and won a big collection of trophies and ribbons to show for her dedication. I have some, but nowhere near as many. She strives to be the best at whatever she goes after, even her baking. Perfection. No one makes chocolate chip cookies like hers.

I love her.

I know she loves me, too.

Bottom line, I want Letty to have a blast and no regrets later.

I won't have regrets, but then, I'm not the one who's married.

If he can fly across the ocean to fuck two bitches, she should have the same right. Letty says she has every right. Right on, girl.

Got to live in the moment. Fuckin-A.

December 17, 1993 (Friday)
Pasadena
Storm

We started off in the family room on the first floor. There was a big bar that looked commercial. Shiny bar, red plaid wallpaper, barstools, long counter, glass shelves and racks with all kinds of glasses, liquor and wine, and a pretty lady bartender to dole it out. A card on our table showed the prices: glass of wine, ten dollars; cocktails twenty dollars; Dom-Perignon by the glass, one hundred dollars; soft drinks, ten dollars; water, ten dollars.

Stone showed us the unisex locker room. The lockers were squeaky clean, honor system, no locks. We took our clothes off and each put on a short white silk robe. The three of us made sexy faces at each other in the mirror and laughed at how we looked. Sexy. Totally erotic. An immediate aphrodisiac. The robes didn't cover our asses. If we had been taller, our asses would not have been covered at all.

A group of four guys walked in as we were walking out. Men, at five hundred a pop. Stone was making bucks hand over fist.

We went back to the bar. Stone made a round to let everyone know that the action had begun on the second floor.

We went upstairs. We had already toured the rooms empty, but now it was like an alien landscape. Neon blue and red lights flashed, and candles burned everywhere. A naked waitress walked around checking drinks. There was some couples and threesomes getting busy, but still lots of room on the floor. We kept walking to the other big room.

There was furniture, but it had been pushed back against the walls. If you didn't want to join in, you could still sit on the sofas and chairs. On the floor, there was such a chaos of pillows that counting them would have been impossible. We found a spot on the floor, lay back on fine sheets, and the three of us started caressing each other. Like in some ballroom, a big mirrored ball hung from the ceiling, rotated, reflecting beams, sparkles, and daggers of light as it turned. In Junior High, they hung a ball like this in the gym when there was a dance. If I stared at the beams of light, I thought I might get hypnotized. Mario had a room downstairs with a ball just like this.

In one corner was a table under a light that rotated changing colors, a sex buffet: a large bowl filled with condoms, jars of KY-jelly, edible lube, thong underwear made of candy, boxes of tissue.

Three young chicks wearing robes were walking around, pointing and giggling when they saw the condoms and KY. They looked at us and found a spot close by, joined us doing what we were doing, playing with each other, waiting for the fellas.

The piped music from the bar made it up here. The music was intoxicating, raising the level of my excitement, keyed to sex, soft sounds thrumming with sexual energy and wild desire. I kissed Tangles breasts, and then felt two hands touch my butt cheeks. I couldn't help tightening at first, but then I relaxed. A strange tongue explored me, and I let it happen. I didn't even turn around to see if it was a male or female.

Letty raised her head on to a pillow, noticed what was going on behind me, smiled and kissed me. Tangles got tired of being the recipient, and got aggressive, jumped in the mix and kissed both of us. The sensation I felt from so much attention, the tongue and probing was, well, no words to describe it. Raw, wild, fiery, incandescent, sultry, penetrating, so penetrating. I didn't need to look for who it was. It had to be a guy. His hands were big, his fingers, oh, his fingers.

December 17, 1993 (Friday)
Pasadena
Lola

Mason rattled on and on. Why had I shot up his car? Why did I come to his home without letting him know? With my gun on my lap, I drove us to the Ritz Carlton-Huntington Hotel, a ten minute drive. I had history there. It's where Mario and I had breakfast after I recovered from being gunshot.

"You'd know if you picked up the phone," I said, "You didn't answer, and I called a hundred times."

"I always answer my phone," he said.

"Bullshit," I said.

I self-parked. Instead of going inside to the coffee shop, I figured we'd stay in the car. Outside, people were walking across the parking lot, going into the hotel, but inside the car, we had our own little cone of privacy.

"Why did you give me up to Olga?"

"I never gave you up. It's been over two years. Never gave you up."

"Don't lie. Are you going to tell me that you didn't know Olga had some asshole trick me on to a plane, drug me, then deliver me to Olga, in

Colombia? Did you know about that?"

"I recently learned about it," Mason said. "I had nothing to do with what happened to you."

He seemed sincere. I put my gun in my purse.

"Was I really in Colombia?"

"You were in Colombia, yes."

"Who is this shithead Art? Where can I find him? I owe him an ass kicking for romancing me and handing me over to the sharks. I fucking trusted that asshole."

"I'm not used to being held against my will," Mason said, his head turned to face me. I figured that was the psychiatrist in him trying to brainwash me with his shrinky superpowers or something.

"I'm not used to being fucked over," I said.

He winced.

"I get fucked out of the five million you promised me, and two years later I get suckered by this bastard Art, wake up tied to a gurney and filled full of pills. I was covered in piss and vomit, humiliated, and repeatedly threatened with death or serious injury. I was pumped full of truth serum, drugged out on some murderous toxic pharmaceutical cocktail while they did God knows what to me, and after that fun weekend was over, I was taken to my apartment in New York, and left naked on my bed. The clothes I had been wearing, and everything in my night bag were replaced with five hundred thousand dollars. Did you know this?"

"I didn't know everything you told me just now, no. And I didn't know you had an apartment in New York."

"All I want from you is to tell me where I can find Art. I want to believe you had nothing to do with finding me in New York and telling Olga about it."

"Like I said, I didn't know you moved to New York or had an apartment there."

"Let's say I buy that. What about Art?"

"I never use that man in my operations. He was Camila's operator."

I practically howled in my fury. "Camila is dead, so he's now Olga's operator."

He raised his hand for me to tone it down. The windows of my car were getting foggy.

"If you were taken back to your apartment in New York and left with the cash as you say, it means that Olga is finished with you. I suggest you leave it be."

"I have no intention of going after Olga," I said. "I want Art. He needs to pay."

Mason got quiet, looked away from me and out his window.

"Mason, I accepted that job from you. It didn't materialize, but I trusted you when I agreed to do it, and you trusted me. Tell me who Art is and I promise I will never tell anyone you told me."

Silence.

He turned to look at me again.

"Apologize for coming to my house unannounced and for shooting up my car."

He made it sound like a demand.

"I'm not going to apologize. Fuck you."

"If you want to know who this operator is, you will apologize."

I took a deep breath and thought about pulling my gun out again. I didn't think Mason would believe I would shoot him. A shrink can read people. We used shrinks all the time to solve issues in a case.

"I'm not sorry I went to your house because I tried calling you at least six times over a period of days. I am sorry that I forced you here at gunpoint."

Mason coughed. I read it as a nervous cough.

"I want one other thing," he said. He looked away again.

I reached over with my hand and gently turned his face to look at me.

"Tell me who Art is, his real name, and where he is."

"I want your body," Mason said, now that he was looking at me.

I felt my body chill from surprise.

"You're pathetic," I said.

"And what about you? What are you?"

"Tell me who Art is."

"And if I don't, then what?"

I reached for my purse. And there was another surprise. A gun pointed at me.

"Driving over here, you are lucky I didn't shoot you," he said. "The gun on your lap. Bad place to have it when you are driving."

"So now what? You think you have the edge?"

"I do have the edge. Your gun is in your purse and mine is right here pointing at your face. You know I'm a private investigator. You should know I pack a gun. Your mind is weakening."

There was his cough again.

"Mason, are you going to shoot me or give me what I want?"

Gun still out.

"I told you what I want," he said.

"You want pussy at gunpoint?" I laughed.

He heard the laugh, grinned at me, and put the gun away. He had a nice smile, something engaging about it. Mischief in his face instead of malice. Fucker.

We talked.

We cut a deal.

I drove the car to the valet, some pock-marked kid probably just out of high school.

I sat in the lobby as Mason checked in. He was a means to an end, but I have a kinky streak that keeps me hungry for action. That, and I hated Art so much I'd do more than just fuck Mason to find out who and where he is. I hadn't walked on the wild side for a while, and there was plenty of kick-ass bottled up in me, primed to explode.

When he walked up to me with a smile so we could go to the room, the stunned feeling was back. What turned him on about me? It has been two years and change since he made me strip while he searched for a wire. He didn't make any strange moves then. I guess the memory played on his mind.

We walked into a beautiful suite. The front room and separate bedroom had matching blue and gold loveseats. Blue and gold like that, it's my favorite. The ceiling was cream, with a touch of mustard mixed in, matching an easy chair next to the sofa. The walls were gold, as was the figured carpet, and the curtains were gold and blue striped. The wood desk, dresser, chair, and bed were all some kind of dark-stained wood, mahogany, maybe. I walked over to the closest loveseat and sat down. From where I sat, I spotted four vases of roses. This was a whole lot of room for a guy just looking to score.

"Big spender," I said. "It's not like we're going to be here long."

Mason laughed.

"You never know," he said. "It's early for a drink, but do you want one?" He walked over to the built-in bar.

"No liquor," I said. "I'll take some coffee if they have a brewer in here."

"They do," he said. "They also have room service."

"Mason, what the fuck is up with you?"

He turned to look at me. He wasn't a bad looking guy. He probably worked out and hadn't aged since I saw him last.

"I want your body," he said. "Lola, Nina, you know what I want. Shut down the business for a few hours, and I'll tell you what you want to know."

"Tell me now," I said, undoing the top button of my jacket. Beneath it, I was wearing a long-sleeved, fitted sweater dress. It was plain, that is, no decoration, a cowl neck, dark ivory, no buttons, zippers, or ornamentation, and it hugged my figure like a second skin. I pulled off the jacket and crossed my legs. He watched my every move, just as he had when he'd been looking for the wire. I reached into the vase on the coffee table and pulled out a white rose.

He took the rose from me, snapped off the thorns, and ran the head of the flower along my jawline, and to my lips. Surprisingly, it was quite erotic, plus I was not expecting such a loverlike gesture from him. I thought about his actions as he hung my jacket in the closet, and on the way back, took a pen and note pad from the desk and handed them to me. Mason wasn't taking any chance writing anything himself.

"Write this down," he said.

"Shoot," I said. "Don't lie, whatever you do."

"I don't lie," he said. The last time he told me that, it had been true. I got the fifty thousand he promised me on the phone.

I wrote down what he told me. Art's name was Gus Bradley. He lived in San Francisco. Mason did not have an address for him because he never worked with him before.

"If you really want to find him," Mason said. "Put your cop nose to work. San Francisco is not so big."

"Ex-Cop," I corrected him. "I'll find him."

Knowing his real name made me fill with emotion. I started to boil. My face burned with heat. I was a riot of emotion, remembering, suddenly, everything. The love I'd felt for Art, because I'd fallen hard; the seduction on the plane; the humiliation on the gurney; the fury at Olga's henchmen, doctor, witnesses. The humiliation, helplessness. The rape. The nightmares. The nightmare of recovery after I was home.

I hated that Mason noticed. The kindness in his eyes was as embarrassing as the events I wished I could erase from my past.

Gus Bradley. Nothing on that piece of paper but his name.

I looked down at what I had written, then up at him.

"Don't do anything too crazy to Gus," he said. "Once you do it, you can't take it back."

"If you can keep it hard, I'm going to fuck you until you beg me to stop," I said.

My libido has a hair trigger anyway, and Mason was working every nerve I had. He was a smooth talker, and then some. After I did him the first time, he ordered lunch, much more than I had selected from the menu. We hung out naked under the hotel robes like we knew each other. I guess by then we did know each other, at least in the biblical sense. We talked a lot about my work as an agent and about his work, his decision not to practice law or medicine and to use both professions in a totally different way.

I never asked about Olga or Camila.

He never asked about the Camacho surveillance detail. Those topics were the great divide, not that it mattered now.

I couldn't figure out, and never would, why a high-profile business-person would risk kidnapping me. Kidnapping is a crime that can result in a death sentence. Maybe that's why she gave me the five hundred thousand. To keep quiet.

We said our goodbyes at the hotel, then I drove him back to his house at seven that night. It was unbelievable that the morning began with me shooting out his car windshield, and what followed was a day of sex and conversation.

"Until next time," he said.

"Yes," I said.

No regrets.

December 17, 1993 (Friday)
Santa Monica
Tangles

I saw Letty get up from the pile of bodies, a guy on either side. One had a hand on her ass, the other around her shoulder. I was getting pumped by a stiff dude filling my pussy with hardness. I wanted to ask Letty where they were headed. Dirty music was pounding my ears. It was noisy, and she wouldn't have heard. I closed my eyes and concentrated on what was going on in me. I figured Letty made a deal with Stone for one of the bedrooms.

When the session was over with Mr. Stiff, I was on my feet. My robe was history, lost on the floor somewhere. I walked naked to the unisex bathroom. A young stud inside was barefoot and naked except for skimpy briefs.

"The line downstairs is shorter than this one," he told me. "Your choice."

We had used the bathroom downstairs when we were at the bar earlier. I headed down the hallway to the staircase. Naked as I was, I felt so free, proud of my body, abs, tight ass and legs and thighs. I was fit and knew it. Letty and Storm and I could not have been more fit, and we had the admirers to prove it. Storm didn't have the abs, the muscle we had, but she was fucking gorgeous. I got a glimpse of her and a dark man on the floor, away from the entanglement of bodies where I had been. I don't think she saw me.

I started down the stairs and saw a youngster coming up, a girl probably too young to walk through the door. Her companion was none other than Matthew Martinez, the lawyer who'd played me until the wife he'd forgotten to divorce ambushed me with a gun in my own front yard.

"You're beautiful," Matthew said, passing me slowly.

"Fuck you, Matt."

He kept walking up.

"I plan to soon as we get a spot."

"Fat chance," I said. "Hey, teenager," I called to the kid he was with, "Have you met Matt's wife? Watch your back. She carries a gun."

Bastard.

I had really been getting to like him until he turned out to be married. According to him, he was divorced. That's what I'd believed until I'd gotten her call. When I'm pissed off, I have trouble peeing. It took me all of five minutes to come out of the toilet stall. Two guys were at the urinal looking over at me, making sure their dicks were visible. I gave them a high five.

The attendant, Sadie, was young and topless, her g-string not doing much to cover her up.

"You are precious," I heard myself say. "I wish I had my purse to tip you."

"It's okay. No one here has a purse. We have bidets in the back if you want to chill out before you return to the action."

A bidet would be fantastic. Sadie pointed me in the right direction. I wanted Sadie. If she had not been working, I would have hit on her, just like that.

December 17, 1993 (Friday)
Zurich
Mario

When I arrived in Zurich and met up with Olga and Riana, a dark-skinned young man opened the door to their penthouse on the thirtieth floor. He led me into the parlor of their hotel suite where they were sitting on a settee in front of a television. Olga turned the sound off before she gave me a solid hug and introduced me.

"This is Dani. He's from Brazil," Olga said. "My butler."

He had the kind of dark good looks Olga favors. If Dani is traveling with Olga and Riana, I didn't need to be a brain surgeon to figure out that he's more than a butler. The night of my arrival, I went to bed with Olga and Riana. After our first explosive reunion, we were all completely naked, propped on pillows, television on, heat on, extra comforter on the bed. In walked Dani wearing white shorts and a sleeveless t-shirt. Outside it was freezing. I get cold just thinking of going out that way, but apparently, it's how he dresses all the time.

Dani sat on the sofa facing the television, his back to us. I looked at Olga questioning his presence.

"He's harmless, Amor. It's okay," Olga said.

"He's here in case we want or need anything," Riana said.

I was reminded of Sami and Jason, both dead now. Sami and I had had an ongoing sexual relationship. Her friend, Jason—who had become my friend too—a voyeur. He only watched us once which had been more than enough for me. I didn't plan on fucking these women with Dani watching.

"Some ice might be nice," Riana said.

He nodded and left. In a couple of minutes, he was back with a gold ice bucket, and matching champagne bucket, both full of ice. He placed the champagne and a couple of flutes on the small table beside the sliding glass doors leading to the balcony. He gave the champagne a little spin, then brought us the other bucket and three hotel glasses half full of ice. He looped the tongs over the side of the bucket, and stood beside the bed looking, in spite of his attire, like something between a waiter and a pet poodle.

"Light a joint for us, Dani," Olga said.

He lit up and handed the joint to Olga. He didn't inhale.

"Anything else ma'am?"

"Relax Dani," Riana said. "We'll let you know if we need you."

"Yes, ma'am."

Dani returned to the sofa, watching the TV as if the sound were on.

Riana hit a switch next to the bed, and, except for the television, the room went black. The three of us sat up on the bed. Olga gave the joint to Riana, who gave it to me. I took a hit. The smoke smelled like my yard when my gardener was burning leaves. I inhaled deep, and the smoke expanded in my lungs. I coughed, and a flickering stream of smoke shot out my nose and mouth. It took a second to get my breathing under control. The room flashed light and dark as the television scenes changed silently. Some German movie. We wouldn't have understood the dialogue anyway, but the way the lighting was changing was affecting my head.

"What happened?" Olga asked, laughing.

I shook my head. "Wow, strong stuff."

"Lightweight," Riana teased.

Dani jumped to his feet. "Sir, would you like a milder smoke?"

I was already buzzed. His quick response made me laugh.

"I can see why you have Dani handy," I said. "Thanks, Dani, I'm fine."

Dani returned to the couch with his back to us.

No longer sitting up in bed, I turned to face Olga.

"Been long time," I said, reaching out for her, though we'd already conjugated once not an hour ago. We kissed, her breasts pressing against me. Her scent was a turn on. I felt Riana behind me, breasts pressing my back, her arm across me, resting on Olga. It all felt very intense, honed more so by the lighting and the pot. This was not a new experience. At home I had Letty and two insatiable chicks who never needed encouragement to join us.

"Amor, I want you on top."

I was on fire as I did what Olga wanted.

"Inside me, now."

I could feel Riana next to us, moving. I didn't know if she was pleasing herself or working on one of us—my attention was on Olga. Her dark eyes sparkled, mirroring the light of the television. The rest of her was shadowed, mysterious. I fell into her eyes, mesmerized by her, by sex.

"So beautiful," I said.

"Amor, it is you who are beautiful."

When we took a break, Dani passed a joint to Olga, then it came to me. We sat on the bed, in the dark. The television was off, but the drapes let in light from outside.

"The hotel will have something to say about the smell tomorrow," I managed to say.

Olga put her arms around me. "I own this hotel, Amor."

I thought that funny. It made me laugh aloud.

Olga laughed, too, and took a hit before passing it to me.

That's when I noticed that Riana was on top of Dani.

I started to object but Olga kissed me, a distraction. Someone took the joint out of my hand and I went deep into Olga. She moaned. She screamed and moved wildly under me.

It was the first time in my life that a man shared the bed I was on.

Olga, Riana, Dani, and I left Zurich in Olga's plane headed for Rome. My plane would catch up to me in two days to fly me home. My last visit to O's house in Rome had been on my honeymoon, not long ago.

We were in the grand living room of her fabulous home. Big showcase of a huge old Italian villa, some place you'd expect to turn the corner and find the likes of Tony Bennet, Dean Martin or Victor Mature pouring himself a stiff one at the bar. Classic antiques everywhere, huge deep fireplaces and an army of servants available twenty-four-seven.

"Amor, Riana and I are going to Portugal for Christmas. Please come with us."

I thought of the big tree, all the Christmas preparations, and more important than the tree, my pissed-off wife.

"I have to get back home."

Riana urged me too.

"What you got in Zurich from us is nothing. Come to my country, and I will show you."

"Tempting," I said with a grin. "Can't do it."

"I can call Letty and tell her we haven't finished our business," Olga offered with a mischievous grin.

I shook my head. I had a feeling how well that would go over.

It seemed that Dani never slept. He hovered around Olga every minute I was around her and then some. But he was a butler, or should I say just hers? Her butler in Milan was ancient by comparison but moved pretty fast when he was needed. Dani, he moved really fast. It wasn't just Olga who wanted this and that. Riana, too.

We had a big dinner with way too many entrees, and the whole ritual left me tired. Riana lit up a joint and then another one less than an hour later. The wine was fantastic. Olga kept plenty of my favorite reds. So, there I was, stuffed to the gills, tired, full of excellent wine, indulged beyond human capacity, surrounded by the lovely Olga and Riana. Full as I was, I did not turn down the massage Olga—or maybe it was Dani who arranged it—for the three of us. On the first night in Rome, I thought that at this rate, I would never get on a plane and fly home.

Eventually it was time to hit the sack. Two hours of bliss left me boneless and barely able to crawl to my bed that incidentally had both Olga and Riana in it.

I loved sex.

I needed rest.

No rest.

But then there was the wine. Wine should slow down a person. I didn't slow down. After the massage, a glass of wine and I was raring to go. Riana didn't push for us to smoke, but we did. She was a joint freak, a true pothead, and when I stayed with them, I'd be a freak too. As it was, we smoke too much at home, but nothing like this. It was hard to tell when Riana was high or what. She was always happy, always laughing. I loved the way she was always up. I never saw her moody or down. I'd known her for years, but I wasn't keeping track. It is all about the now.

By the time I went to bed, I didn't object that Dani was on the bed spooning Olga. She had this big smile, and the lights were all on. Soon I was spooning Riana who was facing Olga, kissing, while Dani worked Olga from behind and I furiously pumped Riana. It was intense, and all about the moment.

I never made eye contact with Dani.

I didn't think of what I would think the next day, or on the way home, or when I got home.

It was about the now.

When we were leaving Zurich, I had called Letty. She asked if I could call her back in four or five hours. She had been out late with the girls and had barely gone to bed. I figured it was seven in the morning in Los Angeles. Just gone to bed. Out late?

I called Letty from Rome on the first day we got there and the next day.

"I'm going home in the morning," I said. "I miss you a lot."

"Amorcito, I miss you too, I mean it, I do."

"Baby," I said with a lot of calm. "What is with this Amorcito business?"

I heard a yawn.

"You told me not to call you Amor. Amorcito has more cariño, you know that."

This was not Letty.

Smart-ass Letty.

"Okay, baby, it works for me." It wasn't, but that's what I said.

"Si Amorcito Querido."

December 23, 1993 (Thursday)
Pasadena
Letty

On December 23rd, Mario wasn't home yet.

I'd had plenty of time to relive last Friday night.

I relived it when Storm was driving us home.

They thought I was asleep, curled up alone in the darkness of the back seat. I touched myself, remembering, and tightened my thighs, tight. At the door to the house, I kissed Tangles and Storm and went straight to my bathroom. I douched, ran a bath. I went to sleep with the gas fireplace burning, snuggling alone in Mario's great big bed that had so many stories to tell, if it could talk. My sore pussy was a reminder that the adventure at Stone's was real.

Every time I thought about Bob and Luke, I felt like a slut.

I thought about them a lot, probably because Mario wasn't back yet.

Bob and Luke. Those were their names. We were strangers, coming in the night. I can't even remember their faces. It was all a blur. They didn't know each other. They just happened on me on the padded floor, first Bob and later Luke. I figured a bedroom would be cool, then I'd head back to the action. I came close to getting off just from watching. The action is on the mats, deep cushy foam mats, inches deep, meant for mattresses. The bedroom door was open to the hallway. Nothing was intended to be private. The draw was sex on a bed instead of a pad of foam.

I remembered this:

"Let's see if we can do it," Bob said.

We were on the bed. I was turned on. I knew they were too because both had their stuff at the ready.

Bob positioned me on top of him. He entered me.

"Come in behind her," he said. "I'll guide you."

"No anal," I said.

"This is not anal," Bob said, his breathing labored.

The mattress creaked. Darkness was around, interrupted by flashing lights, and the noise of the house. I was already at sensory overload, feeling Luke. Feeling Bob. I couldn't tell what Bob was doing with Luke's dick, but I felt the second hardon enter my pussy. I had not done it like this. They went for a long time, the sliding friction, so much sensation. I had at least two explosive orgasms.

It is December 23rd, and Mario is not home yet.

I can tell Mario I stepped out. It's part of our arrangement. To tell him I stepped out with two at a time, how will he take it? Is having two men in me at once, penetrated by two at the same time in my pussy, how is it different from his being with two girls at once? Will he understand?

We worked Monday to Wednesday. Thursday we were all playing hooky to shop.

Still no Mario.

Jamie had been one of the day guards at the house for three years. Late thirties, smart, and rugged looking. I kid him and the other tough guys on guard payroll that I could kick their ass, so they better not mess with me. Tangles said it too. It *is* true, but I always said it in a kidding fashion. One time I did a kick and touched the top of the guardhouse door. Jamie's eyes bugged out in shock.

"We're going to do some Christmas shopping," I told Jamie. "You're elected to accompany us. As we shop, you can haul the stuff back to the car. No uniform. Change into your street clothes."

I could tell Jamie liked the assignment.

Olga had a plain-clothes security detail who dressed in suits and ties unless they were on the plane or needed to blend in with the surroundings they happened to be in with Olga and Riana.

When we left, one of the night guys took his shift. Once when so much bad stuff had been happening, I wanted security. Everything was peaceful now, so I wasn't sure we still needed the guards. Of course, maybe it was peaceful because they were there. Still I wondered why we couldn't open the big gates and leave them open. Turn on the alarm to the house at night and live like normal people. Mario never wanted guards. He hired them to protect everyone else. But Tangles and I, we trained and got to be sharpshooters. With the guns we own, we could hold off a small army.

While I shopped at a Rodeo Drive jewelry store in Beverly Hills for Tangles and Storm, I had them to split to another store. The gifts were from Mario and me, so I used my credit card with my married name, a Carte Blanche card with enough credit to buy a house or two. Mario is big time, no question.

I gave my bags to Jaimie and met up with the girls.

We picked out fragrances for all the household staff, including the guards, two for each. Jaime hung around while the items were gift wrapped and then called to find out where to go next. We did this at a number of stores in walking distance.

By four, we had a trunk full of gifts. I couldn't buy Mario clothes because ready-made does not work for him. He's like a basketball player, too tall to buy off the rack, not as big as a football player but bulkier than a basketball player. I bought him a watch he didn't need, but it was beautiful. A Breitling, blue face, stainless steel and gold band, very masculine.

At Versace, I bought Tangles and Storm dresses that they picked out, gorgeous selections that fit like a second skin. For myself, I picked out a pantsuit, blouse, shoes and a flashy full-length leopard print coat that would keep me warm in the mild California winter. I started to pay for everything with my own credit card but instead used the Carte Blanche. The eight thousand I spent was a pittance of what it cost to keep fuel in Mario's plane. In fairness, GAL footed all that. The plane belonged to the company, and the company was Olga.

I looked at my watch.

"It's just four," Tangles said. "You've been watching the time all day. Are you waiting for something?"

I laughed it off, but I was waiting for Mario. I had been, ever since he left. I was still pissed at Mario. December 23rd and he wasn't back yet.

It was our first married Christmas. We had missed Christmas before when we happened to be somewhere on a plane crash, but it hadn't mattered because we were together.

I wanted Mario home. I had fucked up, but it was because I was pissed off. He had fucked up by running off to see Olga on the pretense that it was business.

Monkey business is what it was. My visit to Stone's house had been on the pretense of checking it out. Who was I fooling, knowing I was ready to fuck my brains out?

All those years I was a single lady living with Mario Luna, and faithful to him even though he never asked for it. I broke out only once for a few months and did what I hadn't done since my arrival at Casa Luna.

Then we get married and I'm out to an orgy and he's back with Olga. What the fuck is wrong with us?

We had made it into the car. We were in the back seat of Mario's Rolls, which is not a limo. It didn't have a privacy glass to divide us from Jaime who was driving.

"A hundred for your thoughts," Tangles said, holding out a bill.

I snatched it out of her hand and tucked it into her jacket pocket.

"My thoughts are priceless." I didn't want to let on I'd still been brooding about Mario and Olga.

Storm whispered in my ear, "You haven't told us what you did that night. You disappeared."

I felt a warmth going through my body.

"Over dinner, I'll tell you, but you got to do the same," I said.

I think I would feel very lonely if I didn't have them. I love them so much. Storm was a relatively new, but I felt like I'd known her forever. Tangles and Pixie are like one of my own ribs.

We ate in the wine room. I entertained them over dinner and wine and told them what I remembered about Tom and Luke. They had stories of their own. Tangles had seen Matt with a minor, and Storm had a marathon session with five girls that I couldn't keep track of, but which she clearly enjoyed. We were all pretty lit when we headed off to bed.

I asked Tangles and Storm to stay in their rooms. I went to bed alone. He had called early in the day. I was hoping that he would come home while I slept, though in my frame of mind, I seriously doubted he would. I lay in that bed. It was cold, though the gas fire was burning. I turned it off because the logs were not what was missing. Eventually, I fell asleep, but it was fitful rather than restful.

A person trained in karate is trained in awareness. I was asleep but not asleep. I snapped awake. The bedroom was dark, and he was quiet, but I sensed him when he walked in, felt the pressure of the room change when he opened the door. Recognized his footfalls. I knew it wasn't Tangles, and it wasn't Storm. I could smell him. I could feel his heat. I kept my eyes closed. If it was a dream, I didn't want to wake. I heard the metal of his zipper, and the soft breath of his shirt and pants landing in the basket, the sway of the bed as it gave to his weight. He took off his socks and tossed a t shirt across the room. Ten points.

He lay flat on his back and adjusted his pillow. I shivered when he hugged me from behind. He pulled me to him, skin to skin, kissing behind my neck, the back of my head, my shoulders. I turned around and hugged him tight.

My mouth found his. It was indescribable to have him back. I could breathe again.

"I love you, Letty. I love you so much."

His hug was tight.

My hug was as tight.

"Mario, you are my life. Thank you for coming back in time for Christmas."

I'd been carrying a burden of tension since before he left. Having him back, and that tension just burst. I had a huge lump in my throat, and tears ran down my face. It wasn't Christmas that made his return so important. It was just his return.

"I missed you, my love."

"I missed you more," he said. "Don't cry. You're supposed to be happy to see me, not crying like your heart is broken."

"Tell me you missed me again," I said.

"I missed you, Letty. Without you, my life is not complete."

We went to sleep practically glued together.

I woke during the night, and he was across the mattress from me.

I wondered what had happened that he said I made his life complete.

I wondered why I wasn't sorry that I'd gone to Stone's House.

I went back to sleep. I missed having a body to hang on to, but I was happy he was home. I was happy we were in bed together.

The doctor's clinic listed in the yellow pages was two blocks from our office, walking distance. I checked in at work, then walked over around ten in the morning. The doctor's receptionist handed me a new patient form to fill out, so I sat in the busy waiting room with a clipboard on my lap. Two other people were also filling out forms. One of the questions was why I needed the services of a doctor.

"I want to test for AIDS," I wrote.

Another question, name and address of most recent medical provider.

"None," I wrote.

I gave the receptionist my paperwork, my driver's license, and my medical insurance card. Her expression did not change as she read over the information.

She looked up at me and smiled.

I smiled back.

A nurse led me down a maze of halls to a tiny bathroom that had a shelf of small sealed plastic cups with instructions to pee in a cup. Above a little niche, a sheet of typing paper on the wall said "Place sample here, and knock." I complied. Someone on the other side of the wall slid open the little wooden pass-through, verified my name, and thanked me. Then the nurse took me across the hall to an examining room. Dropped tile ceiling, brightly lit inlaid lights, poster on the wall advertising sexual hygiene, plastic table model of a female reproductive system, small window covered with blinds that did not show we were on the third floor of a high rise downtown building. On a cabinet, there were a couple of flyers advertising various drugs. I used a stepstool to climb on to the table and commenced reading the magazine I had brought from the waiting area.

More waiting.

The doctor's name was Ralph Hershey, like the candy I use to make chocolate chip cookies. He was young, good looking, his face modeled on high cheek bones. He was the color of a Hershey bar, with eyes the color of almonds. His name was embroidered in blue on a typical white coat. I put down the magazine, and we shook hands. Dr. Hershey smiled. He had a great smile. He was charming, and the handshake was perfect, none of that macho hand-squashing stuff pulled by karate buffs who are trying to show off. He looked fit, but those white doctor coats don't really show much.

"What makes you think you might have HIV?" he asked.

"I'm not thinking I have it. I only want to make sure that I don't," I said. "Years ago, I had a test, something called ELISA or something, long time ago." I never learned the difference between HIV or AIDS, and I didn't want to be a dummy and admit it.

"We can test for HIV, yes. We can do an oral test now, but the blood test is more accurate, and it takes about twenty-one days after contact to get an accurate reading," he said.

I pretended like I really knew what I was talking about. "The test is only going to show if I have it today, if you drew my blood today, correct? And if I was exposed in mid December, it wouldn't be too early for it to show up?"

"Yes, that's correct."

"If I don't have it the day of the test and I fool around tomorrow and get exposed, this test today is not going to mean much, right?"

"If you were exposed tomorrow, it would not show up on a test for at least twenty-one days."

"I want to do it," I said.

Smiling, he said, "No problem. So, you know, insurance does not cover the test."

"It's okay," I replied. "I'll pay for it."

"Do you want to share with me why you are worried about having been exposed?"

For the hell of it, I thought about telling him I got double penetration from two strangers at an orgy, but I didn't say anything. I just raised my eyebrows.

I didn't even have to undress. He left, and a nurse came in and took my blood.

When I got back to the office, I gave a couple of the doctor's business cards to Tangles and Storm. "Tomorrow go get tested."

Both shrugged like they weren't sure.

I went to my office where a bunch of work was piled up on my desk, and a handful of phone messages awaited me.

I skipped lunch and returned my calls. Normally Mario pops into my office, but I hadn't seen him. I called him on the intercom.

"Hey," I said. "I miss you. Where you been?"

He laughed. "Question is where you been? I peeked in earlier and you weren't there. Reception said you were out."

"I had a quickie," I joked.

"Was it good?"

I said, "It was good, Amorcito."

"Letty, don't call me that."

"You know it's a beautiful expression in Spanish, and it's different from what she calls you."

"She is Olga," he corrected me. "You are friends. Don't make it sound otherwise."

"Sorry," I said.

As soon as he hung up, I walked into his office.

He was bent over some paperwork when I walked in. I watched him for a few seconds, as he concentrated on the pages, a serious expression on his face. He looked up and his smile hit me like a sunrise, that smile I fell in love with long ago.

"Did you come in for quickie?" he asked, standing up, and sweeping half the stuff off the top of his desk.

I locked the office door and headed for his desk.

January 10, 1994 (Monday)
New York City
Lola

I knew one thing. Gus Bradley was from San Francisco.

Gus Bradley, AKA Art.

I didn't bother going to my brothers with his correct name. That would leave a paper trail for someone to find in the event something terminal happened to Art, and no way was I bringing them into it. We'd already found out that Art was an alias. I had been thinking with my cunt when I got on that plane. Now I was thinking with my brain. I planned to find Gus on my own.

I put the five hundred thousand with the other cash in my safety deposit box at my bank in New York. I considered letting Art slide. I really tried. All I needed to do is to forget about it, and I'd be done. There'd be no mess to clean up afterward.

I couldn't let go. The fucker had wronged me. He left me in Colombia for dead. He must have known that Olga would pump me for information then kill me, but he didn't give a damn. He delivered the goods and split with whatever payday Olga gave him. I was the goods.

I packed two suitcases and flew to San Francisco.

February 1, 1994 (Tuesday)
Los Angeles, CA
Letty

Tangles and Storm had been spending too much time on distractions, so we'd hired Minnie to assist. She was our secretary, and with her, phone calls were no longer interfering with priorities like spending time with clients ready to order a plane.

"Dr. Hershey's office is on the line," Minnie said on the intercom.

I took the call. The nurse on the line gave me a choice: the doctor could discuss my blood test results on the phone or I could come in. I worried a little because they didn't just say I had it or I didn't.

I chose to do a walk-in. I went alone, and I didn't tell Tangles, Storm, or Mario. If it was bad news, I wanted to hear it on my own.

This visit was later in the day than my first one, and the office was busier than it had been before. Several people in the waiting room showed symptoms of the flu that was going around. Tissues were out, and the piped-in music was punctuated by long choruses of juicy coughs. It wasn't bad enough that I was scared of getting a bad diagnosis. I had to worry now about getting exposed to their nasty illness. How did the doctor keep from getting sick?

This time, I got to avoid the examination room, and the doctor saw me in his office. He welcomed me graciously into the small room, walked me to the chair I sat in, and brought his wheeled office chair around my side of his desk. The office was less fancy than those of the lawyers I'd met while working for Mario. Instead of wooden cabinets and law books, he had a twelve foot tall metallic bookcase all along two walls, and every space was stuffed with medical books. His desk was not of fine glass-topped wood like we had back at our office but was white metal, a little battered-looking, but looked like it would sustain plenty more abuse before giving up the ghost. On it, I saw a beaker of green liquid, stethoscope, computer, phone, and two wire baskets piled high with folders. He had his white jacket on and was as good-looking now as he had been on my first visit. I could hear Tangles's voice in my head, saying 'Ease up cowgirl, you're married.'

"Well doc, I'm here," I said.

"No point in torturing you by making you wait. You're negative. Nothing to worry about."

It wasn't until after he said that, that I realized how tense I had been. My whole body relaxed, and I let out a quiet sigh of relief.

"That means if I behave, I don't have to worry about it for a while."

His smile got bigger. I expected he was going to say goodbye. He had a full waiting room. He didn't.

"I noticed on your questionnaire that you don't have a previous medical provider."

"I know it sounds lame. I had an ELISA blood test done at home along with a group of my friends a few years back, but I don't remember having a doctor as an adult."

"It's good you haven't needed a doctor," he said.

"Well, I did see one after a plane crash off the coast of Puerto Vallarta, November 1991."

"Wow," he said, his eyebrows raised. "You seem to have come through it without any consequences."

"We were lucky, and we had a great pilot. Anyway, I'm in good condition. I don't eat all that healthy, but I'm fit. I hold three black belts in karate."

"I am impressed," Doctor Hershey said. "I don't want to get you mad at me."

I laughed. He laughed too, a little nervously.

"Your questionnaire says you are married. Are you planning to have children?"

"Big question," I said. "We don't know yet. I don't think so."

"Consider doing an exam, a thorough blood work-up, and a pelvic."

As he stood, the wheeled office chair rolled backwards a few inches. I stood up at the same time.

"Think about it. If you decide to, please call Lily, and she will schedule you."

We shook hands.

"If you don't do it here, do it somewhere. It's a good idea. You are a youngster and healthy, but if you want to stay that way, it's good to know what is going on inside."

It was my turn to give him a smile.

"I'll make an appointment with Lily and be back," I said.

He started to call me Mrs. and I stopped him.

"Letty is fine, Doc."

He smiled again.

"Letty, it was a pleasure seeing you."

"The pleasure was mine. Thanks for the good news that my blood tests were negative."

He walked me back to Lily's desk, and then he was swarmed by all the people in his waiting room.

On my walk back to the office, it occurred to me that I waited until I got married to become a flirt. Or maybe not. Maybe I've always flirted. I just never thought about it. It doesn't matter, if I flirt, anyway. It's not going anywhere. Unless Mario makes me jealous....

February 1, 1994 (Tuesday)
San Francisco, CA
Lola

If I only had a picture of Art. I was so over the top about him that I had thought he was too good to be true. That's why I'd originally called my brother to check him out. I doubt he would have let me take a picture of us together, because he had a plan, and a picture would have been evidence. I will make him pay.

I checked in the Holiday Inn at Fisherman's Wharf. The room was spacious, had a nice bathroom and I had a view of the wharf. Since it was still early in the afternoon, I walked over to Pier 39, a touristy spot filled with restaurants and things to do. I found a caricaturist who was twiddling his thumbs. Big dark guy, gold glasses. He looked bored. More importantly, he had a display with dozens of images he'd drawn, and they were all practically photo-realistic.

"Did you do all of these?"

"No, it was my cat, Leonardo," he said. "I cannot tell a lie."

I ignored his sarcasm. "If I describe someone to you, are you good enough to draw the person?"

He perked up, looked less bored.

"At $50 an hour, I am."

"Deal," I said.

When I got back to my room, I had a decent pencil drawing of Art. I had years of experience describing people to artists, and this artist had more than earned his fifty bucks.

In the morning, I went through the yellow pages and found a Xerox copy service four blocks from the hotel. While I waited, the attendant took the drawing and printed twenty 5 X 7 copies for me on hard stock. I was totally pleased with myself now that I had something to work with.

The next morning, I rented a car and plotted my first stop, a private airport. I had found three listed here, and four in Oakland across the Bay Bridge. I had no idea if he flew that big plane he was in back here. If necessary, I would hit the big airports, starting with executive airports.

It cost me a hundred bucks to get through the doors of a private terminal and on to the tarmac. I showed the picture to everyone working in the terminal. No one wants to identify anyone, but all I needed was one person.

One person who saw him.

One person who knew him.

One person who wanted to talk.

I started with a guy moving plane stairs.

"If you've seen this guy, it's an easy hundred for you," I said, with a big smile. Cops don't smile like I just did. Cops don't wear a sexy décolleté black dress slit up the side and spike heels that make tarmac-walking difficult.

"I wish I had. I always can use a hundred."

After an hour of going from person to person, I got in my rented car and drove to the next airport.

"Art, no matter where you are, I will find you," I promised myself.

Five days later, still no luck. I was working on the assumption that he owned a plane. I could be on a wild goose chase. Maybe I should be concentrating somewhere else, not just airports.

I was in a bar at Pier 39 on the fifth night when my cell phone rang.

"Where are you?"

Noisy as it was, I knew the voice. Mason. I got excited hearing him. Excited like racing heart, moist panties, and the temperature in the room raised ten degrees.

"Hold on. Let me step outside," I said.

I made my way through the crowd. I rushed a little, stepped on one guy's toes, and nearly bowled over another dude just getting out the door. I didn't want Mason to hang up.

"What a surprise," I said.

Outside, some boat blew its horn, traffic hummed around me, a plane flew overhead, but it was still quiet compared to inside. Inside were way too many drunks, loud, hungry, horny Californians (and tourists) intent on finding their mate of the night, all yelling over the DJ and the live band.

"Are you in Frisco?"

"I am."

"Did you find him?"

"I can't say that I have. I'm working on it."

"I can help," he said.

"I knew you had his address."

"No, not so. I had to do my own search to find him."

"Mason, give me the address."

"Meet me tomorrow. We can discuss it at our last meeting place."

"I'll do that, but spring the address on me now, please."

I talked for five minutes. Mason wouldn't give it up.

At eleven the next morning, I got a rental and drove it from Burbank Airport to the hotel. He called while I was en route and gave me the room number. Same floor as before, different suite, but it looked identical.

He opened the door.

I was all set to give him a bad time for bringing me all the way to Los Angeles to get the address when he could have given it to me on the phone on my promise. I don't know if I walked into his arms or if he got in my way and just grabbed me. Somehow, I was in a hug—a big, warm, satisfying hug that I didn't want to end—and I won't admit that it took my breath away, and it was just Mason.

"You must be losing your touch. You can't find him."

We settled in the parlor, side-by-side on a loveseat identical to the one we had necked on, before.

"I have no resources," I said. "I'm used to having resources."

I handed him a copy of one of the pictures.

Mason smiled.

"Good job."

"You can have me any way you want," I said. "Give me the address."

"Get that pen and pad on the desk," he said.

"Oh hell," I said. I pulled my dress over my head and tossed it to him. "I don't need clothes to write."

February 4, 1994 (Friday)
Miami, Florida
Mario

I flew to Miami to meet with Michael Taylor, CEO of a commuter flight operator in the Bahamas who wanted to expand his destinations to include Miami, Georgia, and New Orleans. He would need Boeing 737s for that, and I had an option to buy eight such used planes from an operator in Mexico who replaced the planes with new equipment. Unfortunately for me, I didn't get the new equipment lease. Airbus in France landed the business. I had thirty more days to exercise my option to buy the planes or walk.

Michael Taylor came to see me at the hotel where I was staying in South Beach. The Delano was an old hotel, a beauty with a fabulous beach. My top floor suite was done entirely in white, blinding but beautiful. The entire wall behind the bed was padded in tufted white material, the floor was white, plus there were white Calla Lilies in vases, and silver and white-globed sconces over the nightstands. Letty had opted not to join me. It was a shame she was going to miss the room. She would have loved it.

When I invited her, all she said was, "I've got some stuff on the burner and a trip will only distract me. Thanks for asking."

Before I flew down, we checked out Michael Taylor and his company. He was solid, little cash but good cash flow. He reinvested in commuter planes that flew to all the islands. He had two 737s in his fleet that he used for long range flights like Puerto Rico.

Taylor's paperwork put him two years younger than me, married and divorced three times, with three children by his first wife. I met him in the hotel's lobby restaurant. Soaring ceilings, lots of glass, more lilies. We sat at a table facing a patio where some people were dining.

Our waiter with a shock of unruly hair tied tightly back was probably a college kid or a surfer, and was dressed as whitely as my hotel room. He took our orders and moved on to another table.

"You been busy for your age," I said.

"How so?"

"Married and divorced three times."

Taylor laughed. "I believe that married life should not become a sacrifice," he said. "If a marriage doesn't work, you move on. Many of my married friends stay together for the children. I don't believe that's a good idea."

I nodded. "Makes sense," I said, unsure it made sense or not. Children were outside of my experience.

He talked about his kids, his current wife. I talked about how I was almost a newlywed. Our steaks arrived. We started to carve into them and finally got down to brass tacks.

"I can take all eight planes," he said. "What I need is a break on the front-end. I can do ten percent down. That way I am not strapped and can refurb as needed. Judging by the reports and videos you sent me, some can use seats. A couple of them look worn."

"They can all use seats," I said. "The important thing is that all of them are airworthy and have good maintenance records. You run a cheap fare operation. You don't need everything to look perfect. Use the hell out of these, make some cash, then trade them in or make them look pretty."

"Can you do it with ten percent?" he asked, unsmiling, looking a little anxious, in fact.

"I'll do it, but you can't let me down. On used planes we don't go that low, ever. I'm doing it because I like your track record. You know the business. You've never had a tragedy. That speaks a thousand words about your maintenance and pilots."

By the time I finished talking, a smile had stretched all the way across his face. He leaned across the table, grabbed my hand with both of his, and shook it enthusiastically.

"Thank you, Mr. Luna," he said. "Thank you."

More shaking. After a minute or two, he let go, and sat down. I used my freed hand to finish the last bit of my steak.

"Mario is good enough. Are you in for dessert?"

"Always in for sweets," he said.

We each had a slice of the restaurant's signature key lime pie. He was thrilled about our arrangement, and I could see he was indeed a man who liked his pie. I liked him.

Giving him a break on the down-payment didn't leave me feeling like he was taking advantage. I look at the big picture, the long-haul.

Before the sun went down, my business in Miami was complete. I had already called Andrea to give her the go ahead to buy the planes. Taylor had signed the irrevocable letter of intent to lease the planes we were buying. GAL was financing this deal one hundred percent, independent of the consortium. It was a lot of money but not enough to split it with the consortium. Olga had a point that taking GAL public would give us unlimited financing—not that I had ever needed to forego a deal for lack of money. On this deal, Olga would fund GAL with the money needed to buy the planes from the Mexican operator.

She never complained. She simply said, "Keep them coming, Amor."

I called Letty.

"I'm done. It's late to call the crew together."

"Andrea said you closed the deal. Wonderful."

"On paper it's closed, but until he takes delivery and all the contracts are signed, it's not really closed."

"You are so conservative," she said, laughing.

"Careful, that's all. Letting the chickens hatch before I count them."

"You're buying eight planes, and you feel that way?"

"You know it's easy to lease out used 737s. I should have bought them outright instead of getting the option. Anyway, I'm spending the night. What are you going to do?"

"I haven't given it any thought. I'll check with Tangles and Storm."

I went down to the hotel spa and used the sauna. No wet steam. I got an hour's massage, good but much too short. I was in my room before eight.

I'd been to Miami many times. I didn't need a guide. Eight was too early for me to call it a night.

I ended up in a club that was jammed. Half the club had beds, sofas, recliners, all very orderly and nice. The areas were curtained off, but for eating and imbibing, not sex. A waitress served whatever you wanted while you sat up on the split king bed. When each person left, they changed the covers just as they would a tablecloth.

Since I was alone, the waitress left my sheer curtain open. The bed was not long enough for me to lie down, but I wasn't planning on lying down anyway. I sat up, people-watched, listened to great loud music, and drank one of my favorite white wines. The cover charge for a bed was two hundred fifty dollars.

A hot beauty walking by stopped and did a double take. She started to walk away, then stopped again. I was halfway through my wine and smiling by then. So was she. I don't know why she was looking at me. She was the one deserving a second glance. She was one of those very tanned beach girls who looked like she could get a job on a fashion runway. Well, maybe more curvy than fashion likes, but I had no objections. She was wearing not much of a dress, a peachy thing with the kind of sleeves Letty calls spaghetti straps. I was pretty sure that was a bikini under her dress. Her eyes were light, probably green, not that I could tell that much under night club lights.

"Jane is my name," she said, standing by the bed.

I put my hand out. We shook.

"I'm Mario."

"Want a drink, Jane?"

"You got room for me?"

I scooted over. "Yup, plenty of room."

It was too noisy for conversation. Smiles work when it's noisy.

Jane was a lovely brunette. After her first glass of wine, her left hand was on my thigh. I was happy just looking at her, and the traffic of single women and guys walking around the curtained area was pretty entertaining.

Our curtain was open.

Jane said something.

I put my hand to my ear and yelled over the noise, "What was that again?"

She got close enough to me that I noticed how she smelled of tangerines, suntan lotion, and wine.

"I'll level with you. My name is Maggie, I'm from the Bahamas."

"I like both names," I told her during a short pause between songs. "And I'm still just Mario."

Another girl came around the bed, opposite from Maggie. Fantastic face. Big dark eyes, short hair, feathered. Breathtaking, really. She stood with her hands on her hips.

"Move over," she said. "I can use a little wine and loving."

I didn't see how Maggie reacted, as I was too busy looking at the no name girl. I was now in the middle of the sandwich. Squished, actually. Both of the girls were wedged up to me, plenty of space on their other side even though the bed was pretty narrow for three, but I wasn't complaining. No name girl smelled of wine and shampoo.

"My name is Mario," I said.

"I'm Jane," she said.

"No," I said, "Her name is Jane," gesturing to the beauty on my right.

Maggie pinched my thigh, or at least tried, but there's nothing to pinch. "Name is Maggie," she reminded me.

A second bottle of wine was delivered.

I suggested we order food, but if you want to eat in bed, they serve you on TV tables. There was no way the bed would accommodate that.

The waitress secured us a booth that was curtained for privacy. I handed my waitress a hundred and the host a fifty.

Over her plate of alligator bites and her third glass of wine, the second Jane confessed her name was Billie, and she was a Miami girl.

Maggie had stone crab.

I had a filet mignon and a strong craving for a joint, which, I am pretty sure was not on the menu. No way I could pull one out here, even if I had one, which I didn't. It was the youth of the girls making me feel insecure. I'm not old but beside these girls, I felt old. They not have been more than twenty-five. I'd been with ladies younger than me many times, but I was hitting my mid-forties now.

We took a cab back to my hotel.

"Awesome pad," Maggie said.

"Awesomeness," Billie said.

The king size bed was not like mine at home, too short for me, but I found a position for my legs while I devoured these luscious bonbons.

I was doing Billie. Maggie rested.

"You're a beast," Billie said.

"If you're done, I can stop," I said.

"Don't you dare."

Maggie was right there on the bed. I turned to the right every time I filled Billie, and we kissed.

"You're built like Superman," Maggie said. I tried to ignore what she said but couldn't help feeling pleased.

"Not like an old guy at all."

Not so pleased when I heard that.

Billie came noisily under me, then said, "He is superman. I can't take no more."

I pulled out, rolled off the bed, and on to my feet.

Billie was still breathing hard. Maggie was flopped out like a rag doll, her eyes shut, halfway to dreamland. I wondered at their exhaustion. This was no workout.

I gave them each a hundred for cab fare and did not see them out of the hotel. As the door shut behind them, I thought of Lola, maybe because if she'd been with me, she'd still be here, asking for more. The youngsters, they got their nuts off and scrammed. I used to too. I was just wounded by the 'old guy' crack. I walked to the bathroom to check myself out in the full-length mirror. I didn't see any change in the way I looked. Not a single white hair that I could see, my body was toned as it had been for decades, maybe I need to add another day of karate and not just ride a bike or jog. Nah, that's not it. These ladies' figure anything over their age is ancient. From the bathroom door, I looked back at the shambles of the bed, like the laundry room at home had exploded. I thought of calling room service but didn't want the bother. I thought of Letty as I picked the sheets off the floor, shook them out, and threw them back on. Same with the comforter and pillows. How many hundreds of times had the girls had fixed the bedding, especially Letty? I stepped back and gave it the once-over. It looked no way like it had when I'd gotten there, but I was going to sleep, not out to earn a merit badge. Still, I missed Letty. Not her bed-making skill, but she would have laughed with me. I went to bed, tossed and turned. 'Old guy' had stung.

At three Saturday morning, midnight in Los Angeles, I called Andrea.

"Sorry, baby."

"Don't be. What's up?"

"Order the crew. I want to split for home at six my time."

I got to the airport thirty minutes before liftoff. One step into my plane, I smelled coffee.

My crew welcomed me aboard. I accepted a black cup of coffee from Sandy and took a seat. We didn't go through an introduction. She'd attended a flight before this one, but I don't recall which. She was attractive, sleek bowl-cut hair, dark with blond streaks. She handed me a USA Today. Once upon a time, the LA Times classified ads every morning was mandatory reading. How things change. Sandy brought out croissants to go with the coffee, room temperature butter, jam and fruit. She said something about catering for lunch, soup and sandwiches, but I was thinking about Maggie and Billie, picturing them scoping out my plane, bitches that they are. I didn't have the plane to impress girls, but the plane was a perk, no doubt.

The captain and first officer went out to do a walk-around and inspect the plane. Their inspection reminded me of the brutal crash in Mexican waters. Thank God, we all made it. I'd prayed to the Virgin of Guadalupe, for the others to live. Ever since then, for a moment or two before every flight, I think of that crash. I don't fear flying, not at all. That doesn't mean I don't look back at waking up in the ocean, at night. What a memory.

"How about breakfast?" Sandy asked.

"This is fine," I said, over the croissants.

She was wearing Miami casual, shorts and a cute shirt, some kind of uniform issued by the agency. The uniform showed off her tan. I had my own pilots but depended on the agency for flight attendants. I didn't do enough flying to have them on payroll. It was bad enough having pilots on standby. Like firemen, they were getting paid for waiting. My pilots waited for my next flight. Fuck it. The company paid for it, and I was making a lot of money for the company, aka, Olga.

I had a second mug of black coffee and switched out the fruit for two chocolate donuts.

After liftoff, Sandy returned to see if I needed anything.

"You are going to need warmer clothes. It's still winter in LA."

"I got it covered. You're right. It's chilly there."

It was too early for wine and too early to fuck.

I went to the bedroom, changed into sweats, and got the sleep I hadn't been able to get during the night.

Thirty minutes before landing, Sandy came in to tell me it might be a good time to get up.

"Or we could divert to another destination, Chief."

No one called me chief except for Betty. Her father had been a police chief. I thought of Betty with nostalgia. Eventually, she'd called me boss, like everybody else, and now that she was involved with someone, she called me nothing at all. I was still half asleep. I looked up from the bed.

"You mean like Hawaii?"

"Hawaii would be killer," she said.

"If I do that, what's in it for me?"

I think she realized I was serious. I saw a blush.

"You tell me, Chief."

Hawaii wasn't the tempting part. Sandy was the tempting part. I figured she was in her mid-thirties, the perfect age. Letty's age.

I would have nothing to say to Letty if I called her from Hawaii.

"Sandy, I promise, next time you are on board, I'm taking you to Hawaii."

"Promise?"

"Promise."

I got up and gave her a peck on the forehead. I took a shower, changed into fresh jeans, and jammed my dirty clothes in the carry all.

I finished a fresh cup of coffee Sandy poured for me. My plane made a perfect landing. Six hours flight time. The plane came to a stop at our designated hangar where a helicopter was waiting to fly me to the office. I gave Sandy a hug, a kiss on both cheeks, and handed her my business card.

I knew she was watching through a plane window as I got on the helicopter.

We lifted off toward downtown Los Angeles.

I was excited as we circled the helipad for a few seconds, then landed. The engines shut down. I wasted no time going down the stairs. The door to the building opened and there was Letty, arms open.

I swooped her off her feet, cradled her, kissed her passionately at the elevator doors, and then for the three floor ride down.

"I love you, Amorcito," she said, as seriously as I'd ever heard her say it.

"I adore you," I said.

"Hey, that's what she always says to you."

I smothered her objections with kisses.

I hated what I'd done with Jane and Jane.

I hated that I wanted to take Sandy to Hawaii and fuck her.

We were alone in the elevator. I hit the stop button. We necked for a few seconds.

"You smell like the plane," Letty giggled.

"What did you do last night?" I asked.

"Home with the girls. Huge dinner, wine, smokes. We missed you. I missed you."

She tugged at my suit jacket like a little girl.

"How about you?" she asked.

"I had a restless night," I said. "Couldn't wait to get back."

I hit the button and released the elevator. The doors opened. The talk stopped.

We entered the GAL offices.

Tangles and Storm waved from their offices. I had hold of Letty's hand and pulled her into my office and closed the door.

February 3, 1994
San Francisco, CA
Lola

It was not the first time in my life that I had bunked with the enemy. There was always a reason when I jumped across the line. Today it was to find Art, the real enemy.

Mason was sweet. I felt a little guilty thinking of him as an enemy. My attitude comes from trusting a man and then getting fucked around, exactly what happened with Art. Mason is not looking for anything long-term, and neither am I. A long-term relationship isn't going to happen anytime soon.

Good things about sex with Mason: he's immaculately clean, he's not ugly, and he stays hard for a long time. I don't do oral on him, but he does me, and he knows exactly what to do. The doctor in him, I guess.

There were limited available flights to San Francisco, so I took one to Oakland, a hop across the bridge from the airport. I was happy to be back in my hotel room, home for now. I was hungry but too tired to mess with eating, the kind of tired that would keep me from falling asleep on my own. I took an Ambien.

According to Mason, Art lived in Pacific Heights, San Francisco. I drove my rented car by a beautiful old six-story apartment building. Art lived in the penthouse, probably on the entire floor. On my second pass, I noticed a doorman opening the driver's door to admit a woman getting in. I mapped it out and memorized what was where in the small high-dollar community of Pacific Heights.

Parking in San Francisco sucks. In Pacific Heights, no parking was close to the building. No place to park. No place to scope the people going in and out. Surveillance, even for the FBI, would be a fucking challenge.

The next morning, I had a cab drop me off at a restaurant four blocks away.

I dressed like a young man, a warm scarf wrapped around my neck, a long-sleeved shirt tucked into Levis, a to die for belt with a sterling silver buckle, short boots that looked like shoes because they were covered by the jeans. The beanie that covered my hair matched my government issue double-breasted peacoat. My breasts disappeared under tight thermals. I didn't do anything funny with my face except beef up my eyebrows by brushing them the wrong way. I carried a leather backpack instead of a purse and looked like a pretty boy with a thirty-five mm camera taking pictures of the architecture. It took me an hour to amble from the restaurant, taking pictures of the buildings. I took pictures of the buildings on both sides of the mansion. When I crossed the street, I saw the doorman standing inside the entry. He was no dummy. It was cold. He wasn't coming out unless he had to. I wanted the doorman to see me, so I stood in front of the building and waved at him until he waved back.

I took pictures of the buildings surrounding Art's apartment. The doorman came out a couple of times, once to take charge of a car, and once emerging from the parking garage under the building. I had walked a circle around the building, checking out the exits and entrances, and an emergency exit probably from stairs that ran down one side of the building.

"Are you studying architecture?" he asked.

He was an older man, long graying hair tied back, and though his doorman's uniform was almost military, he did not stand like a military man. If I had to guess, I might say he was a retired postman. He had a little cap, a bow tie, and Craig Clark was embroidered on a patch around his collarbone. He wheezed a little, and I might have smelled pot on his breath. I for sure smelled mouthwash.

"I wish," I said in as deep a register as I could manage, without too much effort. "I'm doing a paper on Pacific Heights. I'm from Los Angeles." He should have asked me what the hell was I doing a paper on Pacific Heights if I lived three hundred fifty miles to the South. If he had asked me, I had an answer.

"Hey," I said. "My name is Tommy," I extended my hand.

"Craig," he said, shaking my hand.

My hands are soft, but the handshake was lightweight. His hand felt hot to me, so probably he noticed my cold fingers.

"Craig, any chance I can use the restroom? It's a quickie."

"Sure, let me park this car downstairs, and you can come in and warm up a bit."

"Thanks. You're too kind."

"Gorgeous lobby," I said, ten minutes later, admiring the lobby. "Are these condos?"

"Yes, they are. Tommy, no pictures inside. I could get in trouble."

I put the camera in the backpack. I had more than my camera inside.

My Walther PPK revolver with a silencer was ready for anything.

Craig showed me to the bathroom in the lobby. I went in the men's room. Two spotless sinks, one large mirror, an open urinal, two closed stalls, a strong scent from the toilets, eucalyptus. I did have to pee, and I did, in a stall, sitting.

When I came out, Craig was outdoors. I saw him get in a car, no doubt to park it in the garage downstairs. The man who had been driving the car let himself in, rushed past me to the elevator, and was gone. I don't know if he saw me or not.

I saw neither a directory, nor buttons to press to announce you needed to get in. I assumed the doorman handled that responsibility.

I saw two elevators, both single opening stainless, matching stainless pad with buttons that illuminated. I stepped in the elevator the resident had not used and tapped the 6th floor. The button wouldn't stay lit. I pressed 5. The door closed, and I started moving up. The elevator was far from new, but spotless as well, with signs of wear and tear. Craig would think I walked out on my own. If he had figured me for a bad guy, he would have never let me in.

If the sixth floor was locked out, a key was probably necessary for access. The elevator probably opened into the penthouse. I'd seen that many times.

I got off on five and saw two marked emergency exit doors on either side of an elegant hallway. There had to be stairs going up. Before I used it, I checked that the emergency door wasn't going to lock me out, then I stepped out on the emergency stairway landing. For emergency stairs, these were nice. No bare concrete here, but skylight overhead, nice carpeting, wainscoting, tall ash trays, lighting good enough to sustain a massive palm plant on each floor. There were stairs going down to the ground as well as going up one floor. The sixth floor door might be locked just as the elevator had been. Fuck it. I walked up the next flight and stopped to put on my kid leather gloves. They were not the quality I would have had on the job, but they weren't traceable. I was able to turn the knob, though I did not try to push in. I had no idea if there was an alarm, or if Art, or Gus Bradley, or whatever he was calling himself, was home.

If I got caught, a search would reveal the gun, the silencer, and the permit to carry the gun. Of course, no permit for the silencer. That's a different story. My badge, although clearly marked retired, would temper the impact of an arrest. But I'm not getting caught.

February 5, 1994 (Saturday)
Los Angeles, CA
Letty

We were alone in his office. It seemed as good a time as any to tell him.

"I saw a doctor nearby and had an HIV blood test. I came out negative. Remember when we all got one at the house?"

"That was years ago. I remember. Why did you get it?"

"Amorcito, when you fuck around you should test, even if the test is limited."

Mario gave me a puzzled look.

"I'll walk you over to the clinic. It's only a few blocks."

"I'm not going to test," Mario said.

"You're like Tangles and Storm. They don't want to either."

"How much fucking around have you been doing?" he asked.

"How much fucking around have you been doing?" I kept my voice low, made it sound seductive, even.

"Why are we having this conversation?"

"Robert Reed from The Brady Bunch, Arthur Ashe the tennis player,

Rudolf Nureyev the dancer, Amanda Blake, you know, Miss Kitty from Gunsmoke," I reeled off people I knew had died from AIDS.

Mario looked at me, a blank look.

"You're right. You're right. Never mind. Forget I brought it up."

"Forgotten," he said.

I left his office and headed to mine.

I called Dr. Hershey's office and made an appointment for the works.

I called in Tangles and Storm and asked them to shut the door.

"Have you had a pelvic?" I asked.

"I have," Storm said. "I was having pains or something. Maybe I missed a period. Don't remember. It was no big deal. My mother had an exam every year. Why?"

"I'm going to have one, part of an exam. Aside from the doctor we saw in Mexico after the plane crash, I can't remember going to a doctor for anything."

"You're lucky, you're healthy and always have been," Tangles said.

"Have you had a pelvic exam?"

"I have, twice. First time, the doctor had a nurse in the room. Apparently, that's how it's supposed to be. The second time, no nurse. Doctor went in and swabbed me to test for STDs, opened me up wide. He wasn't abusive or anything. It was me, having his hands on me. You get it? Still remember how I was turned on. Good thing I didn't have an orgasm on him."

"You so fucking dirty," I said, laughing.

Tangles and Storm laughed, too.

"I get it, strange hands there, you're lying down, can't even see him, or can you?"

"If he sits you up on the exam table, yeah. I was lying down, staring at the ceiling, my legs in the stirrups, wide as fuck."

I got turned on thinking of Dr. Hershey exploring me with his hands, lying down looking up and not at him. It would be like having a bandana over my eyes. I felt heat.

What a fool I am to be thinking of a doctor I don't even know.

On the trip Tangles and I took to Rio, we fucked around with guys every night we were there. Maybe it messed up my brain. I haven't been the same since. And the orgy. Fuck. What's wrong with me?

February 7, 1994 (Monday)
Los Angeles, CA
Tangles

His name was Martin Moss Junior, and he called himself Junior. Daddy, Senior, was the CEO of Budapest Air, a flagship airline in Budapest.

I asked Junior about it early on. He said he and his parents were born in New York and moved to Budapest when his father got the CEO job. I didn't know (or care!) about any of the particulars other than that his father took over the airline ten years ago. The credit report we had was preliminary, but I think it was solid. Mario and Andrea felt the same. Solid meant okay. We can lease to them.

For almost three months, my phone conversations and faxes had gone on with Junior who was in charge of fleet acquisition. He was a flirt. After so many calls with me, he'd relaxed his manners and was a bit dirty-mouthed, but not unpleasantly so. I can match or top anything he can throw at me.

I wanted to lease four new planes to them in the worst way.

When I got the letter of intent by fax, I had to run to the bathroom to pee. That happens to me when I'm excited. I received the proof of funds for the down-payment, a letter of credit being held by a Bank of America affiliate in Budapest.

We—Mario, Andrea, Storm, Letty, and me—met in Mario's office to talk about details of the deal. Minnie brought us all coffee and shortbread cookies, then went up front to answer all our calls so we could get rolling. Mario had drawn the curtains over his window. Sometimes the window wall radiated the cold outside, but his office was plenty comfortable.

"Good as cash," Andrea said, looking over the fax.

"Take the Lear and fly over with the contracts. Andrea will arrange for a notary, and that's it," Mario said, a smile tweaking his face.

"Oh you, lucky bitch," Letty said.

I knew she was happy for me. She was beaming.

"Boss, with the Lear?" Storm asked. "It doesn't have the range."

Before he could answer, I said, "We make more fuel stops, dummy. The cost to take a bigger plane is horrendous."

Mario let us talk away while he paged through work on his desk.

"I'll arrange it all," Andrea said. "Figure two days from now, you can leave with everything you need."

"You want her to go alone?" Letty asked.

Mario looked up. "It's good for her. If you want, go with her, and take Storm too."

"I can't go," Letty said. "I have some pending business that might work out. Storm, if you don't have anything pressing, go with her. I feel better if she has company."

"Storm, you can come," I said, "But trust me. I can handle any trouble that will pop up."

Even Mario laughed. They all know how good I am at self-defense.

"I can go, sure," Storm said. "Maybe some of your good luck will rub off on me."

She hadn't reeled in a new lease in more than two months.

"Luck has nothing to do with it," I said. "Been working Junior for more than three months."

"Once he sees you, no doubt he will want to fuck you," Letty said, joking as usual.

"I don't even know what he looks like, and he doesn't know what I look like."

"He does," Storm corrected. "You sent him the company pamphlet with all of our pictures in it."

"Right," I said. "One day at a time. I'm so excited I can hardly wait."

Letty stayed in with Boss, Andrea went back to her office, and Storm and I went back to my office to plan.

Turns out that the beautiful Learjet we were flying on had been Camila's short distance jet that used to sit in New York. Olga had the plane relocated to Van Nuys Airport for Mario until he decided whether it should be kept as a company plane or to lease it out. Mario was in no hurry to decide. It has some sentimental value to him, I guess.

It had no bedroom, but in the main cabin, four seats could be positioned as a flat bed seat. A rare find, apparently the seats were custom made for Camacho. Boss had them on his plane in addition to the big bed in the bedroom.

Near the cockpit were three seats that went flat for the crew to sleep. If we wanted privacy, there was always the back of the plane. Behind a door was a small compartment with a sofa that folded into a queen-size bed.

When she saw the set-up, Storm was all dreamy eyes.

"We can play house here," she said, flopping down on the sofa, and running her hands over the white leather. She pulled open the sofa to check out the sheets that were already on it. Gorgeous, of course, high thread count percale, a pattern and style I am sure Camila had selected.

That's not creepy at all.

I loved this business trip, and I know Storm loved it, too. On board, we were boss. Well, I was really boss, but Storm is my sister from another mother. I wanted her to have a ball on this trip, even if we don't do anything too memorable. Mario gave me leave to take this private plane all the way to Hungary to close a deal I negotiated from start to finish. Having this plane was a huge ego-trip, a power trip, plus I was getting a killer commission. I loved everything about the deal.

"Why do we have two captains and two first officers?" Storm asked.

"Regulations. They're only allowed to fly so long," I said. "The bigger jets have the same regulations, but they fly further faster. It just means we don't have to hang out somewhere while our flight crew takes a nap between shifts."

Our flight attendant was Chloe.

Storm and I sat facing each other, a table between us. The seats turned ninety degrees to make a bed, but we planned to sleep in the rear cabin.

"I'm going to die without a joint," I told Storm.

"How about we get high in cabin where we're sleeping?"

"Yeah, fuck, why not? Camila had a joint every time I saw her. I bet she smoked her ass off on this very plane."

"Right on," Storm said.

Chloe had us buckle up. At seven, we went wheels up. Small planes are noisy mothers, and it is a good thing, too. Plane noise would make it harder for the crew to hear us when we got busy.

"I'm so excited," I said.

"Not even close to how I feel," Storm said, showing me her beautiful teeth.

We had requested simple meals.

Chloe gave us a hot boxed lunch catered by Hamburger Hamlet. Yes, I brought vinyl gloves to eat my hamburger. I brought plenty. Storm accepted a pair, laughing her heart out.

"I never ate anything with gloves," she said.

The hamburger was juicy enough to warrant the gloves. No one wants sticky hands.

The standby pilots had on earphones for their televisions. There was a removable partition between them and us, but it wasn't like there was privacy. They had a toilet next to the cockpit. We had a toilet and a humble tiny shower in the back of the plane, no doubt some upgrade Camila cooked up. I've been in Lear jets before with only one bathroom.

It ended up we didn't need a joint right away. We laughed so much that I bet Chloe and the standby pilots thought we were high on something before we were high on something.

After dinner we hit the cabin. Chloe made the sofa into a bed and left us pillows propped up to watch television on a big screen. Reception wasn't good for TV, so we put on Pulp Fiction. We didn't really watch it, too busy being funny, sipping red wine, and sharing a joint that made it smoky enough that we could see the smoke being sucked out by the ceiling ducts.

Our first fuel stop was Washington D.C. I woke up briefly in Washington, but I was dead to the world when we off over the Atlantic. I went out before I noticed if Storm was awake or asleep.

February 9, 1994 (Wednesday)
Los Angeles, CA
Storm

I'm so happy to be on this plane with Tangles, I want to jump up and down. Thanks to Mario, this is not my first trip. I guess I've gotten braver. On my first plane trip, we crashed. But then a day later, we caught another plane. We had a funeral to get to. I guess that's old news. I've been on the big plane in the big bed. It's just this is so exciting for this trip to be just Tangles and me. I don't even know anything about Budapest except that the pretend Budapest on that old show Green Acres wasn't real.

I can hear the steady breathing of Superwoman Tangles lying next to me. The plane is loud, and I couldn't have heard her if our bodies weren't touching head to toe. I'd love to have this sound in a white noise machine, plus the smell-a-vision of this plane, this moment. I hope I wise up and get the hang of selling. Letty and Tangles are like they've been doing this forever. They're so good. They talk that plane shit like they were pilots or something. I want to be like them in the business sense. I'm never going to have a karate belt, though. I love Mario more every day for giving me all the opportunities that he's opened up since the beginning. He's so good to me. He's so good to all of us.

Before Mario, I struggled to get through massage school and managed to get my license. Back then, I believed that being a massage therapist would provide me with a good living. I would always have an income. Living with Boss and Letty and Tangles has changed what I call a good living, though.

I don't forget where I came from. Before Mario, I was working with Betty for less than living wages and bunking with my jerk of a boyfriend. He and I, we had a volatile relationship. I left him when Mario's plane brought us back from Camila's funeral (my third plane flight). I got home, and he was wasted. I'm not sure he knew I'd survived a plane crash. Hell, I don't think he'd noticed I'd been gone. Letty picked me up at that prick's house and took me to Mario's.

Without Letty's and Tangles's leg up, I might not have left him. Before Mario, massage did provide for me, even though I don't do massages for Mario and the girls. It's like they don't want to offend me. They used to call Betty. Now they call out to an agency to send therapists. Well, that way all of us get a massage at the same time. If I was doing it, one at a time.

I know how lucky I am.

I hope I can contribute something solid for the paycheck I get. Mario was ready to hire a driver to replace me so I can just work at the office. I panicked. Driving is a solid thing I do for my pay. The office thing I need to do better. I need to lease planes to be solid. I have no bills, and I bank everything I make. I saved the (huge) commissions on the planes I closed.

I had so much help from everyone that I thought it was unfair that I got all of my commissions. Mario scoffed when I wanted to share it with everyone who had helped me. It's like I'm insecure, and that's so stupid since everyone goes out of their way to make me feel solid.

In Budapest, a black four door Cadillac was waiting for us after we cleared customs. This trip, customs was an officer who didn't board the plane. He set up a portable table and chair by the plane stairs just for the crew, Tangles, and me. Andrea arranged things like this from Los Angeles. Tangles used to make arrangements, and before her, Letty did. Before that, before she took up singing for her supper, Pixie made all the arrangements, and before that, Jo. Without Andrea's arrangement, we would have had to enter the terminal, stand in a queue, and wait to check in to the country.

Our driver matched the car. He was dressed in a black suit and a hat like an undertaker. He drove us to the Ritz Carlton, an old hotel located in what the driver said was the city center. For old architecture, our hotel was kind of plain on the outside, I mean, fancy white marble, but real square, and the only balconies it had were little fake ones on the side of the building. The church next door was marble too, but all fancy, and it had complicated carvings, gold paint, angels and saints. At two in the afternoon, we got to our swanky two-bedroom suite. Andrea could have saved Olga some money by getting us one bedroom. We had two full-sized bathrooms, a guest bath off the living room, and our bedrooms were identical. Both had gray carpeting with a mod angular design, a gray couch, white striped duvet on the bed, beige bench at the foot of the bed, and white-topped lamps that look like in their last life, they were oversized cola bottles. We both had separate showers and tubs, black and white marble bathroom sinks, which would have impressed the shit out of me, if I hadn't been living at Mario's, where the bathrooms are way cooler, and the toiletries bottles have more than a spoonful inside.

"Why such a fancy place? Boss is not with us."

"Why the private plane?" Tangles asked. "They could have sent us coach."

Tangles got ahold of Junior on the phone to let him know she had arrived with her assistant Storm. To be a good assistant, while she was talking, I assisted by unpacking our luggage. The plan was to meet at the airline head-quarters at ten tomorrow morning. Their offices were in the city center close to our hotel, according to Junior.

Tangles tells me that experienced travelers acclimate to the destination time zone. We did it by crashing fully-clothed for a short nap, but that nap only lasted till Tangles's cell phone woke us up. Tangles answered quick. Letty was freaked out. I could hear her, and she wasn't even on speaker.

We were lying down in her room, blinds open, but it was dark outside. Lots of city lights played through the windows. We were on the top floor, surrounded by big stone buildings that had been there from the beginning of time. Okay, from the beginning of architecture. Buildings in Hungary are way older than the ones East Los Angeles.

"I was worried. Why didn't you call, dodo?"

"Sorry I forgot. As soon as we got to the hotel, we made the plans with Junior tomorrow, and crashed."

"What do you mean, crashed?"

I laughed before Tangles.

"You know. We hit the bed as soon as we walked in."

Tangles handed over the phone.

"Fuck, I wish I was there," Letty said.

"Me too," I said back.

After the call, we both hit the bathrooms. The tub looked fantastic, but I would try that out later. I took a shower, and it brought me to life. I was drying my hair when Tangles came in, wearing a hotel robe. Her hair was slicked back.

"Junior just invited us to dinner. The restaurant is to die for, best wine in the city."

"Fun," I said. "What to wear?"

"He said it's casual. Jeans, sweater, mink coats. It's cold out there. It's Junior and his dad so we can sit boy, girl, boy, girl."

We had both packed long dresses just in case, but I was okay with the jeans.

We met in the lobby. Lucky for us, Junior and Senior were pretty good looking. It was a fancy lobby, white leather easy chairs around marble tables. We shook hands. Old man Moss wasn't that old. I figure fifty, way too young to be called Senior. He was dressed like I picture a banker, gray wool. His shoes were gray too, kind of fancy. I could tell they weren't from J C Penney. Senior grabbed me and kissed me with his cheek. I mean, he rubbed my cheek and kissed the air by my ear. Both cheeks, actually. Junior did the same with Tangles, then shook my hand. It was weird to me getting an Olga kiss from a man.

"You guys are dressed for the office," Tangles said.

"Or a funeral," I heard myself say.

Boss Senior laughed at my wise-crack.

It took a minute for Junior to catch it. He was too busy scoping out Tangles.

Junior was not thirty-four. He looked like a college kid. I knew he'd said he worked full-time and helped manage the company with his father.

Unplanned, we ended up as two couples.

I felt we were going to have fun. Our dates smiled and laughed a lot.

Around ten, as we were escorted to a front booth at the restaurant, I was hoping that Tangles didn't pack vinyl gloves in case we were served anything juicy. I laughed aloud, and conversation stopped while everyone looked to see why I was laughing. I felt my face get hot and didn't explain what was so funny. Junior's eyes just about popped out of his head when we took off our minks. It was like he'd never seen women before.

A band was playing music, some tunes from back home, some Abba, some I had never heard before, in Hungarian. The music was just a backdrop, because the talk was all about planes. Senior told the story of his business, of starting in New York as a ticket counter clerk for Pan American Airlines and moving up to management. Eventually he landed as CEO of this failing Budapest airline. A year after he took his position, he took the airline through a reorganization, a legal thing, like bankruptcy. Eventually he paid off the creditors according to the reorganization plan and ended up with the company. I listened hard and asked no questions. All the while, Junior was gawking at Tangles. It was a hoot. Like me, she was listening to Senior, but while she was listening to Senior, pretending to be all wrapped up, she was watching Junior watching her, and I was watching Tangles pretending to not watch Junior while she was completely aware of him. We both let the men do the ordering. It was small fancy bites of stuff I'd never think to put on the same plate, served with Hungarian wine.

It was fun to be somewhere so fussy and fancy, but I didn't forget for a second that we were there to finalize a lease on planes.

At two in the morning, they delivered us back to the hotel lobby where we hugged and kissed like we had when we met, and like we'd known each other for decades. We were very lubricated with good wine.

"Let's meet tomorrow at one in the afternoon," Junior said before we walked off to the elevator. "That way you can sleep late."

Letty smiled her approval, but I knew she would want to get an early start and finish the deal. We were early risers back home.

You'd think we'd be wide awake after afternoon nap, but no, the wine made us drowsy. We changed in the bedrooms where I'd stashed our clothes. It was cool, perfect sleeping weather. We both put on the flannel pajamas we brought. After I changed, I poked my head in Tangles's room.

"Want to sleep alone?"

"Get your ass over here. How you can ask me that?"

"I thought those two were after our pussies," I said, taking a running bounce on to the bed like a ten-year-old whose parents aren't watching.

"Oh, they were."

"Junior couldn't keep his eyes off you," I said.

"I know, but I'm not here to have sex. I'm here on business."

I said, "Are you serious? He was hot."

I grabbed her pillow and kissed it all over like it was Junior. "Oh Junior, you're so hot," I said. I held the pillow out to Tangles, and she gave him a peck, then a couple more, then grabbed the pillow and gave it the full treatment. I bet no pillow has ever been so kissed. We were both laughing.

"He's a stud, and I'm serious as a heart attack."

"Poor Junior will never know what he missed.

I put my hand between Tangles's legs, a soft touch.

I felt her hand between mine.

For the meeting, I wore a beautiful two-piece red suit. I had red hose, red heels, red costume jewelry, red cummerbund like something Audrey Hepburn might wear, and a red purse. I was all buttoned up, so it looked businessy, but I know I could open a few buttons, and the whole thing would be nightclubby, even though there wasn't a sequin on it. Tangles wouldn't have let me go overboard with false eyelashes and shit, so I took great care getting ready. We made a game of emerging from our bathrooms for a simultaneous inspection, but mostly to show off.

"You ready?"

"I am."

"Me too. Ready, set..."

We each did a big entrance, and a spin for each other. We looked pretty hot, if I do say so myself. I pretended to adjust Tangles's tie and diamond earrings, and she pretended to adjust the angle of the beaded tassel necklace Boss had given me last Christmas.

Tangles looked like a model, or a millionaire businesswoman in her fitted pinstripe suit, vest, tie, and sleek black leather briefcase instead of a purse. She had on high-heeled black boots, the boot leather soft like butter, and fitting as tightly as something Pixie might wear on stage.

Our driver was scheduled to pick us up thirty minutes before our meeting. We came down to the lobby early and went into the Cartier store. Before moving uptown, I don't think I'd ever been in one, but from Mario, I'd learned these toney hotel stores are like candy stores for rich people. I was a little dazzled, and went from glass case to glass case, looking at the various groupings of watches, bracelets, jewelry for women, jewelry for men. Tangles and me, we looked at everything.

"What are we doing here?" I asked.

"I want to get them a gift."

It took thirty minutes to find two pens perfect for men like Junior and Senior. Like the pens, the boxes were showpieces too, each like a red lacquer coffin. I put one in my purse, and Tangles put the other in her briefcase.

"When I give Junior his, you give yours to Senior," Tangles said.

"You got it," I said.

As we walked to the car, I said to Tangles, "A favor, please."

"What's up?"

"I want a picture of us before we change out of these clothes."

"Yes, and let's get someone at their office to take one of all four of us," Tangles said.

"I don't need to be in that one," I said. "This is your deal."

Tangles took hold of my arm.

"You are part of this. Got it?"

I looked at my sister from another mother.

"I love you, Tangles. You are way too nice to me."

The driver opened the door for us. We got in the back seat. Tangles leaned over me and gave me a careful kiss. I pulled out my compact, and checked for lipstick damage, but we were both good.

"On to the airline, James," Tangles said.

The driver laughed. (His name was Ferko, but he spoke English, and was a professional chauffeur so he got the joke.)

We were on the way.

February 11, 1994 (Friday)
Bogota
Olga

"Amor, how are you? How is Letty?" I said on the phone, picturing Mario at his desk, midafternoon. Riana and I were sitting at one of the wrought iron tables outside, blooming in the roses and sunshine in the garden as the sun was about to set. It was February, but in Bogota that can mean seventy degree days. Dani was fetching us a fresh pot of tea. Riana and I each had our own stack of mail to deal with when night fell.

"Olga, thank you," Mario said from his office phone. "We're fine. How about you and Riana?"

"Amor, both of us miss you. I can get serviced anywhere I want, but you spoiled us so in Rome."

"On the contrary, I was the spoiled one," he said.

"Let's do it again, soon, Amor."

"Sure, let me know."

"Amor, I had a nice chat with Storm and Tangles. Tangles got the signatures. I'm so proud of her."

Dani poured tea into pretty bone china cups, lots of gold leaf. I nodded to him, listened to Mario, and looked at the cloudless darkening turquoise sky. The horizon was rimmed in orange, quite lovely, really. I dropped my opened letters in my bag.

"I'm proud of her, too," Mario said. "Storm is coming around. And Letty is kicking ass. She's totally into the business."

"You've always had a good team, even when you were chasing plane crashes. I'm so lucky, Amor. Thank you. GAL is lucky to have you."

"No thanks needed," he said. "You're generous."

"Not nearly generous enough, Amor. Instead of my taking GAL public, I am thinking that LAI can buy the company. I have a team checking it out. If we do that, I'm going to surprise you with the ownership percentage you've never received."

"That would be nice, Olga. Thanks."

"I haven't stepped up to the table like I should've. That's going to change."

I gave the phone to Riana. She talked to him, and then the call was done.

It would have been dark, but the garden lights came on automatically. Riana finished her tea, and we linked arms. Dani followed us back into the house. Before we had even made it inside, kitchen staff had cleared the tables. There was no rush for dinner, which we usually ate around seven.

"I get horny just talking to him," I said to Riana.

"Same here. He's such a stud."

Slowly, we walked back to my room.

"Dani, light us a joint, please."

"Right away."

"About time," Riana said.

"What are we doing tonight? It's Friday."

"Dani," Riana said, laughing. "You first."

Dani grinned, the candles burning in my room reflecting in his eyes, making him look excited and mischievous. He lit the joint for us and handed it to me without inhaling. I took a hit and passed it on to Riana, holding the smoke in my lungs. I patted the bulge in Dani's walking shorts and watched it get bigger.

"He's ready," I said to Riana.

"I can use some of that, Dani," Riana said, not talking about the joint.

"Me first," I said.

Riana got up to turn off the sound. *Pretty Woman* was playing, showing familiar locations from Los Angeles.

"Do you miss California?" Riana asked, gazing at the scene.

"Not at all," I said. "The last few times I was there, I hated the paparazzi. In Colombia, there are so many clubs where we can let our hair down, and no one will pay attention to me being a billionairess. This freedom in Colombia is what appeals to me."

Here, the families that used to be Pepe Camacho clients accept me as a cartel legend, the heir to a cartel legend, kind of a princess without a crown.

Dani stood there, obediently waiting for instructions.

I showered Dani in love and affection, gifts and extra cash. In return, Dani gave back the same and then some. He spent his days and nights pampering and attending to us. I had a house full of help, but Dani handled our personal needs, and I don't mean just sex.

Riana and I still had our personal maids, and Dani was there even when the maids were attending us.

I'd had installed the same kind of intercom Mario had. The cook called and asked what we wanted for dinner.

"You decide," I told Riana. "Surprise me."

Riana took the call.

"I'm suddenly ravenous. It's a wonder we're not fat," I said. "I'm so damn lazy. I used to put hundreds of thousands of miles on planes. I don't know if I could do it again if I had to."

Riana laughed. The joint was working. It was that kind of a laugh, spaced-out.

"Hey, I was with you on those miles. I know."

"Yes, Amor, you're right. I adore you, Amor."

"Back to you," Riana said.

Beside her, waiting patiently, Dani stood at attention.

February 11, 1994 (Friday)
Bogota
Riana

I know everything going on. I can't help but know the business. Olga is constantly on the phone with attorneys and advisers and who knows who else. Business doesn't interest me. I know everything but discovering Lola delivered to us unconscious and tied with bungee cords and zip ties to a gurney in the garage was a total surprise. I was shocked. It was the first time since Olga and I teamed up that I seriously considered going to the airport and hopping a plane to Spain.

I saw Olga kill six men in self-defense. I didn't get sick over it. I've never had a nightmare about it. The circumstances were different. Lola looked small and pitiful on the gurney. I wanted to puke. It's a good thing no cocaine was handy because I would have started using again after years of being clean. If things got worse for Lola, if Olga looked like she was going to have her killed, I meant to step in, even though she was a complete stranger.

When Mario came to Bogota to deliver the million dollar ultimatum from Lola, I was there. It never was clear if she threatened to kill both of them, but when Camila heard the demand, she went ballistic. Olga tried to calm her. Olga had been all for following Mario's advice to hand Lola a million in compensation and be done with it. Camila had been furious, but she agreed to pay. Lola died in a car explosion, or so we all thought. I thought she was already dead when Camila was shot. I don't know who did it.

Olga should not have ordered the kidnapping, interrogation, and subjugation of Lola. It was horrible to witness, maybe even worse than death.

After the interrogation, I believed Lola had nothing to do with killing Camila. The truth serum made her a sitting duck.

After Camila died, I suspected Olga of having it done, though it never made sense.

Even if she'd done it, I loved Olga too much to hold it against her.

I convinced Olga to return Lola to New York, and not empty handed. Lola had already shown her colors the last time she got the million from Camila. I convinced Olga that Lola would get over the humiliation she suffered if she woke up with a million dollars in her suitcase. Olga agreed to give her half that much.

I don't give a fuck about getting credit for saving Lola's life.

Olga was notified that the package, meaning Lola, had been delivered, and all was well. I waited to see if my interference of ordering a stop to the awful interrogation had damaged our relationship. If it had, I'd have dropped everything and gone back to Spain.

There was no such hint. I am still here.

I'm not with Olga because of her money. I have my own millions sitting in the bank. I have a primo portfolio of stocks and bonds, thanks to Daddy.

I took a hit of the joint, inhaled and held it.

So good.

It was after seven, so I told the chef to hold dinner. We moved to the living room. I'd been watching Dani pleasuring Olga for at least thirty minutes, spontaneous sex on one of the sofas in this huge room. When he was done with her, it was my turn. What a life. I love this life.

After Dani and a quick bite so we don't drink on an empty stomach, we would primp to party tonight. It can't get better than this.

February 14, 1994 (Monday)
Pasadena
Letty

It was Valentine's day. While I was waiting, I called Sees, and ordered Valentine candy boxes for everyone, promised a bonus if they could get it there before noon.

Dr. Hershey introduced us as soon as I got in the examining room. Dr. Ida Cummings came in once a week to do the female stuff.

"Don't worry," he said, patting me on the shoulder and leaving.

"Just put on one of the gowns on that bench over there, and I'll be right back," Dr. Ida said.

I was in a different room than before, and though I hadn't sat down on it yet, I saw the table had the famous stirrups I've heard so much about. I stripped down to nothing, put on that unflattering green hospital gown. Dr. Ida didn't make me wait. She knocked before she came in.

I got on the table, and put my feet in. Dr. Ida sat on a rolling stool. Mario would love having that thing in his office, the way it rolls. She rolled to the foot of the table.

"Scoot down," she said.

"Scoot down more," she said.

My knees were bent, and my coochie was wide open to the world.

"Just exactly how far do you want me to scoot?"

The answer was till my ass was hanging off the edge. Why hadn't Tangles and Storm told me about this part?

Dr. Ida did some fiddling around down there, cold metal, gloves, no fun.

"I'm taking swab samples for the lab to check on STDs, sexually-transmitted diseases like chlamydia, gonorrhea, and syphilis," Dr. Ida said from down between my straddled legs.

"Okay." As if I knew the different kinds of STDs.

"I seriously doubt I have any STDs," I said up to the acoustic ceiling above the exam table.

"You are probably right, dear," Dr. Ida said. "We just want to be sure."

I got to sit up, but she wasn't done. She did a thorough breast exam, surprised I had never had one before. She showed me how to do it myself and gave me a pamphlet showing how it was done. She gave me a prescription to get a mammogram. I felt like such a dumbbell making it to adulthood and never doing any of this. I made it a point to keep my pussy squeaky clean, but for all I knew I might have one of these STDs she mentioned. Made me sick.

Sam the x-ray tech did a chest x-ray of my lungs and another of my heart, checking for an enlarged heart. They rolled me in a chair to and from x-ray because I was barefoot.

I dressed fast. Both Dr. Ida and Dr. Hershey came into the examining room together to let me know I would get a call when the results got back from the lab. Dr. Ida reminded me to get the mammogram, just to be sure, although she did not detect anything during the exam.

"You have a resting pulse rate of fifty-four," Dr. Ida commented as she looked over my chart.

"I asked her about that before," Dr. Hershey said with a chuckle. "She's a hardcore athlete, a dozen karate black belts and such."

I laughed. "Not a dozen."

"You are toned," Dr. Ida said. "Good for you. You should do me a favor and speak to my three daughters and get them on a program."

"Sure."

When I was done, I was glad I did it all. Now to wait on the results like when I waited for the AIDS results. Fuck it. It is what it is. Whose line is that? Maybe it's my own.

I walked back to the office after two hours undergoing a 'routine' exam. I had so much blood drawn, I was ready to swear the new doc they sprang on me was a vampire.

I was back at the office at noon. I beat the Sees delivery guy and gave Minnie a fifty to tip him with. I used Mario's shower, but what I needed was to soak in the tub and douche. When I came out, the candy was out on everyone's desks, plus roses for me from Mario. Everyone was on a sugar high and calling like mad. Except Storm. I pulled her away from work. Tangles was on a work bender. She was still jazzed over Budapest.

An hour later I went home. I couldn't stand the stickiness. Storm took me because we had all come together. Emma fixed Storm a lunch. I passed on lunch and wallowed in the tub till the alarm rang an hour later. I dressed again and met Storm in the car. Tangles had stayed at the office.

"I'm sorry I pulled you out of work," I said, "And now I have to drive back."

"Silly girl," she said. "It's okay. How did it go?"

We both laughed when I confessed that I had been looking forward to exhibiting myself to Dr. Hershey on the exam table, how I didn't get the hot exam Tangles described. I got the one Storm talked about, all gloved hands and cold instruments touching me down there. Dr. Hershey was not on the premises. Damn. The doc who did my pelvic was a woman, an OBGYN called Dr. Ida Cummings.

"You are a naughty girl," Storm said.

We laughed some more. I usually ride in the back. Today I got to ride shotgun.

"It's like I stay horny," I said.

"The three of us are," Storm said.

The next morning, I met with Andrea about Storm.

"Do me a favor," I said. "Figure out something to give Storm an edge. Let reception give Storm more new leads, new customer calls, or let her help others close ongoing deals. I want her to feel good about herself. It's not going to happen unless she starts leasing more. She needs more volume from in-coming calls. And Andrea, Storm will never know we had this conversation. It's okay to tell Mario, but not Storm."

I'd never told Andrea anything like that before.

I didn't clear it with Mario. I wanted to see how much weight Mrs. Luna had at the office, if any at all.

Andrea took it like a trooper. "I'll work out something. I want her to succeed, too."

"Love you," I said to Andrea, and blew her a kiss.

That night when the lights were out in the bedroom, when Mario spooned me, I told him about my conversation with Andrea.

"I know, she told me," he said. "I told her it was okay."

"Why that snitch," I said, turning to face him.

It was dark, but not so dark I missed that Mario had a big smile.

"Andrea is lovely, you know that, but she's a snitch. It's just the way she is. Don't you remember when Olga found out we were getting married because Andrea told her?"

"She's such a bitch."

"No, not a bitch. A snitch. That's different because we both love her."

"I remember when she used to sneak out of the office in Milan to meet you across the street and when the two of you would walk to her apartment to fuck."

Mario laughed.

I didn't.

"You make it sound horrible," he said.

"I make it sound like it was."

"That ended quickly," he said.

"It sure did," I said, "After Camila told you to fuck at the house after hours so office personnel wouldn't know about it."

"Why are we talking about this?" Mario half leaned up.

I took a deep breath, smiled, and turned around to give him my back. "Where were we?" I asked,

I felt his arms and body press against me.

"I love you," he said.

"All these years we've been doing it, you never did anal with me," I said. "I know you did it with Andrea. You told me you did in Milan, and probably after she moved to L.A." It was the truth, but I was joking.

"You never wanted anal," Mario said.

"You never asked."

I could feel him behind me, hot and hard. But lover boy said, "Are we doing it or not?"

I scooted away. "I'll pass," I said.

"Suit yourself," he said.

Before we got married, this never happened.

February 14, 1994 (Monday)
Pasadena
Mario

What I didn't tell Letty is everything I told Andrea.

"If Letty comes to you about anything else, don't sweat it. Do it. If she wants it, I'm okay with it, even if she hasn't told me about it. You're okay with that?"

"We're a team and you're the boss. Of course, I'm okay with that,"

"You the best," I said.

Seems to me that Letty has become jealous. She's not jealous of Tangles and Storm who are often in bed with us. I'm going to tell her tomorrow, no more office talk in bed, not about Andrea or anyone else.

February 3, 1994 (Thursday)
San Francisco, CA
Lola

I started down the stairs. Halfway to the fifth floor, I turned and went back. I took my gun and silencer out of my backpack. Without the silencer, the gun fit entirely in my peacoat pocket. If I needed the silencer, I hoped to have enough time to put it on.

I turned the knob. This time I squeezed up my nerve, held my breath and pushed it open, waiting for the blast of the alarm. No alarm sounded. I was in a laundry room which smelled like beer. Correction—I saw a single beer can in the trash. Otherwise, it was immaculate. I moved from the dimly-lit laundry room to a dark hallway, creeping along like it was an FBI training exercise, and my former team leader (who was like a bloodhound who could sniff out one bad guy in the middle of the LA Festival) was watching me and taking notes. It was quiet. All I heard was my heart beating, and the heat coming on. As I walked, I screwed the silencer on the gun. I hugged my back to the wall, and found myself in a large bright living room, windows on two sides. If there were shades, I couldn't see them. Daylight streamed in, a cloudy day but it wasn't raining. At a distance from this sixth floor room, I could see a marina and the ocean. He must have paid a pretty penny for this place. I didn't think anyone was home, but I walked around cautiously. A picture on the piano showed Art. My heart leaped, now that I knew Mason had come through with the right address.

Art wasn't alone in the picture. Beside him was a pretty blonde woman, no doubt his wife, and two children about five and six, both boys.

I was right that the apartment took up the entire floor. I glanced in each room as I walked down another hall, this one bright from all the windows. The doors were all open, neat bedrooms, beds made up. An adjoining hallway was longer. The double doors at the hall's end were closed.

My training kicked in. Expecting the master bedroom, I opened the door like a cop would, covering my back, and doing scan of the room, but when I was active, at least I had backup.

It was the master bedroom. The bed was occupied. King-sized bed, pillows shoved to one side where no one was sleeping. It was afternoon, and a person was crashing on it, covered up, with the HVAC on. I could feel the heat. I saw a lump of clothes in a dainty needlepoint chair, but didn't rifle through, or check out what they were, other than men's clothing. I walked around the bed so that I faced the person.

It had to be him, and not the wife.

I stood there. Seconds passed. Maybe a minute. I expected to see movement under the expensive bedding. No movement. No sound. Ticking of an alarm clock beside the bed.

I leaned over and moved the comforter aside with the silencer. Still no movement.

I lifted the edge higher.

It was Art.

I pressed the silencer to his forehead.

There was no movement.

I froze.

I pushed the silencer harder against his forehead.

Nothing.

I tossed the bedspread back.

Art was in pajamas.

Art was dead.

It took me a few minutes to settle down. I froze in place. I saw that face of his, that jawline, that mouth, the face I'd been halfway in love with before I fell into hate. Now I was numb.

Everything shifted. Everything that he had done to me, everything that he was responsible for was unimportant, even the thought that Olga's men raped me after she released me. I had no recollection but the evidence that I had been used was there when I woke up in New York. When I finally was able to bathe, my vagina was loaded with a nasty residue that had not come from me.

I unscrewed the silencer from the gun and returned both to the backpack. I took my camera out and took a number of pictures of Art exactly as I found him and with the comforter and sheet pulled back, so his entire body was visible. I put the bedding back as it had been. I looked at the carpet where I had been standing. The rug was a pale green low pile that didn't keep imprints when you walked on it. If the Feds investigated, forensics would look at everything. This would be a local police case unless Art was into more. That was possible given that Mason had recognized him as someone Olga had used before.

By the time I was back on the staircase, I felt bad for his family, if that was really his family's picture on the piano. If he did have a family, where was everyone? I never went in the bedrooms, never checked inside the closets, never looked for clothes there other than Art's. I was getting sloppy.

I went back inside the apartment, back to the bedroom and walked in two big closets. One was filled with men's clothes. The other closet was empty except for two overcoats, obviously Art's. All the other bedroom closets were empty. Either the wife was a fiction, history, or the family was stashed somewhere else. Any of these were possible.

I followed the emergency stairs to the first floor, though I saw they extended down past the lobby floor. That meant there was a landing on the garage level. I did not pass any cameras in the staircase and nothing in the garage. I was surprised not to see anything.

I waited until a car drove in. The gate opened. I was able to get out without anyone seeing me. I hoped that there were no cameras in the lobby where I had been with Craig. Even if there was, I didn't kill Art and there would be no evidence to the contrary.

I walked until I found a stop for the trolley and waited.

Did Olga do this and if so, why?

Did Mason know?

I got to my room, changed clothes, checked out, returned the rental car across the street from the hotel, and took a taxi to the San Francisco airport. It was a three hour wait for a non-stop to NYC.

February 23, 1994 (Wednesday)
Pasadena
Mason

I called Olga on her cell.

"Amor," she said. "You hardly ever call me on the phone. Is everything okay?"

"Everything is okay," I said. "I did try you on AIM but could not reach you."

"I'm sorry. Unless I'm at a computer, that will never work for me."

"I'd like to see you," I said.

"I'm in Bogota."

"I can come there," I said.

"When?"

"If you are available, I'll leave tomorrow."

"Do you need a plane?"

"I'll get a charter. Not a problem."

I try very hard to have my affairs in order at all times. I have a will and a living trust with Elizabeth, my wife, but that doesn't tell the whole story, at least not for me. I have a small recording on my desk tagged 'just in case' in which I summarize important things not in my will or living trust. I suggest my survivors go back at least a year on these recordings to learn about assets that we have here and there. I have two safety deposit boxes with more than a million dollars cash in each one. I have bearer bonds in a third bank safety deposit box that amount to more than five hundred thousand dollars.

The night before my trip to meet Olga, I updated my recording.

"Tomorrow I am leaving for Bogota on a chartered flight and plan to return in two days. For a summary of our financial status, listen to the recordings. All bills are paid to date, the mortgage on this place is down to fifty thousand dollars. I should have written a check to pay it off long ago. First thing you should do, if I'm gone, is pay the damn thing off."

I went on for another five minutes.

We have two daughters, thirty and thirty-one, and a son, thirty-four. Elizabeth and I are separated. Five years ago, when we split, she had a choice between the big house in Pasadena or a smaller one in Newport Beach. She preferred the house on the sand. Compared to what it was like living together, our relationship is good. My business has always taken me away from the house. Solving cases abroad often means spending months in other countries while I hunt out stolen art or assets.

When she married me, Elizabeth believed I would practice law. Instead, I kept going to school. I became a doctor, then a psychiatrist. She never approved that I don't practice either of my professions, but the work I do has paid me very well. I can afford two homes. I put three kids through college and still have several million left over in the bank, and income coming in regularly, especially when I do consulting or investigation for the Camachos. After she learned that the son of the cartel chief was held to answer charges in Los Angeles for over a year, Elizabeth never cared for that client.

It didn't matter to her that Pepe Camacho, son of the cartel head, was found not guilty.

I loved Elizabeth, but I love my work. After a year of being separated, we stopped seeing each other. We talk by phone several times a week. On Thanksgiving and Christmas, we have big dinners. Afterwards, the kids go home, and so does Elizabeth.

Elizabeth has a live-in friend. I don't have to rely on my investigator expertise to know it. She lets me know when she shows one the door or invites in another.

I don't do that. I see women in a hotel, but never in the home where my kids grew up, the home in Pasadena that I bought for Elizabeth. I prefer not to have a relationship that would place a woman in my life every day. No live-in for me. I love my freedom. If I wasn't busy, maybe I'd be lonely. The good thing is I stay busy.

I read three newspapers while en route from California to Florida. We had a fuel stop and crew change in Miami. The second leg of the flight was direct to Bogota, and I slept most of the way. I had no alcohol, but I did consume a number of diet cokes.

At the airport, Olga picked me up in her helicopter. She is the sexiest woman I've ever known. Camila was a close second. She hugged and kissed me like we were involved. How nice would that be? Wishful thinking.

Riana was riding shotgun by Olga. I sat behind them in a six-person chopper. I was surprised there were no guards.

"Where is your security?"

"Amor, I don't need them when I'm flying around. They are all back home worried about me when there is nothing to worry about."

"That's for sure," Riana said.

I chuckled into the microphone.

Once we landed at Olga's property, one of the guards took me by golf cart to a guest house where I had stayed many times before, a four minute walk from the main house. I insisted on carrying my own luggage. I took it away from the guard, Brayon Guzman, a face I'd known for a long time. He'd held different positions guarding various of Olga's properties, and was now a regular in the security detail Olga traveled with. Olga wanted me to meet in the main house in an hour. I showered and changed into slacks, white casual shirt with wide collar, and a lightweight casual blazer appropriate to Bogota in March.

Dani answered the door and led me to Olga's home office. Like her home, this was a familiar place. Riana was not with us, but Dani remained.

"Are you drinking, smoking? What can my butler get for you?"

"Mineral water, ice, and lime," I said. "Please."

"Same for me, Dani," Olga said.

Once we got the drinks, Dani was dismissed.

"Mason, shoot. It must be important for you to come right over."

Olga was sitting behind a very wide partnership desk. I remembered that she'd purchased it in Istanbul. I had always admired it.

"It's time for me to leave."

"What?" Olga asked.

"I used to find works of art for Pepe. I came back to work on who was trying to kill Mario, and I never left. I believe I should step back until you have something for me that is a better fit than what I've been doing."

"Hey, that hurt," Olga said, frowning.

Olga is beautiful when she laughs. Actually, she's always beautiful.

She wasn't angry. She was putting on.

"I love you and you know it. It's time for you to behave like the business princess that you are. It's time to stop taking risks. It's not like you to be vindictive. By having me on call, I think it seduces you into doing things that are beneath you."

"Okay, I get what you are saying." Olga put her elbows on her desk, laced her fingers and rested her chin on her hands. "What do you want me to do?"

"I want you to run LAI with your appointed CEO, stop thinking bad about anyone, stop thinking of hurting or killing people."

"You sound like a shrink."

"I am a shrink."

"Art had to go," she said. "He could have fingered me with the Lola thing."

"Before that, he did a lot of work for Camila and Pepe. Before that, he was a good man. He would not have fingered you. I told you he was trustworthy, and you went ahead anyway."

"Mason, I trust you more than any man in this world. You know very well what I mean, and how true it is."

When she'd wanted to get rid of Camila, she asked me to get it done. She never told me not to hire Lola. When she learned I had made a deal with Lola, she went ballistic. In the meantime, someone else, someone unknown, took Camila out. It had not been Olga herself, and she hadn't hired anyone to do it yet. It had not been Lola. No one ever got the five million, at least, not that I know of.

"Olga, I'm a phone call away."

She looked at me, no longer on her elbows. She pushed back from the desk and reclined in her tufted chair, eyes on me.

"A phone call away, only for legal stuff. Right?"

I nodded. "Right."

"What about the Mario business?"

"He's never been bothered again. I never ran into so many obstacles as I did in his case, all dead ends. Good possibilities, but no evidence of anything except the mischief Pepe played. I thought I had one of the neighbors, but there was nothing there. No evidence."

"You think he's safe?"

"He's got protection at home, and as you know he's a walking superman. So is Letty."

I laughed.

Olga didn't like the laugh. She was serious. I saw her jealous face kick in. For her, Letty's name was the trigger.

"Can we still count on you to keep my security people updated on new technology?"

"You got it. That's what I'm good at. Right now, you have all the capabilities that the FBI has. Your man has the equipment and know-how to discover any eavesdropping device, no matter how sophisticated or how secretly it is planted in any environment you frequent."

"Mason, thank you."

"You don't need to thank me. You pay me damn well for all that. Stay careful. Don't say anything delicate on the phone, AOL or AIM. Save delicate communication for face-to-face, in person when it's important."

Olga smiled. "I got it my friend."

"I love you, Olga. You know it. What you asked me to do that time and I agreed, should have showed you where my loyalty lies. Even if it didn't happen through me, it was arranged."

"I understand, I will never forget. I do want to know who killed her."

"Eventually it will come out. I think it will be here in Colombia. It was not a hired assassin. The killer was someone she stepped on, or the survivor of a family she did away with here in Colombia, just like that failed attempt on her life. We found them, outraged family members who had lost family to Camila."

Olga nodded. I knew she had been greedy. She had wanted Camila out of the picture so she could take everything over. Whoever had gunned down Camila had done Olga a favor. She might play at being vengeful now, but it was what she'd wanted.

I wonder what Lola did when she discovered Art was dead. Lola got her wish without having to kill him herself.

Olga had no idea that Lola had been gunning for Art. One day I'll tell Lola about Art's hit. I like Lola.

Olga, Riana and I ate breakfast in the garden. Fresh fruit al fresco.

"If you are all packed, I can fly you to the airport in an hour," Olga said.

But halfway through the fruit plate, Dani brought a phone outside. Olga took the call and handed the mobile landline to Dani to put away.

"Rain check on that helicopter ride," Olga said. "Something has come up."

"That's fine," I said.

Two guards came to the guest house to take me to the airport.

I gave my two pieces of luggage to one of the guards and he stowed it in the trunk of the GMC SUV. One guard drove, another rode shotgun. A guard rode behind me. I paged through a Spanish newspaper. I am pretty good at speaking the language but reading, not too good.

We cleared the gates of Olga's property, and I concentrated on the newspaper.

We hadn't reached the airport. We were stopped in the street, not a car in sight. I felt something hard at the base of my skull. The muzzle of a gun.

"Sorry, Mr. Mason," a familiar voice said.

Everything went black.

February 26, 1994 (Saturday)
Pasadena
Mario

"Amor, did you hear?" Olga said on the land line in my home office.

It was evening, and I was sitting on the sofa by the big window, looking at the sunset. This office is separate from the room the girls used to work in, but no one was using it now.

"Olga, hi. How are you. How you been?" I said, kidding her for launching into a conversation without a hello. She did it a lot.

"I'm sorry, Amor. I'm so torn by what happened."

"What happened?"

I heard a sniff and heard Riana in the background, calming her. There was more noise behind her, Colombian music, an advertisement. It sounded like the television was on, on their end of the line.

"What's wrong? What happened? Where are you?"

I heard indecipherable voices on the line, but no speech directed to me. She took so long that I came close to putting the phone down and calling on my cell.

"Mario, this is Riana. Olga's too worked up to speak. We're in Bogota. Mason came to have a meeting, stayed the night, and in the morning,

Olga's security people were carrying him to catch his flight. He never made it to the airport. The car was peppered with gunfire. The guards were killed, and so was Mason. It's sad."

"I'm so sorry," I said.

I was shocked. I had been standing. I sat down feeling a little numb, like someone had flashed me with a bright light. The sky didn't look so beautiful anymore, but the cool leather beneath me felt reassuring and familiar.

Of all the news she could have had to tell, this was the most unexpected. I wondered if someone was after Olga again. But why would that be? She'd retired from a life as crime princess, and now owned the business world.

I'd had my differences with Mason. I'd never liked his snooping. He wasn't my ally. But except for belonging to Camacho, he was probably a good guy. I was saddened by the news.

Olga came on the line again, calmer. Fewer sniffs.

"I know you didn't like him because he always had men spying on you, but that was only because I wanted you to be safe, Amor. I loved Mason. He was loyal. He was my friend."

She went from sniffs to full-fledged crying.

"I did like him," I said. "I know he had men tailing me, and I know it was to keep me guarded and not to keep tabs of my comings and goings."

When I went to Europe on the spur of the moment, it took a few days for Mason to track me down. I sure didn't like it when it happened, but now that he was dead, I held nothing against him. We talked for a few minutes longer.

"I'm flying him back to his family in Los Angeles on the day after tomorrow. I hope to see you for at least a little while. Si, Amor?"

"Of course. When will his service be?"

"I spoke to his son. He said his father wanted to be cremated, and that the only service he wanted was family only."

"I didn't know he had a son. I would like to do something, send flowers, make a donation on his behalf to a charity or something."

"Amor, there's no need. I will be at the Beverly Hilton. I will call you."

"Safe travels," I said.

"I adore you, Amor."

I swallowed, I don't know if she adored me, but I know I loved her, and she probably only loved me the same way.

"I love you, Olga."

"I love when you call me by my name, Amor."

After the call, I caught up with Letty, Tangles, and Storm in the indoor swimming pool.

"Get in," Letty said. "We're going to beat you like a drum."

"Ouch," I said, standing close to the edge in my sweats.

"I got bad news about Mason," I said.

I don't know if it was my expression or my words that got Letty out of the water and by my side. Tangles and Storm followed a few steps behind.

"Who is Mason?" Storm asked.

"What happened? Tell us already," Letty said.

I repeated Olga's news.

"He was a doctor, a lawyer, and a shrink but all he did was nose around. He was a pain in the ass investigator on Olga's payroll," Letty said to Storm, "but he was an okay guy."

"Whatever he was, he didn't deserve to die like that. How was it? A hold-up? Was it that?" Tangles asked.

"I'm sorry, guys," Storm said. "I mean, my condolences."

"I'm getting dressed. Let's meet in the wine room," Letty said, walking off.

In two hours in the wine room, we polished off three bottles of wine and one joint. That's about a bottle each but in fairness, I drink more than they do. We were feeling no pain by the time we hit the sack. Storm and Tangles went off by themselves.

Letty and I went to bed in the dark. No candles tonight. It was chilly but not so much that we needed the fireplace.

"Lady Olga will be in town for how long?" Letty asked.

"Your guess is good as mine."

"You said she's staying in a hotel. That's good. I don't want to be rude, but I think her days of bunking here have come to an end. What do you think?"

I kissed Letty. Her lips were easy to find when she was right in front of me.

"I agree."

"Are you going to see her? Or is she coming over to visit? Do you know?"

"Baby, stop stressing. I told you all I know."

"I'm not stressing. Really, I'm not."

I kissed her again.

"Bet she'll come to the office."

I sighed, quietly. "Baby, she owns the company."

"Yes, she does. I'll shut up. Want to fuck me now?"

I could feel her stiffen up against me. I wasn't angry, just annoyed. It wasn't even her words. There was an attitude there. "Why are you being this way?" I asked.

She didn't answer right away. I think she would have pulled away, but I kept her close.

"I want you," she whispered. I felt her hands on me.

My lips moved down the landscape of her flesh. She moaned as I nibbled my way down. A kiss here, a bite there. She was warm, and pliant and receptive.

"I love you," I said.

She didn't hear me, couldn't have. Her moans were louder than my words. I wanted her satisfied, and not just by having orgasms. I wanted her to know I love every inch of her body, in case she had forgotten. I wanted her to be happy.

She giggled, she laughed, she hugged me hard, she punched me and suddenly, just like that, she was asleep. She was wiped out, and I was okay with her being wiped out. I didn't toss and turn as they say, but Mason was on my mind. Mason and I had many meetings, mostly on the subject of who was trying to kill me or the occupants of my house. My brain was replaying all the Mason movies in my head.

I went down to the third floor to Tangles's room. I didn't knock. She was sound asleep. I turned away and heard her voice.

"What's up, Boss."

"I'm sorry to wake you. I need a sleeper. Do you have any?"

The night lights showed her crossing to her bathroom. She came back with a water glass and a pill which I downed right away and handed her the empty glass. She followed a step behind all the way to the master bedroom. I slipped into bed, and so did she.

I heard a giggle. Letty is a light sleeper.

"You brought Tangles to finish, you rascal."

"No. Can't sleep. I went to get a sleeping pill."

"Are you jealous, bitch?" Tangles said, laughing.

"I'll kick your ass," Letty said in a low voice. A second later, she was asleep.

How different Letty was about Tangles and Storm compared to how she felt about Olga. And Olga was so nice to her. I hate jealousy, but I love Letty as she is. I would not change her.

I went to sleep between them.

February 28, 1994 (Monday)
Bogota
Riana

We took off from Bogota an hour ago.

"When she wakes and wants you, you'll know about it," I told Dani.

He nodded.

I all but tucked him in his seat in the main cabin. It was made up like a bed, and he curled up on the sheets, looking at me like a devoted Golden Retriever. I love Dani, but Olga needs me right now, not Dani. I came back to the room in the back of the plane and joined Olga in the big bed.

Olga was sound asleep next to me. She's had a rough two days. When I heard that Mason was killed, I wondered if Olga had it done. She never said why he had come to see her. All I know that after the meeting, Olga was angry. She tried to hide it, but it's hard for her to hide her feelings from me. I know her so well.

I asked no questions. I'd seen him at breakfast the day he died. There had been no awkwardness between them, no hint of anything wrong. She took it so hard that I'm beginning to doubt she had anything to do with

Mason's death. Olga does not cry that often about anything. I did my best to console her. She loves to be hugged, loves to be kissed, and loves to kiss back. That's what I came to bed to do, to cuddle with her.

It felt strange to know that Mason is on the plane.

Bogota's police and coroner took crime scene pictures before they released him to the mortuary. We were told there were a dozen bullet wounds in his body, one in the head.

Poor Mason.

May he rest in peace.

The cargo hold was empty except for Mason in the shiny new casket that Olga was reluctant to buy. Olga did not wish to offend his family by choosing a casket for him, but the alternative was putting his body in a box. She was too upset over his death to do that to him.

March 1, 1994 (Tuesday)
Pasadena
Tangles

Letty and I decided to drive our Ferraris to the office. That left Storm driving Mario in the big car. We used to drive separately a lot. Maybe we needed alone-time to think, though I don't know how safe that is during morning rush hour.

Personally, as bad as I feel bad about Mason, I feel bad that I don't feel worse. I had many encounters with him when he came over to see Mario. He'd come over with an entire crew to spend days combing the entire house for eavesdropping devices. I had wanted to see if he'd see me professionally as a shrink, but Letty told me not to. He was too close to Olga, so it would be unwise to arm him with our personal secrets, the kind that you would confess to a shrink. I never been so physically close to a shrink before. I guess that's why I was tempted. In the movies, you lie down and tell it all and then you feel better. I'll never do it with Mason now. He's gone.

I used to just be a masseuse who came to Mario's with Betty sometimes, then Betty set me up with her clients, and she tried working with them, flying around with Letty and Mario. She couldn't hack the job he was doing then, which was talking with a lot of grieving people. She came back, and we switched. I gave her clients back, and Mario put me on the team. So right after I teamed up, I was dazzled by Mario, and Letty, and this big new life. I'd never had opportunities like this before, and I could not understand how nobody was jealous. Olga and her sister Camila had dropped in, and they were in bed with all of us. I don't know what came over me. Mario was Olga's fiancé then. I did not understand how she could love him and share him. I thought it meant she didn't love him. How could she not be jealous? I cussed her out. So stupid of me. Next morning, I apologized. Olga was so nice about it. Then I went home and got beat up by a woman who ambushed me in my own apartment.

She beat the crap out of me, so bad that I decided to get into karate like Letty. I shot the trespasser, the cops put her in jail, then she bailed out and never showed for court. I always figured Olga had sent her to get even. I recuperated at Mario's house.

How great it would be if I ran in to that bitch again? I'd mop the floor with her. That bitch was my incentive to keep going through the rough parts when I was first getting into karate. Of course, Letty was already a martial arts superhero, and she kept me on track. I would never fear someone Olga sent after me again. But maybe it isn't just me Olga went after. Did she have something against Mason? But that's crazy. Mason was her man.

Why would Olga want to go after Mason?

If Letty or Mario knew what I was thinking, they'd argue me down. I'd get rapid fire from both of them. They act like they trust her, but, how can they? I don't trust Olga. Doesn't matter how nice she is, doesn't matter how many gifts she sends. I don't trust her.

I believe in my gut that Olga is raving furious that Mario married Letty.

Letty's no fool. She believes the same. It's not that Olga is madly in love with him. The madness comes from Letty stepping in with Mario, bumping Olga aside.

March 1, 1994 (Tuesday)
New York
Lola

On my flight from San Francisco to New York, I realize I have no one to bounce anything off of, good or bad. When I went into hiding in Puerto Rico, I left behind what few friends I had. I seldom bother to regret a thing I can't change, but now I am sure the decision to hide was a stupid move, and I regret the hell out of it.

I have no one to tell that I found Art dead.

I have no one to tell that I'd been planning to kill him or at the very least, hurt him. As much as I love my brothers, I can't talk to them about any of this. It was bad enough I asked Nico to check on Art. An FBI agent can get into serious trouble for using agency resources for something personal.

Who would want Art dead?

I know nothing about him, other than he betrayed my vulnerable ass, and I hate him for it. If his actions with me were typical, he probably has a lot of enemies who want him gone.

If Olga was erasing evidence tracking to her for kidnapping me, she could have ordered it.

I don't know what killed him. I saw no blood. With gloves on, I couldn't tell much about his temperature to determine how long he'd been dead.

I should feel bad that he's dead.

I don't feel bad.

I'm grateful I wasn't the one who took his life, but I was feeling guilty as hell for not reporting his death. Reporting it, anonymous or not, would be evidence, and leave a trail, and would be dangerous. I wondered if that picture was real, if that was his family, if they were in danger, if they were a target, or if someone had already taken out his family. Who would be vicious enough to do that?

Two days after getting back home, I was seated at my couch, looking at morning game shows, and eating the dry overcooked scrambled eggs I'd fixed for myself. At least I'd used a lot of butter. My phone rang. It rarely rings. Only Art, my brothers and Mason had the number. At least I knew it wasn't Art. I'm pretty sure there are no phone booths where he's gone. I switched off the television.

"You okay, sis?"

"I'm okay. How about you?"

"All good. Did you go apply for the PI job I suggested?"

I laughed. My brother, professional busy body.

"No, not yet. I will, I promise."

"You won't," he said. "But okay." He laughed at himself, then said, "Sis, remember that smart guy lawyer shrink from Pasadena that worked with the Camachos? Remember him?"

If this was a friend, I would have said, Oh, yeah, you mean Mason?

I fucked him for hours in Pasadena.

"I remember. What about him?"

"Apparently he was involved in a shooting. Maybe robbery. He was killed. It happened in Bogota, Colombia."

That it happened in Bogota flew right passed me. I wanted to hang up that second. Wanted to dial Mason, hear his voice on the line, hear him say that the rumors of his death were greatly exaggerated.

My heart stopped. For a second, I found it hard to breathe. I clenched my phone to my chest and tried to inhale. One breath. Exhale. Two. I forced the breath to come and felt my cheek. My cheek was wet. Why was I crying? For Mason? I was still sitting in NYC, on my couch, in front of the stupid game show host and a plate of cold eggs. Why was the whole world feeling so much darker, so different?

I played it off with much difficulty. I stuck the phone to my ear.

"Sorry what was that again?

Nico repeated the news that Mason was dead.

"How awful," I said. "How do you know?" I think my voice sounded normal. It didn't feel normal.

"It's on the wire and in the local paper."

"How awful," I said.

Somehow, I carried on the conversation with Nico until he was done. He hung up.

I found myself lying face down in my pillow, fist pounding the mattress, tears flowing.

March 1, 1994 (Tuesday)
Pasadena
Mario

"I'm only going to be here a couple days, Amor," Olga said on the phone. "I do want to see you. Are you coming over?"

"See us," Riana said in the background.

"Sure," I said. "How did it go with Mason's family?"

"The mortuary sent a hearse to pick up the casket. I talked to his wife on the phone. She thanked me for bringing him back and that was it. I didn't actually see her."

"Seems so cold," I said.

"Amor, I thought they would be at the airport. When I talked from Bogota to his son, I gave him the arrival details and everything."

"It is sad. One day you're here and the next day, you're gone. You never know."

"Right, Amor. That's the reason you need to get over here and visit."

Olga has Dani, the young butler. I remember Olga recently telling me on the phone that she could get serviced anywhere.

Why me?

Tangles was riding shotgun with Storm driving. Letty and I were in the back seat, snuggling. It was still light out, and the traffic was impossible.

"I'm going to meet up with Olga and Riana for dinner," I told Letty on our way home.

"Why didn't you go straight from the office?"

I shrugged. "I want to change. I don't feel like going over there in a suit."

"Are you going in jeans?"

"Baby, I don't even know what I'm going to wear."

"Can I go with you?"

"Sure, you can go."

Letty's posture softened. She looked like an executive in her black suit. She is an executive. I snuck a kiss.

"You guys! Impressionable young people up front," Tangles said.

Storm giggled.

"Eyes forward, people," Letty said to the front seat. "Mind your own business." To me, she said, "You go. If she had wanted me there, she would have called me."

"Riana is with her," I said.

"Of course, she is. You'll do them both, right?"

"Come on, don't be like that."

"Like what?"

I wanted Letty to hold her ground and be the strong person she is. I can't say I liked it when she got like this when it was about Olga. She would be fine if I took Storm or Letty right here in the car in front of her. Why was she jealous of Olga?

"You didn't answer me. Like what?"

I'd be some kind of a dummy to ruffle Letty's feathers. "If you don't know, forget it."

Storm and Tangles were caught up in a conversation about the lunch they'd had with a client earlier today. Letty and I, we rode in silence for a while. Traffic eased and for a mile or so, we covered some ground. Then we hit another blocked lane.

"Is Storm driving you tonight?"

I didn't answer. I hadn't thought about it.

"If you're going to drink, don't think of driving yourself," she said.

"I don't drink and drive," I reminded her.

"Take Raul with you, then."

"Good idea. Pixie isn't here so he's doing nothing."

"What hotel is she in?"

"Beverly Hilton," I said.

"Staying the night?"

"I haven't thought about it," I said. "If I get Raul to drive, he can bring me back so probably not."

"She's going to want you to stay the night. She's going to want you to stay with them for the duration of their trip. How long are they staying?"

It was almost comical. Almost. I wasn't laughing. She wasn't either. She was staring, unsmiling, at her lap.

"Hey," I said, taking her hand and squeezing it. She didn't say anything, or squeeze back, but her hand was warm, and felt like a lifeline. I hated to let go to walk inside, but finally, we were home. I walked ahead of everyone into the house.

A waiter from room service stuck around to serve us in the suite's dining room that had room for a dozen. Olga, Riana and I were also attended by Lydia, a fair and lovely sommelier. She reminded me of Lola and her masquerades. Lydia would make a ton of money as a hooker, but she actually did know her wines.

Dani had been sent into a bedroom to eat a hamburger. He didn't come out again, except for a moment after dinner to prepare drinks, after which, Olga sent him back in his room with a plate of left-overs.

I was the only one to eat steak, a porterhouse that must have weighed two pounds.

The girls had fish.

The dinner was lovely. There were far too many sides, any of which could have been a main dish. Cheese plates, tortilla soup, guacamole, hummus, some kind of salad on a flatbread, calamari, sorbet, a whole black forest cake, and a bowl of strawberries dipped in chocolate. It reminded me of when Miguel first came to work for me, when he was trying to impress me with variety. Being served all kinds of things ain't gonna turn a meat and potatoes guy into a gourmet. I'm just saying I like what I like. The different wines Lydia served us were a learning experience for me, and I've become pretty darn good at knowing my wine.

The dining room is down the hall from the living room. There's a shelf which serves as a bar, and it was pretty well stocked with various liquors. We relocated to the living room as the dining room was being cleared, and the uneaten food stored in the mini fridge. The staff was efficient, and soon the dining room was spotless and we—the three of us—were alone. Olga and Riana were not drunk, but they could put away a lot of alcohol without appearing intoxicated. They chased the dinner with after-dinner drinks.

"I remember when I met you and Camila here," I said, laughing. "She would go out to the balcony to smoke her weed. That's when you didn't smoke much."

"I remember," Olga said, sipping a chocolate liquor. "Thanks to Riana, I smoke too much." Olga laughed.

"We have to be cool. Olga is part of the establishment now. We can't let it get out that Olga gets high. It could damage her rep with the stockholders." Riana gestured with her glass, which was filled with Coco Loco, a concoction Dani prepared for her before he disappeared.

I was surprised to hear something so conservative out of Riana's mouth.

"The wine is good," I said. "Who needs more than that, anyway?"

Eventually we got in bed. Dani was not included. That was fine with me.

Even though his death was the reason for the flight to Los Angeles, Mason was never mentioned, and I, for sure, wasn't going to be the one to bring him up. I was surprised Olga didn't mention him, not even the flight over with him in the cargo bay in a casket as she had told me on the phone.

They had eaten light and drunk heavily. I filled up mostly on steak and skipped the after dinner boozing. We had several hours of sex. I think they passed out from the wine. After they were dead to the world, I showered, dressed, called Raul on cell and told him I'd be right down. I figured Dani was in his designated room waiting for me to leave, but I didn't see him.

I walked into my bedroom at ten after three. I undressed and slipped into bed unsurprised to find Letty awake. Before my head hit the pillow, her arms folded around me in a warm embrace, and she rained kisses all over me.

"I love you," she said. "I'm so glad you came home."

I try not to lie about what I do. If and when Letty asked me what I did with Olga and Riana, I would tell her, but I was relieved she didn't throw the question at me at that moment. Instead, she straddled me so that I entered her.

She lay on me, her lips on mine, my body deep inside her.

"Let's sleep like this," she said in a low voice.

"Yes," I agreed.

"I love you, Letty."

October 1, 1995
Pasadena
Letty

He asked me for a baby.

At the time, we were in Hawaii for a weekend, lying on a public beach near a restaurant where we'd had a late brunch. A couple with children had just walked by. Neither of the parents were anything to remember, nothing that sticks now in my mind, but the kids were amazing during the minute or so they walked past us. There was something about the four of them, two parents, two kids, gamboling in inch-deep surf. They were gathering shells, and we were close enough to hear, for a minute, anyway, the hysterical running commentary of the smaller child. Mario and I laughed aloud over the child's conversation.

We laughed till we were in tears. Chuckled over it the rest of the day. During dinner at Olga's beach house where we were staying, Mario accepted a plate of fruit and fish appetizers one of Olga's permanent staff had handed to us.

"Don't worry," I said. "The main course isn't spam."

"I'm getting older," Mario said, not concerned about dinner. "You're ten years younger. You would make a beautiful mom. Do you want to be?"

Until that second, I wasn't sure I wanted to be a mother. That night. I realized I'd just been fooling myself. I wanted a baby desperately, but never allowed myself to think of it.Now I'm busy at the office, busy planning for the new arrival. I track the days.

I'm six months pregnant, due in January.

Dr. Hershey had changed my thinking about doctors. Since meeting with him, I'm a regular with Dr. Cummings. I get a blood test every four or five months. I've gone out on Mario but only when he escapes to meet up with Olga. I suspect that at least once he met up with Lola.

I didn't ask about Lola because I know he won't lie, and I don't want to be right. I would not be able to stand it.

I planned the pregnancy with Dr Ida, went off the pill, and bang, I got pregnant!

Auntie Tangles and Auntie Storm seem as excited as me. They are constantly bothering me, asking if I feel okay, rubbing my belly, wanting to feel the kicks from the kiddo, asking do I want a boy or a girl. I always say I don't care as long as its healthy, but how I long for a beautiful boy like his daddy.

A local competitor of GAL had a headhunter contact me to see if I wanted to go work for them. You wouldn't believe the bonus package they offered. When I told Mario, he got upset. I told him to chill. It was a compliment that somehow, they found out I was kicking ass for GAL.

Tangles is doing a good job too. Storm is averaging at least one lease a month, which is dynamite. She mostly handles used aircraft. Lots of commission money in used equipment.

About six months ago, for Storm's birthday, Mario and I gave her a new yellow Ferrari. She loves it and was finally okay with us hiring a driver.

His name is Chacho Cortina. He's forty, a retired deputy sheriff who lost his entire family in a house fire in West Covina. He doesn't talk about it. He lives in the personnel quarters in back. I think he likes all of us.

Chacho drives Mario and me to work and brings us back. During the office day, he runs errands that we used to give to messengers to handle. Storm and Tangles drive their cars to work and back, and sometimes carpool with each other.

The rabbit died when I was two months along. Ever since, Mario has needed assurances that sex is okay. Since I was five months along, he wouldn't let me on top. He won't get on top of me. It's now all about side sex.

I get horny like crazy. Good for me, I have Tangles and Storm. I love them more than anything in this world. Well, I love my Tio Miguel, and of course I love Mario.

Except for a really dull stretch routine Dr. Ida choreographed, karate has become history for me, along with jogging and biking. I do waddle endless hours on the treadmill. The first bedroom on the 3rd floor is in constant change in preparation for the baby. Not knowing boy or girl, I bought two beautiful bassinets, decorative as all heck, one blue, one pink. Got it covered. The baby will sleep in our room to start in one of these.

Olga calls me at least once a week, nice and friendly, checking on me, telling me not to push working at the office, not to push working from home, telling me I will get my full paycheck either way. At times I feel guilty for being jealous, but mostly I don't trust her. I trust my gut, and my gut says her calls are BS.

Aunt Carmen who raised Mario (and even Pixie and Lainie for a while) came over on the last three Saturdays to visit. A long time ago, she was a nurse, and she's still a licensed midwife, and gives Lamaze lessons in her home. I hated to turn down her offer to deliver the baby, but I want to be knocked out in a real hospital.

When she offered to deliver the baby. Mario told her, "Dr. Ida's got it covered."

"Love you for offering," I told her.

The only reason I ever met Mario was that way back when Mario first moved to Pasadena, it was because Melina bought the house across the street. Mario and Melina were a thing. She had established a local grocery chain, Marron Markets, and hired her staff culled from people who wanted to work at her grocery. Uncle Miguel who was also supporting me, came to Pasadena to work for Melina, but the job was filled. We were in bad shape. Melina found me waiting in the car during Uncle's interview, brought me into her house, and—well—we got closer than you'd expect. Anyway, she advised Mario to hire Uncle Miguel and me as a package deal. She's had a special place in my heart ever since. Mario and Melina go back a long time. Not too long ago, she lost a baby when she fell down the stairs, her last chance at a kid of her own. She's ten years older than Mario. If she had not let her age issues hold her back, she'd be Mrs. Luna right now. I might be in Storm and Tangles's situation, and not have Mario's ring on my finger. In fact, I bet it would be Pixie and me, and Mario and Melina.

Melina is gorgeous. I don't know if she's done some work on her face, but I don't think so. Since I've known her, she's never aged. She's been over a couple of times with gifts and said she wishes she had not sold the markets. Now she has a pile of cash and is bored to death. She's thinking of opening a chain of hamburger joints throughout California.

I'm six months along and hardly look pregnant. I don't care about my abs now. I'll get them back. Anything for my baby. The time I used to spend in karate is mostly on the treadmill, walking.

In the bedroom, only four candles were burning. They will burn all night and were okayed by Dr. Ida, as long as I don't burn them when the baby is here. I love candles. I used to light up twenty or more candles. Don't need that any more.

Dr. Ida says burning essential oils is not good for the baby's lungs.

"You're going to be a daddy," I said.

"I know," he said. Touched my stomach.

I felt his mouth on my belly. His kisses.

"I love you," he said to me.

"I love you," he said to the baby, his mouth against my stomach. "Hello, in there. Are you a boy or girl? Hello?"

"Did you get a reply?"

He's never without a comeback.

"He's asleep."

"Or she."

"Boy or girl. I can hardly wait, Letty."

He moved up so that we faced each other, our favorite position if we are going to talk. The room is full of emotion. My heart is full.

"Letty, thank you."

"No thanks needed."

We found sleep, eventually.

In bed lately, he stays close. I love it. I kiss his hands. I know he's asleep. He stirs. Like me, like Tangles, we're light sleepers. I leave him alone and let him rest.

I dream of bringing babies to work.

November 1, 1995
Pasadena
Mario

I waited too long to think of having a child. Whenever it had come up before, it was such a distant thought. I could never picture myself as a father. I barely have a recollection of having a dad, just Moonie, Aunt Carmen's husband who died when I was four. I didn't know my real father who had been married to Aunt Carmen's sister Elena. I don't know how to be a father, or what it's like to have one.

Letty thinks I'm hoping for a boy. A girl would be wonderful, a little Letty.

Damn, I love this woman.

I work out with Tangles every other morning. She's no Letty but she's good. We've got Storm working out a little bit, learning some self-defense moves. Last year, Tangles and Letty got her a shooting coach to meet her at Pixie's house where there is a downstairs shooting gallery that Melina put in. After a year, Storm can manage a number of firearms, and she got a carry permit. At first, Storm did not want to carry. What a difference a year makes. She loves to pack.

681   George Hatcher

Going back to when Pixie was here, Melina got the girls their permits. Melina had the connections. She claimed she got her first carry permit from a police chief up north that she fucked into submission. A concealed gun permit in California is very difficult to get, and I never knew if Melina was making up a tall tale or telling the truth. Knowing Melina, it could've been either way.

Casa Luna is fantastic, but making the house kid safe, is impossible. The Santa Monica beach house is too tiny to consider, too small even for just Letty and me to live full-time. I have my real estate broker scouting for listings in Malibu, homes with enough bedrooms for us, the baby, Tangles and Storm, and room for a small crew of house personnel. Not that we're selling Casa Luna. When the baby is old enough, we can consider coming back. We'll never get a house fast enough, but the goal is to get a house before the baby starts crawling.

Breakfast is always a big thing for Emma because no one eats the same thing. Storm usually had pancakes, muffins, biscuits or doughnuts. Tangles drinks some kind of green slime. I usually have lots of protein, eggs, side steak, especially on days when I don't plan to take a lunch. Letty usually eats the same as me, except that Dr. Ida had a food plan for pregnant women, and Letty gave it to Emma. So, now she eats the same as me, plus milk, plus fruit, plus cheese. She starts off ravenous but can't eat half of what Emma puts in front of her.

"Baby, I hate to leave you right now," I said at breakfast. We were sitting at the kitchen counter at seven in the morning. I'd been working out while Letty did stretches, then did some treadmill walking. She called it waddling.

"I'm not having the baby for three months. Not counting the security guards, we have eighteen employees plus the girls to take care of anything I need. Feel free to go. I'm good. In fact, I wish it was me going. It's a big deal. I should have done the deal. Fuck, the commission. Fuck-me."

"When I make money, you make money," I said. "I get a percentage of every lease on the books."

"I know your deal. I was kidding, already."

I was flying for a particular sale. I only travel on GAL business when I am close to closing a deal that requires a face to face meeting. Normally, the clients come see whoever is handling the lease. And me. It didn't matter whose lease it was, I meet the clients, but I didn't travel to the client often.

Juan Carlos operated plane service from Sao Paulo, Brazil to Porto Alegre and other cities within three hours flight time of home base. Juan Carlos was on the verge of signing on a deal for ten brand new 737s, a great deal for GAL.

My personnel get commissions. I don't, but I get a percentage of all lease or sale income. Andrea hand-carried me big deals when they came in. She performed client maintenance, and as far as the client was concerned, he was dealing with me, personally. At some point I had to surface on the phone or in person as I was going to do by flying to Brazil. For two days, I had been anxious about leaving Letty to go on this business trip. She was in good spirits.

As usual, Cacho drove Letty and me to work. Letty went into her office to handle her client maintenance.

I went into my office, and made some calls, including one to Olga about the upcoming business trip. No hotel this trip. I was going to stay at one of Olga's properties in Sao Paulo. I remembered the house Camila had bought in Sao Paulo. Like the other houses, it was huge and gorgeous.

"I'm taking the paperwork with me," I told Olga on the phone. "If Juan Carlos signs, great. If he doesn't, he will eventually."

"He'll sign, Amor. You're the best," Olga said.

"Thanks," I said.

"I spoke to the butler, Carlo. Amor, they are expecting you at the house. You haven't been there for some time, but he certainly remembers you."

"I remember Carlo," I said.

"If you feel like it, stop on your way back. I'll be in Bogota by then."

"Where are you?"

"Milan. Leaving tomorrow."

"You spend a lot of time in Bogota," I said.

"I'm comfortable there."

There was a time when the Camachos had said they were pulling out of Bogota for good. There had been a regime change, and they had been worried that the political upheaval would damage them, but instead it seemed their position improved. Olga uses the military airport to land her planes. They offer her security when she wants extra support.

When I caught my ride to the airport, Letty, Tangles, Storm, and Andrea went up to the helipad. I kissed them all. Letty was last. I didn't pick her up, and she complained.

"I'm not fragile," she said.

"Yes, you are." I patted her stomach.

I kissed her with passion. She kissed me back with such hunger that

I thought about putting off takeoff for thirty minutes. Reluctantly, I took the few steps and leaned down to get through the chopper door. By the time I was in my seat, they were safely in the doorway to the hall. I waved goodbye and didn't get the finger from Letty. She blew me kisses and tossed them at me with both hands.

The chopper came to life. I've been on hundreds of helicopters, but my heart always races a little when I first get on. I put on a headset like the one the pilot was wearing.

"It's your call, Mr. Luna."

The pilot's voice came to me through earphones that also protected my ears from the noise.

"Go for it," I said.

Letty had played at wanting to go, but when I asked her along, she'd said she was too busy. I couldn't take Tangles or Storm when I needed them to be close to Letty. I felt good that they were there with her, all of my dearest loved ones safely together.

The plane crew Andrea had arranged was four GAL pilots and two agency flight attendants. I glanced in the plane's crowded cockpit and shook hands with the crew. The two flight attendants were foxes, both of them dark-haired, dark-eyed and sultry. I wondered if Andrea had chosen them for their looks. The plan was for the pilots to rotate, two on, two off.

Paula, the attendant for the crew, introduced herself.

"I'm here if you need anything, Mr. Luna."

Gigi, my valet on the flight, introduced herself and shook my hand firmly.

"Mr. Luna, it is a long flight. We only have one fuel stop. Please let me know whatever you need. We have good food for you."

"For you and the crew as well, I hope," I said.

"Yes, we do. Thank you very much."

I took my normal take-off seat.

I missed not having someone in front of me. I pictured Letty.

"Please enjoy your flight, Mr. Luna. With your permission, we're going to push back. Wheels up in eleven minutes," the senior captain said on the speaker.

Gigi brought me a glass of red wine.

"Tell him to go for it," I said.

"Yes, Mr. Luna."

"Call me Mario," I said.

She grinned. "Yes Mr. Luna."

Lift off was at 1:35 pm.

I finished my wine when we had reached our cruising altitude of 31,000 feet.

"Gigi, I'll eat later. I'm going to lie down for a bit."

"I will check on you," she said. "Let me run and put the bed down."

"It's okay," I said. "I'm just going to change and lie on top of it all."

"As you wish, Mr. Luna."

I slipped into gray sweats and socks, no elastic, loose and comfortable. I picked a movie called Bye Bye Love, turned the TV on, put it on mute, turned the bedroom lights off, closed my eyes and went out. The movie, which I had not seen at all, was done, so I judged it was at least two hours into the flight.

Gigi let herself in the bedroom.

"Mr. Luna, I brought you ice water. You should stay hydrated. Do you want lemon or lime?"

Andrea could have sent an ordinary flight attendant. She sent two cover models.

"Gigi, thanks." I passed on the lemon and lime, chugged the water, and handed her the glass. "I'd like a glass of the same wine you poured earlier, and a cheese platter if you have it. I'll eat in here."

"Right away, Mr. Luna."

I turned a bedside lamp on and pressed play to start the movie again. It's habit. I need something on the screen. Doesn't matter if I hear it or not.

I sat up. Gigi returned, and presented me a bed table covered with linen cover, serving me the large cheese plate and a glass of wine.

Letty always said the tables we used to use were too small. They were about fourteen inches wide. These were at least thirty inches wide. I don't know where she bought them, but Letty had found them somewhere for home, and for the plane. Thinking of Letty made me miss her even more.

"Gigi, get yourself a glass and have some wine with me."

I saw the smile.

"I have a diet coke. Is that okay?"

"Absolutely," I said.

Thirty minutes later, she was drinking wine from my glass, the sound was on the television. We'd finished *Bye Bye Love*, about divorcing families. She'd picked out *While You Were Sleeping*, a movie which had come out this summer, though I hadn't seen it.

We had our clothes on, a first for me.

Someone knocked at the cabin door.

Gigi and I were both lying on the bed, fully dressed, watching the movie. Gigi jumped out of bed and opened the door.

"Mr. Luna," Paula said, "You have an emergency call. You can take it in the main cabin."

I felt a stirring of alarm, and in my stocking feet, ran into the main cabin and picked up the phone. It was Andrea.

"Mario, there's been an accident. Letty was on her way home with Cacho on the Pasadena Freeway. A cement truck plowed into the back of the Rolls. Tangles and Olga are on their way to the scene. I don't know more. I will call you in a few minutes."

I had a lump in my throat. I could barely talk.

"I'm coming right back," I said.

"I'm on it."

I did not go back to the bedroom. I sat where I had been during take-off.

Gigi was standing there looking at me. "Mr. Luna, what can I get you?"

"Water, room temperature."

Andrea called back in minutes that seemed like hours.

"The news copter on four is over the crash. Letty and Tangles can't even get close to where it happened."

"I want to know about Letty," I said in a loud voice.

"I will do my best," Andrea said in obvious desperation.

"It's too difficult for me to call from here. Tell Tangles to get hold of Melina. Melina knows people."

"I'm on it," Andrea said.

The next call was from Storm, so charged with static, I could barely make out her words.

"Boss, Tangles talked to Melina. She's calling a friend at CHP. I'll get back to you."

The captain came on the speaker.

"Mr. Luna, we have been cleared to head back. We are starting our turn. Please buckle up."

The plane bounced a lot during the turn.

Andrea called again. "Melina is going to call you direct," she said.

Gigi came up several times offering me water, coffee, wine, asking if I wanted to go back to see the rest of the movie. She brought the cheese plate and sat it on the table beside me. Each time she came, I snapped at her, until she left me alone. Finally, Melina called.

"Letty is at Huntington Memorial Emergency in Pasadena. The impact threw her into the front seat. She's alive, critical condition. The driver was dead at the scene."

Melina promised an update if there was one, said everyone would be at the hospital to meet me, told me to be of brave heart, everything would be okay, and hung up.

Okay my ass. The crew was with me, but I was alone on the plane. The weather was fine. The flight was perfect. It was November, and the temperature inside was perfect. But to everything around me, I was numb, and hurting, anxious and frantic to hear the news, and equally desperate not to. I needed to be home, now. The plane was jetting quietly and perfectly through the air. If we had been going at lightspeed, it would not have been fast enough.

"This is a fucking nightmare."

I was talking to myself.

Gigi was sitting in earshot waiting to see if I needed something. I did not call on her.

I was trapped in my mind, worried sick. This was worse than the plane crash into the ocean. Then, I had been in the middle of the crisis, busy staying alive. There's nothing worse than being helpless in a crisis. Nothing worse than not knowing, unless knowing was worse. It had to be good news. They had to survive, both of them. I tried to be optimistic, but my heart was sinking. Nothing I'd heard from Melina had indicated anything good.

I remembered when a stolen rubbish truck had slammed into the back of my Rolls. It had happened in front of my house, and Olga had been a passenger. I always believed that hit had been aiming for me.

Why would anyone want to hurt Letty?

I must be mistaken. I'm crossing the line.

What does critical mean?

What about the baby?

The impact had been enough to kill Cacho. It was catastrophic.

I prayed.

I prayed.

Epilogue

God don't abandon me now. I pray for Letty. Please don't take her away from me. Don't take our child. Virgin of Guadalupe, please hear me, please.

About The Author

Whether George Hatcher is traveling the globe as a consultant/strategist for lawyers in high profile wrongful death cases, running one of his many enterprises, or at home with Molly amid the birds and cats in California, he's always got his eye on the next project. He does a whole lot more than what is mentioned here.

A longer bio is on his website at: www.georgehatcher.com/bio/bio.html